WARRIOR UNDONE

JESSICA RUBEN

WARRIOR UNDONE

JessicaRubenBooks, LLC

229 E. 85th Street

P.O. Box 1596

New York, New York 10028

Cover Design by Sarah Hansen

Edited by Nicole Bailey, Proof Before you Publish

Edited by Jovana Shirley, Unforeseen Editing, www.unforeseenediting.com

Edited by Ellie at Love N Books

Paperback ISBN-13: 978-1-7321178-7-7

E-Book ISBN-13: 978-1-7321178-6-0

Printed in the United States of America

Contact me by visiting my website: https://jessicarubenauthor.com

To the men and women who are currently serving and have served, thank you for protecting our freedoms. Today and everyday, I am grateful for your service.

To Jonathan, who opened up his heart over eggs with olives.

STAY UP-TO-DATE WITH JESSICA

Before you read any further ...

Do you want access to my amazing giveaways? Do you want to stay up-to-date on my upcoming books and hot sales? Join my mailing list! https://jessicarubenauthor.com/newsletter/

READER ADVISORY

Please note that *Warrior Undone* contains fictional characters who deal with gun violence, PTSD, and illegal drug use. All scenes in this book are completely fictionalized. Liberties were taken to fit this story.

PROLOGUE
SLADE

The helicopter descends into the brown-and-gray peaked mountains that jut between the Afghanistan-Pakistan borders. Shifting forward, a tightness fills the circulated air. Systematically wringing my hands, I move them left before right. I'm a man of rituals.

The door opens into extraordinary heat. It rushes forward and seeps beneath layered clothing. As I step off, my head focuses forward while my eyes do a snapshot perusal of the vast earth where people have lived and fought for centuries on end. When I slide on my sunglasses, the bright world dims.

Images of the compound flash on the projector. It doesn't look different from the hundreds we've raided beforehand.

"We're set to clear." The commander's hands move behind his back. He clasps them as he paces. "Marines are coming, too. They'll be inserting with us and setting up a perimeter of defense. Covering while we do our work." A cough rings through the room as coordinates are mentioned. "Intel says they're abandoned."

But first, sleep.

A sudden sensation of falling. Hard grains of sand nestled within the sheets move against my calves and between my toes. It's gritty. It's home.

A hard knock on wood before the door swings open.

Someone shouts, "It's go time, boys!"

I throw my legs to the right side of the bed and rise. Water to the face and brush my teeth. Time to suit up. My heart settles to a steady rhythm as I gather my weapons. The methodical movements are where I find my peace. M24 is strapped to my back. Heavy enough to make a dent but not too heavy to slow me down. An American flag sits on my bed, pre-folded. I place it between my armor and uniform. It settles inside my chest cavity. My body is its cocoon, reminding me of who I am, what I love, and where I came from.

As a team, we enter the thick darkness, a perfect cover.

A few kilometers into our hike, we sit to break. Rex is to my left, his photographic and video equipment resting on his side. He grumbles, spitting on the rocky ground before taking a swig from his green canteen.

"How you doin', brother?" I take a drink from my own.

"Fuckin' A," he replies but not for nothing. Rex hauls some heavy shit. Between the weight of his communications equipment and the high altitude, he is miserable.

He looks up at me. It's so dark, but I can still make out his shining eyes and sharply gritted teeth. Rex is probably the angriest corpsman on the Teams. Yet his complete stability in the face of a firefight has always transcended any anger—probably why we work so well together. Always have and always will.

I rise before holding out my hand. He takes it.

The Team gets back on its feet.

As I'm walking, sweat pours down my face.

Our commander turns to me. "The caves are near, and we haven't encountered a single person yet. Luck of the Texans, eh?"

The sun rises as we reach the complex. It's huge, circular, and wet with riotous colors. Looking up, I imagine who else around the world is staring at it, too.

We start in, four of us entering in formation. Before I step inside, my rational mind reminds me there could be an ambush ahead. This cave could be booby-trapped.

I turn to Rex.

His eyes say, *I've got your back.*

I clench my fists and walk inside.

It's dimly lit, but my adrenaline ... it burns. I pivot.

Wooden chairs and desks are organized neatly in rows facing a chalkboard. I'm in a classroom. Posters line the walls, full of anti-American slogans. Bin Laden's smile graces the largest poster in the center as two planes crash into the Twin Towers behind him. DEATH TO AMERICA!

Lives are dictated with propaganda. The systematic washing of brains.

We clear the room and step out to report.

Onto the next.

It's a fanatical dedication. They're pursuing a brand-new type of combat the free world is only beginning to understand. My father fought in the trenches. He rolled across deserts with huge ground forces. But us? We're up against decentralized cells. Guerrilla warfare on a scale of infinity.

The work is nerve-racking and tedious. Sweat saturates everything from my wool-blend socks up into my North Face jacket. It cools me.

Hours later, our job is complete. We gather what we need before stepping out. Phil rigged each room. When he clicks, it'll all blow to hell.

We easily hike down in a comfortable quiet.

Phil pushes the button.

The explosion causes a wild fireball against the sky, rocking the ground beneath my feet. The world is an echo.

Have I been here before?

The gunfire begins, and the ground shifts again. Liquid black oozes from Rex's mouth, and then his face is ablaze. Through a flaming mask, blue eyes stare as his mouth widens in terror. I move to him but fail to go quickly enough. An enemy comes up behind me. I jump and turn, muscles pulsing. I grab his throat with my left hand and my gun with my right. My mind tells me to forget the gunman and go to Rex, but my body is now on auto. Years of training take control away from my conscience.

He's carrying an AK-47 and a brown wool blanket. Motherfucker is going to die. I squeeze my grip, the world zeroing in on the two of us. He's thrashing. The smell of burning flesh infiltrates my senses as I squeeze ...

Rex. Something in the recesses of my mind knocks frantically. *He's dead. Your friend is dead. You turned away, and now, he's gone. It's all your fucking fault.* I want to scream, but nothing comes out of my mouth. I'm a dying fish.

The cemetery is cold, and everyone is gone. I've killed him. It's my fault. The sun sets, and I'm on the ground. Take me instead.

Open your eyes. Open them. OPEN YOUR FUCKING EYES, my mind screams.

On an exhale, I do.

A room ...

My room.

I drop my gaze. I'm inside a bed where a thick hand is wrapped around a slender, pale neck. My hand? Teardrops pool beneath her pale eyes. The room is still dark, but nature's light illuminates her in sepia. Bare, pointed breasts quiver, and goose bumps cover her soft flesh. I gently let go, my coiled muscles unraveling as my mind recognizes the pace change. Consciousness is restored.

Another night terror. My God.

I trip off the bed before righting myself and flip on the light. "I'm so sorry. Holy fuck," I exclaim. I turn back to her and pause at her unmoving form. Shaking her. "Lilly. Wake up. Wake up."

She's unconscious. I take a sharp inhale through my nose as I check her pulse. Alive. Next, I raise her bare legs over my shoulders to promote blood flow to her brain. Years of boxing and twelve years in the SEAL Teams have taught me a thing or two.

Sixty-four seconds, and her glossy blue eyes open. She's looking at me, confusion in her irises, as though she isn't sure what's happening. I turn my gaze to the bedside clock. It's 1:04 a.m. It takes a few seconds for her puzzlement to leak into fear.

My handprints—I can see them against the column of her white throat. Her breathing is somewhat normalizing.

Sweat drips from my forehead. "I hurt you. I didn't ..." I pause, my hands rubbing against the back of my buzzed hair. "You'll be okay. It's happened to me before. Getting choked out, I mean. You might have a headache later, but you'll be okay."

She stares at me, dumbstruck, not unlike the deer I used to shoot every October.

"S-Slade?" Her voice is hoarse as her delicate hands move up to her neck. She winces, white-blonde hair twisted above her head like a wild halo.

We just met tonight. I stayed until closing, just watching her wipe down the bar top.

WITH A LITTLE T-SHIRT *that shows off her midriff and red-painted nails, she bends down to grab something below the bar. The last few tired patrons leave some cash for her before walking out.*

"They're pulling out their keys." She nods toward the door. "I've got a crazy good sense of hearing."

"My younger brother, Aaron, had a keen sense of smell as a kid. Like a dog, he could sniff what the neighbor was cooking in the house next door. No joke."

I drink more of my beer, and her heart-shaped face laughs.

"Where's he now?"

"Who?" I polish off my drink, not wanting to speak anymore.

I want to get this woman into my bed and lose myself in her body. We've only met tonight, but she's sweet and pretty. Reminds me of the girls I used to know.

"Your brother?" Light eyes squint in curiosity.

"Oh." I clear my throat, rubbing the back of my neck. "He wanted to be like me. Join up. But ..." I lick my lips, not finishing my sentence.

"Oh shit. Sorry." Her gaze nervously darts to the side.

"Yeah." I get off the stool. "Ready to go? My bike's outside, and my place isn't too far."

Presumptuous of me, sure. But women are strange. They claim to want freedom, but most of them just want to be told what to do. Not that I mind. I'm a decent man, but I know what I like—to be in charge.

"Sure. Let me just grab my bag?" *Her voice is hesitant with question, as though I might change my mind. She's sweet but insecure.*

I nod before stepping outside and lighting up a smoke.

When she's on the back of my bike, her fingers grip my waist in excitement and fear. She tells me, "I've never been on a bike before," *as I put a helmet on her head. Yet she trusts me.*

AND, now, look what I've done.

"I don't know what happened. I was ... dreaming. Let me bring you home. You shouldn't stay here with me."

I could have killed you, I think. Another round of sweat coats my forehead.

I jump out of bed and move around the room, steadying my trembling hands as I grab her strewed clothes off the gray-carpeted floor. My place isn't much, but I always keep it spotless and organized.

"Rituals," I mumble under my breath, the word leaving my mouth without any thought.

My dream hits me again, ricocheting around my brain. The force is so strong; it stops my breath.

I exhale, focusing on the task at hand—dressing Lilly. Slowly, I guide long and lean legs back into lacy black panties, trying to remain gentle. Her black miniskirt goes on next as guilt hits me like a freight train.

She's moving slowly but thankfully letting me help. Next, I clasp her bra behind her back and slide her white T-shirt over her head. It says, *Stumble Inn. Have a drink.*

Millions of emotions threaten to take me down, but I tell them to shut the fuck up. Right now, I have to make sure she gets dressed and goes home safely. I'll deal with myself later. When she's clothed, I throw a pair of jersey sleep pants onto my legs and a blue T-shirt with the word *NAVY* in bold white letters.

I help her into my red pickup. Some country song plays on the radio as I try not to drive over any potholes. Like it's hard for her to speak, she tells me her address. I force myself to stick to the speed limit.

Getting to her home, a simple bolted-down trailer, I park the car in front. She opens the car door herself, but I run around to the side before she can exit, taking her hand in mine to help her down. I hold the small of her back as we walk. She fumbles with her keys, a massive chain, but quickly finds them. The door opens to a clean home with white walls and flowery furniture.

Her feet turn toward her bedroom, and I swiftly follow her lead. Hitting the bedroom lights, I lift her in my arms and gently place her on top of the bed, pulling off her short boots. The bedspread is pink. A large framed photo sits on her wooden nightstand. She is smiling in a blue cap and gown next to an older man with a wide, proud grin. Lilly is someone's daughter.

I head to the kitchen and find a glass in the cupboard, filling it with ice from the old white freezer and water from the sink. I take it to her room before asking, "Any Advil?"

"Motrin. Bathroom." Her voice rasps. It hasn't returned.

I immediately find it and remove two pills. Placing them in her hand, I finally ask, "Are you okay?"

She swallows the medicine with a large sip of water, wincing, and then rolls away from me. My cue to leave.

I hightail it back to my place. Shit's been going south in my head for too long, but this is a new low. Dirt kicks up around the car when I pull up to my small home, but I don't wait for it to settle before jumping out.

Within seconds, I'm rummaging through my own kitchen and pulling out a bottle of tequila, twisting the cap open. I need it to function.

"God is watching," my father loved to remind us at our wooden dinner table. He'd built it himself. Chewing his collard greens closed-mouthed with buzzed hair and his back ramrod straight, he'd lecture.

I grew up well. Football captain. Great friends. Church every

Sunday. Both my parents were hardworking and God-fearing. When kneeling for Holy Communion, I'd shut my eyes, just as I'd been taught, regardless of the fact that I was constantly restless from sitting too long. When I confessed to the priest, there was nothing I'd withhold.

I believed in God back then. I still want to, but how can I now amid the shit I've seen?

I take a few more gulps, aiming to drown myself in liquor and old-time memories ...

Aaron beating me in a shoot-out—it was one time, damn it, but he never forgot. That time when Dad drove his truck into a ditch, and the whole football team came to help push it out. Or the time Mom baked that zucchini bread for our new neighbor, but Aaron and I found it sitting hot in the oven, just waiting to be eaten.

"She can make another one," I said.

We used our hands like spoons, shoveling the warm bread into our mouths until there wasn't even a crumb remaining. It was so damn good; we didn't pause to get forks. Mom found us there with our hands in the oven, and boy, did she yell.

I take another swig, laughing. We were partners.

Aaron standing at the door next to my father, watching me as I readied myself to leave for boot camp. His blue eyes were full of hero worship for his older brother, who was willing to risk his life for God and country.

As he was three years younger than myself, life with Aaron was a continual test of strength and strategy. And, by that, I mean, we basically beat the living shit out of each other on a daily basis. Still, we were tight when it mattered.

The Twin Towers had fallen weeks prior, and we'd watched a documentary on television about the strength and pride of our Navy.

After all, good ole boys like us had been raised to represent our country and do it proud.

After I made my choice to go, he swore to join me after he turned eighteen. We shook on it.

On the brick steps leading to our front door, my father hugged me to his chest. "It's what we do," he said into my ear. As a Vietnam veteran, he'd seen and done his share.

My mother's tears weren't silent as I left home. She was proud but terrified.

"I'm proud of you. But what about school? Your football scholarship?" She reminded me of my old plans, worry etched within her words.

"When I come home, I'll finish it all up. I swear." I hugged her, but she shook in my arms as I kissed her good-bye.

Four years later, Dad died of prostate cancer. One year after that, my mama died from breast cancer. And, two years after that, Aaron was gone when a roadside bomb went off in Iraq.

And my world turned.

Some hearts are full of gratitude and joy, eager to make the earth a better place. My heart? It's disfigured, and it can no longer be trusted.

I retired to an empty house with nothing inside but furniture, photographs, and ghosts. In my bed that first night, between stale sheets that smelled vaguely of my high school gym locker mixed with my mom's detergent, I stayed up late to watch TV, hoping to adjust to the time change. A commercial came on for gourmet cat food served in a shimmering crystal bowl. In my mind's eye, I saw children rummaging, barefoot, through trash, looking for scraps to eat. Meanwhile, here in the USA, cats ate salmon out of gemstones.

What is this world coming to?

I became angry.

It took a few weeks, but I called friends to try to reacclimate. Reading the pamphlets, I was urged to reconnect. But it was all in vain.

I called my high school girlfriend, Sally.

She had been the cheerleader, and I had been the football captain. Cheesy, sure. But we had some real good times. We were innocents back then. Not that we weren't partying, having sex, and drinking beers from kegs because we were. I'd always been the type to enjoy life. Still, we were innocent in our thinking. All I thought about were grades, college, sports, and getting laid once or twice a day by my sweet and super-hot girlfriend. It had been a fun life. A simple life.

I picked up the phone and dialed with hope in my chest. Turned out, she was married with three kids. I could barely hear her over the sound of children screaming in the background.

Next, I called Tex.

He told me he was running the town auto shop and married to Jane, his own high school sweetheart. "Let's get a beer sometime."

Sure.

Hanging up, I called Billy. A CPA now living in Connecticut with his wife, whom he'd met at Yale. Always was a smart guy.

Hell, I am, too. But, with no college degree or work experience in the field, I'm behind.

Shannon was next. His mom answered and told me he'd died in a car accident during his senior year in college. I was floored. No one had told me.

Some friends from the SEAL Teams wanted to connect, but I didn't. Could barely look them in the eye after Rex's death. Loneliness and guilt threatened to pull me under at every turn.

Like my father, physical labor was a go-to. I refinished the wooden staircase in my family home, repainted the shutters blue, fixed some shaky white tiles in the bathrooms, and finally sold the house in an auction.

It was time to hit the road. Bouncing from spot to spot, I found myself in New York City and did a little fighting for cash.

"It sucks to have to train these Wall Street fucks," a guy tells me after an underground bout beneath a shitty bar on the outskirts of Times Square. A gash over his blackened eye trickles blood as men yell and jeer around us. "But it's a good way to ease back into the real world after leaving the military. Money and hours are pretty good, too. And the guy who owns the place, Joe? He's a decent guy." Lifting a small, clear plastic cup filled with

water, he swallows it down like a shot of tequila. "He was in the Navy himself. I think Special Forces. He gets it," he adds.

Blood continues to ooze.

"You need stitches." I point to his brow with my forefinger.

He shrugs. "Whatever," he says like it's the least of his worries. "It's just one of many."

I hand him my sweaty white towel. It's better than getting blood in the eye. Lifting it to his brow, he presses firmly to stop the flow.

I PULL the gun from my pants, spinning the black piece on the wooden table. What's the point of life really? My bladder reminds me it's full. I lean against the wall, letting it support me as I make my way to my small, blue-tiled bathroom.

"Want a smoke," I say to no one.

Unzipping my jeans, I lean my hand against the sink to keep steady.

Heading back into the kitchen, I check the junk drawer by the fridge. I push random keys and takeout menus around until I find the pack.

Shit. It's empty. I crunch it in my hand as my phone buzzes.

On shaky legs, I make my way to the table where my phone and gun sit. It flashes red. I've got a message.

Vincent: Yo. Dinner at my place tomorrow night? Eve's cooking.

IT ONLY TOOK a few months of training and sparring with Vincent at Joe's Gym, and I was lucky enough to call the man my friend. As it turned out, Vincent was living in New York while out on parole, but he was in the midst of completing construction on the Milestone, a large-scale hotel and casino complex out on Nevada's tribal lands. When he offered me the job to head security, I jumped at the chance. Even though I had no prior experience, Vincent trusted me to figure it all out. Luckily, my extensive military background easily translated into the security business. I connected with some of my brothers from the SEAL Teams, and together, we began VST, the Vulcan Security Team.

Would I let Vincent down? The Milestone is his life as well as mine. Vincent gave me this opportunity on a silver platter. He and I have a good thing going, and more is yet to come.

Bringing fresh water onto the reservation is next on our agenda, and hiring veterans to do the work will be a great thing.

I continue to spin my gun, dark thoughts pushing through. I wonder ... Why wait? Others can take my spot with Vincent. I'm not afraid of death. In fact, it would be better there. Valhalla. No more nightmares. No more waiting for the last shoe to drop. I almost killed a woman tonight. She could have died. I'm a loaded gun.

My hands shake as I lift my phone. I type and delete. Put it down. Spin the gun. Pick the phone back up again.

Finally, I type, **Yeah. I'll be there.**

Send.

1

Lauren

Las Vegas is completely phony but fun if you buy into its game.

When Sanam said she was getting married to the super-wealthy Reza Nader, everyone begged for a bachelorette party in Vegas. It seemed like it would be a fun idea at the time, but now, I'm seriously regretting saying yes. They're all in amazing places in their lives while I'm stuck in the same spot I've been for the last ten years—a legal secretary at Crier, one of the most prestigious law firms in LA and completely single. I've had boyfriends, of course. But none to love. I'm thirty-two years old, and I want to settle down with a smart, intelligent, kind, and handsome man who loves me. Where the hell is he? I've dated men who checked every box in my credential list. And yet all of them have turned out to be utter assholes.

The heavy rap music bounces against high concrete walls, painted to look like marble, and bursting against my eardrums. Bodies, costumed and practically nude, gyrate on the dance floor. A life-sized metal birdcage dangles from the ceiling by our table. A woman dances inside, if you can call spreading your legs and grinding against the bars dancing. It's Cirque du Strip. I don't want to stare, but it's hard not to. I mean, how the hell does she contort herself in these positions? The theme of the party tonight is Turn a Trick, Get a Treat, and my entire group, along with the rest of the club, is dressed accordingly.

I turn toward my friends, simultaneously cringing at their antics and wanting to make sure they've had enough water. They're all rolling on Molly, and their happiness has reached cloud-nine status. Apparently, Roxy and Allie got it from Sandy, who swears up and down it's as pure MDMA as you can get. The alleged result? The euphoria of ecstasy without any down. I know because I did all the research beforehand. Everyone's been texting for weeks about the party favors tonight, and of course, I immediately looked up all the details. I'm not planning to partake, but I'm also not one who appreciates a surprise. If everyone around me is going to be on drugs, I need to know what to expect.

Sanam moves to where I stand, hugging me with more empathy and love than I ever thought she was capable of feeling. I'm furious with her for rolling on drugs, but her kindness right now makes it hard to be angry. Her expensive perfume moves through my nose, making my eyes tingle. It's the same scent she's been wearing since we were in college, reminding me of when we lived together during our senior year at UCLA. Memories of how we'd find lunch specials from the fanciest restaurants and eat there, waiting for rich businessmen to see us and ask us out for dinner. It was all fun and games for me but not for Sanam. Over time, finding the man with lined pockets became *everything* to her.

We used to be inseparable. But our priorities changed drastically over time, and at this point, we couldn't be more different. I want to still love her because of what was, but it feels as though I can no longer trust her. In fact, everything in my life these days looks and feels like filler, overstuffed with fleeting conversations and pretentious hellos.

She pulls back, smiling. "I know I'm getting married, and you're not. I mean, not for a really long time at least. But we have to stay best friends forever, okay?" Her voice is high-pitched and haughty.

For the millionth time tonight, I ask myself if she has always been this bitchy and I never really noticed or if it's a new development in her personality now that she's about to be Mrs. Reza Nader.

Pushing her thick black hair over one shoulder, she smiles like she just won the lottery. Technically speaking, she has. Reza is rich.

I let out a, "Mmhmm," as I try not to slap her off the metaphoric high horse she's sitting on. Turning my body to the side isn't a choice but done for her preservation.

From my side-eye, I see her duck lips purse. She clears her throat, as though she's trying to get my attention.

"I'm telling you this because I love you. You're getting older, and it's time to wake up. There's no such thing as love. What's real is money. You are beautiful right now, but in a few years, you'll be older. Newer stock is going to rise. Just get in the game and close the deal with one of these wealthy men we know."

I swing around, facing her head-on. "I can't just—"

"Yes, you can," she interrupts. "You can, and you should. I know you believe that love will conquer all and blah, blah, blah. I thought, over time, you'd grow out of it, but you're still stuck in that stupid mindset. Why should you live in a small and crappy apartment with a man who'll eventually cheat on you with some dumb slut in his office? News flash: whether he's loaded with money or poor and hood, they all do the same shit. At least with the rich one, you'll be able to live an amazing life of travel. Parties. Dinners. Private planes. Reza has a lot of friends I want you to meet at the wedding." She smiles excitedly.

Sanam doesn't realize that it's not about money. It's that I'm sick and tired of eating shit from men who think that, because they buy me nice things, I have to say yes to their demands. I'd explain this to her, but how can I? Sanam's entire life is a transaction. She'll be a good wife in the ways Reza expects, and in return, he'll take care of her materially. She's followed this pattern since college. Sure, the trips we took in our twenties to St. Barts and the South of France with handsome and rich men were fun. But, for me, that's all it ever was—fun. As I got older, it became less and less so.

"We've always done everything together. I know we've separated some since I met Reza, but let's get you on my train. All you have to do is pick one of his friends. You're brilliant and beautiful and the nicest girl ever. It's all so simple! The only person to convince is yourself." The look in her eyes is full of honesty.

Before I can reply, Daniela comes over. Long red hair and completely coked up, she's totally out of her mind. She just got out of rehab, but clearly, it didn't help her. Anyway, I heard she's leaving for South America to help her father do some business. Good riddance! She opens the flap of her designer purse and dips a black manicured nail inside. Slowly pulling it out so as not to spill a grain, she sprinkles white powder in Sanam's palm. I try not to cringe over their blatant drug use. I love Sanam, but I hate some of the girls she surrounds herself with.

After she rubs the white crystals on her gums, it's only moments before a bright, demonic smile fills Sanam's face. Still, her crown continues to sparkle. On anyone else, it would look tacky—*Bride-to-Be* spelled out in shining, faux diamond letters. But, on Sanam, it's perfection. She's so attractive that, even drugged up and starving, she looks perfect.

"Most of Reza's friends are assholes," I add.

They're all big in California and New York City real estate, and they come to my law firm for closings. Any chance they get, they hit on me. As the head legal secretary on the real estate transactional team, it's my job to know every single client who works with the real estate attorneys. Unfortunately, it's also my job to make sure they're comfortable and happy. This means that, oftentimes, I have to plaster a smile on my face—even if it hurts.

"And they'd do anything to get into your pants. This has never bothered you before. What's changed?" Her eyes plead before sparkling at someone or something over my shoulder.

I turn my head and groan. There's a man behind me, tall and muscular, with an interested smirk on his face. He stares between the two of us, implication clear that he wouldn't mind some fun with us both. I quickly turn away, not wanting to give him any ideas.

"Anyway"—she brings her focus back to me—"I know your office has strict rules about dating clients, but, girl, get a clue. Every secretary on earth is working to meet a rich businessman. No one is actually working to work."

"I'm not just a secretary. I'm a legal secretary," I huff, feeling defensive. "And, while I'm not crazy about my job, it isn't just to meet some—"

"Whatever. Same difference," she interrupts, circling her hips to the music.

I narrow my eyes, wanting to shake her back to reality and then stab her with my red Louboutin stiletto. Sanam isn't cruel; she's just clueless.

Or maybe it's me who's dense. No. It's her.

The girls around me flit in excitement as some rap song I've never heard comes on. I can feel my despair seeping through my thighs, heavier than I wish they were.

Should I just take some Molly? Maybe, if I did, I could actually be happy again.

I bite my lip, running through my usage checklist for the millionth time. I have no preexisting health conditions. I am not taking any medication that interacts with MDMA. I'm aware of the dosage guidelines, and I know that the positive effects of this drug are maximized between eighty-one to one hundred ten milligrams. I will be sure to drink two cups of water. My costume is thin, which should keep me cool to avoid heatstroke. Molly could be the pause my body yearns for, but my mind won't allow.

Sanam brings her skinny, hairless arms high above her as the music thumps.

"I never really liked this rap music." She shakes her tiny ass as sweat beads at her unlined forehead. "But I love the vibrations. Can you feel it? We're all one. Humanity is meant to become a single body, full of unity!"

I cock my head in confusion at her spiritual words, so unlike her.

"And I'm getting married. And that house he just bought me? God! Can you believe it?" she squeals.

In front of us, Allie climbs up onto the rectangular table over-flowing with liquor and ice. Lowering her own diamond-encrusted hand, she brings Sanam to stand up with her. A few bottles of vodka topple to the ground, the glass shattering near my feet and soaking the floor. The girls only laugh at the mess they made. Reza, of course, is footing the entire bill for the weekend. Meanwhile, they're dancing like they're starring in a porn, making *come fuck me* eyes at any man with a pulse. Okay, maybe not that bad. But still.

Sanam screams to me, "Come up, Lauren!" She's enjoying the attention she's receiving from partygoers, her moves exaggerated and overly sexy.

I click my tongue, turning away. No way in hell am I dancing on a table. Jesus, but I need an escape right now. Still, I wish I weren't the way I was. I want to just take the drugs and be happy like everyone else. I want something to shut me up for once, so I can actually enjoy life instead of questioning and thinking of all the possible outcomes. I want to dance without a care, too. But ... I can't.

Sanam's laughing. She's got that squinting-eye look as her hands clap together, mouth parted. I can't hear it over the loud music, but I know the sound is high-pitched. I tap her slender hip, getting her attention.

I shout, "I'm going to use the restroom!"

She lifts a finger in the air, the universal sign for *wait one second*.

Jayme takes Sanam's hand as she daintily steps off the table.

Picking up a bottle of tequila, she fills a full shot glass and lifts it up between her perfectly manicured fingers. "At least take another drink before you go. I hate seeing you so miserable when we're all happy." She pouts.

Rolling my eyes, I take the drink from her hand and swallow it down in one gulp.

2

Slade

I gave my friends shit when they told me we were going to a costume party, but apparently, this is tonight's hot spot. A well-known rap artist, whose name I can't even remember, is performing.

Hip-hop blasts around the dimly lit club as we step into the throng teeming with sweaty, half-naked bodies. The dance floor is full of women in lingerie and men who look like they just left lockup. People see us walking forward and immediately make way, parting to steer clear. Lots of guys on the SEAL Teams aren't big. But we are.

At the Mile, we work our security team with a single-minded purpose that borderlines on insane. Working for Vincent Borignone means staying in complete control all the time. But, tonight, we're in Vegas to let out some of that pent-up steam, and we aim to tear it up.

I lean on the black lacquered bar. "Three tequila limes."

The bartender wears a black push-up bra and micromini. She's got a throwback 1950s *Playboy* centerfold thing going for her. Retro or whatever the word is. Jet-black hair with straight-cut bangs. A black line on her eyelids that flicks up at the end, sort of like a cat eye would look. She's even got bright red lipstick. I let my eyes take their fill, her practically nude body on display. I'll be able to enjoy it more when I'm drunk enough to relax.

"Anything else you want?" She leans forward against the shiny bar top, putting her massive fake tits closer to my face. Her question is filled with possibilities that have nothing to do with my drink order.

"I can think of a few things. Let's start with those drinks though, yeah?" My voice is gravelly.

She smiles wide. "I'm Candice."

"Slade." I want to grin, but my mouth refuses to turn up. I'm so damn tired. I drank my body weight in liquor last night and slept like shit. My liver is angry as fuck, but here I am, planning on doing it all again. But harder.

Turning around to pour the drinks, she makes a nice show of bending over, showing me her tight, pert ass.

Nice.

Rob rubs his hands together, scheming. "Bachelorette party, twelve o'clock." He points north, his white button-down shirt rolled up to his tatted forearms. "Could be just what we need tonight."

After I choked out Lilly, Rob and I spoke. He hooked me up with some benzos a doctor prescribed to his brother-in-law for anxiety. Men like us don't need to be psychoanalyzed. I can take care of myself. I didn't spend twelve years engaging and prepping for war, only to come home, crying to some doctor who doesn't know shit about shit when it comes to what I went through overseas. If I saw a shrink, he'd smash my head open. Memories that I never want to discuss—ever—would be called out and brought into the real world. And once those demons are freed? There's no putting them back. That would fuck me up more than anything, no doubt. Luckily, Rob understood me perfectly.

The drugs have been a huge help, pausing the never-ending leak of memories that plague me at night. Still, I'm careful not to have any women or friends stay over. While the meds work wonders, they're not foolproof.

I just need a little more time to get myself back under control. I can handle it. I'm going to find a hot girl or two tonight, get laid, and release some of this stress simmering under my skin. It'll work.

I hear laughter next to me and turn toward it. Ultra-slutty attire has my eyes widening. Sparkling white angel wings, lacy white bras, and thong panties. I'm enormously enjoying the view until I see their faces. They're girls, and they all look about sixteen, smiling and taking selfies. My jaw drops.

"Tell me all the women here aren't teenagers," I grumble, rubbing the back of my neck and feeling like a creeper.

"I hope they are," Mike replies with an evil grin, doing his vampire costume justice.

"Sick fuck."

I laugh, lifting my hand to slap him behind the head. He ducks quickly and chuckles as my hand makes a clean sweep, slicing through air.

"Yeah, as if you haven't done some crazy-ass shit yourself, motherfucker. Who could forget Candy, eh?"

We continue to talk smack when my eyes pause on the bachelorette party. I tune out my idiot friends and focus on the bride-to-be, wearing a sparkling crown. A one-night stand with one of these women would be good. Exactly what I need. I admire the half-naked nurse. The slutty devil. Oh, *Risky Business*—always a good costume. And then I pause at the flight attendant, who might not be dressed as scantily as the rest of her group, but whose body is straight-up sexy. Legs for miles into a small waist. Perfect tits. I move my eyes to her face, marked with a scowl, and pause.

Holy shit. *Is it her?*

The strobe lights move across the group, making it difficult to be sure. I wait patiently for colors to shift. Finally, yellow hits her face in just the right angle, and I can confirm. It *is* her. Still hot as fuck, but angrier than before. A hand flies to her hip as she talks to her crown-wearing friend. Yeah, she definitely isn't happy right now. Luckily for her, I can change that.

Her hair is long and wavy, like she just came from the beach. It looks damn good. Last time I saw her, it was pulled back tightly for

Vincent and Eve's wedding in some fancy style. Actually, after I was done with her, it looked a lot like this. I can't help but chuckle at the memory. Was it really only a few months ago? She's just so ... beautiful. Something about the shape of her brown eyes, large and almond, makes my dick twitch. I adjust but keep my eyes trained on the prize.

I asked her what her ethnicity was, but she was shady as hell about it, playing around and never giving me a straight answer. I continue to stare, vividly remembering the night of the wedding.

"LET'S GO FOR A WALK." Grabbing two wineglasses from the wooden bar, I stuff them in the back pockets of my khakis before taking a cold bottle of white from the bartender. "Thanks, man."

We pound fists. He's the son of one of the board members on the tribal council, and Vincent and I both spar with him from time to time. He's never fought competitively, but he is pretty quick on his feet.

"A walk?" she repeats.

I face her and notice her pink lips, nice and full. My eyes trail down to her nipples, which have pebbled beneath her gown. She catches me staring and immediately drops a hand over a slender hip, daring me to keep looking. Good thing I'm not the type of man who hides. I'm not into cryptic shit. If I want something, I go for it. No excuses and no bullshit. The last hour has been spent taking shots and making jokes. It's been great, but I'm ready to move on.

"Yeah," I start. "You know, put one foot in front of the other. Walk." I raise the bottle of wine in my hand and lift my brows, promising more fun. "My truck isn't too far."

"Well, I don't walk in heels like these," she sasses back, shrugging.

I look down and laugh. She wasn't lying. Those shoes are pretty damn high. Strappy and pointy and who the fuck knows what.

"Take them off." I stare at the death traps on her feet. "I'll hold them for you. Why did you even put that shit on tonight? You're in the mountains, if you didn't notice."

She squints. "Shit? They're my shoes."

I grunt, feigning understanding.

Her eyes roll. "You don't get it."

"Guess not." I tip my head, trying to charm my way around the fact that I have zero clue what she's saying.

The women I grew up with had three pairs of shoes—flips, sneakers, and work boots. Lauren wears the kind of fancy shit that I can barely get my head around. I guess they're sexy, but she'd be hot in anything.

She huffs, "Fine. I'll take them off." A flirty kind of annoyance is written on her face. "But only because you served my country. Don't want to seem ... ungrateful."

I laugh, and she bites her cheek, not wanting to let on. This girl. She crouches down, and after a few moments, she stands back up again. She's a lot shorter than what I'm used to. I'm well over six feet, and she looks about five foot three. Surprisingly, I like it.

We walk away from the twinkling Christmas lights outlining the wedding area.

Her bare feet, softly arched, slowly pad forward. "If I get something stuck in my foot, you'd better be ready to remove it."

"No worries. I've got a whole kit in my truck."

"Boy Scout."

"You know it."

I take the shoes from her hands before sparing a glance at the newly married couple, who are so up in each other's love that they can barely see straight. The music is fast, but Vincent and Eve are at their own leisurely pace.

Walking toward my truck, I smell vanilla and citrus. It's her. I want this woman. And it's not just because she's gorgeous. She actually makes me laugh, which is rare. Smarter than she seems, too. She plays it off to be all simple and sweet, but if there's something I've learned tonight, it's that there's more than meets the eye. The fact that she's here for a limited time doesn't hurt either. We can have a great time, and then she'll head on home to LA. No stress.

I turn to her as she breathes in the fresh air around us. It's so dark.

"This is it," I tell her as my red truck comes into view.

She leans against the side, looking sexy as hell. I just spent the last hour trying to make the girl smile, and now, with the way she's staring at me, I feel like yelling, Hooyah! *I love completing a good challenge, and the finish line is so close; I can taste it.*

"So, is this where you wanted me?" Her tongue teases through parted glossy lips.

Before she can open up that pretty mouth of hers again, I lift her round ass into my hands and place her on the car's bed. Her legs spread apart, making room for me. My lips press against hers, and she immediately grabs my back, moaning. Fuck, she tastes so good. Like wine and berries.

I start pulling on the straps of her dress, wanting it off, as I move my mouth to the side of her neck.

"Wait, wait. My dress. The buttons—"

I'm panting. "Huh?" My dick strains against my jeans.

"Don't rip it. It's Mendel."

I remove my mouth from her collarbone. "Mend-who?"

"Like, a serious designer."

I curse. "Turn around. Let me take the thing off."

"You can't do it in the dark, Slade." Again, that annoyed voice.

Why it turns me on, I don't have a clue. The girls I grew up with are down-home and relaxed. Not snooty upper class. I have no idea how a woman like her operates, but right now, I'll do basically anything to make us happen. My dick and I, we're in agreement. We want this girl.

I slide my hand up under her dress, pushing her panties to the side to feel her soaked, hot center. She sucks in a breath as my fingers circle her clit.

"I'm going to fuck you so good. You'd better tell me how to get this dress off before I grab my knife and cut it off," I growl.

She brazenly puts her hand down my pants, stroking my cock while my hand stays up her skirt. I thought I was hard, but her soft hand on my dick has my brain short-circuiting. I can hear her gasp as I reach up higher and curl my finger up, hitting her spot.

"Don't you have a flashlight or something? Isn't survival, like, your thing?" Her voice comes out strangled as she lets go.

I laugh. The combination of wanting to fuck like crazy and this stupid dress has my wires crossed. I lazily pull my hand out of her wet heat before moving away.

I run to the side of my car, pants and belt undone with my dick hanging

out, and pull the flashlight from under the passenger seat. I've got my knife
here, too, but something tells me she wouldn't appreciate this dress getting
sliced in half. I make it back to her and freeze. She's sitting on her knees,
facing the dark mountains. Finally moving her head to me, her brown eyes
blink in amusement.

"Are your parents Middle Eastern?"

God, she's beautiful. That thick hair is a beautiful shade of golden
blonde, but I can see the darkness at her roots.

She smirks. "Just take it off, Slade."

Holy fuck, if this girl isn't the sexiest woman I've ever seen, I don't know
who is.

I move behind her, letting my hands rove over her creamy, nude thighs.
My callous fingers skate against her delicate skin. She's perfect. A large part
of me wants to take her just like this with her dress around her waist. But
the other part of me—the smarter one—wants to get her totally naked.

Button by button, so slowly, I begin opening her dress. I'm surprised to
realize that I've never undressed a woman like this before. I touch her bare
back and kiss the spot between her shoulder blades. She's getting antsy, so I
slide my hand into her pussy again, taking my time. Still soaked.

"You're enjoying this?" she asks, trying to mask her arousal with a
steady voice. She can't hide from me. Her body betrays her—wet.

"You bet I am." I continue to touch her with one hand and open her
dress with the other.

Finally, the last button is undone. She gasps as I blow across her nude
back. She shivers.

"Turn that off?" Her voice is all breathy as she stares at the flashlight,
the mouth on her suddenly stilled to a whisper.

As the straps of her dress fall from her slender shoulders, I'm silenced.
For the first time in my life, I want to make sex amazing for the woman in
front of me. It's not just about getting off and having fun. I don't know what
it is I'm trying to prove, but I want to show her that I can do it better than
any of these prissy fucks she's had before me. Because I'm better than them.
And I'm the best she'll ever have.

"No." I shake my head. "Stand up. And pull your dress off nice and slow.
For me."

I step back to watch, shifting the flashlight to face her. She's on display, standing like a vision from my dreams. Listening to my commands, the way I like. And, just like that, her dress falls. Perfectly shaped breasts. Flat, defined stomach.

"Now, come suck my dick before I fuck you."

"Yo, dude. Earth to Slade. Those drinks are sitting on the bar, man." Mike gestures to the shot glasses sitting before me.

I take them off, holding two in each hand, and pass them out, completely ignoring the bartender, who is expectantly staring at me.

Lauren. It's her.

Walking away from her group of friends, she raises her head. I dart my eyes, figuring out where she's headed while trying not to lose sight of her in the crowd. She has table service, which means she isn't coming to the bar for a drink. Finally, I see the word *RESTROOM* in pink neon letters on the opposite end of the club.

Her shoulders are tight as she presses through dancing bodies. The Lauren I met at the wedding was fun-loving and constantly smiling.

I distinctly remember us talking about anything and everything, joking around as the sun came up while she sat in my arms in my truck's bed. I told her about growing up in Virginia, and she asked me a million and one questions about what it was like to be the captain of the football team in a small town. I asked her about living in a big city and if upper-class private school was as cutthroat as they said. We talked about work and our dreams. She was unsatisfied with her current career, and I told her I was looking forward to handling more at Milestone and expanding my security business. Damn, did we laugh together. I ribbed her about her uptown-girl status but knew that she was totally different than the picture she painted to the world. Actually, she amazed me with how funny and smart she was. It was ... unexpected.

She made it clear that she was looking for long-term, not that I would have been opposed to that option once upon a time. Hell, after she left, I wanted to call her. We were opposites, but there was something real between us. A connection that went beyond attraction.

After the Lilly fiasco, a relationship with a woman can only be temporary. At least, until I regain control of my psyche. Lilly and I spoke after that horrible night. Luckily, she had a father who'd served. She urged me to seek help, and we managed to part on decent terms. As of today, anything more than a one-night stand isn't in the cards. It can't be.

Between memories of war and keeping my day-to-day life maintained and focused, there's no room for anything more than a quick fuck, followed by a drop-off. But tonight and for this particular woman? There are plenty of hours for fun.

I place my drink back on the bar. "Boys, I'm getting some action."

They hoot as I spot her, catching her again with my eyes. I want to get to the restroom line before her. Surprise her. It's impossible to stop my smirk as I turn to leave.

"Wait a sec." Rob pulls out a small baggy from his front pocket. "Brought you more, like you asked. My supply is dwindling. You've got to find a doc who'll write you a script or find a new way to score."

I take it from his hand.

"Just make sure not to touch Ambien. Sleep meds will mess with you in a way you don't need. Trust me."

"Thanks, man. This should be enough." I slide it in my back pocket. "I'll be good. Soon." My voice is confident.

It's been two months of popping benzos at night and crushing half in my morning coffee. Sometimes taking other pills to get me back up again. But I know this is just for now. Just until I get my head straight.

He nods. "Don't doubt it."

We pound fists before I turn away, going to find my girl.

3

Lauren

Pushing through clusters of people and trying to stay above the waves of dancing bodies, I reach the train of men and women who stand, waiting for the restroom. I cock my head to the side, trying to see how many people are ahead of me without stepping out of the queue when my eyes zero in on a great ass. It's high and firm and encased in blue jeans. Shoulders super wide. Waist narrow. Tattoos line his arms. And he's tall. I love tall. Something me and Sanam have always had in common.

Marriage is obviously eons away from me. Maybe a wild night is what I need. Lord knows, I haven't had one of those in ages. Or at the very least, I could use a long, good look. Under normal circumstances, I'd be embarrassed to stare at a man this openly. But we're in Vegas, and the chances of seeing him again after tonight are none.

He takes a phone from his back pocket and sidesteps; I can now see his profile without any obstruction.

Wow.

Hair styled in a clean buzz cut. Straight Roman nose. Strong jaw, highlighted with dark scruff. Full and sensuous lips. Seeing him so straight and tall has me fixing my own posture; I immediately push my shoulders down and back.

He turns, as though he can feel my gaze. We lock eyes—maybe. He's wearing a black mask, covering the top of his face, so I can't entirely tell where he's looking. Ninety-five percent of me knows that he's staring at me. Still, there's that small sliver of thinking that maybe he isn't. Even with his eyes covered—or maybe because of it— my body heats.

I continue to watch as his lips quirk upward, showing me straight white teeth between a gorgeous mouth. And, in my bones, I know that grin is meant for me. Things have been so shitty lately, and it feels *so good* to just be looked at this way. From a sexy stranger, no less.

The manscaped boys I'm used to can't hold a candle to a man like this. With their chests waxed and legs encased in skinny trousers, there's nothing about them that says, *I will fuck the shit out of you and change your lightbulb if it's out.* Nope. This guy, on the other hand, is so ... masculine. I'm all for women's lib, but I can't deny the fact that seeing a man so physically powerful makes me want to jump his bones before cooking him dinner.

The last time I was with a man this hot—or with any man at all for that matter—was at Vincent and Eve's wedding and ... no, I'm not going there. That night was too good, and I refuse to think about what will never happen again. Sure, the sex was off the charts. But I'd made it clear that I was looking for someone long-term, and while he promised to call me, he never followed through.

Whatever.

Slade is totally not my type. He runs adventure races in the wilderness while I prefer the treadmill at the gym. He hunts and kills animals—with a gun—and then smokes them, for God's sake. I barely even eat meat!

I cringe, thinking of those poor baby deer he told me about. Alligators are one thing because, ew, alligators are gross. But deer? I let out a shudder. It was cool when he told me about how he used to hunt with his brother, and we joked around over it. But, after getting back home in LA and having detailed discussions with myself over whether or not I should be the one to call him first, I realized what he'd probably known from the start—we were completely incompatible.

The masked hottie steps out of line and walks over to me. I seductively bite my lip, trying to get my flirt on and head back in the game.

The girlie part of me shakes her ass, screaming, *He's coming over! He likes me!*

As if it's happening in slow motion, he lifts the mask from his face, setting it on his forehead. My jaw slackens as a warm, sexy smile fills his face.

"Hey, Lauren." His voice is like an aphrodisiac to my senses.

I blink, and, of course, that's the moment the alcohol in my blood stream begins to really hit me. I was buzzed, but that last drink took me to an entirely different plane. My memory chooses to remind me of the way he sounded during sex. Saying my name, deep and gravelly, as though he'd die if he stopped fucking me. Raising my leg over his massive shoulders—

Oh shit. My blood travels way down south, pulsing down between my legs. It's unstoppable.

"Um, hey, Slade." I keep my voice steady, trying not to falter.

I seriously cannot believe he's the one I've been ogling. Is he the only masculine man on the West Coast? I let out a small cry over the coincidence, hoping the loud music drowns out the sound.

The first time I met Slade was in the hospital when Vincent, his boss and best friend, was in a coma. I was there to help my friend Eve, who is now Vincent's wife. Despite the horrible circumstances, I took one look at Slade, and my mind turned to jelly. He's just so strong. And his eyes? I look into them and feel like I could get lost and still be safe. Maybe it's because Eve told me he was a Navy SEAL. My mind has obviously gotten mangled between the hero dream man and reality. I mean, sure, he's protected our country, but—

"You're here. In Vegas." His voice is sure. Friendly even. So warm.

"Looks like we both are."

The hours we shared in his truck at the wedding? Arguably, the best I've ever had. Maybe I need to look on the bright side. Sure, my friends and I have hit a crossroads, and, at this rate, I might never find love and marry. But I've got Slade in front of me—also known as the best sex of my life. He doesn't want anything long-term with me—this I know to be true. Maybe God is throwing me a bone for the night. Who am I to say no to a miracle?

A finger taps the center of my back. "That one's free."

I turn to the bald guy behind me, who points to the second door on the right.

"Ladies first." Slade grins. "I'll meet you by the sinks."

I walk into the hallway, lined on each side with individual bathrooms, and try not to sway. I can feel Slade's eyes trained on my backside and give myself a mental high-five because I know my ass looks good tonight. I'm not dressed as slutty as most of the girls in this club, but my costume still shows that I've got the goods. When I step in, the door shuts behind me. After sliding the mangled silver lock closed, I finally let out the scream I was holding in.

"Slade! SLADE! He's here!" I do a little dance, careful not to let my legs brush against the nasty toilet, but I curse when I realize there is no mirror in the stall to evaluate how I look.

After finishing my business, I step out to the communal sink and check myself out in the large, horizontal mirror.

I'm glad to see my shelf life is still kicking with no expiration date in sight. My eye makeup is smudged, but it looks dark and smoky. My hair is in tousled waves, which is perfect for a hot and sweaty night. I switch the part in my hair to give it a little extra volume, noting that I'm overdue for highlights; my black roots are showing more than usual. No thanks to my Persian heritage, my naturally jet-black hair is crazy thick and difficult to handle.

I turn on the sink and begin washing my hands when Slade moves up next to me. There is no soap, so after drying my hands with a paper towel, I pull out a small bottle of Purell from my bag. His eyes squint in confusion as I squeeze a few drops into my hand.

"Want?" I lift the small bottle like an offering when he gives me a shit-eating grin.

"You carry hand sanitizer?"

"Of course I do. There's no soap in places like this." My voice comes out more defensive than I intended.

"You realize you're in the middle of a nightclub in Vegas. It's almost one o'clock in the morning, and you just took a piss in a communal restroom."

I grimace from his word choice. "And?"

"Well"—he chuckles—"good to know you never lose your sense of hygiene."

He puts out his hand, and I squeeze some in the center of his huge, callous palm. He presses his hands together.

"Ready? Or are you planning to floss, too?" His lips quirk up. "I can wait, if you want." He crosses his huge arms in front of his chest.

"You're funny, Slade." I shake my head as though he's ridiculous when, really, I'm holding back my own laughter. Because I do in fact have a miniature floss in my bag. What can I say? I'm serious about clean teeth.

We both turn to leave when a tall, lanky man exits the stall to our right, sweaty and panting as though he just sprinted ten miles.

"I can make you feel good," he says in a singsong voice, coming at me with yellowed teeth as his grabs at his crotch. Dark, beady eyes roam over my body.

I'm ready to yell when Slade steps to my right, pulling me into his thick chest. "Back up."

It's only two words, but they're said in such a way that the guy spins off, running.

Slade just laughs. "You should have seen your face."

"He could have killed me!"

He pushes an errant hair from my face. "Don't you know never to worry when I'm around?"

I look into his eyes and know he's telling the truth.

"You need a drink." He smiles playfully, breaking the moment and throwing a heavy arm around my shoulder. He bends down, putting his lips near my ear. "Let's go."

I can feel his breath, hot in my ear.

I should play hard to get, right? I take him in and pause. Oh, who the hell am I kidding? There's *no way* I'm turning him down. He's so hot; I can't even pretend to be unsure.

I open my hand as he reaches for it, and he takes us away from the restrooms. I'm drunk, and he doesn't want a future. But that doesn't mean I can't have fun tonight, right?

We step onto the dance floor, but this time, I feel no anxiety. I'm hanging on to a man who my bones know would never let me get clobbered. Slade, in all his bigness, plows through dancing fairies, badass-looking demons, and jumpsuit-wearing jailbirds. He's a man on a mission. My drunk mind wanders to how he probably looks in his uniform. And then without the uniform. The images swirling through my mind have my temperature rising to new heights.

We finally get to the bar where he pulls me close to his side. "Gin, vodka, or tequila?"

I press against him. "Tequila. It's what I've been drinking tonight."

"Hey, you," the bartender purrs to Slade, cat eyes glowing with interest.

I look between them, trying not to look jealous or territorial. The way she's staring at him makes me wonder if they've hooked up.

"Two tequila limes," he requests, not unkindly.

I step up closer to Slade, wanting her to know he isn't alone. At least, not anymore. She takes a nice, long look at me, and I her. Her eyes are judgmental, telling me to step down. I raise my brows, as if her wordless request is laughable. Pursing her red lips in annoyance, she grabs two shot glasses and fills them to the brim. My friends in LA are the hugest bitches on earth. If she thinks an evil glare is enough to shake me, she has no idea whom she's dealing with.

"I'll add it to your tab," she tells Slade, seductively inching closer to him.

I've got to give her props; she doesn't give up easy.

I put my hand on his arm to regain his attention. When he turns to me, a liquid smile moves across his face, and I know I've won. The bartender, no matter how high her tits are pushed up or how little she's wearing, doesn't stand a chance. Clinking our glasses, we shoot them back. I make sure to look at her from my side-eye. She's watching—and now, she knows. I wrap my arms around his thick neck and press my lips against his. They're hot and full and so good. Tonight, this man is mine.

The strobe lights fly across the room in riotous colors. We've been dancing and drinking nonstop. His heavy hands roam over my body on the dance floor when I realize I haven't had this much fun since we were together at the wedding. As I bite my cheek, my smile won't wane.

I'm the type of girl who pictures all possible outcomes before I get myself involved in anything. But, with Slade, I'm somehow free. With him, I don't feel the need to know every detail or potential result. Maybe it's because he and I are so different, and a future between us is so improbable that there's nothing to think about other than the moment. Whatever it is, I love it. And, by the way he's acting, he does, too.

"So fucking glad you're here," he says again, pulling me back to the bar to order more shots.

We don't have time to sip on drinks. We want to get drunk and *dance*. Perspiration beads at his forehead, and I get another flashback of how he sweat above me in the back of his truck. His smile tells me he knows what I'm thinking. At this point, all embarrassment is gone. I'm glad he knows. I want it again.

We clink our glasses together—I think it's my third and his fifth—and swallow them down before he moves his hands to my face and angles it upward. Our kiss is scorching. His tongue, so hot in my mouth, is a direct line to my panties. I'm soaked.

Back on the dance floor, I give in to the hip-hop music, letting my body burn from the heavy beat and dirty lyrics.

"Bend over and spread 'em, girl ..."

I drunkenly laugh because regular Lauren would be disgusted by what's coming out of these rappers' mouths. I mean, to call these lyrics raunchy is an understatement. But, right now, I can't even be bothered to care.

I lift my eyes back to his. They shine.

"Want to get out of here?" His masculine, deep voice is a growl.

"Yes," I yell, needing him to hear me. If I sound overly excited, it's because I am.

His hand takes mine as we move back to the bar.

Raising his hand, he nods to the nearest bartender, who immediately comes over. "Close my tab." The request is brisk.

He signs the bill, and my mouth waters from need.

We start moving again through the throng, but a sound goes off like firecrackers around me. Is it just the music? Something feels off. In my gut, I know it's not drunkenness. My mind sobers as my internal alarm beeps. It's a slow and steady rhythm that won't let up. The air is restless. The faces of some partygoers look strange, too. Are they on drugs? Or is it me? I rub the side of my head. Before I can squeeze Slade's hand, wanting to ask if he feels the change, he stops in his tracks and pulls me into his chest in a move meant to secure. He scans the room. He senses something is off, too.

The music blasts while people around me turn left to right, seemingly confused as well.

"What's going on here?"

The strobe lights have the entire room painted red.

My eyes pause on a woman dressed like a Catholic schoolgirl, dancing on a high pedestal. It feels like slow motion when she drops, falling to the ground like a rag doll. People jump back until I have the perfect view of her splayed on the floor. With long hair twisted behind her and spray-tanned legs awkwardly bent, her white button-down shirt bleeds, turning black. Is the light playing tricks? The blood begins pooling around her like spilled ink. It could be motor oil but for the smell—a putrid copper. A deep shiver moves down my spine, undulating over each disc in my back.

People scream, pointing at the girl, as Slade pushes me behind him, shielding me from what's ahead. His body, while stationed, pivots left to right. The heavy bass pounds straight up into my chest. I want to run and hide. I want to tell myself that, of course, this is just part of the game. It's Vegas. Everything is a mirage. It must be a play of light. Everything is fine.

I count to ten and will myself to lift my head. I want to confirm that nothing is wrong. Slade wrings his hands together before tensing up. He's completely still now, barely breathing. Shouldn't we be moving or running or ... something? My breathing picks up. It's panic. People are running, but we aren't.

The murmuring grows louder until it drowns out the music in my ears. Person by person, happy turns to mortified; it's a domino effect. Club security comes barreling toward us as partygoers flood toward the exit. Slade and I seem to be cemented in place. That's when the music shuts down.

A horrible silence descends among the crowd. I raise my arm and squeeze his shoulder, but still, he doesn't move. It's as though he's in a trance.

The ringing in my ears continues to echo, pounding straight into my heart.

A unified quiet before a mixture of, "What the fuck?" and, "Oh my God," fills the void.

A voice, dark and heavy, comes on a microphone at the DJ booth. It towers above, in control. We're the tiny ants below, crushable.

The club, like a collective, tilts their heads upward. A gasp bounces off the walls, the sound rebounding. Slade continues to methodically wring his hands together, left to right. I'm holding on to him, a solid and straight wall.

The man breathes into the microphone, and the sound cracks. His mouth opens as he yells, "There's only one ruler on these motherfuckin' streets!" He points a gun to the ceiling.

It dawns on me that I've never seen a real gun in all my life. Is that really it? This tiny black handheld can ... kill?

He pulls the trigger into the crowd; it's thunder.

"No!" The word tears from my lips into the world around us. A pit, the size of my fist, flies to the center of my throat. I want to breathe, but I can't.

The blood in my arteries flashes to molasses.

That's when the shots begin to spray.

Slade grabs my arm and runs.

"No, we're going the wrong way," I scream, trying to stop him.

But he won't allow me to turn or pause, and it's as though he's been taken over and turned into a robot. I'm tripping over my heeled feet, being dragged behind this massive man-machine who won't let me go. While everyone in the club seems to be going left, we're moving against the tide.

I keep yelling, "I'm going to get trampled," but Slade continues to push forward, his hand like a vise around my wrist.

A man dressed like a police officer runs toward me with his mouth foaming white, and I shriek as he makes direct contact with my body, knocking me down and running over me, his heavy feet stomping and running over my arm like he's hitting a parked car.

Then, more people come toward me, but Slade drops to his haunches, and like a wolf, he raises his huge, muscled arms and knocks people down because anyone who dares to come close will be removed. They're falling backward from the force of his upper body while I'm still here, on the ground.

His eyes are completely vacant and dark when he says, "Grab my neck," with a mechanical voice.

A woman to my right drops onto the floor—not from his arms, but from something else, as if she was hit with a bullet. My mouth gapes open, but no sound comes out.

Finally, Slade yells, "Get on my back now!"

A horrible chill moves through my body as I grab on to him, just like he told me to, and his large hands wrap behind the backs of my knees. He stands to his full, enormous height and begins to really run. With adrenaline pumping hard, I can't feel anything but his energy bursts. His body is so hot that it's practically steaming as he jets through the shrieking masses, crouching his form, likely to keep from being a target because he's bigger and faster than anyone else, weaving expertly while shots spray all around. I have no choice but to shut my eyes from the sickening view of people dropping, but after a moment, I open them again because I'm too afraid to not see. We reach the opposite end of the club where Slade pushes a huge metal door wide open, stepping out into the night.

The humid air spins around me as the door slams shut behind us.

It's so dark. We're in a back alley with nothing but desolate concrete and cries. There's an ambulance in the distance. Slade sets me down. My knees buckle, but he immediately holds me up beneath my arms.

"Can you stand?" His voice is still robotic, a complete change from the man I was with a minute ago.

Or was it hours ago?

With nothing other than sheer will, my legs manage to straighten. Slade anxiously wrings his hands. I look down at my calves, seeing splotches of black against my tan skin. It's blood. Mine or someone else's? My arm pulses in pain. Chunks rise from the back of my throat, and I turn around, sprinting toward the alley wall. Dropping to my knees, I vomit alcohol.

I can feel his body behind me.

"Shouldn't you go back in? Help people?" Trying to stand, I desperately grab his forearm, my voice cracking. I might faint.

His eyes are asphalt black. He's Slade in body but not in mind. The man I know is seemingly gone.

He spits out the word, "No."

My hands tremble as though it were thirty below while sweat streaks down my face. "What about the rest of the people in there? I saw a rush into the—"

He cracks his knuckles and blinks wildly. Exhaling, he turns left and right with his eyes in a squint before stuttering, "J-just try to relax. I'm sure the police have been notified. You're safe." The mechanical beast has morphed into a man, bewildered.

"Slade?" I'm dazed. What's going on here?

He places a warm hand on my damp forehead, pushing my hair back, away from my face. I expectantly stare at him.

"You're okay." With those words, his eyes soften. "I'm not carrying," he continues, keeping his hot hand on me. "But, if I go in, all commando-style, the cops will see a man they don't know who looks like he's got a plan. They might shoot me, assuming I'm an enemy. But you're okay, right? Are you hurt or just scared?" His eyes flit over me in assessment, as if he didn't see what just went on inside the club. As he lets out another long breath, his gaze bores into mine as though he's willing me to understand. His confused eyes now look ... sorry?

A stray hair gets caught against my lip. "I-I think so." And then it registers that I just threw up. My thoughts are jumbled and delayed.

"How can you be calm right now? My friends—" I gasp. "My friends are inside. I'm supposed to be with them."

We turn around as a group of people comes flying out of the exit, panting and talking in unison over each other.

A girl screams, "Where is Ryker? He was next to me, and now, he's gone." Pause. "He isn't answering. Can you guys try him? I need to go back for him!"

"There is club security," Slade starts again, forcing my attention back to him with his deep voice. "Trust me."

Trust him? Yes, he saved me. But something about him changed in there. He was cold and completely robotic. Nothing like the man I'd thought I knew. Maybe it's me? I'm too out of sorts to think clearly. Everything is a horrible blur. My memory can't be reliable. No, it isn't.

"I'm staying a few hotels down on the strip. Let's go." He moves to take my hand.

"Now?" I ask, eyes wide.

He takes my palm in his, lifting me from the ground. The sounds of ambulances and fire trucks increase in volume. Flashing red lights come closer as cold sweat pours down the side of my face. My makeup must be dripping. I turn back, seeing mayhem amid the giant, brightly lit buildings.

"You aren't going back there." His voice is firm. "And it isn't a good idea to stay in this area either."

He squeezes my hand, and we walk away. The balmy night sticks against my skin. I should ask him more questions, like where we are going, but I can't seem to gather the words. Screams of terror echo around me. Is it my fevered imagination or my memories? Or maybe it's all happening in real time? But Slade's hand is in mine, and somehow, my legs move.

The Slade I saw in the club has vanished, and in his place is the man I know who is solid, strong, and in control. I shake my head, feeling absurd. I was under extreme stress. He was only trying to help me. His eyes didn't darken; my mind was playing tricks. I grip his hand harder, not wanting him to let go. Slade is amazing. It's me who's unhinged.

Silent but quickly, we make it to his hotel. Which one it is, I still have no clue. The main floor rings with the sounds of gambling —*cha-cha-chinggg*—while carpeted floors in wild colors make my heart pound. Does no one know what's happening a mile down? Faces here are all normal. Glazed and staring at the slots in front of them, barely blinking. I see a group of people hollering at a craps table. A woman in a white dress calls out for a miracle before rolling dice. The crowd around her cheers, fists pumping into the air.

"Security is everywhere," Slade comments. "I know the guys who run this hotel."

A man in a dark suit stops us with a neat smile as we make our way across the floor. He's shorter than Slade with hair trimmed to his skull. The men comfortably shake hands, like old friends.

"You coming from the club? Just heard about the shooting. Got a call from Rob a few minutes ago. Your boys are on their way back here, too."

"Sounds good. We're going up to my room."

After pounding their fists, we move on. Sanam's face plunges into my brain, and I stop moving.

"Hang on, babe. We're almost upstairs."

"My friends—"

"I know. When we get up, you'll call 'em."

Entering the elevator, he slides a white card through the reader before pressing the number nineteen. Walking to the end of the corridor, we stop at room 1952. He swipes the card again in a reader on the door, and the light flashes green. Pushing it open, he holds the door for me to walk through. I don't. Instead, I wait for him to go before me. His brows turn down.

I swallow hard. "C-can you go in first?"

"No problem." His body softens in understanding.

He circles the room. Rationally, I know everything is fine. I mean, the shooting wasn't even here. Still, I need this reassurance.

"We're all good," he calls.

I step inside. He holds the door as it shuts, avoiding a slam.

Waiting in the middle of the room on gray wall-to-wall carpeting, I'm awkward and upset, wishing I had a sweatshirt or something. I'm freezing in this tiny outfit.

"Come here." His voice is so strong and sure. Bending down toward a small duffel, he takes out a white Hanes T-shirt. "Wash up and change. Bathroom's there." He points to his right.

"I can't." I touch my arm, and suddenly, it hits me. I'm in *pain*.

His eyes move straight to it. "Let me take a look."

He presses his hands against my bicep, and I wince as he massages from my shoulder down to my elbow.

"You're going to bruise pretty badly. Nothing feels broken though."

He moves to the bathroom. The sound of running water comes through the door. Moments later, he's back with a glass full of tap water and two pills. "Just some Advil."

He hands them to me, and I swallow it down.

Are people back at the club, still waiting for help, while I'm here in a hotel room, drinking water? I stare at him, open-mouthed. I feel like I should apologize for thinking he was a monster in the club. How could I have thought that of him? He left more quickly than he should have, and it's my fault. He should have stayed. I'm a terrible person. I need to thank him. I need to say a lot of things. But, most of all, I want to roll into a ball and cry. As I stare down at the blood splatter on my calves and thighs, my stomach rolls. How am I going to clean myself up? Whose blood is this? I feel dizzy.

He takes the glass from my hand. "I can help you wash." His eyes are knowing yet gentle.

"No, it's okay. I can do it." My voice comes out shaky and small.

"Your arm hurts. Let me help you."

He turns around, reentering the bathroom. Hesitantly, I follow behind.

Moving to his knees, he turns the tub faucet on. He runs a hand beneath the spray, presumably to check the temperature. Satisfied, he lifts a small bottle off the bath's ledge and squeezes liquid into the water. Bubbles immediately spring up. Blinking, I stand there, staring. Should I stop him? The smell of vanilla wafts through the air.

"Don't worry. I've got you." His voice is strong, deep, and soothing, like a balm.

I can't tear my eyes away from him.

"You think you can get undressed on your own?"

I shake my head, biting my lip and trying not to cry. My arm hurts so badly, and just the sight of my bloodied legs has my stomach turning. "I can just get inside the bath with my clothes on. That might be easier for me—"

"I'll undress you. Looks like we've got a pattern between us, eh?" A little smile sits on his lips.

"You realize you're making a joke right now?"

The smile finally reaches his eyes, green with swirls of blue. Nothing about them is dark. He's *gorgeous*.

Holding the top of my dress with his left hand, he drags the front zipper down with his right, not breaking eye contact. *Trust me*, his body seems to say. His hands don't rush, as though he's trying not to startle me.

Still, I shake.

The dress is undone, but his hand keeps it from falling. Slade takes a towel draped over the tub and presses it against my chest when I gasp, "I was supposed to call my friends."

He holds me in place. "The police must have gotten over there quickly. Call now."

He lets go, and I jet back into the bedroom, finding my purse on the floor. I tear it open, pulling out my phone.

I dial, and she answers after the first ring.

"Sanam?" My voice cracks with relief.

"Yes, it's me. Oh God, Lauren. Where are you?"

Keeping the towel up with a shaking hand, I turn to face the wall. This is my small attempt for privacy. Tears well in my eyes, tickling my nose. If I allow myself to cry hysterically, it will be impossible to stop. I swallow hard, trying to control my emotions when I ask, "Is everyone okay?"

"Yes. We were hiding under the table. But you ... you were gone," she sobs. "Shots were everywhere. It was gang-related. A rap feud. They said a gunman went into the bathroom—"

"No, I wasn't inside at the time," I assure her.

Wetness slopes down my face.

"Thank God," she whispers like a prayer. "Reza is sending a jet for us in a few hours. Come meet us. No one wants to stay in this horrible place for another second. It's hell here."

I should leave and tell Slade thank you and good-bye. But I can't go back home to my quiet and empty apartment. It's just not possible, not yet. "No. I'll head back tomorrow, as planned." My voice comes out surer than I actually feel. "I bumped into a friend."

"Someone you trust? I'm not so sure this is a good idea. You've just been through a lot, and we're all leaving—"

"Yeah, I trust him." I squeeze the towel between my fingertips.

Any of us could have died tonight.

"S-so glad you're safe." I can hear her short and choppy breaths, as though she's slightly hyperventilating.

"Okay. I'll see you back home tomorrow."

I put my phone away and step back into the bathroom. My chest is tight. I feel relief but also dread. All the what-ifs are still fresh in my head.

He reaches out, touching the side of my face. "They're okay?"

I lean my head into his palm when I remember he wasn't alone either. "Did you connect with your friends?"

He shrugs casually. "I'm sure they're fine. You ready?" His fingers dip inside the tub. "I added some hot water." He puts his wet palm out to me before averting his head.

I take a hard swallow and drop the towel. My dress falls off with it. Trying to remove my strapless bra, I wince. I stop and go for a second attempt, this time using only one arm. I move my upper body for easier access, but it's tricky.

He seems to notice my discomfort. "What's wrong?"

"It's just my bra. It's taking me a minute with only one hand."

"Turn around." His voice is gruff.

I slowly pivot.

Not a second passes before his deft fingers settle on the center of my back. "I won't look, okay?" Unhooking delicate white lace, he removes the bra from my breasts. His fingers then move to the top of my panties.

Oh God.

He slowly drags them down. I shiver as his callous fingers slide down the outside of my thighs. I bite my lip, both nervous and turned on. I could have taken off my underwear without his help. He's doing this because he thinks I can't. I should stop him. But he's doing it, and I'm—

They're on the floor, loose at my feet. I lift one foot and then the other, leaving the scrap of white lace behind.

"I'm going to turn around and give you my hand again."

Slowly, I circle back. His hand is out and body turned away, as promised.

I use my toes to push my underwear into the corner. Gripping his fingers, I step one foot at a time into the steaming tub. Once covered in soapy suds, I sigh, "I'm inside, Slade." Not for the first time, I realize how good his name feels in my mouth.

"Did your friends have any information?"

"It was a rap feud. Sanam thought I was trapped in the restroom, which I wasn't. And I—you and I, we ran away." Again, it dawns on me that I'm safe and sound while others are hurt or dead. "And you left the scene because of me. We should go back. I shouldn't be here, in this bath, while others are—" My voice breaks off as I grip the side of the tub, ready to sit myself up.

I could have done something more. I should have pulled people out with me.

His hand touches my shoulder, keeping me down. "No. The only person's safety you need to worry about is your own."

"I know it's stupid to say"—I laugh sardonically—"but I really didn't think something like this could ever happen to me."

He licks his lips. "No one ever does, Lauren. That's how it always goes."

Slade turns around, and I swipe the tears falling down my face with warm bath water. He sifts through puffy white towels, searching for something. When he doesn't find whatever he's looking for, he leaves the bathroom.

"Hello. I need hand towels please." Pause. "What do you mean, you've run out? I need one." Pause. "No, I can't use the large ones." Pause. "Forget it." The phone slams.

Coming back into the bathroom, he's rubbing the back of his neck. "It's hard to use a huge towel in a tub. It gets wet and heavy. It will be hard for you to clean yourself up. It's all right. Just lift your leg up for me."

"I can do it myself," I whisper.

My stomach churns when I remember my legs are bloodied. That's why he pulled off my underwear. He was trying to spare me the view.

Oh my God.

"Let me clean you. Don't be afraid, okay?"

I can only blink.

Trusting him, I raise my left leg against the edge of the tub, cringing at the blackness strewed about my legs.

"Just close your eyes. Don't look at it."

He grabs the soap from the edge of the tub, and my eyes screw shut. The towel presses warmly against my leg. I open my eyes, unable to stop myself from looking at Slade. Slightly open-mouthed and face in concentration, he wipes the towel against my skin. *Cleaning me* with careful strokes.

Bending forward, he asks, "How is your arm?"

"It hurts."

Moving the edge of the towel up higher and higher, he reaches the juncture between my thighs. My body quivers.

"They're scraped up. I see bruising starting to form on the right. Can you lift your left arm for me?" He coats the corner of the towel again with soap.

I do as he said, letting him wipe off evidence of the night. How can a man so huge be so gentle?

He moves methodically, as though he's done this all before. I want to ask if he has. With hands so sure, without any trembling or fear, it's as though he was born for this role. Slade moves, walks, and stands with utter assurance.

I'll take care of everything; his body seems to say.

Soon, I'll be clean. And then we're going to sleep. And then I'll wake up and say good-bye.

No! my mind shouts.

His large form looms over mine as he turns the hot water back on. The sound batters against the older water. "Warmer?"

I want to stretch out my arms and tell him to come inside with me. I want to feel him, his body, and his stability.

Instead, I gingerly lower the first leg and raise the second. Some of the bubbles part as I lean my head back, reveling in the warmth. My nipples peek out from the water, but he doesn't stop to stare. Swallowing, he adjusts his seat and continues his task of cleaning me.

"Let's do the arm that's bothering you."

I shake my head. "No. It'll hurt."

"Come on, Lauren." He's so gentle. "Trust me, okay?"

Shakily, I lift it. Lathering soap on his own hands, he then touches my skin. His motions are whisper soft. All I can do is watch in amazement.

"All right. You ready to come out now? If you want to hang out here longer, that's fine. Just call me when you're ready."

"No, I'm ready now. Exhausted really." I swallow.

Pulling out another large towel from the pile, he raises it like a shield in front of his eyes.

Taking his hand again, I rise and step out of the tub, straight into the towel.

"You're very lucky, you know." He tightly wraps me before his eyes reach mine.

"I know."

Following him into the bedroom, he lifts his white shirt from the bed. Handing it to me, he steps to the air-conditioning unit, pressing buttons on the keypad. The sound of blowing air stops.

"The bed looks good." I longingly stare at it. A huge, fluffy white comforter and too many soft pillows make it look almost cloud-like.

"Can you get yourself inside?"

I nod.

"I'm just going to wash myself up then."

After he leaves, I gingerly slip his shirt over my head, taking care not to move my arm too much. It takes a few moments, but I manage. I can already see a bruise starting to form on the top of my bicep. Climbing into the bed, it's thankfully as soft as it looks. I curl up under the cold sheets, waiting for him. I shouldn't wait. I should just sleep and have this night of terror be over. But I can't. I'm scared to be without him. A chill slides through my body. I'm freezing, my wet hair chilling the back of my neck.

Slade steps back into the room in nothing but a pair of beaten-up jeans. My eyes scan him from his bare feet up to his wet hair. I've never liked tattoos, but his are so passionately drawn, as though every piece of ink is there for a reason. I shiver.

"I like your tattoos."

His body language somehow hardens with my comment, and I bring the sheets higher up on my body, needing more warmth.

As he waits at the foot of the bed, we're at an awkward standstill. His eyes look reddish and glossy.

"I've got a good artist," he replies curtly.

We were so open with each other, and now, it's as though our energy is no longer in sync. What happened? He's thrown down an emotional curtain, and I've been shut out.

I'm unsure what the protocol is for a situation like this one. "A-are you coming to sleep?" My voice is hesitant as I slowly sit myself upright.

Maybe he isn't planning on staying. Maybe he's going to crash in his friend's room and leave me alone in here.

He steps to the small desk at the edge of the room and lifts up a white room-service menu. "Are you hungry?"

"No, not really."

"I think you ought to eat. Stress is amplified if your stomach is empty." With his back turned, he calls and orders what sounds like half the menu. After hanging up, he lifts the remote. "TV okay with you?"

I shrug. "Yeah, sure." My voice comes out small.

He moves into the bed. We're both sitting up, but my legs are tucked under the covers while his are over them. He's purposely keeping his distance.

"You're still in your jeans." The words crack as they leave my mouth.

"Yep," he states quickly, changing the channels. He stops at *Forrest Gump*.

I look at his legs. "You don't have to keep them on if they aren't comfortable." I move an errant hair behind my ear.

"Yeah?" He stares at me as though he's making extra sure it really is all right with me.

"Mmhmm." I pray my hum comes off relaxed because, in reality, I'm anything but.

Swiftly hopping off the bed, he unbuttons his jeans. I want to shut my eyes from embarrassment because he's just so crazy hot. But, when a man like Slade undresses and the lights are on, it's a sin not to look. The last time we hooked up, it was so dark. Too dark.

He drops his pants like he's just getting into his comfort zone, not like he's trying to be sexy.

I want to ask, *Who the hell has a body like this?*

I have seen all sorts of good-looking men who are in shape. But, with Slade, it's more than muscles. He's strong because he protected our country. He didn't lift weights to look good at the beach. His body is corded because it's who he is as a man—his strength representing abilities that almost no one else on earth has. The man is a true hero. And, holy shit, does it bring his sex appeal up ten thousand notches. Maybe he is strong enough to avert his eyes while I'm nude. But I'm not.

I'm shaking, staring at him in a pair of boxer briefs as he moves to his duffel to grab his phone. I should turn around because I might pass out from this visual.

Oh, who am I kidding? I'm human.

My eyes? They're peeled. The V—*oh my God*—those cut muscles in his abdomen pointing down into his underwear. The eight pack above it. The perfect smattering of chest hair. The riotous tattoos in all sorts of colors. The bone frog on his chest, signifying his Navy SEAL status. If I wasn't already in a bed, I'd be searching for one.

He moves close to me and lifts my chin up, so our eyes connect. "You all right?" He looks like he wants to laugh out loud, but his eyes are still distant.

I want to retort. I want to say ... something. Anything. But I can't because I'm stunned. He smells unbelievably good, too. Dark but slightly lemony. The idea of speech right now is laughable. I just want him to lie on top of me, so I can breathe him in.

"Slade," I manage to stutter, my voice scratchy. I need him—so badly. My core pulses.

"Lauren, we're not doing this tonight."

"Yes. We should." I nod my head because this is a great idea. I need to forget.

"Look, I know tonight was intense. You're going to have a lot of emotions. But this"—he gestures between us—"isn't happening."

His face is completely relaxed, as though his mind is totally made. I search his eyes to see if there's more behind his words. But he's unreadable; I can't tell.

I feel as though I'd been slapped. My fragile ego trembles. But, considering what I've been through, I decide I've got nothing to lose.

"I'm an adult. And I know what I want and what I need. Right now, after what I've been through, I'd like nothing more than to lose myself in you. We're good together. You turn me on like no one else."

I pull his shirt off of my body, trying not to wince, and touch my breasts, warm and full. I tweak my nipples, and they immediately harden. I know from the night of Vincent and Eve's wedding that he's a boob guy. Throwing myself at a man is completely out of character for me, but my body has a mind of its own right now.

He lets out a hard breath with no words, and it spurs me on.

"Don't deny this. If tonight's events ... if they hadn't happened, we'd be in this room anyway." I barely sound like myself, but I can't stop.

His eyes flicker, roving across my body. He wants this. Wants me. I crawl to the side of the bed. At this point, I'm not above begging.

He raises his hand up, stopping me in my sex-crazed tracks. "I'm no saint." He takes the shirt from the top of the pillow and slides it back over my head. "But you aren't the type of girl to fuck after an attack of that magnitude. If we had sex, you'd wake up upset tomorrow. Plus, your arm is hurting. So, let's not do this." His face is set to marble.

I swallow hard. "Well, can you at least hold me?" A shiver runs through my body. I need touch. I want someone to remind me that I'm alive. I need—

"Yeah," he sighs, sternly pressing his lips together. "I can do that. But first, clothes."

I feel like crying again as I slip my arms through the shirt's sleeves. I lie down on my side, facing away from him when he turns off the TV and then the lights. He moves behind me. Even though he's huge, he repositions himself with so much agility that he barely shakes the mattress. My back sets against his warm front, and my entire body feels safety, security, and all good things.

For a few moments, we're silent. But then the tears come.

He presses his lips over my damp hair. "Don't be upset, Lauren." His heavy body moves against mine.

"Did all of that really happen?" I sniffle.

"It did. Don't hide the truth or pretend it wasn't so. It happened. Know that and deal with it."

"Do you believe in love?" The question leaves my mouth before thought can intervene.

"What do you mean?" He places a hand on my leg. It isn't sexual, but it's so comforting.

"Do you believe that, regardless of who you marry, your problems will be the same? And you might as well marry for reasons like money or looks? Or is there more?"

"Why do you ask?"

"Because Sanam said, no matter who I marry, he'll cheat and lie. I might as well go for someone who can give me a life full of material things." I listen to his paused breath. "Slade, are you asleep?"

"No."

"I thought of you a lot. After the wedding. Is that okay to say?"

He shifts, holding me closer. "I thought of you, too. More than I have any right to."

"But why didn't you ca—"

"Shh," he murmurs, wrapping my hair in his hands.

Maybe I should press, but I don't have the energy.

"I want to thank you. For saving me tonight. And for taking care of me."

He remains silent as I stare at the inky darkness, trying to imagine my life back in LA. All I can see in my mind's eye is his strong body behind mine.

His hand moves up and down against my leg. It's a move meant to soothe. "My parents were in love. We didn't have too much as far as material things, but life was real good, growing up."

"Are they still in Virginia?" I recall him telling me about it in his truck at the wedding.

"Actually, they all died. My brother, Aaron, too." His words come out matter-of-fact.

I'm stunned, remembering the funny stories he told me about himself and his brother and the drama they'd stir when they were together. "I'm sorry."

"No need to be. Life is full of events we have no control over. We're all just breakable things. I wake up every morning, work out, shower, and remind myself that I'm just a man and that men die. It keeps my expectations on par."

I feel his breaths, steady against the back of my neck.

"As for love?" he continues. "I'd categorize love with allegiance and brotherhood. Those bonds aren't breakable—in theory. In reality, no matter how hard we try, I think we'll all be let down eventually. And we all let others down, too. Nothing good can ever stay."

I turn around, so our lips are only centimeters apart. My hands move to his angular face. "True love is flexible and forgiving. Even if your lover lets you down, the love won't break because it will bend for the other person."

"That sounds about right. But still, almost impossible to find. So impossible that you might as well say it doesn't exist." His hands move behind my neck.

I close my eyes, breathing him in. "Maybe you're right."

I press my forehead to his, and he doesn't back away.

"Hey." I can feel the brush of his lashes against my nose.

"Yeah?"

"You should keep looking, Lauren. Don't stop until you find it. You're a great girl, and you deserve to find love. Don't sell out."

"What about you?"

He exhales, and I part my lips, wanting to breathe him in.

"Nah. I'm on my own."

"But your parents had it?"

I lift my hand, letting my fingers graze against the tips of his clean, buzzed hair. He leans into my touch.

"They did. But I've seen enough to know we all have a different lot. That was theirs. This is mine."

"But why?" I exclaim. "You're—"

"Don't push." He rears his head back. "You don't know me, Lauren." His terse reply doesn't invite a response. He averts his eyes to face the ceiling.

"Okay, maybe not that well. But I know enough. I mean, we had so much fun at the wedding. You told me you saw yourself having a family one day."

"You're great. And I know you're looking for love. But I'm not the one. Please don't try to tell yourself that I am or that I could be. I'm not."

For a few beats, we're quiet. His words burn.

"Look," he starts again, moving his face back to mine, "now isn't the time to think about such things. You've been through tremendous stress. Just promise me that what happened tonight won't make you go from the funny, cool, sweet girl I know to someone more anxious. Find a way to let it go. Remind yourself that you were in the wrong place at the wrong time, but by the grace of God, you escaped harm. Don't let what happened drag you low."

My eyes water as I stare at him. Because, even though his words and actions are incredibly kind, his eyes are so sad. Tortured even.

"What's your story, Slade?"

He lets out a dark, contrived laugh. "My story? I went off to fight for our country. Saw lots of crazy shit. And came back."

"Is that all you're going to give me?"

"Yep," he says, the word clipped. "So, why were you looking so upset tonight?"

"And how do you know how I looked?" I questioningly lift my brows.

"I saw you. Watched you with your friends."

I sigh before swallowing hard. "I just don't fit in anymore. We used to all be on the same page when it came to having fun and going to great dinners and meeting guys. But, now, they're all getting married and moving on. And the trouble is, they're choosing a type of man who isn't for me. Sanam wants me to marry one of her fiancé's friends, of course, but I don't want that. And so, I'm just in the same spot while everybody else is changing."

"What do you think you're going to do? Just turn your back on them and go your own way?"

"No. Yes. I don't know. The thing about my friends is, you've got to stay in the same phase of life together; otherwise, the relationship will end. At the same time, I can't just get married to stay within my social group. I guess our priorities have changed. Vacations and clothes are enough to satisfy them but not me."

He nods solemnly. "Those don't sound like good friends. And, the way you make them sound, I want to tell you to lose them. You're more than they are. Actually, you're more, period."

My heart pauses. No man has ever said that to me. I've always been the hot girlfriend or the arm piece as a date to whatever gala. Never the *more*. He makes me want to be.

"Learn to stop hanging on to things that aren't working. Life will be much simpler. You're better than those girls."

With his words, a strange feeling comes over me, like a warm hum. His thumb rubs the center of my lips. For Slade, they part.

"You'll find it." He pushes my hair back away from my face. "Just make some new friends. For a woman like you, it's easy, right?"

I choke up as my mind roves in hundreds of directions. The shooting. This man. My life as it currently stands. All the friends, all the bullshit.

"I guess I'm not too good at change or falling behind."

He smiles, his straight white teeth glimmering in the dark. "You aren't behind. You aren't lagging either. You're at a crossroads. Gotta use more mental strength, babe."

"Is that Navy SEAL talk?" I smile.

"You know it."

"Is it true that they tie your hands behind your back and bind your feet together and then dump you in a pool to swim?"

He smiles. "Sure is." A hint of a Southern accent peeks through.

I feel absolute wonderment. "But how?"

He laughs. "You've gotta get mind and body on the same page."

"Right now, my mind and body are scattered."

"I know. Just sleep."

I press my lips to his. At first, he doesn't move. But, when he opens his mouth, I have the strangest feeling. A sense that I'm meant to be in this exact moment in time. My hands grip the back of his head because I don't want to let him go. With Slade, I feel so alive. Our kiss deepens as he takes control, but then he pulls back.

Breathing heavy, he turns me around so that he's spooning me again. He puts his head into the back of my neck, inhaling. I shudder.

We might not be having sex, but still, he holds me. The heat from his body transfers into mine, the connection soothing and perfect.

I fall asleep with his mouth on my mind, and blessedly, my dreams are nothing but static.

* * *

I WAKE UP WITH A START. It's 6:03 a.m. The events of the night before come tumbling back. The club shooting. The dead girl, blood drenching her clothes. All of the screaming. Slade washing the blood from my thighs.

I turn to my right. He isn't here. The pillow doesn't even have an indent. I sit up, spotting him on the floor on the left side of the bed. He's lying without a blanket or pillow, head directly on the carpet.

I gasp. Am I that bad? I threw myself at him, and he denied me. And, once I fell asleep, he ran away.

The room service that I never ate sits untouched on a folding table at the foot of the bed. Slade must have stayed up. The smell of cooked burgers and fries makes my eyes burn.

I look down at my wrist, stamped with the club's insignia. Hopping out of the plush white bed, I make a run for the toilet where I drop to the cold marble floor and throw up bile. When I'm finished, I lean my sweaty head against the tiled wall, knowing that I've got to figure out what I'm supposed to do. What if the police are looking for me? Would they do that—have questions or something? What if Slade wakes up, and things are crazy awkward? Actually, considering the fact that he'd rather sleep on a carpeted floor—in a Vegas hotel room, no less—instead of sleeping next to me, I'd say that's a sign he's completely uninterested or borderline disgusted.

Our night together at the club was so much fun though. He was interested then, wasn't he? And, at Vincent and Eve's wedding, too, it was clear he liked me.

Self-preservation tells me not to waste time thinking. I've got to get out of here before he wakes. I've looked pathetic enough. I couldn't even take my own clothes off or wash myself. And it all felt so intimate. He must have only done it out of pity. I need to leave Las Vegas as soon as possible. Whatever his reasons for leaving the bed and sleeping on the floor, they can't be good.

I silently lift my dress off the ground—if I can call a scrap of red-and-white material a dress. Well, flight attendant it is. I won't waste time in going back to my hotel—clothes, shoes, whatever I left be damned. I need to get out of this city. After putting my costume back on, I slide the shirt I slept in over it. It smells like a mixture of Slade and myself. I tear up. The night was insane, but I thought we had something between the two of us. I guess I thought wrong. It's not the first time. The outfit looks ridiculous, but at least I'm covered.

After rinsing my mouth out with mouthwash and scrubbing my face with soap, I use hand cream and a tissue to remove the mascara and eyeliner that's fallen beneath my eyes. I look like shit and feel even worse. My hair is a rat's nest on top of my head, and I don't even have a comb. It feels as though there is a timer on me. I need to leave.

Rummaging through my purse, I find a lone piece of gum, still wrapped. I pop it into my mouth before checking my phone. A slew of missed calls from my parents cover my home screen. I've got a full voice-mail box and more texts than I can read right now. I'll just go home and figure it all out. I'm sure, when he wakes to see me gone, he'll be relieved.

Sneaking out, I take one last look at the Adonis on the floor and flinch, the truth hitting me between the eyes and sparking the headache from hell. After almost being killed, I had one of the most tender and intimate moments of my life. The feelings were one-sided, but still, it felt almost perfect to me.

I can't think about it now. I don't have the mental capacity to deal. Turning out, I move as fast as my legs will take me down the hallway and into the elevator, escaping my hero.

4

Slade

I crack my knuckles, raising my eyes to the young clerk. "Marlboros."

He turns around, searching for my poison among the cartons filled with different brands of death sticks. I used to smoke casually, but these last few months, the habit has gotten heavier. Smoking has a way of calming my nerves.

The clerk's hair is brown, shaggy, and long, falling into his eyes like a stringy curtain. I'm not sure how he'll find it. Still, he locates the white pack and drops it on the counter. I hand him a twenty, collect my change, and head back out.

Walking out to my bike, I hear giggling. Such an awkward sound when women above the age of eighteen laugh like little girls would. They're leaning against the glass show window, staring at me in excitement. I ignore them, removing the film from the pack and pulling out a cigarette. I need a moment of peace. God knows I need one after the shitshow in Vegas.

Sienna, one of the blackjack dealers at the Milestone, saunters over. Long black hair sways behind her. "Need a light?" She slowly blinks her blue eyes. Girl knows she's hot.

Placing the cigarette in the corner of my mouth, I nod a hello. Putting my hand in my pocket to pull out my own light, I find it empty. "Shit. Yeah, I actually do."

She giggles, the sound grating on my frayed nerves. Lifting the pink Zippo in front of my cigarette, she lights me up. "So, hard night? I can make it better." Her eyes dart to the zipper on my pants.

I consider taking her home. She's super hot; that's for sure. And willing, too. She wouldn't care if I dropped her off when we were done either.

Still, I'm nothing if not a man who follows my own rules. I don't fuck girls from the Mile—not ever again.

I thought Colleen, one of the cocktail waitresses, was cool, hot, and easy. She knew my background in the Navy and swore up and down that she just wanted to have some fun. I dropped her off at her apartment late at night after hooking up at my place. Hell, I even kissed her good-bye, thinking all was well.

The next week, I heard from Mike that she was crying by the employees-only restroom with Mary, the craps dealer, bitching about how I'd fucked her and never called her again. I can imagine Mary's red hair and scrawny finger lifted in front of her face.

"Forget that Slade," she'd say. "These Navy men are all the same. You need a good Christian boy. My Sam's just graduated from the top of his class at Cornell ..."

A week after that, Rob overheard Sienna complaining about me at The Blue to Della, one of the waitresses.

"Slade is such an asshole!" she cried. "He thinks he's too good for me? Screw him!"

My phone buzzes. I look down, glad for the interruption.

Vincent: Yo.
Slade: What up?
Vincent: Problem at the Mile. It's waiting downstairs. He got caught cheating in poker three times over the last two weeks. Keeps comin' in though. Man needs a lesson.
Slade: On way.

With a nod of thanks to Sienna for the light, I put my helmet on, shutting the clasp beneath my chin. Turning on my bike, I let out a long breath, letting her know in no uncertain terms that there's no chance. Pulling out of the lot, dust kicks up behind me. When I ride, all of my senses are magnified. My emotions feel as though they double. I am alive.

Considering the places I've been and dangerous things I've done, I should be dead by now. Instead—and God only knows for what reason—I'm still here on Earth. For whatever reason, Lauren then enters my mind.

I hope she's okay. Left without a goddamn word this morning. Probably woke up, found my ass on the floor, and thought I didn't want to be near her. Girls always think everything's about them. Then again, what else could I expect her to think? That I'm too fucked up in the head to sleep next to a woman? That I can't be near her and sleep? Otherwise, she might wake up choked out or, even worse, dead. I shudder but do my best to keep myself in check. And that arm of hers. Damn, it looked rough. I'm sure she'll be carrying some bruises on it for at least a week.

Her body was killer. Long, shapely legs that I already knew were soft and strong. Her tits in that tub ... *Christ!* My self-control has clearly reached a new height. Watching that kind of beautiful throw herself at me and denying it? I mean, shit. They should saint me for keeping my dick in my pants. But she was so shattered after the shooting that only an asshole would have hit her up in that kind of mental state. I like all kinds of women, but they've gotta be of sound mind.

Lauren is a good girl. She's happy and funny, and she isn't the type who uses sex as a tool to forget. I like that about her. She'd be better off discussing her issues with friends or taking a vacation, sipping strawberry margaritas on a beach. Not having sex with a damaged guy like me. It's not pity for myself; it's just reality.

This was a horrible event for her, a one-off. Sure, it's shocking to any human with a pulse. But still, it was something that was not prolonged over days or even hours. I have no doubt, she's strong enough to move forward.

As I ride on, I see a black SUV slow down. Maybe the driver's looking at a cell phone to check directions or reading a text message. That's when the white truck behind it plows straight forward, slamming the car from behind. The crashing sound ricochets through my head, and somewhere in the back of my skull, a spark is born.

I pull over to the side of the road, needing a moment to breathe and refocus. My hands wring together as the memories steamroll over my psyche.

THE STAIRS ARE CRACKED *gray concrete. We walk up, the four of us welcomed with open arms. As I enter this home, rich with the smells of fresh bread and spices, relief fills my lungs. Ahmad is a friend. Girlish laughter is everywhere in sound but hidden from sight. He has four daughters, all gentle.*

We sit on the floor, cross-legged, as his daughters come to serve us. Hair covered in black cloth and pink lips silent. Asal leans to serve me, holding back a smile as she dips the serving spoon into the large plate. Her green eyes connect with mine, asking if I want some. I nod without words, watching as warmth fills her oval face. The men joke, hungry but calm, as she makes her way around, head downcast. Rex grumbles, staring at my plate 'cause I've got more meat than he does.

A child starts to scream from outside, and we all pause. Something's wrong. I blink, setting down my plate and moving toward the corner of the window.

Shots fly through. Our reflexes razor sharp, we're all crouched in position with our weapons drawn.

But she didn't know. How could she?

I watch the widening of fearful green eyes before she drops. Blink.

· · ·

THE AMBULANCE SIRENS BLAZE, and I'm shaken back to life. *Christ.* I forgot about that day. That firefight had gone on for hours. I was called to leave soon after that. Never even made it to her burial.

I want to remember what happened at the club, but I *can't*. Last thing I'm sure of was the rapper claiming to own the streets. After that, it's static. But then Lauren threw up in the alley, looking at me, all frightened. And it was as though I snapped awake.

I get off the bike and pace back and forth on the grass bordering the highway. Pulling on the ends of my hair, I want to kick my own teeth out. Lauren was afraid of me. What did I do in that club?

Whatever it was, it's done now. My memories are all fucked up, things sliding in and out of my consciousness.

Did I carry her in my arms or on my back? Did I just pull her forward? Did I hurt her? *Fuck.*

I lift my head to see the car crash still needs assistance. Shit. I'm so wrapped up in my own shit. Pulling out my cell, I dial 911 and give them the coordinates of the crash. While I'm talking, an ambulance arrives. I gather myself and pull back onto the highway.

The ride up to the Milestone is smooth and fast. I do my best to think of nothing other than this drive. A floodlight blares down, illuminating the center of the employee lot. I make sure to park where it's good and bright, so no one will accidentally hit the bike. Walking through the employee entrance, I focus on what I'm going to find down here. I'm going to focus and get my job done. Be a man.

My phone vibrates.

Vincent: Fucker is downstairs. I'm on the floor now, dealing with some other shit.

The basement is dark, but there's light shining from the small holding cell that no one other than Vincent and me know about. I follow it, steps sure.

After growing up in the Mafia, Vincent knows how to handle pieces of shit who cause trouble. But, since he left the family and began the Mile, he does his best to keep his hands clean. As the head of security here, I'm often called on to handle the dirty parts of the business. I don't mind.

The door creaks as it opens, and an excited shiver runs down my spine.

"So"—I rub my hands together, left before right, as I stare at the shitbag sitting before me, a shock of bright red hair on his head—"you cheated at cards. Not once or twice, but three fucking times. Here are your choices."

His blue eyes widen as they take in my form. Seated on a plastic chair, he bounces a fat leg up and down, his white button-down shirt sticking to his chest from what looks like sweat. "Are you going to hurt me? P-please. D-don't hurt me. I won't come back again. I swear it." He pants.

I chuckle, ignoring him. I've got my own agenda. Kick the shit out of him, go home, pop my meds, and sleep. "I can bring you into the authorities. As the Milestone is on tribal land, that would be the Tribal Council. They can deal with you as they see fit. Or"—I pause, cracking my knuckles as I watch my words sink into his head—"I can kick the shit out of you. Either way, you're never coming back here."

I've used this ultimatum many times. But, tonight, I've got a load of tension I need to expend, and my bet is, he'll take the beating. I'll rough him up some, scare him good, and then he'll disappear from our lives.

"Just get it over with," he says, his voice cracking.

"Feel free to fight back," I add. "It'll be more fun that way." I laugh, knowing he's got nothing on me. "Get up."

He stands as I pull off my shirt; blood is hell to remove. His eyes widen at the sight of me, although the truth is, they shouldn't. Muscles aren't always equal to strength. Unfortunately for him though, I'm as tough as I look. The bone frog tattooed on my chest? Evidence.

My fist connects with his face, but I don't give it my all. Not yet.

He shuffles backward with his pale hands raised, as though he's trying to escape. I stalk toward him. He made a choice, and now, he's going to pay the price. A real man doesn't make a choice and then run away from it in fear.

He tries to duck a few times, but it's too easy. Anger begins to pulse. Why won't he defend himself?

I suck in a hard breath, my hands wringing together. *Rituals.*

"Get one in, asshole!" I scream, my voice echoing around the concrete walls. I barely sound like myself.

THE MOSQUES BEGIN PRAYERS; song echoes all around. But this alley is good and dark. No god is watching.

He punches my face, fist weak. It doesn't make a dent. I throw my gun off to the side. I want to feel contact. I want to know my fists killed him. I hit him in the side of the head again. He drops to the ground. My feet scuff against the concrete littered with sand. I kick him hard in the ribs.

"You ready to die?" I growl. "Motherfucker!" I yell. "Get up! Get the fuck up! Fight like a man."

I drop to my knees, punching his ribs. He's frozen in fear. Crying for his mom—Arabic words I've learned by heart. My body is on auto, fury trained on this body lying on the ground. I want to kill him. He's going to pay. No one takes my brother's life without punishment. My muscles vibrate as I go in for punch after punch. Retribution isn't sour. He thinks he'll get away with ambushing us? He thinks he can shoot my brother and walk off into the fucking sunset?

A BIG PAIR of arms moves behind me, pulling me back. "What in the fu—calm down, Slade. Holy shit, man." Vincent's voice is behind me yet feels far away. His words ricochet between past and present.

I'm grabbed beneath my arms and thrown off to the side. It's Vincent. He's shaking me. My head clears, and I see what's before me. I'm in the Mile's holding cell. A red-haired man is spread on the floor and beaten to a bloody pulp.

I turn to Vincent. His chiseled face is drawn with worry. I open and close my mouth as he steps away from me and moves beside the guy, feeling for a pulse.

"He's still alive." His voice is full of relief.

My eyes go dry. I lean my head against the cold cement wall, tightly shutting my eyes. I can hear Vincent calling a doctor.

"What's going on with you?" He drops the phone into his back pocket and sits to his haunches next to me. "The last few months, I've noticed changes. You aren't as focused. You're zoning out. Have you been sleeping?"

I look up to see his dark eyes, shining, concerned. I don't respond because what the fuck am I going to say? The truth is that I'm losing my grip, and it's getting worse. I'm living in this horrible in-between, where my past keeps invading my present. They're twisting together, turning my life into a fucking nightmare.

He exhales. "Normally, you kick the shit out of them. Fine. But not like this. You're spiraling down. No one else might see it, but I do."

"Nothing's wrong. I'm not spiraling anywhere." My voice is rough, the lie tasting like shit on my tongue. I clench and then open my fists, feeling the rawness in my knuckles. The hands hold a lot of tension, and mine feel tight.

"It's time to take a few days, yeah? Get off the rez. Eve and I want to visit Utah on Wednesday. Chill on Lake Powell. Why not come with us?"

"Third wheel? Nah." My throat is sore. I turn my face away from him.

"Don't worry; we won't share a room."

He laughs, but I don't make a sound.

It dawns on him that I'm not playing.

"Truth is, there is only one goddamn answer to this question. You're coming. After the stunt you just pulled? You need to clear that head of yours. A change of scenery is good."

"I'm in control," I reply, straightening the muscles in my face.

If he only knew I was at the shooting in Vegas, he'd be dragging me to the VA hospital to get my ass committed. No way that's happening, not to me. Luckily, Rob and Mike agreed with me that Vincent didn't need to know the details of our night.

I'm trained to stay straight in the face of mayhem. I refuse to allow a few difficult months to break me down. I've spent years building my barriers, and with a little time, I'll have them reconstructed. This is a dark phase. I'll get through it on my own.

"No"—he slowly shakes his head—"you're not. I know what control is. And that"—he points to the man crumpled on the floor —"isn't control. That shit is bad for business."

"I've beaten up plenty of guys down here before." I sound defensive.

"Yeah, but not close to death. Christ. You're supposed to rough 'em up and scare 'em. Not actually commit murder."

With a hard scar running down from his eye to his jaw, jet-black hair, and eyes so dark that they're practically black, you'd think people would see Vincent and run. Not the case. He is the only moth-erfucker I know who, even damaged and dangerous-looking, still gets more come-ons by women than any man I've ever met.

I clear my throat. "Listen, GQ—"

"Not the time to divert. I see you, Slade." He points a finger at me. "I know you put the mask on every day. Don't hold that shit inside, or you'll burn. Why don't you speak to a doc—"

I turn my face, unwilling to listen. He puts a hand on my shoul-der, and my body stiffens.

"Don't fucking lecture me." I throw his hand off, standing up to my full height.

He rises, too. It's a standoff.

"I'm fine. I did twelve years in hard combat. I don't need a goddamn shrink prodding at my psyche. Or you."

Vincent shakes his head, as though he's disappointed. "Let's just start with some time off. Figure out what you're going to do to regain some discipline."

"Time off isn't good. I work."

"Not up for discussion."

The guy on the floor lets out a painful moan, and we both turn toward him. Vincent looks back at me, a dark eyebrow raised. He won't let it go.

The breath I was holding slowly comes out through my nose. "Yeah. All right."

"Help me drag him upstairs."

"Before we go up, I think you should hit me." The words leave my mouth, and I can only pray this works.

"What the fuck?"

"When the doctor comes up, we'll say he got aggressive with me."

"I'm not hitting you."

"Why not? We spar all the time. But you've gotta punch me hard. Real hard. Just not my nose 'cause, you know, it's nice."

He chuckles, rubbing the back of his neck. It's one of Vincent's tells that he isn't completely opposed to an idea. "You're a sick fuck. Come up with another story. How about we say we found him—"

"Nah. This is the easiest story. Come on, Vince. Time is ticking. And the good doctor you hired needs a decent and believable story."

I tried telling him that we needed a shady doctor on our team, but he refused, insisting we keep the entire operation kosher from the ground up. This means that, if any shit goes down that isn't legal, he and I are the only ones privy to it.

He shakes his head as he rolls up his sleeves. Vincent's tough as fuck. I know he tries to stay clean, but the man has done so much bad shit in his life that it's not that difficult for him to handle darkness when he has to. He's been there and done it all. The perfect man to hurt me without any emotional strings attached. After what I just did, I know I deserve this beating.

He rears back and smashes his huge fist against my face once, twice. I see stars, and in my gut, I know that justice has been served. I keep my hands balled into fists at my sides because I need to bring my head back to focus. With the pulse of pain comes a twisted kind of relief, as though I've paid my price for fucking up. I know it's crazy to feel good after getting punched, but … I do.

Laughter hits me.

"You're wacked." He chuckles, shaking his dark head from side to side. "Now, let's get this idiot upstairs."

My face pulses with bruises to come as we drag the limp body onto the emergency staircase. Neither of us blinks at the absurdity of this moment. We're each gripping a chunky white arm as we trek up to a small room on the sixth floor, permanently reserved for situations such as this. The top of his brown loafers drags against the concrete steps; man's a dead weight. On the list of horrible shit Vincent and I have done, this doesn't even rank. Finally dropping him in the small living area of the room like a beaten doll, we pound fists. If this isn't brotherhood, I'm not sure what is.

Seconds later, the man groans again, his voice a low rasp. "H-help."

"Shut the fuck up." Vincent steps to where he lies, looming over him like a shadow from hell. "You see, when you cheat at my casino and get aggressive on the gambling floor"—he looks to me, smiling, before getting back into the man's space—"we have no choice but to contain you. And if you think to add any other details to this story?" Vincent bends over lower, pulling his gun and pressing it to the side of the man's head. "I'll kill you."

Piss leaks from the guy's pants, making a small puddle on the carpet.

"The doctor is on his way," I add for good measure, pulling out a beer from the glass bar. "Make sure to get housekeeping up here, too. Can't stand the smell of piss."

"Oh, the places you'll go," Vincent says as he drops the gun back into the holster around his waist.

We laugh, talking shit to each other.

The phone rings. I answer.

"Doctor's here, sir."

"Send him up." I hang up as it dawns on me that I'm low on meds.

After saying bye to Vincent, I pull out my phone and text Lion, the president of the Death Crusade MC. He's been asking me to gather some information for his club. Most of his boys are veterans, so we've known each other for a few months now. I've never agreed to helping him out, but now, he's got access to something I need.

I quickly type out the text, not reading it over before pressing Send. Moving my phone into my back pocket, I realize just how fucked up I've become. The good ole boy of my youth has been replaced—for now. Just until I straighten out. Soon, I'll be back to myself. *Soon.*

5

Lauren

I came back to my apartment this morning and immediately show-ered under a scalding hot spray. My shoulder feels tender, but physi-cally, I'm fine. The rest of my day was spent watching reality TV. Just needed to forget about my own life, if only for a little while.

My parents are over now, having brought dinner. My round glass dining table is packed with food—my mom's way of making life better. Unfortunately, my favorite Iranian dishes taste like cardboard in my mouth.

"Do you want more?" My mom points to a plate of saffron lemon kabobs.

I want to say no, but Slade was right about one thing. A full stomach does in fact help level out stress. My freezer, once full of ice cream and now empty, is proof.

"Yeah, okay. Just a few though."

She stands, adjusting her cream-colored pencil skirt before adding a few more pieces of chicken to my plate. Her thick black hair is styled straight to her shoulders, skin flawless and perfectly unlined, and outfit beautifully matched.

"Did you speak to your boss?" My father rolls up the sleeves of his blue-and-white-checkered button-down shirt before my mother pours a ladle of hot tomato stew, overflowing with mushrooms and eggplant, over a bed of rice on his plate.

I wonder if Slade has ever eaten Persian food. I sigh, dropping my head with the thought of him. He'd probably run screaming if he knew my heritage. Not that I have any evidence he'd react negatively, but there's a general bend against people of Middle Eastern heritage in this country since 9/11, and that's a fact.

I still haven't called or messaged him to thank him for saving my life. As it turned out, nine people died, two of whom were trampled to death while exiting the club. But I was safe, and it was because of him. My mind continues to replay how he knocked over anyone who came into my path. And then how he took care of me all night, his face in concentration and control as he *cleaned me.* Slade is a better man than any I've ever known.

"Did you hear me?" My father's face is stern but worried.

I'm not usually one to zone out, especially when he speaks.

"No, I won't tell him." I shrug. "I went away for Vincent and Eve's wedding a few months ago, and even that was a huge ordeal ..." My voice trails off.

"Oh, right. Your friend Eve who married the man who built the Milestone?" My mom smiles wide. She knows the answer but is trying to keep the conversation light. She places a hand on my father's forearm. "We should go there, Farzad. I heard it's amazing."

"Yes, that's them." I stick my fork in a piece of chicken and place it in my mouth.

"How is she? Your friend Eve?" Standing again, she pours stew in a bowl for herself—no rice. I don't think my mom has had a carbohydrate in the last twenty years.

"She's good. Really good." I swallow. "Started this safe house for abused women and helps them legally separate from their husbands and get jobs."

Talking about Eve makes me miss her. She is the one person in my life who is both strong and honest. She used to work at Crier as one of the associate attorneys but left for Nevada after rekindling her romance with Vincent. I brought the jokes, but Eve brought the real. I miss having that in my life.

"I agree with you," my father chimes into the conversation, voice decisive. "Don't take any time off. You've got to just let this go and put it all behind you. Worrying about what could be won't fix anything."

"But, Dad"—I shake my head—"it's not about worrying about something that might happen. It's the memory of what did actually happen, and—"

"Why don't we just take it all day by day?" my mom chirps.

I shut up, privately caving in on myself.

"Have you sent out your law school applications? I've been waiting to review your essay." He cuts into a piece of lamb kabob, the dark hair on his head perfectly gelled.

My girlfriends all used to tease me that my parents are the Persian version of George and Amal Clooney. It's annoying but true.

"No, I haven't."

"You're delaying. If you miss the application deadline again this year ..." He continues his lecture, but I tune him out.

I want to push back at them, scream, but what's the point? My parents are good people who love me. They've paid for all of my fancy education since I was three years old. Came to all of my dance recitals as a child. Watched me cheer at my high school home games. Hell, they even held my hand when my first boyfriend broke my heart. In fact, they did all the right things, all the time. But they also micromanage my life. It used to just annoy me, but lately, it's suffocating. Love isn't the issue, but boundaries are.

I began working as a legal secretary because my parents wanted me to have experience in the legal field before applying to law school. But, as time went on, I've realized I don't want to be an attorney like my father. Still, I can't upset him. I hate disappointing people. I keep saying that, yes, I'll apply because I want to make him proud. But it's not what I want.

The result is an awkward in-between where I keep saying, "Yes, sure, of course, Dad," but then tear up all the applications the moment I'm alone.

It makes me look like a liar or procrastinator when, really, I'm just unable to tell him no.

I press my fingers against my eyebrows, massaging them. I'm a thirty-two-year-old woman with a life and a job and a steady paycheck, but I'm still tied to expectations that I feel obligated to fulfill. Meanwhile, my father still tells me what to do, ordering me around like I'm fourteen years old. He loves me, and I love him, but I need space.

The rest of our dinner is eaten with comfortable, shallow conversation led by my sweet mother. "Did you see the new bags Gucci put out this season?"

The girl who always says yes feels fed up with all of it—the shopping, the buying, the never-ending quest of physical beauty. Quite honestly, I'm sick of her. And something tells me that this change in me, sparked by the shooting, is irrevocable. I'm tired of running to meet expectations that I don't care to meet. I want to set my own.

After a cup of freshly brewed black tea, my father stands to leave. After kissing me once on each cheek, he hands me a prescription for Xanax. His name is handwritten on the orange tube.

I shake my head.

"It's just a little Xanax," he urges, pushing them in my palm. "If you wake up tomorrow too stressed out, it'll help smooth out the edges, so you can work."

"But I—"

"Just take it with you, Lauren. Just as a precaution." He hugs me into his chest.

"Yeah. Okay."

My mom hugs me next, tears filling her eyes. "I love you so much. I'm so glad you're okay." She swallows, blinking hard, as though trying to keep her face from crumbling. "*Alhamdulillah*," she whispers in my ear before wrapping a cashmere scarf around her shoulders.

With two long presses of her lips to my cheeks, they leave.

. . .

MY MAKEUP IS FLAWLESS. Outfit, perfection. I remind myself of these details over and over but still cannot manage to walk out of my bathroom. I don't care about how I look. I mean, what does it even matter? But still, before the shooting, looking great was important to me.

After a long discussion with myself after my parents left, I decided that I should at least try to get myself back on track. After all, I don't want to make any rash decisions because of a traumatizing event. If I really want to change my life, I need to figure it out while levelheaded and calm.

I open my medicine cabinet, pulling out the Xanax prescription. Pushing down the cap and twisting it off, I pour the pills down the toilet and flush, like they do with drugs in the movies. *Wait, is that just for powder? Whatever.* I'm definitely having a hard time, but I'm not going to take drugs to fix it.

In my small black BMW, I drive to my favorite coffee shop, a few blocks from my office. After pulling into the parking lot, I drop the visor above my seat and stare at myself in the small mirror for a long while. Large brown eyes look back at me, blinking and filled with anxiety, pupils dilated.

"Everything is fine," I repeat out loud for the hundredth time. "Whatever happened is over now. It's done. I'm fine."

With a firm nod, I step out of the car like I've done millions of times before. I press the lock button on my key, and the car beeps.

Standing in line, I do what everyone else is doing and pull out my phone. I haven't checked any news or my social media accounts since Vegas. I'm about to scroll through my news feed when Leigh, my usual barista, asks how I've been.

"I'm okay. Just super busy. You know how it is." I chuckle awkwardly. "I'll have the usual—green tea with no sweetener. Large." I'm putting on a performance as the old Lauren, even smiling at the end. If I pretend long enough, it's bound to level me.

Leigh calls out my order to the guy behind her, who is hustling to make drinks.

"I still can't believe you work for Jonathan. What a shithead," she says in a conspiratorial whisper, making me laugh.

My boss is known to be a complete asshole. Unfortunately for me, his reputation is completely warranted.

"I know. I ask myself why every freakin' day." My eyes roll playfully as I hand her my card to swipe.

After taking it, she points to the TV in the corner above a small stand selling artisanal coffees. "Can you believe that shooting in Vegas over the weekend? Is this the new normal? I mean, who knows what's next?" She lets out a visible shudder before adjusting the black visor on her head.

I turn to stare at the monitor, and the blood drains from my face. A video taken with someone's phone was uploaded onto Facebook and is now front and center on the news. Shots spraying out into the crowd. Costumed partygoers running and screaming. A woman wearing large, sparkling wings falls to the floor. People run. It's a mass exodus toward the door. They're being trampled. I was there. My hands shake.

"Oh no. Lauren, a-are you okay? Shit. Don't tell me you were at that club. Or someone you know?" Her eyes widen.

I'm completely stunned.

Somehow, my legs bring me to the other end of the counter. Flashes of Vegas hit me like a freight train. Feeling down about no longer fitting in with my friends. Dancing with Slade and drinking tequila. His hot lips on my neck. And then the shooting. He pulled me out. Practically dragged me.

My life has been sliced in two. With one event, I'm on a different trajectory. I can't even imagine going back into work. What's the point? Why am I even still alive right now? I could have died.

The office must be exactly how I left it—cold, organized, and perfectly functional. Jonathan will run to my desk in his tailored suit with one hundred and one questions. I wouldn't have even sat, and he'll be on top of me, barking orders.

My mind jumbles. I'm sweating. I roll up the sleeves of my favorite DVF printed blouse, trying to get more air onto my skin. The strap of my Chanel bag digs into my shoulder, reminding me that I'm out in public. But I'm shutting down, my breaths labored.

The walls feel as though they were caving in on me. Since I got home, I've been functioning on autopilot. But it's all coming out now.

"Lauren!" the guy across the counter shouts out my name, alerting me that my tea is ready.

I step forward like I've done so many times before, taking my drink off the counter. "Ahhhhh!" I drop the paper cup to the ground as boiling water splatters all over the floor.

The people around me quickly step back.

"I'm sorry. Oh my God." I cup my hands over my mouth as the scorching water burns my bare ankles.

"It's my fault," he says in a rush. "I forgot to use the sleeve."

He chews his lip when a short guy with cropped hair comes running toward me with a mop.

"No worries, ma'am. Just step aside. I've got it."

I want to move, but I can't. My jaw is locked open. I look down at my white Louboutin pumps, which are now tinged with green. Should I be crying?

Leigh shows up next to me, taking my arm. "Is there someone I can call?" she whispers, ushering me to the side.

I feel unhinged.

"R-restroom?" My voice comes out in a stutter.

She helps me to the back. I focus on a shelf full of old books lining the wall.

"This is the one we use. It's cleaner. Look, I'm not sure what you went through. But take your time, okay? I'll tell everyone it's out of order."

I nod my head before closing the door behind me.

I'm about to bawl. I slide down the wall and sit on the restroom floor, tears covering my entire face.

Eve pops into my head. She's the most solid and real woman I know. Can she help me? With a shaking hand, I find her number in my Contacts and press Call.

"Hey, girl."

I can feel her smile across the line.

"Eve?" My voice comes out tiny. I swallow, trying to get my bearings.

"You okay?" She knows something is wrong.

It's eight thirty on a Monday morning. Typically, I'd be behind my desk right now, organizing the week and fielding phone calls.

"No, I'm not." I break down, telling her about the shooting. The deaths. I want to tell her that Slade saved me, but I can't even get into that right now. "I'm so anxious. What am I going to do? I can't go back to the office—"

"Okay. Take a deep breath."

I open my mouth to inhale and hear her doing the same.

"You need some time off. Go tell Jonathan you need a few weeks."

"But I can't. I'm terrified of going home and being alone. I'm ... I need help, Eve."

"Why don't you come out to Nevada for a while? I could use you at the Center, and you could use a break. Come for as long as you can. Two weeks. A month. A year. A lifetime! Whatever you want."

"I don't want you to tell Vincent. Or anyone. If I come, I don't want to see it in their faces."

"No problem. My lips are sealed." Her voice is confident.

I stare at a frame against the restroom wall with the words, *You Only Live Once*, written in lime-green script.

I'm not really living my life right now. My two brothers have both moved out to New York with big careers and families. And me? I just wake up, go to work, and focus on looking great, so I can meet a guy and get married and have kids. And then, one day, I'll die.

I tried calling Sanam yesterday, but all the girls have scattered, clinging to their boyfriends and husbands. And here I am, all alone, with no prospect for more. Even my job is a dead end. Do I want to be a lawyer one day like my father? No. Do I want to stay as a legal secretary forever? No. So, what exactly am I doing?

"Okay," I finally reply. "Yeah, I'll come."

"Good. Do you want the jet?"

I already know that the Milestone, being one of the most high-end resort and casinos in America, has a private plane.

Eve clears her throat. "You were there for me at a time when I needed it the most. Let me help you now."

"I just need to get out of my head," I stutter out.

"Trust me; I get it. More than you know."

"Okay," I say again, sounding like a broken record.

"Now, go to work. Tell Jonathan you need two weeks. Actually, no. Ask for three, so he'll bargain down to two. The flight will be around five. Let me just make some calls and make sure it works. I'll call you back to confirm." Eve's no-nonsense voice rings clear, and it chokes me up.

When we worked together, she was always tough in the office; we used to call it her bitch mode. But the thing with Eve is, she's always a straight shooter. I've never had to worry if what she says isn't what she means. It is always real. In my gut, I know being near her will help me.

"I'll be ready," I reply with as much strength as I can.

"Good. Talk later."

She hangs up, and I clench my fists. I need to get through today. Just one step at a time.

THE BLACK TUMI suitcase is opened up on my queen-sized bed, filled with two weeks' worth of clothes. My hands shook while packing, but I refused to let it ruin my neat folds.

I stare at my handiwork, feeling confident that I have what I need for this trip. Readjusting a shoe to make space for a cashmere sweater that's waiting to be settled in, I notice a tag hanging on a shirt. I gently pull out the blouse, not wanting to upset the rest of the clothing. I turn the tag around and see it—*$425.00*. My jaw drops. How could I have spent this much money on a shirt? For the first time in maybe ever, I feel sick to my stomach over the amount of money I spend on material items. I pull off the tag, wondering just how much cash I have sitting in material items.

I turn from the bed and enter my closet, tearing shirt after shirt off their hangers and flinging them onto the floor. Shoe after shoe.

And the bags. Thousands of dollars of Yves Saint Laurent. Chanel. Gucci. God, all of these things that I used to save up for. I used to covet these items, but what do they even mean? They're nonsense, and right now, they're making me ill.

My mom told me it'd get better. Will it ever?

I walk into my kitchen, taking out three extra-large white trash bags before turning back around and grabbing a fourth. With a Sharpie pen, I write *Clothes, Shoes, Purses, and Shoes again* on each and begin to methodically fill them, making a mental note to drop them off at my local Goodwill as soon as I return from Nevada.

I'm sweating by the time the work is done, but I feel amazing and somehow lighter. Relieved. That's when I decide that I'm going to get through this. I will take a little time and figure out what I'm going to do next, but no matter what, I'll be okay. This incident is causing me temporary suffering. Still, it's temporary. It might change me, but I'm still me, and I always will be.

6

Lauren

I'm drinking a beer with Eve at a restaurant and bar called The Blue. It's pretty cool, styled like an old-school New York City deli. With a long and high counter lined with red leather stools and dark wooden booths on the main restaurant floor, it's the kind of place to relax. I enjoy the comfort of my surroundings as Eve chats about a woman and her three kids who came into the Center this morning. The woman's husband, who'd randomly dropped into their home during the week for check-ins, physically abused her. The cycle was endless —until she came to Eve for help.

"Have you filed the restraining orders?" I flip my hair to the side and immediately feel oil gathered by my roots. Whatever. I can add it to my list of Things Gone to Shit in the last two days.

"Yes, of course I filed them. But you know," she continues, straightening her black tank top, "I can seriously use some help. It's crazy busy, and sometimes, I get so bogged down in filing the necessary legal paperwork that I don't have enough time to spend with these women. I need to do more than the legalities, but I don't have the hours."

An idea sparks. "What about clothes?"

"Clothes?" Eve's face spells confusion.

"Well, I bet a lot of these women are trying to get back on their feet. They need to interview but don't have the right wardrobe. Everyone knows that dressing the part is half the battle for both confidence and getting the job. While I'm here, I can work on that."

"I love that idea!" she exclaims.

"Oh, you know what else?" I'm excited! "A haircut. I mean, imagine how these women must feel after the abuse they've endured. A fresh cut would give them that quick boost. I can speak to some stylists in the area. Maybe I can arrange for someone to come once a week."

"Brilliant idea." Eve claps her hands together. "I'll handle the legal elements, but you can handle the personal ones. We've always made the best team, right?" Her eyes shine, genuinely.

"Too bad I'm only here for two weeks." I shrug. "Luckily, I did as you said and requested three. Jonathan negotiated down, obviously. I'm just praying this break will be enough to get me back on my feet again."

"Maybe you won't go back to him at all. Crier is toxic. And, at the Center, you can use all your skills to actually better people's lives. Great for the résumé when you go back to California. Imagine what we can do together." She raises her hands together in prayer.

"But ..." I sigh, trying to figure what I should say. "It's not that I don't want to stay here longer, but I'm just not ready to throw down and quit work and tell my landlord I won't be back. It would be a huge change."

"Let's use these few weeks as a trial run."

"I don't know." I lean my head in my hands and exhale. "I can't make any choices right now. Of course, I'll help you while I'm here. I just need to get back to myself before I make life changes."

"There's something in the air here that's healing. And, remember, my door is always open, and the Center would love to have you. But still, Lauren, you deserve more than that bullshit law firm. Jonathan is such an ass—" Her voice breaks off, and her eyes move to the door before lighting up.

I turn to see what she's looking at. It's Vincent. But wait ...

Oh shit! Shit, fuck, shit, shit, shit!

Beside Vincent is a wall of a man. A six-foot-something, tatted-up, military man. I knew I'd see him while I was here, but I figured it would be a few days into my stay and after I got myself together—or at least did my hair, wore some makeup, and put on a cute outfit. Instead, I'm a mess.

The men stride toward us, their presence shrinking the entire bar and restaurant. Has Slade always been this big?

"Hi, baby," Vincent murmurs, putting his nose in Eve's hair after sliding into the booth.

I haven't seen him since the wedding, and I'm absolutely struck stupid at how handsome he looks. Hair like black ink, dark eyes, and tan skin. Sure, he's got a deep scar down his face that wasn't there the first time I saw him. But, somehow, it only adds to his dark and dangerous appeal.

Slade effortlessly moves his huge body next to mine, maneuvering over two hundred pounds of muscle with ease. My body is completely rigid and awkward from nerves. Slade, on the other hand, looks barely affected by the fact that I'm here.

"Lauren, hey," he says calmly, casually draping an arm behind my chair while looking back, presumably to find the waitress.

I glance at Eve, finding her eyes pinging between Slade and me. She smirks before turning to Vincent, whispering something in his ear. Moments later, they both stand.

"I've got to call my sister, and it's too loud in here. We'll be back in a minute." Eve winks.

"So, how've you been? We didn't get to talk after ... you know. You ran out on me." The rumble of his voice is firm, eyes creased in the corners.

"Things have been hard the last few days, obviously." I clear my throat. "So, I came out here for a little break. Was planning to message you later tonight actually." I do my best to keep my voice and body steady.

The art of bullshit and acting calm when there's a riot in my chest is second nature to me at this point. I try to find something about his face that bothers me, that should settle the ache between my legs and the awkwardness in my heart. His nose is too straight. His lips are too full. His jaw is too chiseled. Damn him!

"Yeah. It was pretty crazy." His gaze moves down to my lips and back up again. "Still doesn't seem right though—to run away. You had me pretty worried for a minute there."

"Well, I didn't think you'd mind, considering the fact that you'd rather sleep on the floor—which was probably dirty as hell, by the way—than sleep next to me." My voice comes out snarkier than I intended as I hold back a glare.

His eyes? They darken. There's more he wants to say, but the man is in complete control of every word that comes out of his mouth, and for whatever reason, he decides not to answer.

Slade is the kind of man who doesn't spew bullshit. If he says something, it's because he thought about it and chose to talk. And, if he doesn't speak or respond, it's him consciously deciding to refrain. I haven't known him long, but this is a trait of his I picked up on right away. Slade's ability to control himself is both frightening and powerful.

I take another gulp of my beer, reminding myself that I have nothing to worry about. Sure, I ran away with my ego bruised instead of sticking around and thanking him like a proper adult. But, in my defense, the situation was stressful. And what would any woman think after seeing a man she threw herself at sleeping on the floor of a hotel room instead of in the huge and plush king-sized bed? I mean, please!

Suddenly, the image of his huge, hulking body cleaning me in the tub flashes before my eyes, and I feel like an absolute jerk. I can't believe I ran out on him after what he did for me. Guilt runs over my insides. I could have bought him breakfast or, at the minimum, left a note.

Another swallow of my beer, but this one goes down over a pit in my throat.

The waitress brings another large pitcher, setting it on the center of our table. Before I can refill my glass, Slade picks it up and begins filling mine just as Vincent and Eve come back to the table. They are still preoccupied, talking quietly to each other.

"Listen, angry girl," he starts, lip twitching, "you were under a tremendous amount of stress. Don't worry about the fact that you wanted to fuck. Lots of people do after something like that." His mouth quirks fully upward.

Is he messing with me right now or serious?

I turn my gaze to Vincent and Eve. Did they hear? Luckily, they're focused only on each other, seemingly in deep conversation.

My head swings back to Slade. "I—what—you—"

He slowly nods his head, looking all cocky and laughing under his breath. He's making light of the whole thing while I'm guilt-stricken.

Asshole!

"I did not—I mean—of course not!" I whisper-yell under my breath.

"Yes." He fiddles with the watch on his wrist. "Yes, you did. You wanted me pretty damn badly. If I remember correctly, you pulled off your—"

My hand slaps against his mouth, shutting him up. His warm breath coats my palm with his laughter.

"You finished now?" I grumble.

His eyes are green with flecks of blue, and they're amused. I'm either going to slap him or straddle him, but the jury is still out.

I peel my hand away, and a smile fills his face.

"Did you tell her I was there?" His eyes flash to Eve before he leans back into the seat, completely nonchalant and in charge.

"No. I didn't mention that," I reply, shrugging. "I told her not to tell him"—my eyes quickly flicker to the couple—"what happened to me either. I need to feel like myself right now and don't want pity or questions."

"Good. Let's keep it quiet, yeah? Don't need anyone meddling in my business either." His voice comes out slightly hurried.

I tilt my head, confused. What does he have to hide?

I didn't mention anything to Eve because Slade's part in the story was almost too much to discuss. For one thing, Eve doesn't know we had sex at her wedding. It didn't feel necessary to tell her, considering the fact that he never even called me afterward. And his role in the shooting just hasn't come up. At least, not yet.

Vincent leans forward. "You should help Eve at the Center. You can probably get a lot done for these families. She's always chirping in my ear about how you do more than most attorneys she knows."

I try to ignore the fact that he's barely said two words to me since he sat down. Vincent isn't warm. As I learned at his wedding, he isn't even nice. He's all serious, all the time. Unless, of course, he's with Eve, who he'd kill for.

"Let's start again, Vincent." Slade shifts his heavy body, elbows leaning on the table. "Hey, Lauren. Good to see you again. Have you thought about possibly staying longer and working with Eve at the Center?" He opens his hands. "See, it's easy."

My mouth drops in happy surprise. I can't even remember the last time someone stood up for me. My life in LA is an animal farm; everyone eats who they must to climb socially.

"What are you? The manners police?" Everyone laughs, and Vincent turns to me, his demeanor noticeably softer. "Hello, Lauren. So great to see you again. Love your earrings, by the way. Tiffany?"

"Ha!" I laugh out loud. The smile on my face wouldn't wane even if I tried.

The man behind the rough exterior is the man Eve loves. My heart lurches with want. Not for Vincent, of course, but for what they have. I want someone to love, who will love me in return.

Where is he?

Slade's thigh shifts against mine, but my head turns down. I continue to smile, trying to cover up the sadness blooming in my chest. I know I'm blessed to have my health. My family is supportive and wonderful. And I have one good friend, Eve, which is more than a lot of women can say. Maybe I'm being too expectant. Maybe God sees that I've been given enough, and my limit of his goodwill has been reached.

Keeping the emotion from my voice and sitting tall, I reply, "Thank you, Vincent. It's good to see you, too. I'll help Eve while I'm here."

I turn to Slade, as if to say, *Did we do well?*

He smiles.

"Vincent has this way of pressuring people," Eve explains, opening her palms to the ceiling.

"Why not? Pressure can be good. Come on, Lauren, stay longer." He pulls Eve closer to his side. "I bet we can get you to extend." He kisses the top of her head with so much gentleness.

Seeing them together ... it's almost too intimate to watch.

"I'm not so sure. Jonathan only gave me two weeks, and, you know, I've got things to do at home." I stare at my nails, doing my best not to notice Slade's tatted-up, muscled forearms.

"Everything you need, you can find here. Trust me." Vincent's voice is so commanding that I can do nothing other than look up. His eyes are so serious and knowing that it makes my stomach churn.

I need to divert this conversation. "So, Slade, do you also ride a motorcycle?" My voice is higher-pitched than usual.

He nods. "Sure do."

"Oh shit." Vincent sighs, eyes shifting to the front door. "Stalker incoming."

We all turn at the same time to see a girl strutting into the bar with low-slung jeans and a silvery crop top. She looks like she's in her twenties with that young and carefree attitude and pierced belly button. While she might not look like she stepped out of *Vogue*, she's hot in that trashy, stripper sort of way. She makes eye contact with our table, her long, pin-straight black hair swaying and eyes blinking blue. Her beauty is startling.

"Hey, baby." She places a hand on Slade's huge shoulder and rubs up and down.

The touch is intimate, and my eyes widen. He turns to stare at their point of contact before bringing his gaze back to her. She immediately steps off, as if chastened. The man is scary when he chooses to be.

"Sienna." His voice is curt.

Turning her head to the other side of the table, she smirks. "Hello, Mr. Borignone." Her glossy mouth smiles.

She isn't trying to seduce Vincent, but with the way her eyes move between him and Slade, it's clear she's aiming to make Slade jealous.

"How are the tables going?" Vincent asks politely.

"You know me. I make sure the house always wins." Opening her purse, she takes out a stick of blue gum and places it in her mouth.

Vincent nods sternly, and I inwardly steam. Eve looks barely affected—so obviously confident in her relationship.

It's easy to forget that, while Vincent looks rough, he's actually an Ivy League–educated man who built and runs one of the most successful casino and hotel operations in the country. Sure, he did a stint in federal prison. But then again, so did Martha Stewart.

"Come have a drink with me, Slade." Sienna twirls the bottom of her hair. "We didn't get to talk after we shared that cigarette on Sunday."

My heart pauses. After our horrifying weekend, he hung out with this girl? I have no right to feel hurt, but I do.

Asshole!

He stares at her but again stays silent. Slade is not a passive man, but he's clearly trying to keep this interaction under control. We're all looking between them, nervous yet interested in what's to come. Not me though. I want to tear her hair out and throw her tiny ass out the door.

She smiles, taking no offense at his *get the fuck away* demeanor.

"You'd better not leave without buying me a drink tonight." She flips her hair to the side, as though everything is great. "See you later, boys. And you"—she points a sharp red nail at Slade—"find me when you're done." Her eyes flit up to mine, ice cold, before she walks away.

An awkward silence resides over the table.

"Can you fire her already?" Eve whines.

"Nope. She's one of our best dealers." Vincent shrugs, lifting his drink.

"Best dealer or best at other things?" The implication is clear as she all but growls, giving Slade a penetrating stare.

Slade lifts his hands up in mock surrender. "Don't fuck where I work. Learned that lesson a long time ago. Doesn't change the fact that some of these girls can't take a hint."

Am I one of those girls who can't take a hint? Shame washes over me.

His pupils widen, as if he knows what I'm thinking, and he feels ... bad? We're engaged in this weird staring contest, and I need it to stop before I lose myself.

"I'm going to use the restroom," I say out loud, defusing the moment.

Slade immediately slides out of the booth so that I can step out. Holding my black YSL purse tightly to my body, I make my way to the back of the bar.

Before I can enter the ladies' room, I'm pulled over. It's the blue-eyed bitch.

"You're hooking up with Slade?" She giggles, placing a hand over her hip. "I can see how you'd be something exciting to him. Rich girl you obviously are."

Her eyes scan my clothes, and I roll my eyes. Turns out, girls like these exist in every walk of life, from the rez to Rodeo Drive.

"I'm not hooking up with him. But, even if I were, it wouldn't be any of your business." I push past her, making my way into the restroom.

Unfortunately, she follows right behind me. "You can try all you want. But I know men like him. My brother was Special Forces, too. Delta."

I hiss, "So?" I make a mental note to look up what Delta is when I get back to my room.

"Slade was special ops over in Afghanistan. That changes a man. And a girl like you, all prissy?" She stares at my tight jeans and soft blue T-shirt in disgust. "You could never understand him and what he went through. For years, he was prepping or engaging in war. He's seen things your stuck-up little brain can't even fathom. You should back up now before you find yourself under some rubble."

I want to speak, but the words won't come. What could I possibly know or understand about Slade and his past? She isn't wrong. I can hardly imagine what Slade must have gone through. Does he agree with her? Out of my high school class of one hundred and fifty students, zero went into the armed forces. It's embarrassing, how little I know. If not for a few random documentaries over the years and movies, my knowledge would be zero.

Feeling satisfied by my dumbstruck expression, she turns to leave. I'm staring at the door when Eve steps in.

"You okay?" She puts a hand on my shoulder.

I smile. "Yeah, I'm cool." Lifting my back, I shake myself out of my daze.

"I saw some sparks between you and Slade." She smiles wide. "I've always liked you two together."

"He's cool." I smile.

There is so much she doesn't know. I have to fill her in but not here in the restroom and, surely, not now. She opens her mouth to ask more, but before she can, I enter a stall. Luckily, she gets the message. It's not like me to avoid discussing a man, but Slade isn't a normal guy. At least, not to me. What we went through in the night-club was ... intense. In some fucked up way, it bonded us. We were there *together*. Survived *together*. My feelings are conflicted, but he was literally my personal hero.

After I wash my hands, we walk back to the table. Slade and Vincent immediately stand with our arrival, letting us back inside the booth.

"No camping," Vincent says, sitting back down. "Sorry, man. I tried to convince her, but she's still scared of snakes after that small one we saw—"

"It wasn't small, Vincent. It was an actual rattlesnake. And this guy," Eve continues, pointing to Vincent, "jumps over it like it was nothing while I clung to our guide. I mean, who jumps over a rattlesnake? We're from New York, not the Amazon!"

He laughs, pulling her head under his chin. "Lauren's coming, too, yeah?"

I questioningly look at Eve.

"I forgot to tell you, but we're leaving tomorrow to Anam, this gorgeous resort in Canyon Point, Utah. We'll stay there for two nights and spend the day out on Lake Powell. No camping." Eve's eyes sparkle in excitement.

"Wait." I pause, looking around the table. "We?"

I'm supposed to stay here, in Nevada, and unwind. While I love traveling, it's something I need to mentally prepare for. I'm not the type who likes spur-of-the-moment anything. Even flash sales on websites give me anxiety. Like, what do they mean, *only twenty-four hours to shop these items, or they're gone*? A girl needs time to weigh her options!

"It'll be so relaxing," Eve promises.

Slade shifts in his seat.

"Are you sure? If you guys had plans, I don't want to impose."

"No!" Eve exclaims. "I want you with us. We all do. Right, guys?" She looks around, silently asking them to chime in.

"Sure, you should come along," Vincent replies.

Still, Slade doesn't utter a word. I turn to him, waiting for his acceptance.

"Not up to me." He shrugs. "You should come if you want. Don't come if you don't want."

I lick my lips, deciding that Slade is right. I was invited by Eve. I don't need his permission or anyone else's but my own. "Okay, yeah, I'd love to come. Why not?" I turn my eyes back to Slade. "I'll be there."

A small smile fills his lips as Eve claps her hands together.

The waitress strolls over, pulling out her small pad and a pen. With skin the color of clay and lines around her sunken brown eyes, she looks exhausted. "What would y'all like?" Her smile is forced.

I'd guess she is in her mid-forties, but then again, living in LA, it's safe to say my age timeline has gotten skewed. With all the plastic surgery, strict diets, and workout fanatics, it's gotten hard to tell who belongs to what age group. My own mother looks forty when, in actuality, she's in her mid-fifties.

Slade lifts a hand in greeting. "Hey, Candy. How's Jim? Hope he's doing better."

She shrugs as her features darken. "He's all right. Still catching those damn dizzy spells."

"Is it vertigo?"

"Yep. He isn't able to work right now either. I'm taking on more shifts."

"Ah, shit." Slade presses his lips together in a thin line. "I think I know someone who does acupuncture out here, off the rez. I hear that helps." He lifts his phone and begins to scroll. A few moments later, he finds what he's looking for. "Ready?"

She flips to a fresh page on her small pad, writing as Slade spouts off a number.

"It's Dr. Shcherbakov. He's helped a few friends of mine for other things."

Her eyes fill with thankful tears. "Got it. Thank you, Slade."

"Lauren?" His eyes, slightly shadowed, flit between the menu and me, silently telling me to order first.

I clear my throat, looking up at Candy. "What salads do you like? It's my first time here, so I'm open to any suggestions."

"The chicken Caesar is pretty good," she says slowly, moving her pad to a fresh page. "Had it just last night, too. It's a favorite."

Finding it on the menu, I do a quick skim of the ingredients. "Perfect. But would you mind holding the anchovies and keeping the dressing on the side?"

"Sure thing."

I hand her my menu.

Vincent pipes up next, ordering salmon with a mixed green salad for Eve and an eight-ounce steak with steamed veggies for himself.

I tell Eve, "Oh, that sounds good!" Turning back to Candy, I ask, "Can you swap my chicken for salmon?"

She nods as she writes. "And you, handsome?"

Slade scratches the back of his neck. "Burger, whole wheat bun. No cheese or onion. Baked sweet potato, dry. Let's also get steamed Brussels sprouts and spinach."

"Got it." With a grateful smile, she steps away.

"Look at us," I tell the table. "Poster kids for health and wellness."

Slade chuckles at my joke, and I try not to let the warm, slow rumble affect me.

Our food comes quickly, and we all dig in.

"Good, eh?" Slade takes a huge bite of his burger.

"Mmhmm." I nod, surprised at how delicious it is.

"So," Slade starts, "you've looked better."

I smack his wide shoulder, and he just laughs at my lame attempt to hurt him.

"I'm kidding, jeez. You look good. Even rumpled and tired."

His eyes twinkle before taking in my body. I want to overthink this moment, but I bite my cheek.

I whisper, "Seriously though, I shouldn't have left like that. It wasn't right."

His eyes dart back to Vincent and Eve, who are thankfully now focused on Vincent's phone. "Don't stress," he says quietly. "We're cool."

I open my mouth once or twice, but my mind won't let me ask.

"Catching flies, or you've got a question?"

"You slept on the floor, and I thought you didn't want to be near me," I say in a rush.

"I'm not good with sharing a bed. I kick a lot." He smiles jokingly, but it doesn't reach his eyes.

Slade isn't about to explain himself or get into any truth. That much I know is true. It's a bullshit response.

"In that case, thank you for sparing me." My voice is sarcastic.

"If you only knew how true your statement was," he mumbles under his breath.

Instead of replying, I dig the fork back into my salad.

Vincent and Slade begin talking about bringing water to the rez and when the construction is supposed to begin. I'm enthralled by their conversation. Vincent and Slade work so hard and clearly make a ton of money. But they're also trying to better people's lives. Slade mentions hiring veterans for the project, and Vincent wholeheartedly agrees.

"I'm getting tired," I sigh, taking my last bite. "I just got in today."

Slade checks the sporty-looking black watch covering his thick wrist. "I'll bring you to your room." His reply is quick and easy. He turns to Vincent and Eve. "Going to bring this one to the Mile. See you all tomorrow for the trip." He drops money on the table and slides from the booth, waiting for me to follow. When I put my hand into my purse to take out cash, Slade shakes his head. "Nope."

"But why?"

"I already paid for us. Let's go."

Too tired to argue, I stand awkwardly with the table pushing against the center of my thighs as I lean across the booth, hugging Eve.

She's half-standing as well and squeezes me back. "Sleep well. And, if you need anything, call reception right away. They know you're there."

"Sure. Thank you. And bye, Vincent!"

"Don't forget to think about staying," he adds as I scooch to the left, exhausted but relieved to have someone bringing me home.

7

Slade

"I just want to get one thing straight," Lauren starts, stepping through the exit and into the chilly night. "We didn't have sex this weekend because ..." Her voice trails off.

"Because you were in a bad headspace, and I'm not a piece of shit." I open the passenger side of my truck, helping her in. Shutting the door behind her, I get into my own seat and buckle up.

"All right then. Fine. And you slept on the floor because you kick in your sleep?"

She obviously doesn't buy my excuse, but I'm not about to tell her the truth.

"Right again."

The car is dark, but I can see her beautiful profile, down to the shape of her heavy, round breasts. I can't stop my eyes, taking glances at Lauren every other second. Everything about this woman just does it for me.

"You cold?" I turn on the truck's heater, making sure the temperature inside is warm enough. Evenings here can get pretty chilly.

"Thanks."

My eyes continue to flit between Lauren and the road.

"You're staring at me, Slade." She giggles, her voice half-tipsy from the beer.

"No, I'm not," I reply too fast.

"By all means, look all you want." She sits up taller, smiling and sighing, showing her body off for me.

"Is that what you want? For me to look at you?" My eyes stay on her for a moment longer. Even though it's dark, I can imagine her flush.

"Maybe." Her voice is whisper soft. Nervous even.

All thoughts of why this is a terrible idea flee from my brain as all the blood in my body moves south.

"I'll look. I'd like it more if you touched yourself though. Would you do that for me?" I lick my lips like a wolf.

We've already hooked up once, and I know she likes the way I take charge.

Her eyes shoot open in surprise at my request. "W-what do you want me to do?" Her voice trembles, but she'll do what I ask.

I know I'm not the kind of man Lauren is used to, but she likes that about me. A lot.

"Spread your legs for me. Just sink into the seat and get comfortable."

"I've never done this before."

"Good. Don't want to think about you ever doing this with anyone but me. All you have to do is listen and do as I say." My voice is her command.

"Mmhmm. I can do that."

"I want a visual of what you've got on underneath your clothes. Tell me."

"My bra and p-panties are matching. Just simple nude lacy thong and push-up bra."

"Lift your shirt for me. Let me take a look."

As she gingerly raises the soft cotton top, I harden, seeing all that girlie cream lace from my side-eye. She winces, and I pause.

"Your arm still hurting?"

"It's bruised, but I'm okay."

"Take it off."

"My bra or the shirt?"

"First, the bra. Then, the shirt. And do it slow."

I tap on the brakes to slow the car down as she opens the clasp. I'm not typically a man who appreciates a slow reveal. Something about Lauren makes me want to drag everything out. Savor it. I'm a lot of things, but dumb isn't one of them. A woman like Lauren offering herself to me in this way? It's once in a lifetime.

It slowly comes off, and I groan, trying to make out her large cherry-red nipples peeking through her thin T-shirt. I can see the natural slope of her heavy breasts and those hard, pointed peaks, begging to be sucked. I slow down even more, letting myself drink her in as she finally takes off the shirt. She's topless and wanting. It's misery to my arousal.

"Now, the pants. Quickly take them off, Lauren. I don't want to wait anymore."

She unbuckles her seat belt before undoing her jeans. They're tight as skin. She has to keep wiggling around to lower them in the seated position. Her breasts sway as she squirms, fumbling like an innocent.

Christ, it's hot.

Finally, the denim is down to her calves. Bending over, she pulls each pant leg off, one at a time. Laughing, she says, "Sorry that took so long."

I swallow my groan. She has no idea how sexy she is. The fact that I'm pulling her out of her comfort zone, making her do something those assholes she's had before me would never do, it turns me on like nothing else.

Fuck this. I need her—now. I pull over to the side of the road and unbuckle my belt. It's only seconds before I'm pulling her on top of me.

"Goddamn, Lauren. Fuck." I suck hard on the base of her neck, wrapping my hand around her breast and tweaking her nipple, as she grabs the back of my head, urging me on.

She's shaking, nothing but her panties on while I'm completely dressed.

"Need more space."

I lift her to the passenger seat before jumping out of the car and into the back. Slamming the door behind me, I take her hand as she climbs over the center console to join where I sit. So close to nude, she moves directly onto my lap. I grab her ass, pushing down. She grinds against my rough jeans and hard dick. I'd drag her back onto the car's bed, but it wouldn't be warm enough for her. I can smell her want, and it's got my head muddled.

"Lie down," I instruct, moving myself to the far edge of the seat and lowering my mouth directly to her core.

Moving the small scrap of lace to the side, I blow. Her legs shake.

I let my tongue lap around her clit before sucking hard.

"Ahhh!" she screams, the sound low and guttural.

I lift my head. "Yell all you want. No one here but us."

I put my lips directly on her glistening heat and suck. She screams loud enough to wake the dead.

I lick up and down, and she moans, "Slade," from the back of her throat.

I don't normally go down on women. I always like to make them feel good, of course, but this act is intimate. For Lauren though? I want nothing more than to inhale her.

"You're so hot. Your perfect tits high and nipples hard. Do you like it? Do you like the way I eat you?" I get deeper with my tongue. Her sweetness intensifies. "I wanted to drag you into the restroom at The Blue. Screw you against the wall." Lick. "You would have liked that."

I suck harder, and she goes almost wild, body so hot that the windows are fogging.

The visual, combined with her taste, has me out of my goddamn mind. I move my hand to the back of my jeans, needing a condom. It's empty, so I try the next.

"Fuck!" I curse.

Fumbling up, I open the console, but it's empty. Reaching forward, I open the glove compartment—empty again.

"What's wrong?" She's splayed out on the seat, naked and pink and quivering. So close.

"I don't have condoms on me." I lift my hand to touch the roof of the car, heaving with annoyance. "I can drive us to a gas station. There's one about seven minutes away."

"Let's go back to your place," she says, body quaking as she sits up.

I lean back on the seat again, and she crawls back to my lap, kissing me with absolute abandon. Gripping the back of my head. Moaning with her scent all over me.

This woman.

Her hot tongue sliding into my mouth with need. I want to pull off my jeans and slide inside her, but I won't. Couldn't disrespect her in that way.

"Let's just drive and pick those condoms up," I groan, wishing my car could fly.

"Okay." Kiss. "And then how far to your place?" Kiss.

"No." I grip the back of her neck, sucking on her bottom lip.

Panting, she asks, "Huh?" Her eyes settle in confusion as she pulls back, away from me.

"I don't bring women back to my place." I grit my teeth, remembering Lilly in my bed and what I did to her.

Fury brews at the fact that Lauren wants more. It's irrational, but she's asking for things I cannot give her, and that pisses me off.

"We'll finish this here. Trust me; it'll be amazing." I press my lips to her collarbone, wanting to kiss this gorgeous woman who is somehow magical to me and say, *I'm sorry, baby, but we can't. I'm dangerous and not to be trusted. Please, just take what I can give.*

But she turns away, oblivious to my silent pleading.

"Excuse me?" Her brows lower in the offensive. Bending down to take her clothes that have been strewn around the car, she turns her face away from mine, hands covering her full breasts.

"You heard me," I repeat, my voice low and deep.

I want her, but it's got to be on my terms. For the sake of her safety, there is no other option.

She leans down again, picking up her bra that hangs from the headrest of the front seat. "So, that's how you see me? Some easy lay? Good enough to fuck in a car but nowhere else?"

I pause. She's completely wrong. I'd like nothing more than to screw her brains out in my bed. In my shower. Over my kitchen counter. But, if she enters my house, she'll want to stay over. I can't provide what she wants. I'm incomplete and fucked up. I'm a man who's been altered by war. I'm not the man she thinks she knows.

"Oh, that's great, Slade. You're silent? Screw you."

"Lauren, come on."

Her jeans come on first and then her bra and top. I can do nothing but watch her redress.

We both make our way back to the front seat, and I bring her back to the hotel in silence. I can feel her angry thoughts stewing, but there is no defense. At least, none that I'm willing to say out loud. I can barely speak the truth to myself.

When I pull up to the hotel, she unbuckles her belt. "I've always been honest. I understand you aren't interested in me long-term. I knew it when you didn't call after the wedding. I'm a big girl who can handle sex without strings, but I won't be disrespected or treated like a girl you just want to fuck in your backseat and dump. It's never been me, and it won't be me. It's a line I won't cross."

I grip the steering wheel and face forward, not wanting to see the look on her face when I deliver the truth. "All I've got to give is this. If you don't like it, there's nothing I can do."

"So, now what?" Her words are final but also questioning.

She wants me to fight for her or change my mind, but it won't happen. It can't. We haven't known each other too long, but we've been through a lot together. She deserves more than a quick fuck in the back of my car. But she also deserves a decent life, and that's something I can't give her while my head is in this state. My mind is made.

"Now, nothing."

When I look at her large eyes, filled with hurt, my chest freezes.

Right now, Lauren's almost childlike. She's so trusting and open, waiting for me to change my mind.

I want to yell, *Don't trust me! Don't come close to me! I'll hurt you.* But I don't. Instead, the warning sits on my tongue like bitter acid.

After a moment of hesitation, she leaves.

I slam my hand on the steering wheel, cursing as she runs into the hotel—away from me, as she should. Suddenly, my anger starts to blow. I want to break something! I slam my hands down over and over again, yelling like a lunatic. Part of my mind knows this is crazy and irrational, but I can't stop myself.

With shaking hands, I take three pills from my glove compartment and swallow them dry, needing to calm down. There is no other way.

8

Slade

The hotel is the epitome of rest and relaxation. The only colors around us are white and cream. Oh, and beige. Who can forget good old beige? And, at the rate I'm being asked if I want a hot towel, cold towel, or my bags taken, it's clear there are at least three staff for every guest here.

For a fact, Vincent hates this shit. But he's got it in his mind to take Eve to the best places in the world. Apparently, it's something he swore to do a long time ago.

This is the second time they've dragged me to one of these fancy resorts, and I can safely say I officially can't stand them. I'm too big for places like these. Don't even get me started on the food. The plates are two bites each. Not least, I can't take a step without worrying I'll knock something or someone over.

A few months back, we flew to Paris to meet with potential investors for the Milestone. Vincent and I stayed at the Four Seasons where I made the mistake of sitting on a silver couch in the lobby. How was I supposed to know it was an antique and not actually for sitting? The concierge ran over to me, red-faced, cursing my American ass out.

The trip over here this morning could have been awkward, considering last night's clusterfuck, but I did my best to stay out of Lauren's way while she zoned out on her e-reader. Last night, at The Blue, I'd wanted her to come on this trip. For Lauren, nothing could be better than a trip of rest and relaxation on the lake. Obviously, I'm regretting it now. After the car last night, I'm twisted. I want her badly, but it can't work. She'd expect answers, as she should. But I'm not in my right mind to give her those things. I can't give more than what's available.

Vincent and I step up to reception.

A boy, suited up and dressed as a man, waits with a smile. He swallows hard, trying not to show anxiety. "Hello, and welcome to the Anam."

"We need another room," Vincent says brusquely. "It's under Borignone. We've got two right now, but we must have a third."

Vincent pulls out his phone, checking e-mails, while I stand a step behind him and survey the area. I'm not technically his personal security now that the mess with his past life is behind us, but old habits have a way of sticking.

The concierge types on the computer before blanching, eyes flitting from the flat computer screen to Vincent. "I'm sorry, Mr. Borignone, sir. But we're completely booked. There aren't any e-extra rooms," he stutters.

Vincent was sure there would be space for Lauren, but as luck would have it, there isn't. I cross my arms, hoping that a little intimidation will magically open a room.

"You have two reserved," he continues. "One master suite with a king bed and another suite with two queen beds."

"Two beds?" Vincent repeats before lifting two fingers up to me.

I vehemently shake my head, mouthing, *No*.

Vincent turns away from the concierge, whisper-yelling with teeth gritted, "Don't be an asshole, Slade. What do you want us to do, send her back to Nevada?"

Both of us look at Lauren, who's relaxing on one of the white chairs in the lobby, holding her e-reader. Her brows are furrowed, as though in concentration. I try not to stare at her long legs, casually crossed. Is she in another lace bra and panties? I swallow hard before finding Vincent staring at me with a smile.

"The answer is no," I tell him, gathering myself. "You should have thought of rooms before you brought us all out here. I'm not staying with her."

"Just a second, sir," Vincent says politely, obviously trying to soften his hard look.

He throws a heavy arm over my shoulders, pulling me into a private corner of the hotel lobby. "What's wrong with you? There are two goddamn beds. Grow a pair. You obviously want to get with her. And she wants you, too. You should be fuckin' cheering right now that you have to share a room."

I should tell him that Lauren and I were just together in Vegas, but if I did, he might ask about the shooting. Lauren told Eve not to tell him, but Eve and Vincent are crazy tight. Maybe she did?

I froze when the shots started. Can't even remember how I got us out of the club.

I'm not in denial about my issues; I know there's a screw loose in my head. But I won't seek professional help because I know that, with time, I'll fix this on my own. I don't need someone psychoanalyzing me. Someone who doesn't even know me and has no idea about what I went through overseas. I can handle this myself. Vincent knowing what happened would earn me a one-way ticket to the VA hospital. But having a girl like Lauren sharing a bedroom with me? Also, a bad idea. The question is, which bad idea is the better one?

I straighten my shoulders. "We already hooked up at your wedding," I reply easily, knowing that I need to give some truth to shut him up. Vincent is the kind of man who reads people easily. A lie won't cut it.

"Yeah, so what? Even better." He looks at me like he doesn't understand what the problem is.

"She's into me. And I don't want to give her any ideas." I maintain direct eye contact.

"Lauren's an adult. Keep it in the pants or don't. Just don't make promises you don't intend to keep. I know she looks flighty 'cause she's cute and into fashion, but she isn't. She used to help Eve on huge cases. She's sharp as a whip and really intelligent. She's not some clingy moron."

I look back at Lauren as she adjusts her white sweater. It falls over one shoulder, showcasing the smooth line of her collarbone. Vincent isn't telling me anything I don't know.

"There are two beds," he continues. "It's just a few nights. Not a big deal." Placing his hands on his hips, he waits for an answer.

Vincent would be right if he were talking to a normal guy who didn't medicate to control dark memories. I need to weigh the shit-show that would go down if he put the pieces together about Vegas versus having her and me share a room.

My job would be in flux if he figured out what I'd been dealing with—or worse, he'd throw me into therapy or rehab. On the other hand, Lauren could witness a night terror and be in harm. Then again, there are two beds in the room, so she wouldn't be directly next to me. And, with my meds combined with a good amount of liquor, I'd be able to conk myself out well enough to keep her safe. I try not to mix drugs too often, but it's okay. I'll do it. Staying with Lauren is my best bet at keeping the image of myself steady.

"Fine," I find myself replying with a silent, *Please, God don't let this blow up in my face..*

"Fine?" He looks at me funny, as though my sudden agreement surprises him.

"Yeah, man. Fine. We'll share the room."

I dare you to argue with the fact that I agreed.

He easily reads me and backs off.

9

Lauren

I slide my large, round Chloe sunglasses over my eyes. Not that it's sunny, but I don't want Slade to see my face right now. I'm nervous to be staying with him. I'm good at faking things but not *that* good. Plus, it dims everything around me. I don't want to see his huge body and handsome face. He's almost too much. After leaving me on the brink of a deep orgasm, followed by his admission that I'm nothing more than a one-night stand, unworthy of being in his bed, I feel frustrated, insecure, and angry. I begged Vincent and Eve to find another room for me, but the hotel is completely booked.

The bellboy trails after Slade and me as he brings our bags to the room. My black suitcase is full-sized while he has nothing but a small green Under Armour duffel bag. Figures.

We enter our beautiful room, and I do my best not to clap in delight. Two plush white queen-sized beds are on either side of the rectangular room as serene black-and-white photography of a mountain sunset adorns the space between. A large white desk sits at the opposite corner alongside a cream couch. A black-and-chrome Nespresso coffeemaker sits atop a beautiful cream-colored dresser.

"The bathroom," the bellboy announces, opening up a door to a huge double-sink marble bath.

I peek inside, feeling utter relief. This is exactly what I need to relax my nerves.

After the bellboy gives us a detailed description of the beautiful amenities of the property, including handing me a schedule of group workouts on the property, Slade opens the minibar. Leaning in, he seems to scan the items. I can see the top of his boxer briefs; the black elastic band is nice and tight around his firm waist.

"Everything in here is alcohol-free." Shutting the door, he turns back to the bellboy in fury.

I'm taken aback by his attitude. I love a glass of wine as much as the next person, but Slade looks legitimately angry.

"That would be right, sir."

I'd bet sweat is taking up residence beneath his uniform with the way his eyes have widened. I glance between the two of them, unsure.

Slade crosses his arms, apparently waiting for a reply.

"Utah state law a-affects alcohol service, sir. The m-minibar must be dry because it is complimentary, and complimentary alcohol is illegal."

"Shit," he says out loud, clenching his fists.

After pulling out a bill from his wallet, he hands it to the shaking kid, who hastily makes his exit. There's a moment of awkwardness as the door slams shut. His exaggerated response makes me feel uncomfortable.

"Which bed do you want?"

He calmly raises his brows, and I take his cue. Brushing the incident under the rug works for me.

I drop my purse on the bed that is closest to the bathroom, staking claim. We need to have a conversation about the fact that we're stuck in a room together. I want to relax, and here I am, instead stressing out over my temporary roommate.

"Sunshine, you look like a bug right now." He chuckles.

"Sunshine?" My heart pauses at this potential term of endearment, but then I process the rest of his sentence. "Wait. Did you just call me a bug?"

"Yep. What are you wearing those ridiculous glasses for? The sun isn't shining in here. You aren't hungover either."

"I can wear my sunglasses anytime I want to." I cross my arms over my chest.

"Sure you can. They take up half your face though. Very round, too," he adds.

"So? Round is stylish." My teeth grind together.

"Well, if you're going for bug-style, you've done it."

I tear the glasses off my face, and there he is. No longer darkened by my lenses, but full-blown. Perfect. And then he smiles, and my heart sinks.

"There you are, Sunshine," he croons.

"Why are you calling me that?" I huff, trying to ignore how sinfully hot he is.

"Because you are."

"No. Right now, I'm a dark cloud."

We both pause, and then he starts laughing—from his belly, no less.

"Lauren, you're goddamn hilarious," he stutters, clapping his hands together.

Dark cloud? Could I have come up with a dumber line?

He's laughing at me. I want to laugh, too, because, fine, it was a stupid retort. This man calls me on my shit like no one else.

Jumping onto the bed near the window, he lays comfortably with his big body practically taking up the whole mattress. When he sweeps his tongue across his full bottom lip, I try not to salivate. I need to say something to clear the air. We're stuck together for two nights, and I don't want awkwardness.

"Just so you know," I start, "I'd appreciate it if we could just move past last night."

"Don't sweat it, Sunshine. I'm past it. We're here, sharing a room. I can keep my dick in my pants."

"Right," I exclaim, feigning relief. "I'm glad we're on the same page."

Silence takes over the room as he grabs his phone and begins typing.

I begin unpacking my stuff when he says, "I noticed last night. It looks good, by the way."

I turn to him, and he gestures to my arm.

My stomach warms. "Yes. You were right about that. It's still bruised, but it's okay." I inhale, his smell invading my senses. Stepping back, I need to make more space between us. I'm here to find myself and figure out what the heck I'm doing with my life—not fawn over a completely inaccessible man who doesn't see me as anything more than a good lay.

"Let's just have a good time. Friends?" I plaster a smile on my face, hoping he agrees. If I can play it off as though he didn't massively offend me, I can get through this vacation in one piece.

He smiles, but it doesn't quite reach his eyes. "Of course. Like I said, we're cool."

My phone pings, and I pull it out from my back pocket to check.

Eve: Hey there. Everything okay in the room? Not sure why both of you were so opposed to sharing, but if you want, I can have Vincent and Slade stay together, and we can share a room.

Lauren: Nooo. No way. You have your romantic weekend. I'm fine.

Eve: Are you positive? We'd have fun. I don't want you feeling uncomfortable. You're here to rest.

Lauren: I'm all good. Trust me!

Eve: Okay. Love you, and if you need me, call the room or text. Xoxo.

Lauren: Are we having dinner together?

Eve: I think Vincent and I are going to lay low. Unless you want to go out?

Lauren: That's okay. I'm exhausted, too. See you tomorrow morning.

I turn back to the massive man before me. "Turns out, we aren't meeting for dinner."

I pull the tie out of my hair, and it falls around my shoulders. His nostrils slightly flare, but other than that, he remains completely stoic.

"Yep."

When he moves his thick arms behind his head, I bite the side of my cheek.

"Well"—I lift the class schedule in front of my face and skim through the times—"looks like a yoga class is starting in ten minutes. I'm going to go."

Calmly, I bend down to find my exercise clothes. This hotel is gorgeous and the epitome of tranquility. I plan on using the time to clear my head.

"I'll join you." He sits up.

I drop my hands to my hips. "What?"

"I do yoga." He opens his own bag, pulling out a fresh pair of black shorts and a T-shirt.

"You do not," I practically scream. Clearing my throat, I repeat myself in a calmer tone, "You do not."

"I do." He smiles. "And I'm coming, Sunshine."

FIFTEEN MINUTES LATER, we've both changed into exercise attire. I'm in a white sports bra, cropped white T-shirt, and gray lizard-print leggings. I try to keep my head up and off the fact that his shorts show off his dick imprint. Long, thick, and utterly perfect. I inhale and exhale, trying to get my breathing under control.

He's a jerk. An asshole. I hate him. I repeat these lines like a mantra.

Slade pushes the down arrow for the elevator. It lights up in red. "How long have you done yoga?"

"On and off over the last seven years. And you?"

I begin braiding my hair, moving it to the side. His eyes trail my fingers.

"Not too long."

"Well, you can watch me if you need."

He chuckles. "I'll be sure to do that."

I could swear, there is a twinkle in his eye.

I keep my back straight as we walk soundlessly to the studio.

With floor-to-ceiling doors opened wide and facing the mountains, the room is the ultimate in peace, just what I want. Slade takes two beige-colored mats from the corner of the room, handing one to me. I lay it vertically on the wooden floor, facing the windows. We're side by side, stretching, as four other people enter the room.

"Yoga's good. I wish I did it more."

"I try every morning for at least fifteen minutes. It just clears my head in a way nothing else can," I reply.

And then the class begins. It's slow at first, but the flow increases.

Slade effortlessly moves from position to position. At first, I'm impressed. But it doesn't take long for annoyance to take hold. I've been doing yoga for years, focusing on the elevation of my practice. Instead of concentrating on myself right now, all I can see is his huge, muscular body contorting in positions that even I have trouble doing.

"Let the pose ground you," the instructor says, gliding between the two of us. "But don't go beyond your edge or push yourself too far," she adds, staring at me. "Feel your apana moving downward through your body as you settle into your squat."

"Fuck my life," I whisper under my breath, watching Slade fall into a perfect position.

"What was that?" he whispers, smirking.

Sweat drips into my eyes, the salt burning my pupils.

"Don't talk to me. I'm centering," I hiss under my breath.

"Get lower in your squat, Sunshine."

I glance up just in time to see the tease coating his eyes.

Asshole!

That's it. I've had it. I pick up my mat and move behind Slade, so he no longer has the perfect view of me. Unfortunately, that means I'm the one with the view.

When class is over, the instructor flits over to Slade, asking him where he studies. I decide there is no reason to sit here and watch them flirt. I need a shower.

I arrive back in our room in a huff. Stripping my clothes off my body, I step angrily into the hot spray. The nerve! Pouring shampoo into my hand, I scrub my hair. With each pass over my scalp, my anger intensifies. And, surprisingly, it isn't because of the fact that I was just in the midst of a mass shooting. Actually, ever since I came out here, I've been feeling a whole lot better. The cause of my anxiety is tall, muscular, and moody. The man who saved my life and washed the blood off my body is gone. In his place is a smug and cocky asshole, who's probably fucking the yoga instructor right now—in the back of his car! I can only imagine the positions she can contort herself into.

Bitch.

My soapy hand glides over my nipples, and I shut my eyes. Flashes of his face, smile, and body overwhelm me. The truth is unstoppable. I want Slade because he's hot and cool and kind. And so smart. He makes me laugh and makes me happy in a way I haven't felt in ... ever. And he doesn't want anything with me other than sex. It *hurts.*

A loud knock brings me back to the present.

"Can you get out already? It's been over twenty minutes."

I quickly rinse the conditioner from my hair, wrapping one white towel around my body and a second one turban-style around my hair. When I exit the bathroom, steam billows behind me. He's waiting, leaning against the doorframe in a casual stance with some clothes balled in his hand.

"It's about time," he drawls, a slight tinge of a Southern accent coming through. His eyes wander from my toes up to my face.

I tighten the towel around me, trying not to glower. "I'm surprised you're back so soon with the way that yoga teacher was checking you out." I raise my brows.

There's no reason I should be so furious right now. Rationally, I know this. But it doesn't change the truth. I like him despite the fact that he doesn't think highly of me. I know I'm acting like a child with an unrequited crush, but I can't help myself. Deep down, I want to show him that I'm more than he thinks. Instead, it's all coming out as anger. I finally get out of my head enough to notice his gorgeous chest is bare.

"Don't worry. She's not my type." And, with one last good look, he steps by me and walks into the bathroom. The door shuts with a thud.

"God help me," I moan, face-planting on the bed.

He comes out freshly showered and changed into a pair of soft, worn-looking jeans and a white T-shirt, feet bare and smelling clean and soapy warm. His hair has grown out some, the strands shiny and thick.

The doorbell rings.

"Hope you don't mind, but I ordered us an early dinner. Can't stand to eat late at night," Slade says before opening the door.

The waiter sets up the food on our small terrace where he pulls out plate after plate, each with a silver cover. He seems to have ordered enough food for five. After signing the bill, he takes out a bottle of white wine from the minibar.

I gasp. "How did you get that?"

"I've got my ways." He chuckles.

"And here I was, thinking you were a good and honest all-American boy," I joke, trying to shake out my earlier fury.

"You thought wrong, Lauren. I'm anything but good."

His eyes move to mine. What I see surprises me. I see ... pain. I think about Sienna and what she told me. Is that what this is—a post-war agony?

He sits tall, placing a large Caesar salad in front of me, topped with roasted salmon. "Hope you don't mind that I got this. I remember you ordered it at The Blue."

I nod my head, overwhelmed by his thoughtfulness. He remembers what I ate. That's a good sign, right? Or maybe he just has a really good memory.

"Why are you looking all worried?" He opens the cover from one of the plates and digs into his chicken, placing a large piece in his mouth.

"It's nothing."

He uncorks the wine and pours it into the empty glass in front of me.

He smirks. "Yeah, sure. Have some of my chicken. It's better than your salad." Cutting me a piece, he transfers it onto my plate.

"Hey, don't give me the leg. That's the best part."

"You should always have the best." Our eyes lock until he looks away.

We eat quietly. It's filled with warmth and comfort.

You like him, my brain reminds me. *So, so much. But he won't ever give you more than his backseat*, my heart reminds me.

"So, your parents are from Iran?"

My silver fork drops, clattering against the plate. "Who told you that?" The quiver in my voice is unmistakable.

He laughs out loud. "I asked Eve." *Simple,* his silence adds.

My eyes narrow, as I feel oddly betrayed. How could she have told him this?

Never in my life have I been ashamed of my heritage. All is well on the coasts where the left-wing reigns, and cultural diffusion is typical. But, in the rest of the country, I'm considered the *other*. And here is this man, a military man, who fought for my freedom.

It worries me to believe that he would see me and think, *She's the enemy.*

Not that he's ever given me a reason to believe that, but I'm still worried he would.

Food rises to the back of my throat as tears prickle my eyes. I continuously swallow, trying to get rid of them. Luckily, I manage to bring the unshed tears down to the center of my body.

True, my parents didn't arrive via the Mayflower. But my Persian heritage is part of me, and I refuse to show any kind of embarrassment. I have nothing to hide. If he thinks worse of me, then he isn't worth my time. And anyway—

"Sunshine, it's fine." His words interrupt my thoughts. "I know your parents aren't terrorists." He lets out a dark, full-bellied laugh, assuring me that all is well. "Some of the best men I've ever known are Middle Eastern. You gotta think better of me, right? I know who you are, Lauren."

Does he?

His words echo around my ribs, tapping on my heart.

"Seeing as you're the way you are, I'm sure your parents are wonderful people, too."

I nod, still not trusting myself to speak. I didn't realize the extent of my worry until now.

"And don't get mad. I asked Eve an innocent question, and she had no reason to lie. Is that why you didn't tell me when I asked at the wedding? You were afraid I wouldn't like it?" he teases me, smiling as he cuts up more of his food.

I burn from embarrassment because he's right. I thought he'd run away if he knew.

"Don't mock me about this, Slade. I was worried. You're right. But there's a lot of hatred in the world. And how would I have known your views?"

"I'll try not to be offended." He continues to eat, finishing his chicken and moving on to a steak with sliced beefsteak tomatoes on the side.

I'm having my salad slowly and quietly, watching him eat every last bite until his plate is wiped clean.

Standing, he pulls a pack of Marlboros from his back pocket. Pulling out a cigarette with two fingers, he drops it between his full lips before bringing up a lone match, lighting it up to a shining amber. "You don't mind if I smoke, do you?" He sits back down.

"No, I don't mind."

With my agreement, he exhales.

I'm not a fan of smoking. I want to live my best and healthiest life. But watching this huge man spreading his long denim-clad legs out in front of him, relaxing with a cigarette, does something to my insides. It's undeniable. With his huge, muscular arms, tatted so well, and his heavy soldier's body, I find myself clenching my thighs together. Intensely staring at him in the dim light, I swallow hard.

"You should talk to someone about the shooting." He takes a napkin from the silver holder and wipes his hands, cigarette dangling between his lips. "Don't hold it in." His voice is low and deep.

"Actually, I think I'm doing okay." My voice comes out surprisingly upbeat. "I had a bit of a breakdown before I came out here, but I feel a lot better already. How about you?" I take another bite of my salad.

"Me? What about me?" He wrings his hands together.

"Well, you were there, too. And I thought I saw you freeze up for a—"

"Of course I'm fine," he spits out. "Never been better."

He lets out a dark laugh as he takes a hard pull of his cigarette. His demeanor has my guard moving up, but I tell myself to stop my overreaction.

"Really? Because I noticed, when the shots first went off, you—"

A stone face flashes to mine. "Don't," he snaps.

I questioningly tilt my head to the side. "Wait. Why are you getting so upset?"

The chair scrapes against the ground, and he stands to his full, hulking height. My jaw drops at the outburst as my heart lurches in my chest. What the hell is going on here? Maybe he's the one who hasn't dealt with his shit. He's all about being helpful and doling out advice, but when the tables turn, it's complete shutdown.

I hesitantly stand, unsure if I should run away or wait this out. "I won't press." My voice is a whisper as I raise my hands in surrender. Part of me wants to run, but my heart won't let me move.

His eyes are suddenly dark and so empty. "There's nothing to fucking press." He bares his teeth and steps closer, raising the stakes and morphing into someone else entirely.

He wouldn't hurt me, right? I know Slade would never, but this man isn't the Slade I know. I shiver, as though my body knows something that my mind refuses to register.

"L-let's just enjoy our dinner, okay? Let's not talk about that night anymore. I'm okay. You're okay. Everything's great," I whisper, as though trying to calm a rabid animal.

I should run, get the hell out of here. But I don't. The swirls in his eyes, normally flecked in gold, have darkened. Seconds pass in silence. I'm frozen while he continues to fume.

A moment later, I ask "Slade?"

Taking a risk and reaching out my hand, I touch his arm. Suddenly, his eyes soften. He opens and shuts his mouth, eyes darting around our small balcony before settling on me. He's sad and angry and something else I just can't name.

He retakes his seat, and I let out the breath I was holding. Whatever gripped him a moment ago has passed.

Slade has a dark side with a temper. I know it, and my body knows it, too. The night of the wedding, he seemed to be okay. But something happened, turning the fun and cool man I'd thought I knew into someone else.

I swallow, my mouth feeling dry as he lights up another cigarette, blowing smoke into the night.

"I scared you." His eyes flit back over to my face, assessing me.

My heart pounds because, yes, I'm scared as hell. Still, I don't want to back down. Not from the man I know, who is filled with so much decency and kindness.

"I'm still here, aren't I?" My voice shakes, and yet I sit taller.

Smoky white wisps billow from his mouth as he nods his head. "You need to hear me now. I'm not the man you think I am. I'm not a savior. I've done some horrific shit, and now, here I am, living my life. You want to meet a good man, so you can get married, start a family? I can set you up. But it's not me. I didn't call you after the wedding because it would have been for nothing. You're a great girl, but I'll never be able to give you the white picket fence."

A pregnant pause wedges itself between us.

"I don't even know what to say to that."

"Say you'll stay away. We had a few fun times, but we're not suited for anything more. I need to know you understand." He turns his head to mine, eyes blazing. "I see the way you look at me, like you're dying to fuck and then meet my mom for dinner. You've got to stop that. Seeing as you're Eve's best friend, the last thing I need to do is screw around with you and piss her and Vincent off. So, do us both a favor and just back up." He casually exhales, as though he didn't just knife me with his words.

I open and close my mouth in shock and hurt as heat rises into my face. Men see me as hot. They want my body, but they never want *me*. I thought maybe Slade was different, figuring we had a connection that went further than mere attraction. I was wrong. Tears well up in my eyes. I'm not asking for yachts and travel and fancy dinners. I just want someone who'll open the covers in our bed when our kids come in the middle of the night. Someone to know and love the real me. I'm sick and tired of all the phony bullshit that surrounds me. But something about me magnetizes the wrong men. Something about me says, *I'm good for one thing—and it isn't talking.*

"Do you hear me? Say yes, Lauren," he commands, sitting forward with his elbows leaning on his knees. His voice is sure, confident, and ice cold as he stares at me like he wouldn't mind grabbing and shaking me.

I feel so vulnerable and defeated by his anger.

"Y-yes." I sound scared because I am.

He went from calm to scary and then to cruel in a matter of minutes.

He pours himself more wine, and I let myself back inside, leaving my food for him to clear.

I turn on the water in the shower, feeling ill as I take my clothes off piece by piece. I'm clean, but I need to clear my head. Soft black jersey leggings, white V-neck T-shirt, and a pair of lacy bra and panties sit in a heap in the corner of this luxurious white marble bathroom. All at once, I straighten my back and make another conscious decision not to listen to him. I'm an adult. I refuse to allow his opinion of me—or any man's opinion, for that matter—affect how I see myself. I've spent too many years hanging my self-worth on a man's opinion, and I'm sick of it. I guess, in some twisted way, I can thank the shooting for that.

Slade believes I'm nothing more than a beautiful outer shell? Well, fuck him! Any man who believes that is missing out on me—a woman with intelligence and kindness and more love and loyalty in her pinkie than any of them have in their entire bodies. The right man is out there for me, somewhere. I just haven't found him yet. Just because Slade's decided I'm not valuable doesn't mean my fate is decided. He can kiss my perky ass.

10

Slade

Lake Powell is a sight to behold. White houseboats line the sandy shore while kids play in the water, drifting down slides and balancing on colorful noodles. Once upon a time, I would have wanted a life just like this. Beautiful wife. Few kids. I crack my knuckles, refocusing. None of that is meant for me.

I'm holding a plastic bag filled with two six-packs of Corona that we picked up from a bodega on our way. Vincent's got the bag of lunches and drinks the hotel packed for us to take on this excursion.

"Oh my God!" Lauren exclaims, pointing toward the boats. "Those are so awesome. Eve, we should totally rent one of these houseboat thingies one day. Do you see how the slide is connected to the boat? I love it!"

I can't help but smile at her exuberance. Lauren's personality is bent toward happiness. Hands on her slim hips, she looks around with joy. Being near her reminds me of what I'll never have. She'll wind up happy—so long as she stays far away from me.

I'm a shithead for talking to her the way I did last night, but it's for her own good. She needed to know the score. And my temper? I lost complete control when she asked me about Vegas. Just another event pointing to the fact that I'm fucked up in the head and losing control of myself.

ONCE SHE STEPS off the balcony, I let myself out of the room and chain-smoke off the property for hours, polishing off a six-pack of beer. When I finally get back to the room, she's sound asleep, curled beneath layers of sheets. Face calm and relaxed, as it should be. I pop a few benzos in my mouth, ensuring that I'll sleep like the dead.

At six a.m., my alarm goes off. I'm on the carpeted floor and completely fogged up. Forcing myself awake, I drink a few cups of water out of the sink before changing my clothes and heading down to the hotel's gym. The machines look completely new. The weight section seems as though it's never been touched with rows of silver kettlebells in a wide range of weights, sitting neatly in size order.

Running six uphill miles on the treadmill, followed by six sets of fifty plyo push-ups on the floor, my entire body drips with sweat. The fog begins to lift. Vincent shows up midway through my workout. He must realize I'm not in the mood for conversation because he leaves me good and alone without anything more than a nod hello.

Back in the room, I still feel like a damn criminal with the way I treated Lauren. Coffee brews while I wash up in the hot shower, trying not to think about her as I soap my body. Lifting her small black shampoo bottle and opening its top, I inhale. Leaning against the wall, I drop my head against the cold marble, trying to fight through the turmoil I feel inside. But I can't. My mind is shattered, not to be controlled. I curse, stepping back to the spray. I want this woman so fucking much, but I'm nothing but a lowlife. I refuse to live in some fantasy where Lauren would be enough to eradicate all the shit I went through overseas. In actual life, I have no choice but to drink and take meds if I want to sleep anywhere near her. I might have lost control, but I'm not delusional.

Sitting on the terrace, I make sure to position my chair, so I can see her, but she can't see me. After my third black cup, she wakes with swollen, bee-stung lips and perfectly braided hair. Lauren sleeps in soft pink cotton shorts and a matching shirt. I stare at her long legs and beautiful arms, the bruise still wrapping around the left. A small sliver of stomach peeking out between her top and shorts has me salivating. Pulling out a cigarette, I let the smoke push down my craving for her.

I want nothing more than to mark her. Establish ownership of her body and mind. She thinks I have no clue who she is as a woman, but she thinks wrong. She's intelligent, not selfish or simple in the least. I see how she acts to everyone around her with kindness and grace. Always reading. Making sure to check in with work so that the girl covering her doesn't drown. Still, I need her to hate me. I don't deserve the love of a woman like her, nor am I in the state of mind to have it.

She returns from the bathroom and glances around the room, presumably noticing my absence. Grabbing some clothes, she reenters the bathroom. Is she locking the door to keep the monster out? She should. The absence of her in my line of sight makes me feel strangely desperate, but I sit and wait.

She comes out, looking fresh and gorgeous in a short yellow sundress with red strawberries that look painted on. Those round bug-glasses I ribbed her for sit above her head. I stare at my phone, making her think she's far from my mind's eye.

She steps onto the balcony. "I'm leaving." Silence descends as she turns on a gold sandal.

I nod, although she can't see me. Not that I deserve her eyes.

A MAN WEARING a captain's hat stands on a boat, waving us over. Even though I insisted we didn't need a guide, Vincent wouldn't budge.

"THIS WAY, we'll enjoy ourselves without worrying about where we're going," he tells me over the ridiculously nice breakfast buffet, complete with a section of rare fresh fruits and cheeses, an entire spread of breads that would rival any bakery, and a section of different salads.

An omelet station stands to the left where a chef is ready to make any egg concoction one could dream of. Of course, there is also a menu to order from, if you don't feel like getting up. The excess can be fun when in the right mindset, but sometimes, it's straight-up sickening. Just imagining the waste of this hotel while the world hungers makes my anger rise.

Lauren eats a cucumber, tomato salad on the left side of her plate and scrambled egg whites with spinach and feta cheese on the right. She drinks her coffee hot with a drop of skim milk and no sugar. My behavior is obsessive, even for a man like me who is always paying attention to everything. But I can't stop myself.

"Hey there!" the captain greets us, white linen shirt bright against his leather-tanned skin. His voice shakes me back into the moment. "I'm Randy. My boat is ready for you. We got bodyboards, tubes, and water skis." He shakes each of our hands.

Eve jumps up and down, unable to contain her excitement, while Vincent smiles like he won the goddamn lottery. Making Eve happy is his kryptonite. Lauren smiles wide, too. I'll never be the one to make her smile like that; I can't be. The thought is the ultimate in sobering. And yet, each time she blinks, my fixation with her grows.

The happy couple gets on first, Vincent's arm wrapped around his tiny wife. I step onto the speedboat after them, putting out my hand to help Lauren on. She might hate me, but I don't want her falling. The boat shakes, but she refuses to take what I'm offering. I should be glad. Whatever it takes to get her to move on is a good thing. This is what I wanted, and this is what I got.

Lifting the top of the cooler, I drop the beers inside before stepping to the back of the boat.

"Who wants to tube first?" Randy smiles as he puts the boat in gear.

In unison, Lauren and Eve scream, "Me!"

Vincent laughs, and I try to smile, needing to act like a normal guy who's well-adjusted in the world. A regular guy who is vacationing with his best friend and a beautiful woman.

"No problem, ladies. You're both small enough to share."

The captain drives approximately ten minutes into the center of the lake. The temperature outside feels around eighty-five degrees.

He stops the boat to grab the tube while Lauren does a little shimmy out of her short sundress. I want to stand up and cover her or tell her to keep it on. She lifts it from the floor and neatly folds it, placing it down on the seat. Her bathing suit is cherry red and shows the tops of her breasts. I sigh in relief because it's a one-piece and not a skimpy bikini. Her fingers move deftly as she braids her shining hair to the side, laughing at something the captain said. Lauren weaves each section of her hair together until she looks like a bona fide mermaid. How she does her hair like that, I'll never know.

Turning around to face the water, she holds the top of the silver ladder that leads to the lake. I stare at her back, and my jaw drops. The suit dips all the way down, reaching the top of her perky ass. The bottom isn't much either. It's not a thong, but it's small. Like, really fucking tiny and barely covering. I want to run up with a towel and cover her before anyone can see what I see. That she's perfect.

I need to calm down. "Yo, Vincent, grab me a beer."

He opens the cooler and takes one out. "Not too cold yet."

"It'll do."

I catch his throw. It pops open with a hiss, and I drink. It's warmish, but I'll take what I can get. Leaning over the edge, I watch Lauren climb onto the black-and-white-striped tube. On her stomach, she holds on to the small black grips, long legs behind her. I wish I'd checked the tube before he placed it into the water. What if it has holes?

The girls scream their heads off with glee as Randy turns the engine on high, turning the boat left and right in an attempt to get them to flip. My throat dries as I continuously scan the lake. What if there are hidden rock formations, and the tube hits one? A million terrible scenarios pass through my head, all ending with Lauren hurt. The tube pops up against the water over and over again, making a popping sound. My hands start to shake.

· · ·

"Get low!" someone yells as gunfire sprays.

Rex and I drop down, the rocks on this dingy mountain digging into our stomachs.

We've got a good spot, I think as I tighten my hold on the gun in my hands. I'm ready.

"Whoever is shooting these guns doesn't know how to use 'em." I look over, and Rex laughs, heavy equipment surrounding him like toys on Christmas.

The shots ping past us, hitting nothing but air.

I chuckle as we wait for the firing to end.

I blink quickly, clenching and then unclenching my fists. I'm here. On Lake Powell. I'm here. On Lake Powell ...

Pulling out a cigarette from my back pocket, I quickly light it up. Hell isn't a place. It's memories—and I'm living in them. The nicotine helps to settle my nerves, but I wish I'd brought some extra pills with me, too. Just to soften the blunt edges. I popped two this morning, but clearly, it's not enough. Not anymore.

"You've really picked up the habit." Vincent helps himself to a cigarette while he chastises me.

I exhale. "Guess you could say that. Nothing like a smoke and a beer and a boat."

I light him up.

"Did you contact Veterans Affairs? Make sure you give them our timeline, so they know when we'll begin hiring. There are always delays, so give them a few months out."

"Already done."

On a scream, the girls flip over, and my heart skids to a pause. I'm ready to jump in the water to grab Lauren when she pops up, giggling. My rational mind knows she's wearing a life vest. But, until she's back here, next to me, I can't stop stressing.

Vincent puts out his full cigarette into the cup I'm using as an ashtray and dives headfirst into the water. Eve swims hard, trying to get away from him. Within two strokes, he's caught up and grabbing her into his arms. The other day, Eve mentioned that it was Vincent who'd taught her to swim.

The water sparkles around Lauren as she does the backstroke toward the boat. I feel relief in my chest when her soft hands grab on to the ladder.

She's okay.

After a few hard pulls, I put out my cigarette, too.

Randy points north. "The slot canyons are there. We'll head over now."

I finish my beer and open another as the girls dry off with fresh towels and scroll through their phones. Lauren mentions something about skirts and dresses. They seem to be shopping.

"Oh, I love these pumps." She turns excitedly to Eve, handing her the pink crystal-looking cell phone. "Comfortable, too, because the heel isn't too high and super classic, too. It'll be perfect."

What the heck is a pump? Lauren's got a vocabulary I just don't understand.

Vincent gets on the phone, yelling to his attorney about rental payments from one of his retail spaces.

The boat pulls over before Randy takes down three blue paddle-boards and oars.

She tucks her phone between the folds of her sundress before lifting her hands to the top of her eyes, shielding herself from the sun. "I can't believe I forgot a hat," she complains to Eve. "I'm going to age, like, ten years from the sun here."

I immediately pull the hat off my head. "Here," I offer.

"No, it's—"

"It's cool." I tighten the back and hand it to her. "You'll burn. And who wants sunspots?"

She tries not to smile. "Are you messing with me right now?"

"No. Just wear it."

Hesitantly, she puts it on. *NAVY* in bold letters stares back at me.

"Looks good." I clench my fists, trying not to enjoy the fact that she's wearing something that's mine.

"Thanks." She gives me an undeserved smile.

I eat it up like a starving man given a morsel of food. I never knew how hungry I was until Lauren.

We paddle through the slots as the girls marvel at the colors and light play. Vincent once told me that this part of the country made him believe in God. I finally understand why. It's centuries of evolution written in rock formations. Every detail here was made by nature alone.

"Basically, what happens"—Eve's voice echoes—"is there's a crack in the rock. A heavy rain comes down and seeps into that crack along with sediment and natural debris, which then carve away at the inside edges."

Sharing a board, Vincent quickly paddles himself and Eve around the bend as they continue their discussion. I slow myself down to brush my hands against the red-and-orange-striped wall. It's so smooth.

Lifting my head, I notice that Lauren's no longer ahead of me. Turning my head, I see she isn't behind me either. Still, I didn't see her rush ahead with the others.

"Lauren?" I call out.

No reply.

"Fuck." I want to spin my board around, but the slot is too narrow. Paddling faster, I try to reach a wider section but can't find one. I get off the board, starting to swim. The water is cold as shit, but I couldn't care less. Did she fall? The light dims as I swim around, dunking underwater and swimming deeper to see if she's there. I can't see her.

I pop back up.

"Boo!" she screams.

My eyes widen in surprise as I turn. "You—"

Her laughter is song. "You were zoned out, and I hid behind that section. Never thought I'd get you into the water though," she says happily on her board, pointing to a small bend on the right. "Looks like you're too slow, Slade."

I want to grab her. Tear her clothes off and show her how fast I can be. Instead, I climb back on the board and tightly grip my oar. "It's dangerous. You should never sneak up on someone. Especially not on a man like me." My mouth dries out, words sounding like a threat.

"Oh, is that right?" she sasses. "You might have scared me last night with your temper and tough-guy attitude. But, in the light of day, I see you're nothing but an asshole. You don't scare me, Slade. Not one. Little. Bit. Oh, and here's your hat." She throws it at me, and it lands straight at my chest.

Eve calls out, "You guys coming or what?"

Lauren paddles away, ahead of me, cursing under her breath.

Shit.

Back on the boat, Vincent pulls out our lunches, packed by the hotel. Mine is a crusty baguette filled with ham, cheese, and honey. Lauren seems to have taken one with vegetables and cheese.

"Vincent, you were right on this one." I take a huge bite while the sun beats down over my shoulders. "Bringing food from the hotel was a total win."

We're sitting on the couch beds in the front of the boat while the girls scroll through their phones, showing each other some more clothes. Finally, Lauren opens her sandwich, picking out the vegetables inside like a bird might do.

"You have something against bread?" I open another beer. My third.

"Um, of course I do." She shrugs, munching on a slice of cucumber. "My body doesn't process grain."

"What the hell does that mean?"

"It means that bread makes her fat." Eve laughs, and Lauren grabs a small white pillow, hitting her in the shoulder.

"People are hungry in the world, Lauren. You shouldn't waste."

I'm back to acting like a dick, but I need to stop my feelings. She yelled at me a few minutes ago, and it only makes me want her more. Her strength and confidence are a turn-on like nothing else. I'm protective of her. I want her, but I can't have her. And that makes me mad.

"Seriously, that makes no sense. Regardless of whether or not I eat this bread, children are still hungry."

Vincent takes another bite of his sandwich, staring at me a little too closely. "What the fuck does it matter to you if she eats the damn bread?"

"Yeah, Slade. What does it matter?" Lauren parrots, picking up a sliced tomato and placing it in her mouth.

She's … taunting me.

I take another drink. "You're wasteful. There are people around you who are unfortunate, but you couldn't be bothered. Girls like you are selfish, sitting on an expensive boat, barely touching the fresh food prepared for you by a chef, and shopping, for fuck's sake."

Her face guts from my insult. I'm branding her as a materialistic and selfish bitch with my comment. It's fucked up, and it's mean. Most of all, it's untrue. But I need to create distance, and I don't know how else to keep her away. It's a sick attempt at short-circuiting the electricity I feel for her.

"I can't stand you," she spits out.

"All right, you guys. Let's all relax." Eve comes over, placing her tiny self in Vincent's lap before whispering, "I hope this is your version of flirting, Slade. Because you're being an absolute asshole. Lauren doesn't deserve the way you spoke to her."

I take my food and walk to the back of the boat, uninterested in hearing shit from Eve. Vincent's glare reaches me, but I pretend not to notice. Lauren leans against the front, seemingly watching the water. I want to force her to turn her body, so I can watch her face and not her back. I hate her hiding from me.

I watch her like a stalker, memorizing the way she stands with one foot slightly ahead of the other. I can't look away. My mind teases me with memories of how she moaned beneath me in the backseat of my truck. The way she tastes, like soft, salty caramel. Dancing at the club, her sweat slick between her full breasts. My dick pulses.

I'm in a trance when she steps in front of me, bringing me to the moment.

"I was going to ignore your disgusting comments, but I can't. I've been looking at clothes all this time with Eve because I'm planning on helping some of the women from her shelter find appropriate attire for job interviews. I'm not selfish, and I do realize there are people much less fortunate than I am." She's on the defensive, obviously hurt.

"And the bread," she huffs, brown eyes shaded by her hand against her forehead. "I saved it for you to eat. See? No waste."

She practically throws it at me. I stare at it, feeling like shit. The way I've been acting isn't me, but how can she know that? She was supposed to hate me for the way I'd behaved—not save the bread, for God's sake. I want her to understand that my life is not my own. My memories have a strong hold over my life.

I swallow hard, feeling every bit the asshole that I've been. I don't want to be a dick. I just don't know how else to keep her away. "Look, I didn't mean that. My behavior ... it was fucked, all right? I've been going through some rough shit lately. Work's been hectic. It's not about you."

"Yeah. But, when you treat me like shit, you make it about me. You think I'm nothing more than fluff. I hear you loud and clear. But get this, Slade; I couldn't give a shit what you think about me. So, stop trying to shove your opinions about who I am down my throat. I won't swallow them."

She stands up tall, daring me to argue.

"I'll stop. I know you aren't fluff." I inch closer to her, but she doesn't budge. "Last night, I overstepped. I just need to make sure no lines are crossed. I don't hate you. Just need to be sure you know the score. And I lost my shit about the food, but that's my own hang-up."

"I asked you about how you felt after the shooting, and you freaked out. What line was I crossing then?"

"I'm just not interested in answering personal questions. But, Lauren, I mean it when I say, there's nothing here for you." I open my arms wide. "I'm not available in the way you want or need or deserve. We've got something be—" I pause, letting out a long breath. "I'm not a typical guy. I've seen things a girl as sweet as you can't even imagine in her worst nightmare. I do only casual. This means, no bed-sharing —ever. This means, nothing but casual sex."

Lauren is everything I wish I could have but can't. And I'm not a man who is used to not getting what he wants. I work hard for what I get. Every muscle on my body. Everything I've ever accomplished. It's been hard work and dedication from start to finish. But this? Being with a girl who isn't just a one-nighter? It's not possible for me, and the truth is infuriating.

"Slade, calm down. I'm not asking you for anything. You have your own life, all right? I'm just here temporarily. After this trip, we never have to see each other again. You don't have to be an asshole to me. We can be civil." Her voice is a whisper, as though she's begging me to be kinder.

Why does she have to be so nice? So sweet?

Her words are hard, but her heart still opens for me.

"I'll stop acting like an asshole."

She exhales.

Before I can think it through, I tell her, "Let's sit together and watch the sunset. It's going down soon."

"You want to sit. With me?" She purses her lips. "The girl you have nothing in common with?"

"Come on. You know that shit wasn't true."

She takes a hard swallow. "But you said it."

"Come on." A cushioned bench lines the perimeter. "No one here but us." I gesture to the couch.

She rigidly sits down, raising her legs in front of her before invitingly opening them. She taps the space between her knees. The sun lowers, casting an orange glow over the boat.

Hesitantly, I sit between her legs. I twist my torso to face her. "You're not going to strangle me, right?"

"I considered it." She raises her brows at me. "But, no, I won't."

She pulls me back by the shoulders, so I'm resting my head in the juncture between her thighs. Part of me wants to jump upward, but her fingers move into my hair, and it feels so damn good.

"You aren't a materialistic bitch either," I add. "I know you're not."

"Thanks." Her voice drips with sarcasm. "I know who I am. Now, straighten your head, so I can massage your face. Lord knows you need something to calm your domineering ass down."

She drops her thumbs on the bridge of my nose, pushing down and out over my cheekbones. I let out a sigh.

"Am I allowed to ask you what it's like in Afghanistan, or are you going to chew my head off?"

I tilt my head up to see her. "Lots of good people. Some bad."

"On the way to Utah, I ordered a book on my Kindle about Adam Brown. The Navy SEAL. I've been reading it."

I melt from her hands. "Did you now? Adam was a good man." I close my eyes and try not to smile at the fact that she's trying to learn more about me. Shaking off my attempt to keep her away, I find myself in a warmth I can't fight. I don't deserve it, but fuck if it's not the best feeling I've ever had.

"You knew him?" She sucks in a surprised breath, her fingers pausing.

"Knew of him, yeah. We all do. Total badass."

Her hands continue to rub up and down my face. "You're a good man, too, Slade. When you aren't being a huge asshole, I mean."

I chuckle. "I'm all right. And I'm sorry, okay? I said fucked up shit that wasn't true. I just wanted to be firm and make sure we were clear, but it wasn't necessary. You didn't deserve that."

"I should just ask for no bread, so I don't waste. You're right about that, and I—"

"Oh no." I put my hands on her, stilling her words. "You don't have to finish everything you eat. It's a weird thing I have after the shit I've seen. You don't have to take it on."

"No. You're right. I should ask for less, so I waste less."

When I let go of her hands, she continues her ministrations. I let her take care of me. I'm not sure why I was being so difficult. Sure, she's a sweet girl who deserves more than me. But she isn't a child who can't make her own choices either. Best part is that she isn't planning on staying here; it's just for a short time. I need to cool off and calm down, stop fighting everything and let it all ride. She knows the score now—of this, I'm absolutely positive. My body sinks between hers, and for the first time in what feels like ages, I feel peace.

11

Lauren

Back at the hotel, we're all exhausted from fresh air and sun.

Slade and I get off the elevator and turn left while Vincent and Eve go right. I can feel Slade's steps behind me. It's as though he's stalking me like a predator. I stop into the bathroom, locking the door to create some distance. Gripping the side of the sink, I dip my head down.

On the boat, he watched me so closely. His eyes were always trained on some part of my body. He made some horrible accusations, but I believed him when he said that he just wanted a line between us. On one hand, Slade says these cruel things, but then, on the other hand, his actions say he *cares*.

He wants me, and I can feel it. I'm not going to lie to myself and say I don't want him. Because I do. I've wanted him from the moment I saw him. And the truth is, I have nothing to lose. Less than two weeks remain before I go back to the real world, back to California. This is just a small break from my life. I was worried that getting involved with him would affect me getting better, post-shooting. But I actually feel okay. In fact, being with him might do me some good.

My body is my own. If I want a meaningless fling with Slade, why can't I have it? He doesn't want to share a bed? Well, that's okay with me. We have two beds in this room, and I like mine just fine.

I haven't been with anyone since Slade at the wedding. I never did the drugs with my friends, but Slade might be the exact trick. He can be the one to calm me down and give me a modicum of happiness before I have to reenter the lion's den at Crier and go on date after bad date via the five different websites I'm subscribed to, each promising to find my "perfect match."

I step back outside the bathroom, wanting to make my move. His shirt is off, and he's in nothing other than board shorts. Rippling abs and that perfect, hard ass. Like an athlete. Can I really do this? Maybe not, but I want to try.

"You all right?" He scratches the back of his neck. His chiseled face is colored with sun. He's so sexy.

I hesitantly lick my lips. "I was thinking, why don't we just hook up?" My voice falls out in a rush, as if my mouth knows that, if I don't get to it quickly, it'll never happen. "I know you don't do anything serious. And, right now, that's the last thing I want in my life. Less than two weeks to go, and I'll head back home. I think we both want each other. So, why not stop the asshole routine and just give it a—"

In just one step, he presses me into his arms, and his lips fall on mine. The first thing I feel is warmth. It's consuming.

"Can't stop this," he groans, pressing his dick against me. It's hard and so good.

I open myself, letting him take. He lifts me up as if I weigh nothing, pushing me up against the cream-colored wall.

"Just while you're here," he pants between laying heavy kisses down my neck.

"Yes," comes my breathy reply. "Two weeks." A shudder moves through me as his hands make their way up my dress.

He pulls back. "Shit, the bathing suit."

After he lowers me, I undo the bathing suit's halter top tied behind my neck.

"Keep the dress on. I love it on you."

He drops to his knees, pulling the suit downward. It's around my feet in mere seconds. The fabric of my dress rubs against my nakedness, brushing against my hard nipples.

Lifting the dress up around my waist, he sucks and licks around my belly button. I'm whimpering as his big hands dent into my thighs, spanning from the inside out. Grabbing his hair, I pull him closer, wanting and needing more. I ache from the way we left things in the back of his car, but my desire burns me from the inside. It rages like a wildfire.

His hands rove down to grip my ass, and all I can do is pray he'll touch me exactly where I need. But he doesn't. Instead, he stands back up, cupping my face in his huge hands.

"Wait. What? What are you doing?" I'm confused and frustrated.

He'd better not tell me he's stopping or that he doesn't have a condom.

"Remember back in the truck after The Blue?"

He kisses me again, deeper. Undoes the zipper of my dress. It falls as his tongue plunges into my mouth. I'm completely nude before him.

"Fuck, you tasted so good. I remember how tight you were. You were so close to coming in my mouth. I wanted you to come on my dick though." He presses a muscled thigh between my legs, pushing slow and deep.

"Oh God," I gasp as he takes my hands, holding them hostage above my head, so I'm pinned to the wall.

My brain is shocked by his words, but my body has a different reaction. I'm completely soaked, gyrating against his heavily muscled thigh as my wetness drips. I want to reach forward to bring his body to mine. I want more and can't wait. He doesn't budge.

"You think I don't know what you want?" he whispers again into my ear, tongue darting out before his teeth nibble on my lobe. "I know exactly what you need. The question is, are you going to be a good girl and listen to what I say?" He brushes my hair out of my face with his free hand. "Will you listen like a good girl, Lauren?" he repeats.

I want to scream yes, but my mind-mouth connection has been severed. I can't stop my body from swiveling against him.

"Y-yes," I manage to stutter out.

His hazel-green eyes hold mine. Scruff lines his face, as though he forgot to shave for a few days. He's so serious. He slightly shifts his body, so I can feel his hardness. It's huge. I clench my inner muscles, panting for release. He's an animal right now but in complete control.

"I want you begging for my dick. I want you shaking so hard; you can't speak. I am going to ruin you," he growls.

He brings his mouth closer to mine. I snake out my tongue, needing to taste him.

"Oh ..."

He's pure sex. The ache he brings out in me is so acute; I could cry.

His mouth attaches onto my nipple, and he sucks hard. Holy shit! This whole thing with Slade is crazy. I'm vanilla. I wear heels every day and get my hair professionally blow-dried twice a week. I don't do casual sex with an ex-Navy SEAL. Who am I? I tried to convince myself I didn't want him. He's an asshole! But this asshole feels so. Damn. Good. Tremors rack my body. I'd take a lifetime of casual sex with this man, if I could.

In a rapid movement, his lips move to my other nipple. I want to grab his head and force him to move harder and faster, but I'm still completely at his mercy. Moving his lips away, he blows cool air against my hot breasts. My body trembles like it's forty below.

"How is this possible?" I groan as he licks and sucks my wet nipples again and again, alternating and playing with them in his hot mouth.

I can't stop moving. Moaning. I don't remember ever sounding like this before—so wanton. At the wedding, we were in his truck. The party wasn't close but not far either. He shushed me as I bit through his shirt, praying not to shriek through my orgasms. But, now, we're in a hotel room. *Privacy.*

I can only imagine how I look. My hair down around my shoulders. Nipples distended and soaked from his tongue. My lower half undulating against his heavy thigh. My throat already feels raw from my deep, guttural moans. That's when his hand lowers itself from my breast and goes down and down.

"Oh no. Oh God. Slade."

"Yeah, baby. Yeah."

I'm shaking from my toes upward. I want to tell him to wait a minute. As it is, everything feels too good. It's too much. I'm so close. I bite my lip as his thumb presses directly against my clit, and another two fingers slide straight up inside me, curving. My head bangs against the wall as I come so hard that flashes of light dance in front of my eyes. My head drops down, only to see him on his knees with his mouth on my pussy, drinking me in.

Oh my God.

My legs tremble so hard that he has to hold each of my thighs in his hands, so I don't collapse. I might die.

When I come to, I'm on the bed, too satisfied to even ask how I got here.

"We're not done," he says.

"Done? What? Where?" My voice is raspy as I try to get my bearings. I turn to Slade and can't stop my smile. "I have the hottest man I've ever seen next to me right now—whoop!"

He chuckles. "You make me laugh, you know that?"

"Like, ha-ha, we're laughing together, so funny? Or like, ha-ha your face?"

He claps his hands. "Who are you? I swear, I've never met anyone like you."

"Surprise?"

His huge arms pull me into his body when I finally notice he's still in his shorts.

"I thought you didn't do *the bed*."

"Well, it's not to sleep."

I hum, "I'm so tired."

Lifting my arms up over my head, I stretch like a cat against the soft sheets. He watches my breasts shift with rapt attention.

Grumbling, he nestles into my neck as his hand snakes out to hold mine. For a man who isn't into cuddling, he sure knows how to tangle himself up.

Wrapping my legs around him like an octopus, I feel free to enjoy this time without worry and speak my mind without anxiety that I'll screw something up.

Last year, I dated this doctor, Jordan. We had been set up by mutual friends, and I really believed we could fall in love. When we had sex, it was terrible. But I couldn't be vocal because, if I were, he might get offended, and the relationship would be ruined. I figured, stay quiet now, and once we were married, I'd finally be clear about what I wanted. But this isn't the case with Slade, whom I have no future with. If he pisses me off, I shouldn't have to bite my tongue.

Yes, I want him. Then again, he was an asshole. Maybe I need to stand up for myself. It's a bit late, but an idea takes shape in my head.

"Ready for more?" His voice is rough.

He takes my hand, trailing it down his muscled abs and down to his heavy cock. I want it badly, but my self-esteem has other plans.

I smile. "No, I don't think so." I quickly let go of his hot length before I change my mind.

"Huh?" He rolls onto his side, propping up on an elbow.

My eyes move to his gorgeous, wide chest, and I swallow, telling my body to shut up. Intelligent Lauren is in control right now and will take the reins.

"Sorry, but no." Taking a look at my nails, I see a chip.

"Why's that?"

I turn back to him. His gorgeous hazel eyes look confused.

I huff. "You were mean last night and on the boat today." I drop my hand to my side.

"Mean?" he repeats, lowering his head.

"Yes," I huff. "I'm a lot of things, but I won't be treated like shit by you. I've gone down that road before with other guys, and I don't want to do it again. You aren't long-term, and I'm not trying to find love with you either. If I don't want something, I'm saying no."

"First off, you should always say no if you don't want something.

But are you sure you don't want me?" The look of confusion on his face intensifies.

"Well, no, I don't. I mean, I do want you, but I'm still mad."

"What does mad have to do with us right now?" He scans me up and down. "You can be mad, and we can still—"

"It means that I'm finally doing what's right for myself and not putting a man first. I'm not going to pacify you to keep your feathers smooth."

"But you were mad before, right? And we still—"

"Yes, we did. But, now, I've changed my mind." Do I sound wishy-washy? Sure. I sit up, touching the back of my matted hair. Must have gotten tangled from rubbing up and down against the wall. Under normal circumstances, I'd comb my fingers through the strands, making sure to smooth it out before he saw. But I'm not playing that game—not anymore and not with Slade. If he doesn't like my crazy hair, he can go elsewhere. I smile, liking this new development. Maybe there's some merit to this no-possible-future thing. I can finally just be myself and do what I want without worry.

He puts his hand on my back, and I pause.

"You're sexy as fuck. Now, stop being a baby and get your fine ass over here. What's right is for you to have another orgasm."

"That might be true but not right now. The answer is no. You made me feel inferior, and I'm not."

I cross my arms below my breasts, and his eyes move straight to my lifted cleavage. Quickly, I drop my hands and pull up the sheets for cover. For the record, it isn't easy to be haughty in the nude.

"You're beautiful inside and out, Lauren, okay? That's the truth. The shit I said out of anger wasn't the truth."

"Luckily, I don't need you to explain that to me. I know who I am, Slade."

"Yes, I know that. But I know who you are, too."

I clear my throat, trying not to let his kind words affect me. "Yes, you apologized. And I appreciate the clarification. But that doesn't mean I have to forget it. By the way, thank you for giving me the best orgasm of my life. I appreciate it."

Off the bed I go, strutting into the bathroom, naked, as his perfectly chiseled jaw drops. For the first time in a long time, I'm proud of myself.

A FEW HOURS LATER, we're both showered and well-fed, courtesy of room service. We ate quietly, but the silence wasn't antagonistic. It felt like he was giving me space, which I needed.

Cozy in my soft, blue cotton pajamas with white lace piping, I have no choice but to keep my eyes averted from Slade. If I look at him, I might jump his bones. He's wearing nothing other than a snug white T-shirt and beaten-in jeans, typing away on his laptop and checking in with work while sitting casually at the desk in the room. Okay, fine, I'm staring. But I'm really good at not letting him see—I think.

"You think I'm blind?"

"Hmm?" I lift my head from the new book I'm reading from Leigh Ford, acting like he just interrupted me in the midst of a chapter. I typically can't tear my eyes away from her romances, but Slade is giving me a run for my attention.

He moves next to me, massaging the top of my thigh. "Have you cooled off some?"

I can't look at him. "Mmhmm. I'm all good."

"Lauren," he starts, tearing the Kindle from my hands, "what the hell happened here? It's just us. Let's have fun with the time we've got. I know you wanted to show me you aren't some pushover. But the thing is, I know you're not."

I sigh, finally looking at gorgeous eyes. There are about a million things I want him to do to me. And we've only got so much time to work it all out.

"Feel like brewing me a cup of decaf?" I finally ask, unable to stop my smile. I swear, all the man has to do is look at me.

"Yes, ma'am." He winks before jumping off the bed and stepping to the fancy coffeemaker on top of the dresser.

Minutes later, two white mugs are filled with a dark roast. Slade brings them to our small balcony, and I follow him outside. It's pitch-black but incredibly soothing.

"What drives you?" I lift the hot cup to my mouth and take a sip, curling my legs beneath my butt. "I mean, what gave you the strength to be a Navy SEAL?"

"It's always been about achievement. I think we're all able to accomplish anything we set our sights on, and limits are simply a game our minds play. Limits are excuses. I like to test those limits and break them. Our internal dialogue makes or breaks our success in war."

"War is chaos," I add.

"Yet someone's gotta fight them," he replies simply.

"But why? Why can't we all just live in peace?"

"War is good sometimes. We can all live in peace, but that might mean our country is turning a blind eye to atrocities. Would you rather have lived in alleged peace while the Nazis killed millions of Jews? Would you rather have fought no war but had African Americans still enslaved? War is necessary."

"But the youth! War kills future generations. Sometimes, once war is opened, it's like a terrible can of never-ending filth. It takes a toll."

"War is just a means to an end, Lauren. It's a tool," he interrupts.

"So, are you the tool they use? The government has you risking your life to achieve its politics abroad."

"Yes. That's right. But you can't imagine the shit people eat in other countries. You talk like you think everyone is living in la-la land, and we, the United States of America, waltz in where we're not invited. You don't realize that there are children scavenging for food and eating from the trash due to oppressive governments that don't give a shit about the people so long as their own pockets are lined. Fathers selling their daughters into marriage. Brothers who, after hearing of their sister's rape, will pour acid on her face. Do you realize that, in Afghanistan, ninety percent of women don't leave their homes? When they wear a burka, they essentially turn themselves invisible. These women are controlled by men. Sure, the men are happy—because they're in complete control. And lots of women don't know better. How can they? They can't imagine a better life when even the television stations are controlled by their government."

"You have to respect the choices of these women."

"That's where you're wrong. Women in those countries don't get a choice. You're viewing their life through an American lens, which is a mistake."

"Getting involved hasn't always worked. I mean, look at what Jimmy Carter did in Iran. The fall of Shah Pahlavi put the entire Middle East in flux. The shah's government was secular and pro-Western, not Communist."

"Disaster of an administration. Absolute disaster." He shakes his head in disgust.

"So, are we supposed to just go with the whims of these politicians? What if they're wrong?"

"Yes, that's a risk. But what about all the amazing things that happened for women here in the USA due to the fact that the men were off fighting? Women finally left home and entered the workforce."

"Yeah, but that's over now."

"Is it?"

"We don't need our men off at war to finally be able to be independent."

"Yes, but we did initially. So, war has had benefits both here and abroad. I mean, war has helped pull us out of recessions."

"I'm not going to agree with you. I mean, I'll always support our troops. God bless you guys for going out and fighting for our freedom. But that doesn't mean I agree with sending you all off in the first place. Especially under a regime that Americans do not understand. You can't walk into the Middle East and say, Voilà, *welcome to democracy!* The people are so far from that, they wouldn't know what to do to handle the freedom."

A few beats pass in silence. I want to say something to soften our conversation.

"More coffee?" My voice is hesitant.

He chuckles, and I sigh from relief.

"Nah, let's go inside. You must be getting cold."

We brush our teeth side by side. Staring at our reflections in the mirror, I see how physically opposite we are. He's huge, whereas I'm on the smaller side of average. He's white and all-American with those hazel-green eyes and buzzed hair, whereas I'm of Middle Eastern descent. My hair at the roots is black as night, and my eyes are a warm brown with golden flecks. Still, we look good. Really, really good actually.

He smiles at me through the mirror. "You're gorgeous." He spits into the sink before turning on the faucet.

I roll my eyes, wanting to tell him that he's the hot one. But the man doesn't need anything more to feed his ego, so I just shrug. "Thank you."

I climb into my bed as Slade sifts through his small duffel, pulling out a little bag before taking it into the bathroom. I want to ask what he's doing, but that would be overstepping. He's got a thick red line, and the last thing I want to do is cross it. We seem to have a good thing going, and I don't want to ruin it.

A few moments later, he returns, sitting in his own bed without a shirt and nothing other than boxer briefs. I do my best not to ogle.

"You should be proud of yourself, Lauren." He leans back onto the bed. "After the shooting, you had a rough few days. But, now, look at you."

He flips off the light by his bedside, but I can still feel his gaze in the dark.

"You decided you would be okay; that's internal dialogue. You told yourself you would be all right, and now, you are. You sleep well. You eat well. You're smiling and laughing. Sure, what happened might have shifted your perspective on some things. But you're okay." His words fill up this spot in my chest I never knew was empty.

"Are you saying I'm ... strong?" My voice comes out more upbeat than I intended.

He chuckles. "I am. You have more mental toughness in you than you let on. I see it though."

"Th-thank you. I appreciate that." My heart thumps.

"Well, I, for one, would never want to cut you in line for a sale at … Prada—or wherever it is you shop. You'd probably smack me upside the head for taking the last size seven shoe."

"Oh," I exclaim, unable to stop myself from laughing. I won't fill him in on the time I did in fact get into a fight with another woman over the last pair of red Louboutin heels, which are now sitting pretty in my closet. "What can I say? I play to win."

"Is there another way to play?" I swear, I can feel his smile as he says, "Good night, Lauren."

"Slade?"

"Yeah?"

"We head back tomorrow."

"Yep."

"We'll continue this, right?" I cross my fingers beneath the covers.

"If you want, yeah." He pauses. "Just till you go."

I want him now. Badly. "You have condoms?" My voice squeaks, as I'm nervous to initiate. But, after the stunt I pulled, I have to assume he's waiting for me to reopen the door.

"Fuck yeah, I do." Jumping out of bed, he rifles through his things, pulling out a pack. "Now, take off your clothes and spread your legs for me how I like."

I quickly strip off my pajamas, doing as he said.

"That's right. How I like it, Lauren." He walks toward me like a predator, abs flexing with his steps.

I swallow hard, doing as he asked. My hands shake, but I've never been so wet before in all my life.

12

Slade

"Ugh, I hate listening to nineties grunge." She clicks her tongue. "If I hear 'Black Hole Sun' one more time ..." Her voice trails off.

I chuckle. She thinks she's being coy as she shadily taps the volume on my phone, trying to lower it.

I glare as though I just caught her in the act, and she lifts her hands in mock surrender.

"I get it, okay?" Her leg bounces up and down. "Don't need Mr. Built Like A House getting angry with me; that's for sure."

She tries to hold back a smile, and I laugh.

"Well, get used to the music. My car, my rules. And we've got another forty-five minutes of nineties grunge I plan on playing."

"Great," she replies sarcastically. Her arms angrily cross in front of her chest. "It's not really your car though," she mumbles under her breath.

"I'm the one who signed for the rental, so technically, it's mine for now."

"Yeah, yeah."

Vincent and Eve wanted to stop somewhere using the plane, so

Lauren and I decided to drive our way back to Nevada. With the windows of the 4Runner down, her long hair blows behind her. I can faintly smell her, vanilla and citrus and something else I can't name but drives me insane with want. She keeps trying to tame the silky gold strands with her hands, but it's not working. I love ruffling her feathers. She's even hotter when she's angry or annoyed.

A red-and-yellow sign for fast food shows up ahead. With my stomach growling, I put on my blinker and move to the right lane to exit.

Nirvana's "Smells Like Teen Spirit" begins when I pull into the drive-through. Ordering half the menu, we get our food and park.

The paper bag crinkles as I stick my hand inside, pulling everything out. "Your side salad and Diet Coke."

She grudgingly takes it from my hands. I took the liberty of ordering her a chicken sandwich and two more burgers. I know she likes to eat well and clean, but once in a blue moon, enjoying food is all right, too.

I unwrap the foil. "Have some of my burger." I take a bite and lift it toward her.

She adamantly shakes her head. "No." Her eyes are both hesitant and full of longing.

"Come on. It's so good. I eat it and still maintain my figure." I shrug, taking another huge bite.

Her eyes follow the food as it enters my mouth. She licks her lips.

"Fine. Give it." Eyes widening at first, she moves closer to me. Shutting them, as though she can't bear to look, she opens her mouth and bites. "Mmm," she moans. "So good."

When she's done chewing, I hand it to her. "Please. Eat the rest," I beg. "But only if you keep moaning like that with every bite."

She giggles. "Oh, Slade." She takes another. "This meat." Her eyes move from the food to my dick, and I start to laugh. "Just want a taste …" she sings, licking her lips.

"That's it, Lauren. You've really gone and done it now." I unclick my belt and grab her by the ass, dragging her onto me.

"We're doing this? In a fast-food parking lot?"

"You bet we are."

"Fine, but only if you'll buy me another burger when we're through. Now that I've committed, I don't want to eat it cold."

I drag her hand into my pants, and she grips the base of my cock.

"See?" I ask, voice strangled. "Still hot." I tickle her ribs, getting a roar of laughter. "I already got extras, you crazy little thing."

Her lips press against mine, and I sigh into her mouth. I only had to take a few pills today. Less than usual.

Maybe being with Lauren is enough.

"WE'RE FINALLY BACK!" she squeals, unable to hide her excitement as we pull into the lot of the Mile. "If I never have to listen to your music again, it won't be too soon."

She gives me a classic Lauren eye roll, and I laugh.

For the millionth time, I scan her amazing body, focusing on her gorgeous tits encased in a blue spandex top. Our trip should have taken roughly half the time. But, after fucking in the backseat like teenagers, we each ate our weight in hot burgers and washed it all down with icy milkshakes. I can't even remember the last time I had this much fun.

After parking my truck in the hotel's lot, I help her out of the car.

"You don't have to help me. They have someone at the front." She drops her head, as though she's suddenly gotten shy.

"Nope. I've got you." Next, I pull her suitcase from the backseat and carry it to the front door.

"You know it's on wheels, right? You don't have to hold it."

I smirk. "Guess I'm just strong like that."

"Or you didn't know it had wheels," she sasses back.

We strut through the hotel lobby. The concierges all wave to me, and I nod in return.

"Everyone seems to like you, huh? Not sure what the hell they're thinking ..." She pinches my side, but I don't pause.

"Maybe they're thinking you and I just—"

She jumps to her tiptoes, throwing her hand over my mouth. "Can you stop doing that?"

"I love embarrassing you," I say into her hand. She lifts it from my mouth. "So cute how you get so scared. Sorry to break it to you, Lauren, but with the way you're always looking at me, with those wide brown eyes, they all know we're doing it."

"Doing it? What are you, a teenager?"

"Well, we did just have sex in the rental," he laughs.

I press the elevator button to go up. I shouldn't walk her to the room. We just had a lot of time together, and some space would be good for us to keep our situation clear. The problem is, I want more. Can't seem to get enough of this girl. When she's with me, I feel *free*.

We enter the room that is freshly made, thanks to housekeeping, and I lift the suitcase on top of the dresser.

I raise the bottom of my shirt, wiping the sweat from my forehead. "It's hot."

"Yeah. You can use my shower if you want ..." Her voice trails off. She wants me to stay.

When I pull the shirt over my head, her eyes go wide. It's a look I'll never get sick of.

"Sure thing."

I finish soaping when she steps into the spray.

"Whatcha doin', followin' me in here?" I joke, hardening at her nude, lush body. I grip my dick, unable to stop myself. Can't wait.

She drops to her knees, maintaining eye contact.

"Fuuuuck," I curse as her hot mouth envelops me.

13

Lauren

I'm going into Eve's office in two days, so I've decided to spend today and tomorrow just relaxing. Even though I'm on call at the office and I have already gotten about fifteen hysterical messages from Carla, who is covering my desk while I'm gone, I'm able to help her without ever leaving my lounge chair. Nothing in life is perfect, but this comes close.

The pools here at the Milestone are absolutely gorgeous. Around six in the evening, I get a message from Slade that he wants to pick me up. Running back to my room, I change in record time, just casually throwing my hair up and sliding on a T-shirt and jeans. He takes me for a long drive where we enjoy each other's company and the magnificent mountain views.

Stopping at a small diner off the highway, we sit side by side in the blue booth, unable to take our hands off each other. My head rests against his chest. His thigh presses against mine. He feeds me half of his burger—whole-wheat bun, lettuce, tomato, hold the onion—and I give him half of my chopped salad, kitchen sink. We each have our own waters, but for whatever reason, I keep drinking from his cup.

Eating only lasts twenty minutes before he drops some cash on the table and drives us straight back to my room where we don't even bother to turn off the lights. His body is so amazing. I've decided to forget about my own insecurities and just enjoy what it is I've been given—this gorgeous man, for a short time.

It's after midnight, and that means it's time for him to go back to his own place. I'm wishing he could just stay the night, but ... it is what it is. There's no way I'm going to do something to jeopardize the great thing we've got going on together.

"Bye, Slade." I sigh, leaning against the doorway.

We've been saying good-bye for the last ten minutes but keep derailing his departure with kisses.

His mouth presses against mine before he says, "Tomorrow night?" Kiss. "Let's do something." Kiss.

The man is a flood. Once I opened the gate, he found his way into every part of me.

"What kind of something?" I ask excitedly, grabbing his shirt and hoping that he has some plan for us.

I know our time is limited, and it makes me want to spend every available moment with him. Sure, I haven't forgotten the other darker side. But it seems that, so long as I don't cross any of his boundary lines, he'll stay in his natural state—cool, calm, controlled, and sexy as hell.

"I can take you to a nice spot for dinner."

"Okay. Well, what should I wear?" I bite my lower lip, trying not to appear too eager.

"The less, the better." He winks. "I'll be back to pick you up at nine." He pulls out his phone from the back pocket of his jeans and scrolls through something. "I've got a meeting that should end around eight thirty."

"Okay. That sounds good."

He backs up away from my mouth, and I sigh again, dazed.

. . .

THE NEXT DAY is perfect pool weather, so I spend it again just lounging and answering e-mails. Around five o'clock, I look down at my nails and sigh. So many chips in my polish. After heading back into my room, I dial the spa and make an appointment in thirty minutes for a manicure. Jumping back into the shower to actually wash my hair, I do a quick shampoo. The conditioner sits in my tresses as I shave from my ankles upward. I typically prefer to wax, but there's no time for that. After blow-drying my hair in waves, I run downstairs to take care of my nails.

"What color would you like, miss?" The manicurist smiles, her white uniform perfectly pressed. With beautiful, long black hair braided like a rope down her back and high cheekbones, she is a true Native American beauty.

I feel a surge of pride for Vincent, whose hotel and casino has employed so many tribal members.

I'm scanning the rows of colors, like I've done millions of times before, but nothing is feeling right. "Actually, no color. I just want all of my polish removed and my nails buffed."

"Are you sure?" Her eyes widen in surprise. "Not even something simple like Ballet Slippers or Marshmallow?"

I smile. "Absolutely sure. I'm Lauren, by the way." I take a seat in the cream-colored swivel chair as she fills a small green bowl with warm water from the sink behind her.

She sits in front of me. "Tina."

As she takes off my nail polish with white cotton balls dipped in remover, we chat about what I'm doing here in Nevada. I spill about the shooting in Vegas. How Slade saved me and cleaned me and then held me all night. I also mention how amazing he's been, lightly dropping in the fact that he's had a few random outbursts, which terrified me. But, overall, it's been dreamlike.

She places my left hand in the warm water as she begins pushing back the cuticles on my right. "You need to be careful, Lauren." Her face darkens in warning.

"W-what do you mean?"

She holds my free hand in hers like a mother would.

"Some men go off to war and come back and can adjust. Others, they can't manage life back at home. Don't you think that maybe he's pushing you away for your own safety? Or possibly acting in a way he can't control?"

I shake my head. "No. No way. I don't think it's as serious as you're saying." I smile, but somehow, it all feels rehearsed. "Yes, he has been through hard times. But I think he's just a man who likes things a certain way, and he doesn't want commitment. Okay, so he doesn't want a woman in his bed. But maybe that's his thing. I know he can get aggressive, but maybe that's just how these types of men are. Right?" My voice is jovial, but my chest tightens. The truth circles around my insides, but my heart won't let it enter. *No! That's not him.* "Anyway, in Vegas, he hurt others for me. But he'd never hurt *me*."

She looks at me, face tight but eyes slightly narrowing. There is more she wants to say, but she doesn't. With a hard swallow, she lifts my left hand from the water, dries it off with a plush white towel, and places my right inside the water bowl.

When she's finished, I'm happy to realize that I don't need to sit under a dryer for twenty minutes. With clean nails, I exchange phone numbers with her and promise to get lunch while I'm here.

"Lauren, please be careful, okay? You're a great girl. But I'm not so sure you understand the gravity of—"

"I'll be careful," I exclaim with a smile, cutting her off mid-sentence.

Back in the room, I plop on the bed, feeling absolute relief. How long has it been since I've just gone natural without all the fuss of makeup? In LA, there's so much emphasis on my looks and attractiveness. Sitting at the front of the real estate department, a client walks in, wanting to see *the girl* so that he can feel like *the man*.

I lift my gigantic silver makeup bag, emptying it all out on the beige bedspread. Highlighters and bronzers to show off my cheekbones. Coal and liquid liners for eyes and creamy nude liners for lips. Seven separate brushes, all for different parts of my face. I turn from the pile of makeup, frustrated at what I have to do to maintain my womanhood. Always, I plaster makeup on myself, but tonight, I'm going to say, *Fuck it.* No one on earth cares what a man looks like. All he needs is some swagger, and the world swoons.

Sticking with my *why the hell not* philosophy, I apply a moisturizer on my skin and tinted pink balm on my lips. I feel pretty good. Without the mask of makeup, I'm only myself.

Shuffling through my clothes now hanging in the room's closet, I decide to go with tight jeans, a white tank top that shows off my boobs, and short Rag & Bone booties in black suede. Am I ready? I hope so.

Slade knocks on the door exactly on time. I open it, wrapping one foot behind my opposite ankle. He lets out a long, slow whistle as he stares at me from my feet up to my face.

I shrug happily, bending my head down almost shyly. Now that he's here, I'm wondering if I really should have done more with my face. Some lip gloss at least. Meanwhile, Slade looks sexy and casual in dark jeans and a navy shirt, his hair freshly buzzed.

"Ready?" After a flicker of a moment, his eyes lower. "What's wrong?"

I open and close my mouth a few times, but nothing comes out. What to say to this man?

Oh, I normally never walk out of the house with so little makeup but had this weird epiphany that I didn't care. But, now that you're here and I want to impress you, I think I might have gone the wrong route.

I straighten my back. Well, what's done is done. If he doesn't love the way I look naturally, then there's nothing I can do about it now. I won't be ashamed of myself.

I grab my bag off the edge of the bed as we head out toward the elevator. "I wanted to bring my bike but thought you'd be more comfortable in the truck late at night."

My chest inflates at his thoughtfulness. "Either is okay. I tried to be casual tonight."

I risk a look at his face. His eyes are warm and happy. The monster from days ago is gone.

"Yeah, I like it." He nods slow, taking me in again. "You look hot, no matter what, but this laid-back look ..." His voice trails off as I wait for his answer. "I like it more. I like to see you."

"You do?" My eyes widen.

He smiles warmly, moving a stray hair away from my face. "Yeah, babe, I do."

I want to lean up and kiss him, but he's not giving me the option. Standing at his full, huge height, he's just so physically intense.

We leave the hotel, where the valet guy stands in front of Slade's truck. Slade gives him a back pat with some cash and holds the door open for me.

Stepping inside, I immediately notice how fresh it looks. "Did you just get it cleaned?"

"Yep." He nods. "I don't like things to be unorganized or dirty." He shuts the door and walks to the driver's seat.

I look at my nails, giving myself a pat on the back that they're nice and neat.

We drive with the windows open, the air filled with a warm, dry wind. Slade seems to become agitated, clutching the steering wheel at random intervals, as though he's filled with anxiety. I stay quiet, not wanting to make it worse.

Twenty minutes and an entire playlist of grunge later, we pull up to a small and dilapidated-looking house. This can't be the restaurant, can it? The gravel driveway crunches beneath the wheels of his truck. I look around, trying to find a name, but it's unmarked.

"Wait. What are we doing here? This isn't the restaurant, is it?" For reasons I can't comprehend, my own anxiety builds.

"Just stopping here to pick up a few things. Wanted to come earlier but the timing didn't work out. Be back in ten." Moving a heavy arm to the back of my seat, he turns his head to back into a spot. Stopping the car and turning off the engine, he hops out, slamming the door with a thud.

I want to call out to him, ask more questions, but my sense of self-preservation tells me to shut up and be quiet.

The car beeps as he locks me inside. That's when I notice a row of bikes in black and chrome sitting together like a foreboding gate. My heart quickens.

Oh shit. Is this a motorcycle club?

I pause, staring at this derelict den and wondering what the hell he's doing inside this place. Slade seems to say a few words to the guy at the door, wearing a black leather vest, before entering. I sink low into my seat, hoping not to draw any attention to myself as I wait. I grip my phone but won't turn it on, for fear that someone would see the light and know there was a lone person inside. This is dangerous, and I feel it in my bones.

14

Slade

The kid hanging out by the door is youngish-looking with a tough, acne-ridden face and leather vest with one small patch on the front that says, PROSPECT.

The farmhouse is smoky and full of club members and their friends. I look around, trying to find Lion in the crowd. Quickly spotting the shaved head, leather cut, and trademark smirk, I walk over.

"Get the fuck outta here," Lion growls, baring his teeth at some girl with long black dreads hanging down her back.

She's wearing nothing more than a white T-shirt and jean shorts so small that I can see the underside of her ass.

"You're a piece of shit," she hisses. "I'll never give him up."

"Bitch, that's my son. You can die in a ditch for all I care. But, if you take my boy away ..."

He lifts his hand, grabbing the base of her throat. The woman's face is stricken with fear, staring at Lion as though he were the devil incarnate. He isn't choking her, but she is scared to death.

Her breaths are labored when he says, "Alicia, if you take my boy from me, I'll fucking shoot you in the head myself." Her body shivers so hard that I can see the tremor moving through her small frame. "Deliver our son to the clubhouse at noon on Sunday. And get out," he yells.

When he lets go, she scurries away, running.

Not a moment later, Lion notices me and happily exclaims, "Slade!" He stands up, greeting me as though he didn't just threaten a life and saying, "Hello," like we're one and the same.

"Hey, man."

We bump fists.

Under normal circumstances, I'd run after that girl. Make sure she was okay. But I've got business here that can't wait. It's just a one-time thing. I won't need more after this.

Sweat beads at my brow.

I met Lion after moving out here. A few former Marines introduced us after a few drinks at The Blue. As an aggressive motorcycle club president who expects nothing but complete loyalty to the hierarchy he's created, veterans easily gravitate to Lion. Still, I was honest about the fact that I wasn't interested in the brotherhood. He asked if I could be a friend to the club if they needed it. As the head of security for the Milestone, I'm able to get information on people much quicker than they can. Not one to make enemies, I was evasive with my answer.

Last week, he requested some information from me. I was ready to say no when I realized there was something I could use in return. I named my price. He accepted. And here we are.

The music is loud, but he doesn't shout when he says, "Glad to see you came around."

Another woman walks by in a bra and panties, medium-height with gigantic fake tits and red lipstick. Sweat, like slick oil, beads between her breasts. She's coked up to the gills. Lion's beady eyes dart to her, tongue flicking to the top of his mouth.

Grabbing her by the wrist, he says, "Don't move from this spot. I'll be back."

She nods.

I hear a loud moan. Turning to see where it's coming from, I find one of the club's members with long and stringy black hair fucking some club slut on one of the tables for all to see. My stomach rolls. This entire situation is fucked. If Lauren were here, she'd be revolted. My heart pounds with the thought of her name, but I push it away and focus on the task at hand.

Lion and I walk together into a back room when I check my watch. Shit. It's already been twenty minutes. A small and round wooden poker table sits in the center of the room. We take seats on opposite ends.

I light my smoke, and he does the same. I'm here tonight because he needs some information on Tom Maione, the Mafia boss of Kill Incorporated, known on the street as Kill Inc. And I need something, too.

"Word is," I pause, clearing my throat. "Tom is running the enforcement arm of a few Italian American families. He's handling contract killings and running small businesses on the East Coast—some legal and others not. I'm sure expansion is on the horizon now that Antonio is out of the picture."

"Antonio Borignone, that crazy fuck. Ran a tight ship though. Which families is Tom doing work for?"

"Mostly Italian American gangsters based in Brooklyn. The boys grew up together. Childhood friends. The Bonannos and Luccheses. He's also got his own guys working under him. None of the old-timers."

"Your boy Vincent, he knows 'em?" He ashes in a small black tray.

"Vincent doesn't get involved in this shit. Ever." I sit up to my full height. "My boss is completely uninvolved and always will be."

He chuckles. "Yeah, yeah. The reformed prince. Ivy Leaguer. Builder of the famed Milestone. I know all about him." Smoke leaves his mouth in a hard exhale, a dark smirk filling his remorseless face.

"That's right." My mouth is straight, but my heart secretly beats like a wild drum from within my chest.

If Vincent knew I was here ...

I've got to go.

Sensing my unease, he says, "Wait." He stands and exits the room, only to resurface minutes later with a baggy filled with tablets. "This shit is harder than you're used to. I've got a feeling you'll like it. And thanks for the info. You hear anything else, let me know."

I take the bag, trying to steady my hand. *This isn't me. But it is me. It's just for now, so I can get myself straight. I won't be back here again.*

His dark face shadows, like he knows something I don't. "Men like us, we're cut from the same cloth. I served, too. Saw crazy shit. Came back to a country that could never understand me. They want me to follow laws I can't abide by. Muscle like yours is valuable to me, Slade. Working with a man like you, who understands honor in the way I understand honor, could be a real good thing for us both. If you're going to need this on the regular, we can make a de—"

"No. This is a one-time thing."

I flinch, my conscience screaming, *Lie!* It's subtle, but the look on his face tells me he noticed.

He cackles. "Sure it is. If you want to straighten out, I can help with that, too. Show you other ways to channel those demons. Or not."

I turn to leave the room as his voice calls out behind me, "I'll be waiting for your call. I can get you more anytime, son."

I don't turn back even though my muscles pulse to knock him out. *I'm never coming back here! Never. This shit isn't me.*

But Lauren's waiting in the car, and I need to get to her. Her face moves through my head as I become more and more frantic to get the hell out of this place and back to her.

I walk back through the party and strut directly out the door to the lot. Unlocking the car, I step inside, mind flashing back on Lion's words to me.

"Cut from the same cloth," he said.

NO!

"You're an asshole!" Lauren screeches, greeting me with a yell.

"I'm back now."

She's breathing all heavy, hurt lining her eyes.

"Calm down, Lauren." I grit my teeth, stressed over what just went down. The last thing I need right now is lip.

"Did you just tell me to calm down?" She vibrates. "Fuck you, Slade." Opening the car door, she steps out.

I pull down the window. "There isn't any Uber here in this neck of the woods. It's me, or it's nothing."

I grip the wheel, praying she'll come back inside. Lauren doesn't know what these men are capable of. For the first time, I realize how stupid it was to bring her here. Someone could have seen her in my car, all alone, and smashed the window open. They could find her now and take her from me. My chest tightens with the image of my woman in their hands.

"Get in the car, Lauren." My voice cracks.

"Fine. Whatever." She throws her hands up. "Take me home."

She gets back in but slams her car door with force. The sound jars me. In the driver's seat, I begin to wring my hands, left to right.

Rituals.

Blood trickles from my eyebrow, settling into my mouth. The copper taste moves up into my nose. I press my fingers against my coarse brow, now wet and slick to the touch.

What the fuck?

I bring my hand down, noticing a substance like slick motor oil between my fingers. The blood, it keeps pouring and won't stop! My breaths shorten.

A ROCK IS THROWN DIRECTLY into my face, hitting my head. I hold my tongue, even as blood drips hot, not wanting to curse or escalate the situation. Sometimes, kids don't realize that we're a force of good around here. Still, my head bleeds from the sharpened edge, trickling like raindrops onto the sandy gray street.

The village outside Kandahar is dusty and full of Taliban. An elderly gentleman waves to us, toothless and seemingly friendly. I motion for our interpreter to follow me. I'm going to him.

"Ask him if there are Taliban around here," I instruct.

The interpreter goes ahead and speaks, and the man immediately responds with hands gesturing wildly.

When he's finished, the interpreter says, "Yes, when Taliban are here, we must be with Taliban. But, today, America is here, and so we are with America. You will allow us to farm, yes?"

Another rock hits me, but this time, it's straight between my eyes.

"Slade?" A soft, far-off voice wakes me.

I come to in a small and dirty cot, huddling under a blanket.

Rex. Where's Rex?

"SLADE?"

I hear her soft voice again, but this time, I'm back to the moment. I flinch as Lauren's warm hand moves to my arm as my eyes blink wildly.

"Slade, are you all right?" Her face is a combination of anguish and nervousness. "You zoned out." Her earlier anger has turned into worry.

"Yeah." I push the gas and drive, my skeleton shaking beneath my skin. Holding the steering wheel, I attempt to get ahold of reality. "Don't stare at me like I'm some goddamn freak show," I growl, my fear disguised as anger.

The streetlight turns red, and I lower the sun visor in front of my seat, slightly tilting my head to get a good look at my face. No blood. Nothing anywhere.

I shut it as the light changes to green. "Look, it was just a few minutes. It wasn't a big deal." I try to soften my voice. I'm losing my grip, acting totally off the wall.

Who am I? Who the fuck am I? My mind moves in fast-forward.

"Yes, it was a big deal." Her angry voice is sad now. "How could you just leave me there? You shouldn't have brought me. I was scared as hell, sitting in your truck in the middle of this dark lot in front of some dilapidated house and all these motorcycles. It was a motorcycle club, right?" The question rips from her lips.

"Most of them are decent guys," I lie, clenching my fists around the steering wheel. "I wouldn't have brought you somewhere dangerous." My chest palpitates.

Reality is, I brought her with me to a horrible place just so I could score drugs. My life is fragmenting, but how else can I stay alive? How else can I keep myself from drowning? I need to numb the part of my brain that's deserted the rest of my psyche.

It isn't me.

But it is me.

Putting on my signal, I turn right. I'm taking deep breaths through my nose, trying to bring my head back to the present. "Look, Lauren, nothing happened to you, and we're okay. We won't ever go back there, all right?" I turn my head to see her, but all I get is the back of her head. "I won't ever bring you back," I repeat.

A few minutes pass in silence, and I can only hope she's calming.

She shifts in her seat. "It's not like *Sons of Anarchy*, is it?" She turns to me, a small grin on her face.

Is she ... playing?

"If you're looking to meet Jax Teller, the answer is no."

She laughs out loud, and the darkness between us dissipates.

Lauren, God. I want to yell with relief.

"Well, that's unfortunate," she grumbles. "Don't tell me they're like the Bandidos or the Hells Angels."

"And what on earth do you know about those guys?" I move my eyes between her and the road, needing to see her beautiful face. Her face steadies me.

"Well, I saw this show called *Gangland*, and they are really scary. Like, flying gang colors and torturing each other in prison and making these things called shivs—"

I laugh out loud, and she tilts her head in mock confusion.

"What's funny about that? Tough men like you aren't afraid?"

"You're just crazy cute. Yeah, they're outlaw. I'm sure they do illegal shit, but they'd never mess with me." Another lie. God must be making tally marks.

"But what were you doing there?" she presses. "What kind of work could you possibly have with a—"

"That's none of your business." I hold my breath. I want it to be her business. I want everything to be her fucking business. But it can't.

"Well, you left me there in their parking lot. I hope it was for something important." She purses her lips. "Wait. These guys aren't the same ones that had trouble with Vincent, right?"

"No," I say vehemently. "This club is a mixture of guys with a heavy veteran contingent. Some men discharge and just can't reacclimate into society. They do better under a different set of laws. The brotherhood is something men understand after leaving war." I wonder if it would have been better for me, too. Meeting Vincent derailed that potential though.

"Well, I guess you're right that it's not my problem. I mean, I'm leaving in a little more than a week. And it's not like you're my boyfriend." She says this to the window.

I want to move her face around, so I can get a better read, but she doesn't face me.

Panic fills my chest at the thought of her leaving. Nine days left. Has it only been five days that we've been together? It feels like so much more.

The baggy in my front pocket is heavy as a brick.

It isn't me. But it is me. Who am I?

I take her palm in mine, and finally, she turns back, brown eyes wide in surprise at the fact that I'm holding her hand. Now that I've got her, I'm going to keep her near me.

Mine, my head, heart, and dick all pound in unison.

She just satisfies me in a way I've never had before. It's great sex, but it's also more than that. She's funny and sweet, and she somehow brings me peace. I won't fuck this up. I'll do whatever I have to—drugs, drinking, anything—to keep her while I can.

"You hungry?" My voice is slightly hesitant.

Kissing her knuckles, I silently vow to keep her close to me. That's when I notice leftover would-be tears sitting on her lower lash line. She must have swallowed them, not wanting me to see. They shine like diamonds in her eyes.

"I'm sorry. Lauren, I'm sorry I brought you there. I shouldn't have."

"You aren't sorry." She turns back to the window, crossing her arms in front of her chest.

"I am. I swear, I am. I wasn't thinking straight." Leaning over, I take her hand again. "You feel me? I don't hold hands." I pull the car over to the side of the road and unbuckle my belt. "Look at me, Lauren."

She does.

"I'm sorry. I haven't been good to you the way you deserve. I won't fuck up again, okay?"

"I wish you'd stop doing and saying things you don't mean."

I lift the ends of her hair, soft and like painted gold. "I know."

She doesn't reply, but her hand tightly squeezes mine.

"There's a small Italian place nearby that we can go to."

"I don't think so. I'm actually really tired, and I have to wake up early to work at Eve's Center. Would you mind just taking me back to the Mile?"

Her expression is so pained; I can't fucking stand it. I shift my body over the console and unbuckle her seat belt, bringing her into my arms so she's in my lap.

"I'll bring you back to your room. But tell me you forgive me." I grip her head in my hands.

"I forgive you," she whispers, finally giving me her eyes. They swim with emotion as I bring my mouth to hers, kissing her lips.

"I'm worried about you," she whispers against my mouth.

I don't reply. It takes every ounce of strength in my body to push back and not take her here and now in the seat. But I've put her through enough tonight.

When I pull back, we're both breathing heavily.

"I really like you, Lauren. I want us to have a good time together."

She pleadingly looks at me. "Okay, but you can't pull this shit, Slade. It was wrong on so many levels."

I close my eyes for a split second because the shit I pull isn't always in my control. "You haven't known me for too long. But, if you give us this time together, I promise, I'll make it worth your while."

"You'd better." Her relief is apparent in the cadence of her voice.

I smile, and for the first time in God only knows how long, it's full blown. After I help her back into the passenger seat, the rest of our drive is quiet and warm. Dropping her off, I vow to keep myself under control. I'll do whatever it takes.

15

Lauren

"Lauren, your one p.m. is here," Eve sings out melodically, knocking on my door.

I'm helping Eve out at her Center this week. It's a nice-sized, newly built house on the rez with small apartment-type residences attached to the back.

With a small but clean communal indoor playroom for the children as well as an outdoor jungle gym, a hang-out living room area for older kids, and a tearoom for the mothers, the Center is a safe house in all senses of the word. Even the newly built apartments are perfectly constructed.

My makeshift office is filled with brown boxes, which have been pushed to the back corner of the room. But, with a small, square folding table and chair, a phone line, my own small laptop, and some pens and legal pads, I'm already knee deep in work. It hasn't even been one full day, and yet I'm already feeling the fantastic pulse of making a difference. Not least, working with Eve is second nature to me. After years of working for her at the law firm, I know exactly how she likes things done and know what she needs done before she even asks.

Seeing abused women with their children isn't easy, but I've already begun organizing cases and scheduling updates and reminders. On the boat in Lake Powell, I managed to order a nice closet filled with clothing, shoes, and even undergarments for these women to keep. Having a crazy rich husband like Vincent, who wants nothing more than to make Eve's dreams come true, means a lot of financial support. Eve wants these women to get jobs and have a few articles of clothing to start them off? Done. Eve wants a beautiful, clean library, so the kids can have a safe place to read and relax? Yes. Eve wants a daily cleaning service to ensure everything is always spotless? Check. I'm not sure why she hasn't hired an assistant to help her yet. Eve says she wants to learn all aspects of the Center herself before she hands it out to someone else. But, clearly, as evidenced by how much work I've been doing, she's ready for that now.

After last night's drama with Slade, I took a thirty-minute shower. The entire episode scared the hell out of me. First, the motorcycle club. And then his zone-out in the car. Can I even call it that? I could see him compulsively touching his brow before moving into a trance. His eyes fluttering, as though he was seeing something I couldn't see. I wasn't sure what to do. I waited, frightened. Then, I touched him, and it was as though he was shaken out of it.

I'm just not sure which way to turn. I'm having an amazing time with him, but there's something lurking beneath his surface.

Pushing away thoughts of Slade and my impending departure, I stand up on shaky legs but straighten myself out. I'll deal with my personal stuff later. Right now, I've got to focus on helping Mary, a woman who's been staying here for the last two weeks. Eve has already filed the necessary paperwork to keep her abusive husband away from her and their children. But it's time for us to discuss ways to get her back on her feet.

I'm turning the corner to our small conference room when Eve stops me.

"Tomorrow night is the opening of Hook. You're coming, right? Vincent has some fancy-pants PR firm working the event."

"I'll be there with you. So long as you promise we can have a few drinks together. I seriously need it."

One more week—that's all I have left. I want to break down and tell her about what's been happening with Slade and how badly I need some girl time, but we're at work, and I know Eve too well. She would not appreciate coffee talk at a time when a client is waiting.

"Perfect. You'll love it. It's not casual," she says with laughter. "You'll get to doll your gorgeous self," she adds with a wink. "Oh, and by the way, I got a threatening letter from one of the ex-husbands, so just make sure you stay focused on what's around you."

"Don't you have security?"

"We do. Slade also comes a few nights a week to make sure all the locks are secure and families feel safe."

"He does?" I can feel my eyes widening.

"Yep. He's awesome like that." She smiles knowingly.

I want to have a good game face, but I don't. My face blushes crimson.

Turning on my red Gucci loafers, I step into the small conference room that is designed to look like a warm den. Eve believes a setting like this is more comfortable for these women as opposed to a cold, rectangular table and too many chairs. Mary is already seated on a floral love seat, face filled with worry at seeing my new face.

"Hi, Mary. I'm Lauren. I've reviewed all the paperwork you filled out, and I'm ready to discuss possible job placement for you. But, before we get into that, tell me how you're all doing."

Tears fill her eyes as she describes her older daughter, already sixteen, who, yesterday, brought her a college pamphlet for the local community college that she'd gotten from the teen room. "It's only been a few weeks, but we already feel like we're going to make this happen."

"I can promise you, things will happen for the better. I've brought my computer, so I can show you how to scan for career opportunities here in your area."

I take her to the job search website and give a small tutorial. The Milestone shows up with opportunities in housekeeping.

"I wouldn't mind working as a cleaning lady. Do you think they'll hire me? I hear they're even building houses for their workers. And benefits, too, right? I'd love to get that job."

I smile. Eve never advertises the connection between herself and Vincent. "I bet we can arrange something. I am friends with the owner."

"You are?" Her eyes widen. "That man is a saint!"

"He's a good man." I try not to roll my eyes.

Sure, Vincent has done amazing things. But the man is not exactly warm and fuzzy.

"You'll be with me every step, right?" She worriedly inches closer.

I sigh. "No, actually. I only have another week, so I'll do the best I can until then."

"But why?"

"I'm only here temporarily ..." My voice trails off.

"That's a shame. You seem so sweet."

"Well, we'll work together while I'm here. Let me just print out the application form for the Mile housekeeping staff. And then we'll call and hopefully get an interview date."

She nods vigorously.

Eve already told me that these women were looking for kindness plus strength. They want us to be kind and gentle, but they're also in a sensitive place and need someone strong to trust, who they can hang on to. Who would have thought it would be me?

BY FOUR O'CLOCK, I'm desperate for a coffee. I knock on Eve's door. "Hey. Coffeemaker?"

"It's here." She lifts her head from a file, smiling at me in relief. "I am so glad you're with me. I really wish you'd stay. I've tried to hire other girls, but no one is ... you. So nice and friendly and thoughtful but also smart. Mary came in before leaving and told me how warm you were with the women who were in today."

I flush from her praise, but it is what it is. I add water from her liter bottle of Poland Spring before adding a paper filter and scooping in the ground beans. "My apartment is sitting there, collecting dust. My parents are there. My ... friends ..." I try not to choke on the word.

I haven't heard anything from any of them. It's not really a surprise. We have nothing in common. All we had was our looks and our mutual enjoyment of shopping and parties. That kind of glue always stays wet.

"What about Slade?" She presses her lips together. "It's obvious you guys have something going on."

"You don't know the half of it." I swallow.

"Well, start talking."

And so, I do—sort of. I tell her the general story from her wedding, the outline of the shooting, and skim through the drama without giving too much away. As much as I want to tell her every gritty detail, it would be a betrayal to Slade for me to give too much information about what I'm sensing about his internal life. And, anyway, what if I'm wrong? I'd be spreading things to his friends that might not even be true, and that wouldn't be right.

Her eyes widen with worry when I run through last night at the motorcycle club and his erratic moods, but otherwise, she stays completely quiet.

"I would stay for him," I continue, "if he gave me even the hope of more. You know I would. I like it here. A lot. And he's an amazing man, but obviously, he has some issues, right? Maybe I'm being paranoid, but I get the feeling he's hiding something. And, anyway, our entire relationship right now is built on the fact that, when I leave, we're done. I'm getting older though, and I need to meet someone real. I want kids. I want a man to love me back. I want more than two weeks of no strings, and that's something he's made clear he isn't willing to give." I finally pause my rambling.

"Honestly, I agree. You deserve a future, Lauren. You really do. If you want to go back to LA, I'd never blame you. And, if you change your mind and realize you'd rather be here, you always have a spot at the Center. There are other men here, too. I know Slade is special, but at the end of the day, you've got to be on the same page. I'm convinced most of life is timing."

"You're right. But, with Slade, it's different. I feel that electricity between us, and it's not just sexual. It's more than that ..." I exhale, letting my voice trail off. "Then again, maybe I'm just not used to a good man who's authentic. Like, maybe this is just how he is?"

"Yes, he's a great guy. But you aren't one of those girls who imagines things. If you feel that connection, it's because it goes both ways. But that doesn't mean he's ready to face the fact that he has the best girl ever in front of his face."

I know Eve has my best interest at heart. I pour us each a mug of coffee, and we drink in a warm silence like the best friends we are.

"But, Eve?"

She takes a sip before replying, "Yeah?"

"Don't tell Vincent what I'm telling you. It's Slade's private life, and if he wants to tell Vincent, he should be the one to do it."

"The stuff with the motorcycle club sounds shady, but I'd never interfere. Slade is like a brother to me. I haven't noticed anything out of the ordinary with him. Then again, I've been so involved in my own world that I'm not paying attention. I'm going to start though."

"I'm sure Vincent already knows anyway. They're so close, right?"

"Right. Best friends. Whatever is going on, I'm sure Vincent is on top of it." She bites her lip, mannerisms opposite from the confidence in her voice.

We turn to a hard knock at the door. Eve questioningly looks at me and with slight anxiety. Is it an angry ex-husband? She stands tall, pulling out a gun from her drawer, and my eyes widen.

Holy shit! Eve has a gun?

My immediate instinct is to hide and pretend we aren't here while hers is to take out a weapon. Do I know this woman? She moves toward the door.

I flail my arms, mouthing, *No!*

Eve ignores me and quickly opens the door, as though she needs to act before changing her mind. It's Slade.

He sees the gun and immediately raises his arms. "Whoa."

We both stare, open-mouthed and shocked. Speak of the devil

...

Eve lowers her gun, hand shaking.

"What's wrong?" He looks between us in confusion, and we burst into laughter.

"We thought—you were—a killer ex-husband—but instead—it's you," I speak between fits of laughter.

A few seconds later, I get ahold of myself. But Eve cannot stop laughing. I know she has this issue; when she starts with the nervous laughter, she cannot stop.

"Here we go again." Slade chuckles. "Lauren, get this woman some water. For God's sake, Eve." He laughs himself.

She wipes tears from the corners of her eyes, but her body is still going at it.

"Care to tell me what's so fucking funny? I'm not the psycho husband. Maybe we should do a special code word, so you know it's me."

"How about just a text letting us know you're coming?"

He smiles at me. "Smart girl."

"It's you!" Eve laughs. "We thought—"

She's cackling as Slade and I roll our eyes. The girl is losing it.

"Well, I'm here to check up on you all. Not kill either one of you. But, Eve, I might have to take matters into my own hands if you don't stop laughing. Christ!" His body shakes from his own laughter. "This shit is contagious."

Eve turns to face the window, taking large, heaving breaths.

"So, all is well?" Slade asks me.

In unison, Eve and I say, "We're great!"

She looks at me, ready to crack up again.

I point a finger at her. "Don't laugh, Eve. Take another breath," I speak slowly, wanting to keep her from another giggle attack.

"Oh, you! Get to work," she stutters out.

"Yes, boss." I leave her office, and Slade follows behind.

"Come to my place for dinner tonight?"

"You want me to come over? To your home?" I try keeping the shock from my voice, but it's there.

"Yep." He stands straight and tall, full of confidence.

"Oh, um, Eve told me there was some restaurant opening."

"That's tomorrow night." He leans against the wall, legs crossed casually.

I nod. "Okay, I'll come. Do you want to pick up any food from the supermarket? I can cook."

"No. I'm cooking. I'll pick you up from here. Seven thirty?"

"That sounds good." He kisses the top of my head before leaving, strutting out like the self-assured man he is.

I'm shell-shocked. Slade just asked me to dinner. At his house!

AFTER SEVEN, Eve asks my plans for tonight. The work here is never-ending, but it is more fulfilling than anything I've ever done.

"Slade is picking me up."

"Is that right?" She lifts a beautifully arched dark eyebrow.

"Yes." I sigh. "What am I going to do?"

"You're going to be careful. Enjoy yourself. And call me if you need me."

Sometime later, I check the time on my phone. It's almost seven thirty. It turns out that time flies when you're working on something you care about. I pull out a brush and a small mirror from my bag, checking myself out and redoing my hair when Eve reenters my room.

"Don't go back to LA," she begs.

I drop the brush back into my purse before straightening out my desk. "Can we not mention it?"

"Yes. One day at a time. But you've been so helpful, and I love having you with me," she exclaims before defensively raising her arms and adding, "Just saying."

I roll my eyes, not unhappily.

"And you look beautiful," Eve adds.

"Thank you." I smile. "And I love working here, too. The circumstances that brought me here are terrible, but I'm glad it led me back to you."

We hug before I leave the Center. With my eyes on my phone while I delete junk e-mails, I walk through the exit. Pausing at the curb, I raise my head. Slade is here, casually leaning against his huge motorcycle with a smirk meant just for me.

"Hey, you," I call out, trying to stop myself from sprinting to him.

When I reach him, he presses a kiss on the top of my head before securing a black helmet beneath my chin. He gets on first and helps me on. I'm scared to death, but I trust he'll get us to his home in one piece. Luckily, I'm wearing flat shoes. I make a mental note that pumps on a motorcycle would be a terrible idea.

We take off. The ride is exhilarating. The wind and the fresh air ... oh, who am I kidding? Screw nature. I have Slade, the hottest man I've ever seen with a body to kill for, sitting in front of me. I'm squeezing his muscled midsection as the rumble of the bike shakes between my legs, and I have to do everything in my power not to moan out loud. He's in an amazing mood and bringing me to his home, and I don't have too much time left. I'm going to capitalize on the positive and ignore everything else.

We pull in front of his home. It's small but freshly painted with a square yard in front and a driveway where his truck is parked. Helping me off the bike, we walk hand in hand inside, where I'm pleasantly surprised. Slade's home is clean, tidy, and organized. It smells like a delicious dinner has been cooked. The living room has a nice, large gray couch in an L-shape with a big screen TV mounted on the wall. I poke my head into his kitchen on the left. At a quick glance, the appliances look brand-new.

"Left is the kitchen, here's the living room, and on the right is my bedroom." He points to the back of the house. "I've got a porch and grill out there."

"Do you mind if I use the bathroom?"

He walks me into his bedroom. No clothes are strewed on the floor, and the bed is neatly made. "There's one over here, on the right."

I head inside, locking the door behind me. As I stare at myself in the mirror, my bliss is so extreme that it's all I see. You hear about happiness shining through? Exhibit A: me. When Slade and I are good, we're so, so good.

I reenter the kitchen to find Slade with black oven mitts, pulling food from the oven.

"Can I help?" My voice is cheery as he puts the hot glass dish over a hot plate.

He asks, "Red, white, or beer?"

"White."

"In the fridge, and the opener is in that drawer." He nods to where it is before pulling out extra virgin olive oil and white vinegar from a cabinet. "Would you mind grabbing me a beer?"

I open his refrigerator, shocked to see the detailed level of organization. Everything inside is fresh and organized in Tupperware containers marked: grilled chicken, grilled vegetables, meat, fried onion. On the lower level, there are larger containers filled with cut-up vegetables. Shredded cabbage and carrots. Spinach. Lots of hard-boiled eggs.

No wonder his body is so good.

Typically, in my fridge at home, I have hummus, condiments, and wine. My pantry is filled with rice crackers, chia seeds, fiber thins, and other shortcuts to skinny. My girlfriends and I always tote about health and fitness, but the truth is, all these diet fads are just ways to control calories.

"Did you get lost in there?" He laughs.

"I need to take notes on how you organize." I pull out a bottle of Stella and a small bottle of pinot grigio before shutting the door.

"Oh, yeah?"

"Yes. I mean, you premake everything?"

"Sure do. Sunday nights, I take care of food for the workweek."

I open the beer and hand it to him, noticing a few black mugs on the windowsill over the kitchen sink.

"Why don't you mix the salad and grab some silverware from the drawer next to the oven? I'll get the chicken and rice on the table outside. It's pretty warm out still, so I figured we could eat there."

"Sure." I use the spoons already in the salad to mix it all up as he props open the door.

When we sit down, I notice how much food he's prepared. Two whole chickens perfectly browned and surrounded by carrots, celery, and potatoes. A large plate of brown rice. And, of course, a salad filled with spinach, cabbage, celery, carrots, and cranberries. For all his gruffness, the man obviously has a way in the kitchen.

"How did you learn to cook all of this?"

"I hated eating out all the time. Learned some recipes and then figured it out from there." He lifts my white ceramic plate, filling it with food. "My parents cooked a lot also. My mom had a huge book of her recipes I brought with me."

After giving me back my plate, he takes care of his own. I dig in and smile. It tastes even better than it looks.

"So, how was work today?" he asks, all domestic-like.

"I actually loved it," I exclaim, unable to stop the smile from filling my face. I tell Slade about all the work I accomplished for Eve and how I met with one of the abused women. "She wants a job at the Mile. I've got to talk to Vincent about that."

"Sounds good. Nevada suits you."

"Does it?"

He nods, seemingly pleased.

The rest of our dinner is full of laughter and jokes. He tells me a bit about his years overseas and the different trainings he's done. I sit in utter awe of this amazing man in front of me.

"Lauren, I know we don't have much time left together. But, while you're here, I want to be with you. And, when you leave, I want you to know you can always call me."

"Is that what you are? Mr. Dependable Friend?" I sit up and lean forward to get closer. I'm not expecting him to say we're more, but right now, it feels like it.

"Yes. Everything good starts like this." He puts his hands on the small wooden table as though getting ready to stand. "I've got some fruit for dessert. Interested?"

"Let me get it." I rise.

"Grab me another beer, too, will you?"

With a polite nod, I head back inside.

16

Slade

She comes back to the patio and hands me my drink, already opened.

I look down at the beer before staring back at her, my chest expanding when I say, "Thank you." It feels good to have her with me.

"So, when did you have your last relationship?" she asks quickly, words laced with curiosity.

I take a long pull, the need to be truthful rising above all else. "Not since high school. When I joined up with the Navy, I had someone. It felt good to think she was at NYU, studying and waiting for me, but it turned out, she wasn't actually waiting. I learned from another friend that she was cheating on me with some New York City stockbroker. After we broke up, there were women who came and went during my time off. But nothing steady."

"Was it lonely?" Her brows lower with worry for me.

"Sure." I shrug, taking another pull from the bottle. "But, for my friends who had wives at home, it wasn't too easy for them either. They were always worrying. Waiting by the phones. E-mailing. I was more comfortable being on my own. Helped me to focus. I think, if I had a family to worry about, it would have clouded my judgment."

She takes a sip of her wine before I ask, "And what about you? What's the trail you've left behind?"

"There have been men in my past. But no one too serious. I think I always picked the wrong guys. They looked like the right ones, but then, somehow, they weren't. The truth is ..." Her voice trails off.

I sit closer, waiting for her to finish.

"There has been no one since you at the wedding." She nervously looks up, waiting for my reply.

"Is that right?" For whatever reason, this sounds like good fucking news to me. The best news actually.

Lauren's epic eye roll is followed by, "Yeah."

"I knew I rocked your world," I exclaim, my voice exaggerated.

She laughs out loud, throwing her napkin at me. It sails onto the table and falls back on her plate.

"Let's clean up and go inside. Movie?"

"Sure."

We clear the table together and head back into the kitchen. I take the serving platters, leaving them on the counter, while Lauren picks up the plates and silverware off the table. She moves to the sink, rinsing off the dishes and putting them in the dishwasher. She moves so comfortably, as though she belongs here.

After I put the extra food back into the refrigerator, I grab a cigarette from the junk drawer.

"I'm going to step out to have a smoke. You make yourself comfortable on the couch over there. Remote should be on the side table by the couch."

She looks over her shoulder, smiling at me while continuing to rinse. "Sure."

Outside, I light up and listen to her movements in the house. It feels so good to have a woman with me. A spot in my chest that I never knew was empty seems to be filling, and I feel it. I know it in my fucking bones that having her with me is right. I know it can't last, and I can't let her in. But still, the truth is there, written clearly for me to see. In another life, she'd be my only.

I put out the cigarette and head back inside. I want another but don't want her waiting too long.

"I'll make us some popcorn," I shout into the living room.

A minute later, I pour it into a large bowl and take it with me. Shoes off and barefoot, she sits with her hair piled high on top of her head. I pause and swallow.

She belongs here.

She lifts her hand in hello. "What do you feel like watching?" The remote is in her hand as she scrolls through channels.

"Why don't we go somewhere?" I speak before I think.

"Where?" She looks between me and the bowl of popcorn.

"The sun is setting soon. There's a spot."

"Yeah. Okay." She stands up, sliding her shoes on. "Let's do it."

"It's about half an hour west of the strip. Red Rock Canyon. You cool with riding for that long?"

She nods enthusiastically.

We get on the bike together and ride. Her hands trail all over my stomach as I drive. Her touch is a brand. It moves like fire straight into my dick and my heart and even my brain. We get there just as the sun sets over the canyon, painting everything in shades of orange.

I help her off the bike, walking us away from the parking lot and the highway.

"It's like God is putting on a show for us," she tells me, almost breathless with awe, staring at the mountains. "The rocks are incredible. And these colors!"

"Time and erosion does wonders."

Taking a long inhale of mountain air, she smiles at me.

"Wish I'd brought a tent for us."

"Oh no." She nervously shakes her head. "I don't do camping."

"Why not?" I lean back against a large boulder, bringing her between my legs.

"Well, you heard Eve before. I don't like snakes and the wilderness. All those noises. Animals that come out at night." She shivers.

"With me, camping would be different. I've been here on my own tons of times. Sunrise is spectacular."

I pull her body closer, showing her with my actions that I'd protect her. I would use the words, but I can't. I don't want to make promises I can't keep or talk about things that can never be.

A terror creeps into my psyche and pierces my brain. Memories of war sit on the back burner of my mind, waiting to come back. How much time do I have until the next onslaught? But then, next week, she'll be gone.

I imagine other men touching her and loving her back in LA. Lauren looking up at them, brown eyes large and sweet, like she's doing with me right now, agreeing to long drives and fancy dinners and a huge diamond ring ...

"Tell me more about how it would be different." Her soft voice interrupts my thoughts.

She is looking for clarity. She knows what we have between us, but she wants to hear it line by line. She wants me to work it out in my own head. But I can't. I need to keep us as a jumble, so I can deny what I'm feeling. Deny the fact that I can't see past next week, when she'll be gone, without wanting to break something.

She seems to know that I'm conflicted because she swiftly changes the subject. "Did you camp with your family? I always wanted to do that, but my parents aren't the type." She smiles. "We've traveled all over the coasts of the US, Europe, and Hawaii, but we've never done something as simple as pitching a tent."

"Yeah." I nod. "We used to camp all the time. Dad, Aaron and I used to love building fires. Mom didn't always want to come along though. It was our time."

"If we stayed here together, give me a play-by-play of how it would be." She nestles into my body and leans her head against my chest, the smell of her skin filling me up.

"I'd pack everything we needed. Set up the tent. Lay out the sleeping bags inside. Build us a good fire. We'd cook over it." I put my hands in her hair, gripping the back of her head to tether her to me. "I'd hold you. In the morning, we'd watch the sun come up. My mom used to tell me that, wherever I was in the world, I should look at the sun and know she was watching the same one." I bend my head, gently kissing her lips.

For the first time since I've been home, I feel it like a hole in my gut. I miss my mom.

"That's beautiful, Slade. She must have been a special woman."

I nod because my mom wasn't just special. She was incredible. "She was a nurse but never missed a football game of mine. Always had a home-cooked meal ready for me after school even if it was sitting in the refrigerator for me to heat up. When I left for boot camp, she cried so hard. Wanted me to go to college. I had a scholarship for football."

"It's not too late to go back to school, Slade. You can go and do that now. We're in America, aren't we? And this is what you've talked about—mental strength. If you want something, I have no doubt you'll make it happen."

I want to respond, but the words won't come. I'm too overwhelmed by her support and thoughtfulness. "My mom would have loved you," is all I can manage. In fact, I have no doubt that my whole family would have. I'm a hard man, and I was a tough kid, but I was raised right in the kind of family that was God-loving and full of warmth. I wasn't always this broken.

Lauren expectantly looks back up at me.

If I asked her to camp with me now, she'd say yes. What if I asked for ... more?

Instead, I say, "Let's head back."

I pull her back toward the bike and lean her against it, sliding my hands over her shoulders and beneath her loose blouse. She tilts her head, and I can see the vulnerability in her face. This is the innocent side of Lauren. Her eyes, they yearn.

"Maybe I can't wait for home," I whisper in her ear, playing with the buttons on her ladylike shirt.

Impatience thrums through my blood. I want her so badly; I can't stand it. It's a basic urge to mark her and take her as mine. Before I can kiss her, something passes over her face. It looks something like disappointment.

Before I can think another thought, I say, "Home. Let's go home."

She lets out a tiny exhale as I fasten her helmet and get on the bike, helping her on after me.

BACK IN MY DRIVEWAY, we barely get off the bike before we lunge for each other. The softness of her mouth sends chills down my spine. She pulls back for air, but I don't let her go. I can't. Lifting her into my arms with her legs wrapped around my midsection, I bring her into the house, our mouths fused as I hold her gorgeous ass in my hands.

She whimpers as I shut the door behind us. I bring her into my bedroom, dropping her onto my black bedspread. I lean onto her, and her legs spread to make room for me. Palming her breasts over her shirt, I know I need her completely nude. With the way she's shaking, she needs me, too. We have a response to each other that's off the charts. I wish I could find a girl who means nothing and expects nothing and have this kind of heat. But I can't. It's *Lauren*.

She groans as I stand up, pulling down my jeans and my underwear at the same time. My cock springs free, and I fist it in my hand, watching her eyes widen and smolder. I take off my shirt next, pulling up from behind my neck. She sits up, peeling off her own clothes. When she's undressed, we both pause to stare, breathing heavily. She's looking at me like I'm her king.

I drop to my knees in front of her. "You're beautiful," I whisper.

She moves her hands around my head, hugging me into her chest. I can't remember the last time I was truly hugged, skin-to-skin. Yes, she's stunning. But she's more. Lauren is everything.

I sit back up, finding lips while gently rubbing my thumbs over her nipples. They harden from my touch. "So fucking hot."

I let my dick slide up and down over her bare pussy, coated with slick wetness, until we're both groaning. I want to shift and get inside. Just one more minute of this perfect torture. I keep sliding, my dick passing over her clit back and forth, driving us both insane. The sound of her juices is a goddamn aphrodisiac.

"Condom." Her voice breaks.

I curse, spinning around and opening the small drawer by my bedside. Pulling out and opening a square packet, I unroll the condom over my swollen length.

The sound she makes when I enter her is enough to turn me mindless. I'm growling like an animal, my need so desperate that it's shocking. I want to mark this woman and take her over on every single plane. I'm dizzy with the thought of her being mine.

Mine!

"Oh!" Her pussy tightens, squeezing my dick so hard that I'm shaking.

I grip her firm ass, plunging into her, and my movements become more erratic. Her full, big, nippled breasts. And the heat of her moans.

Christ!

She's whimpering now from the pleasure as I throw her legs over my shoulders to get deeper, but I don't slow down the force—can't even if I tried. My finger moves down, as I know what she needs, and it circles around her clit. She screams out as sweat breaks in the valley between her breasts.

"Oh God, Slade ..." Nails score my back up and down.

"Take me deeper. Raise those legs higher. Spread them for me." I bend low, sucking on her neck and breasts so hard that I know I'm leaving bruises.

She gives it to me, offering herself. I take it all. I want anyone walking near her to know she belongs to me. A fizzing sensation builds in the back of my neck, growing until, finally, I explode. I come so hard that I barely contain my own shout.

While we steady our breaths, she caresses my hair and kisses my shoulder and runs her fingers up and down my chest, as though she can't stop herself. I'm so overwhelmed with this feeling, like she's flowing into me. Clear as day, I know this woman has the power to give my life meaning but also to utterly destroy me.

I stand up, taking care of the condom before getting back into the bed. Bringing her into my arms, I press her warm, sweaty body to mine before rolling back on top of her, kissing every inch. She squirms, laughing and asking me to stop tickling her.

"Stop?" Kiss. "How can I stop?" I lick a circle around her tiny belly button, waiting for her eyes to connect with mine. "Have you seen yourself?" Down her perfect body I go.

If I ever wanted to stay away from Lauren, I should have drawn the line at Vincent and Eve's wedding. I never should have brought her into my truck. Once I got a taste, it was as though I physically and emotionally bonded with her. There are depths within Lauren I haven't even begun to understand. But, God, I want to.

I move between her legs, spreading her wide, wanting to inhale her essence. My last rational thought before I press my mouth against her heat is, *Eight days left.*

She replies with a guttural moan.

I finish her off before kissing back up her glistening body. Lauren has a figure that's straight out of my dreams. Heavy breasts. Small waist. Toned hips.

I squeeze her thighs, and she says, "You're killing me, Slade."

"Just the beginning, baby." I grasp the back of her head, locking our eyes. *Stay*, I silently beg.

Her eyes smile, but she stays quiet, just as I have.

"So, we're in your bed, huh?" She can't resist the question.

I lean up on my elbow. "We are."

In my bed, with the thin shades lowered, we spend two hours talking about everything. Joking around and moving to serious topics and then laughing again. We have another round of sex but slower and deeper. My nose, eyes, hands ... all full of this woman who feels made for me.

"Do you feel my heart?" she whispers beneath the covers, lifting my heavy hand and putting it against her chest. It beats so quickly.

"No, babe. I think that's your stomach growling up into your chest cavity," I joke, feeling her stomach rumble.

She laughs, swatting my chest.

Her body is so hot to the touch and coated with our sweat. The steady beat of her heart against my hand has me light-headed.

"I can put some food together for you. Just gotta get out of this jail you've set for me."

"Sure." She untangles her legs from mine, and I immediately feel the loss.

I get out of bed, sliding on a pair of shorts before leaving the bedroom. Opening the fridge, I pull out some already-cooked taco meat and a packet of soft tortillas from dinner two nights ago. I toast the tortillas while I warm the beef and then put together two over-stuffed tacos filled with saucy meat, shredded cabbage, and carrots. It's nothing fancy, but I know it's delicious. After filling a cup with ice water, I bring it all into the bedroom, expecting to see her gorgeous, naked body in my bed.

When I enter the room, she's gone. A rush of adrenaline surges through my chest. Where the hell did she go? I put down the plate and water on the desk by the bedroom window and put a hand on the wall to steady myself. Our mingled scents are still on the bedsheets, turning me to fury. Did she run? But where? I break out into a nervous sweat, my hands shaking as I practically sprint to my front door. Did she leave while I was warming her food? I turn the door handle, but it's still locked. That's when I hear the faucet running from the bathroom.

I drop into a seat at my kitchen table, pulling out a cigarette and smoking it in record time. And then another. I don't open any windows but just smoke and smoke to calm my nerves. I need to keep this woman near me. How can I let her go? I know I'm fucked up, but I've lost the strength to push her away. With her soft body and eyes, I'm done for. I fill a glass with vodka and quickly drink it down before grabbing a few mints from my junk drawer and chewing them.

With a fresh cigarette dangling from the corner of my mouth, I go back into my bedroom and open my bedside drawer, popping three white-and-yellow-coated pills and chewing them quickly. Need this right now. Need to keep her with me tonight, next to me. *How else can I do it if not this way?*

I finally knock on the bathroom door, wondering what's taking her so long. "Lauren?"

She opens it, smiling, crazy sex hair piled up on top of her head in a sloppy bun and completely clothed. I lean against the doorframe, brows raised in confusion as to why she's fully dressed.

Inhaling the smoke, I try to keep myself from unhinging. "Where do you think you're going?"

Her face turns down. "I thought you'd take me back to the hotel after we ate something."

"No. Get back in the bed." I slowly shake my head because there is no way I'm sending her home right now. I've already taken the drugs and had a drink. It should be enough to put myself out completely. She'll be safe, and I'll get to keep her. Win-win.

"Really?" Her voice is full of nervous question.

"You'll stay here tonight. With me."

"But I thought you said you didn't do sleepovers." Her voice is small but hopeful.

"Well, tonight, that changes."

The happiness that fills her face is so beautiful that I'm floored. She walks back into the bedroom, pulling off pieces of her clothes as she moves, her gorgeous heart-shaped ass twisting with her steps. My heart rate begins to slow as my body calms.

I'll be okay. She'll be safe. Please, God, I need her right now.

I pull off my shorts and get into the bed, bringing the food with me.

"Slade, I seriously love you right now." She smiles, pulling a taco from the plate.

My heart pauses. She's just joking around because I brought her tacos. But ... love. The word is like a small seed, pounding against my rib cage and then expanding into something more.

She moans, biting into the food I've made her as the saucy meat drips from the other end into the plate. She's messy and fucking gorgeous.

"Want the other?" she asks.

"Sure. Let me just ..." I lift my thumb, wiping the corner of her lips.

She blushes shyly.

I go ahead and take a large bite. When she's finished with hers, I offer her the rest of mine. She tries to take it with her hands, but I shake my head from side to side. From my hand, she eats.

The drugs begin to settle into my bones as I put the empty plate back on my desk. She drinks from the glass of water I brought. When that's done, I drag her into the center of my chest. Having her near me is relief and warmth and joy, all rolled into one. Lauren. She's here right now, and she's mine.

Slowly, my thoughts crackle. Fragments of memory join together like magnets as I'm pulled down into a heavy sleep.

I HEAR A WOMAN'S VOICE, but it sounds muffled, as though she's talking through a sheet. I think I know who it is, but I'm too tired to confirm. Has cotton filled my ears? The voice is more urgent now, but I only sink deeper into my bed where sand sits between my toes. I want to tell whoever is talking to just stop. I'm here where I'm supposed to be with Rex in the cot next to mine, snoring. Lead coats my bones, turning them to an unimaginable weight. And there's nothing to do but let it ride.

17

Lauren

I woke up this morning while Slade was still in a deep sleep. I've already showered. Made coffee. Cooked eggs. And still, he sleeps.

Tiptoeing into his room, I take a look at his face, paler than usual. His breaths are so light. Too light?

"Slade," I whisper-yell, shaking him.

But he doesn't move. And then he opens his bloodshot eyes, oozing redness.

"Sla—"

He grabs my upper arm and pulls me to his body as a gun moves to my head. The whole world slows down. I can feel the beat of my heart.

"Slade?" I stammer. I want to scream, but I can't. My entire being is frozen in fear.

He lets me go, puts the gun back beneath his pillow, and throws his legs to one side of the bed before standing. His entire body is coated with a sheen of sweat, but he shivers, as though it were ten below. Darkness circles his eyes. I'm so terrified. I think I might collapse to the ground.

On shaky legs, he enters his bathroom, shutting the door behind him as though I were nothing but air. Like he didn't just pull a gun on me. A gun! A weapon!

The sound of him puking into the toilet has me running out of his bedroom and into the kitchen.

Shifting from foot to foot, I ask myself, *Why did I stay here last night in his bed? Am I insane?* He warned me to stay away. He told me he never shared a bed! But I ignored him, like a fool. I need to get out of here and never return. My life isn't perfect, but I'd like to keep it.

Slade is the best man I've ever known, but something is *wrong*. All of this between us is just temporary, and sure, I like him more than I should, but the truth is, I'm scared of him. Should I be? He pulled a gun on me, but I was the one who surprised him. I should have known better. I should know that shaking a sleeping man like him would be dangerous ... like poking a bear, right? I start to laugh. Something in the back of my mind tells me I'm losing it, but I just shake my head. I had the best night of my life last night, and sure, this morning has been ... frightening, but it's nothing I can't handle, right? Because he's fine and I'm fine and all is well. But, no, it's not well. A gun was pulled on me! Shit. My life doesn't make sense anymore.

My thoughts are on speed, denial battling with reality, when he casually walks into the kitchen, huge and imposing with spiky wet hair, low-slung black jersey pants, and a white T-shirt showcasing his tats and muscles. The red in his eyes has somewhat cleared, but he looks ... hungover. He looks hungover, and we didn't drink last night. This means ... this means nothing; that's what it means!

Or ... it means everything, my psyche reminds me.

Leaning against a wooden cabinet, he pulls out a glass and fills it with ice from the freezer and water from the sink. The coffee I made sits hot in a small carafe. He stares at me, drinking, but no words are spoken.

Pouring the hot coffee into a mug set on the counter, I risk a long glance at the man before me. My first thought is how handsome he is, even with misery written all over his unshaved face.

"Morning," he croaks.

His first word is mine.

A cigarette moves into his lips. He lights up.

I bring my own coffee to my mouth, needing something to do. He stares, not giving any indication whether or not we're going to discuss what just happened.

"I'll take you to your room at the Mile and then drop you off at the Center for work. You're working today, yeah?" His eyes are now guarded, silently adding, *Don't say a word about it.*

I want to ask him, *What are you hiding?* My inclination though is to smooth it all over with a smile and brush problems under the rug. Not let him feel bad or awkward or push him where he doesn't want to go. But how can I do that? Something dark is happening with this man, and the fear I feel is real. Am I allowed to discuss it with him, or will I lose him if I do? His good parts are so good. But ... this is way beyond the realm of okay.

I hum my assent as he lets out the breath he was holding. We have to talk about this, but I want to think it all over before I speak. I care for Slade more than I have any right to. Still, I don't want to lose this time we have. I've got to just get out of this house as quickly as possible.

"I'm going to grab my stuff?" It's a comment, but I'm so nervous that it comes out like a question.

He nods, and I scurry into the bedroom, gathering my things like a bandit.

THE DRIVE back to the Mile is quiet. He sits and waits in his truck as I run upstairs to the room to wash up and change. I use a shower cap—no time to wash my hair. Dry shampoo will have to be enough. Quick makeup. Black shift dress. A nice pair of black heels. When I come back downstairs and into the parking lot, he's smoking against his truck. I wait, watching his movements. He looks as though he's deep in thought, staring at the mountains. When he's done with the cigarette, he takes out another. How many has he had? I could swear that, each day, his smoking increases. I pull out my phone. Should I tell him I'm getting a ride with Eve? With tentative steps, I walk toward him. It's just a ride. I'm a big girl. I can handle it.

"Hey." I wave, making sure he sees and hears me from a decent distance.

He nods, opening my door and throwing the cigarette stub onto the floor, stepping on it. I climb in. Again, the ride is quiet. His strong hand holds the gear, gripping it so firmly that I can see the flexion in his muscular and veiny forearms.

"I'll come get you from the Center at six to bring you back to the Mile." His voice is firm and nonnegotiable. He's the warrior right now, in complete control. He pulls up in front of the newly built stucco Center. "The opening of Hook is tonight. I'll have to work during it, but I'll pick you up from your room at nine and walk you down."

I turn to him to reply. I want to tell him that we should take a night off from seeing each other. I want to scream, *You pulled a gun on me! What the fuck?*

Before I can get a word out, he grabs me and kisses me.

"Baby, I'm sorry." Kiss. "I won't ever do it again." Kiss. "I lost control, but I've got this. Just wasn't used to having a woman by my side." He tightly holds me as though, with sheer will, he can erase the memory of what I witnessed this morning.

All my words and nerves are swallowed in his mouth, which begs me not to let us end. I find myself pressing inside his chest, simultaneously wanting to run and yet never wanting to let go.

"It's okay, right? We're cool?" He's so soft right now. Warm.

I want to believe him so badly.

I don't answer because I can't. I turn mindless from his lips; he erases my dark thoughts with the rhythm of his tongue. The trusting side of me gives in. I want this. I want him. And he's sorry. That's enough, right? My chest softens as his kiss deepens and slows. We're okay, cool, just like he said. I raise my hands, dropping them to the back of his neck. He lets out an audible groan of relief.

I'm here, I tell him with my body language.

He pulls me closer, up into his lap. I open my eyes to see his are shut tightly.

His mouth is at my neck when I see the time flashing on his dashboard.

"I'm late," I grumble, wishing he'd dragged me into the backseat of his car.

He pulls away with a flushed face. "Later?"

"Yes." One more closed-mouthed kiss, and I open the door to leave.

When I'm at the front of the Center, I turn back, finding him staring at me through the passenger window. My breath stops. From this angle, Slade looks almost white. It's as though I'm staring at him, but I can see through him as though he were a ghost. A twisted shiver moves through me before I turn myself away, entering the clean building.

At first, I'm still in the post-make-out haze. But, within an hour, the mind fog clears. Hours begin to move in a warped speed, the fear over Slade this morning plaguing me.

When he first opened his bloodshot eyes, my gut told me it was drugs. *Drugs!* The word zings through my head, but I push it out. I won't think it or say it because Slade is too smart and too good to get wrapped up in something like that. Right? But, holy shit, he pulled an actual gun on me. Was it loaded? I feel ill.

My throat tightens. Me, a girl who has never even seen a gun before the shooting in Vegas. And I slept next to one all night. This is so fucking bad.

The file of Jane Simble sits on my desk. I need to review it before calling her for a check-in, and I don't want my personal shit interfering with this job. I read through her history, getting my mind in order. I dial her number, pushing my own emotions back. Eve insisted follow-ups were necessary, and I agree.

Jane answers on the fourth ring, and I put on my happy face.

"Hello, this is Lauren Amini, assistant to Eve Petrov. We're just checking in to see how you've been doing. How are the children?"

She replies, and I listen intently, jotting down notes.

I continue burying my feelings within the work. The load is unimaginable but also incredibly fulfilling. These women need help, and it's amazing to be able to play a part in their safety and freedom.

After eating a large salad with turkey that Eve picked up, I open the window in my box-filled office. The air is so fresh, almost briny. There's no ocean here, but somehow, the air feels salty. Even the sky is fresh—clear blue with puffy white clouds. Perfect really.

Eve comes into my room in a pair of straight-leg khaki slacks and a soft white blouse, showing me dress options for the opening of Hook. I vote for the tight red one because her boobs will look best in that scooped neckline.

She smiles. "My sister said the same thing when I showed her via FaceTime. You think Vincent will like it?"

"Like it?" I scoff. "The man won't be able to function!"

She laughs, and I do my best to smile.

All is well! Lauren is always happy! That's what my face says. It's what I always say even if my insecurities and fears are currently ravaging my insides.

"I was thinking"—she lifts her pen, clicking the back—"have you considered going back to school for social work?"

"Social work?" I repeat, squinting my eyes.

"Yes. You can help service some of the kids who come in here when their parents aren't in the right place to care for them. Even if you don't come back here, I can see you continuing this work back in LA. It suits you."

I nod. For the first time in countless years, an idea about my career feels right to me. "It's a great idea actually. You know my dad is still pushing law school—"

"You've got to be kidding," she huffs. "Why would you do that? You've never wanted to be a lawyer. If you did, you would have done it by now."

"I know. But it's what he's always wanted for me."

"So?"

"What do you mean, so? You can't understand. There's a cultural expectation. I need the advanced degree. And my father has wanted me to follow in his footsteps for so long." The words sound ridiculous, coming out of my mouth, and I can see the expression on her face is one of incredulity. But it's the truth nonetheless. "Even Sanam has a master's in real estate. I've got to make something serious of myself, above being a legal secretary. I know it's good work, but—"

"First of all, you'd be getting a master's," she interrupts. "And, if you're going to spend your time and hard-earned money, do something you actually care about. Otherwise, you'll be miserable. I see the difference in you here as opposed to back in California. Your work is better, too. And the reason is simple; you like it. I don't want you to be underneath me here. I want a partner, Lauren. That could be you. Work during the day at Crier and get your degree at night. Or just move here and work with me while you do your degree online. You're competent and smart. Let's do this."

I bite my lip. "Look, I just came here for a break. Let me go home and figure it out."

She sighs. "And how are you since the shooting? You look good."

"I am good. Great really. And I'm going to seriously consider the social work thing. I can't promise I'll move here because I'm just not sure where my life is headed. But school is a good direction."

"Do that."

And then she does the unexpected and full-on hugs me. She smells clean and sweet, and I grip her back, loving this new Eve. Back in LA, she was brilliant at her job, but so cold and focused. With her living here and married to the love of her life, it's as though she's revived.

Checking my clock, I realize it's two p.m. Letting go of her, I gather the paperwork for Alicia, a new woman I'm meeting today. I'm going to get down her entire story and organize it, so Eve can then file the necessary paperwork. It's amazing how we've gotten back into our old flow so quickly.

We leave my office together, and I head into the small den where Alicia is already waiting, sitting in one of the cozy floral chairs. Her back is curved and head drooped as though in thought. She hears me enter the room, and her head pops up, on alert. With hair worn in dark, heavy dreadlocks and eyes a sharp black, she silently assesses me. Acne scars and dark spots mar delicate pale skin. She's not perfect but still beautiful.

"Hi, Alicia. I'm Lauren. Do you want any water or coffee or tea before we start?"

She nervously looks me up and down, and I remember Eve's warning to look soft, calm, and gentle. Setting my hair back in a clip, I smile.

"Yeah, sure. Coffee's good." Dark circles mar her eyes, as though she hasn't slept in weeks.

I place the notepads on the table and step out of the office, letting out a breath. This woman needs help, and it's written all over her face. Pouring the coffee in a pink mug and grabbing a few servings of creamer, I step back into the room.

I place the coffee in front of her, explaining what it is I'll need today.

"Well, I'm here because ... I'm afraid for myself and my kid."

"You're in the right place." I sit forward and pick up the large yellow pad, wanting her to know from my body language that I'm listening and taking her seriously. "Why don't you tell me why you're afraid?"

"It didn't start too bad. He's always had a temper, but I figured, high-stress life and all that. But the rage has gotten worse over time. Sometimes, we'd be talking and all was well, and then boom!" she yells.

I grip the arms of my chair.

"It's like the man I knew became someone else. After six months or so, the lows with us got lower, and the highs got lower, too."

"I see." With a shaking hand, I start scribbling some notes. "Did you keep a log or journal of when these incidents occurred? Any photographs perhaps of physical assault?"

"Yes." Opening her oversize black purse, she pulls out wrinkled papers, handing them to me in a heap. "Sorry it's not organized. I hid them under some stuff in my underwear drawer. But a lot is there."

"No, this is great." Opening the first sheet, I see a date for three years ago. Photos, too.

"You see, I love him. He's a good man. A great man. Fought for this country. But"—she pauses—"he's dangerous."

I swallow, my throat suddenly drier than dry. "And you have children with him?"

"We have a son." She shakes her head, tears welling in her eyes. "I was pregnant again last May. But he came home in a dark mood. I asked him a question, something stupid"—she chuckles—"like, 'How's your headache?' because I knew that he had taken a few Tylenols that morning. And he flew off the rails."

I swallow hard, moving the pen to keep myself focused, although my hands are shaking uncontrollably. My handwriting has turned illegible.

"And he—he threw me. Against the table, stomach first."

Bile rises.

"It wasn't always like this," she says in a rush, eyes wide as though she's ready to defend him. "He's an incredible man. So loving. No one takes care of me like he does. I don't want to run like this, but my life is ... it's gotten out of control. He's so possessive. It used to be flattering really. He'd pick me up and drop me off. He'd always come to check on me. But then it became ... crazy, like he'd just show up at my work to watch me and send his friends to check on me, and I can't live like this." The tears drip down her face. "I want a life. A new life. I know it might be impossible to leave, but I have to try. And Devon"— she visibly shakes—"I can't have him near his father. I can't. Even if he's never laid a hand on Devon, I don't want his influence, and I don't want Devon paying for his father's sins. In our world, there's always payment."

I shake my head, trying not to emotionally crumble from her charged words. "I hear you. And we're going to take every step we can to keep you safe."

I take her hand, and she looks up, eyes filled with water.

"But, if he knows I'm staying here," she continues, "he's going to look for me. For his son. He won't let us go without a fight. He told me to come over and bring Devon to him. I texted him to get out of it. Said I was going to visit my sister on the outskirts of Vegas. But my sister doesn't live in Vegas anymore. She used to dance, but then she married Jacob, and he made her quit and move to Utah. But Marcus doesn't know. Not yet at least." She raises a skinny arm, staring at a thin black watch on her wrist. "And he's already threatened me. He knows I want to go ..."

"Listen, I know it feels like you're the only one, but you're not. Eve Petrov runs this place. And she has helped so many women just like you escape abuse. You have to trust in her. The rooms are clean and fresh. You and Devon will be safe here. There's security, too." I quickly jot down a note that we'll need increased security for Alicia and her son.

"What about school for Devon? He's in first grade."

"Once we file the paperwork, his current school will be notified that he is not allowed to be picked up by anyone other than you."

"How quickly can that be done?"

"Very quickly. Eve has connections at the courthouse. She'll handle it today."

"But Marcus, he's not your average bad guy. There's something else you need to know." Her face darkens.

"What is it?" I ask, my voice a strangled whisper.

"He's a biker. His road name's Lion, and he's president of the Death Crusade, MC. Most of the brothers in the club are veterans. They're good at tracking. They'll find me."

We both pause, but before my silence can be construed as fear, I tell her, "You'll be safe here. Trust me."

"He'll kill me and take my son. He wasn't always like this—"

"We're going to set you up and make sure we do what we need to ensure your safety and your son's. Give me a few minutes to sort all of this, and I'll be back. Do you want another coffee?"

She shakes her head, crying into her knuckles, and I step out.

Locking myself in my office, I lean against the door. The parallels. I feel them. Is this Slade? Is this what I'm doing, too? Slade has a temper and a dark side. Slade is erratic. Dangerous even.

"No," I say out loud.

I'm totally fine, and Slade is nothing like this biker, Lion. Absolutely not the same man.

Oh God.

Reentering the room, I bring my focus back to the task at hand, separating myself from this woman, who is not me, nothing like me, and Lion is nothing like Slade, and I handle her situation like the strong woman I am.

WHEN SLADE COMES to pick me up from work, I find him hanging out on a park bench, smoking a cigarette. When he spots me, I give him a small wave, and he runs over, fiercely hugging me. I'm so emotional. Relieved to see him, angry that he is back here to pick me up. I remind myself that I'm not Alicia, but then again, what if I am? What if I'm just like her, and Slade is just like Lion?

"Missed you," he says into my hair.

I dig my nose into his chest. He smells like laundry, smoke, deodorant, and something uniquely him. In his warmth, I calm down, reminding myself that Slade isn't long-term. He's just for now. In this moment, things are fine. I want to enjoy it. I smile up at him, wanting to be enough for this man. Wanting to heal him. Wanting him to talk to me about last night and this morning and to tell me I'm just overreacting. He's nothing like these disturbed men I've been hearing about. He made a mistake, letting me sit alone in a shady parking lot. I surprised him by waking him up, and he sleeps armed because that's how he's been trained. He doesn't realize it yet, but I know how much he cares about me. I can feel it. Am I making excuses? Yes. But they are all valid.

His eyes are still tinged with red. He looks so broken that I can't bear to ask. I can't afford to lose him or to cross some line that would have him turning from me. Not when we only have a week left. The clock ticks with my impending departure. I thought that an end date on this relationship would mean I could feel free to do as I pleased or to say what I wanted, but now, with the way I feel about him, what started out as a selfish affair has turned into so much more. I want him, but he's so damaged that I don't know what he's capable of. Hurting me? Loving me? Which is it?

He opens the car door, and I step inside.

A few minutes into our drive, he asks, "You okay?" His eyes move between me and the road. "You're quiet."

"Yeah. Just met this woman today, and it shook me up."

"Want to tell me about it?"

I shrug. "She came in near hysteria. Her husband is this guy, Lion. He's the president of a motorcycle club."

His eyes show nothing, but a small tremor moves through his neck. Are these men connected somehow?

"I don't want you anywhere near that woman." His voice is hard and worried.

"Why?" I poke. "That's the work Eve does. She helps women like her." I need to know if there's something between these men. I see their parallels, but what if it's more than that?

Abruptly, Slade pulls the car over. "I said, stay away from her, do you hear me? I know that guy. He's fucked in the head. Did he threaten to find her?" His brows lower, breaths shortening.

I nod, staying silent. He's ... anxious for me.

He curses. "I'm going to add some of my guys to do rounds in the area at night and during the day. You call me right away if you ever feel off."

"You're worried?" My voice comes out breathy and confused.

"Of course I'm worried. I care about you, Lauren. More than you know. I realize you're helping these women, and they've got bad lives. But I happen to know that Lion is worse than most. Promise me you'll call if you even feel the air change. Always trust your instincts, okay?"

I stay silent, watching his anxiety ride over my safety. Holding my hand, he gets back on the road. I feel satisfied that the parallels between Lion and Slade start and end with the fact that they're both veterans. Slade would never harm me the way Lion harms Alicia.

I'm sure of it.

We pull up in front of the Milestone.

With a chaste kiss, he tells me, "I'll see you later."
After I get out of the truck, he speeds off.

GETTING BACK TO MY ROOM, I decide I'm going to stop stressing and take a load off. My mind has been moving so quickly between Slade and work that I feel exhausted.

I order a spread from room service, strip off my clothes, and put on one of the hotel's soft terry-cloth robes. It feels heavenly against my skin. When the food comes, I eat the roasted chicken with grilled vegetables and a hummus plate with pita chips while watching back-to-back episodes of *Real Housewives*. It's as though all my years of borderline starvation have caught up to me. Maybe it's the fresh mountain air or all of the incredible sex. Oh, who am I kidding? It's the stress of Slade that's gotten me so turned inside out. Nothing but food will settle me.

Whatever.

I'm absolutely famished and enjoying every single morsel entering my mouth—guilt, calorie count, and stress be damned. Meanwhile, the show has me simultaneously laughing and yelling at the TV. It's keeping my mind occupied on nonsense instead of focusing on reality.

TWO HOURS LATER, I'm plucked, shaved, and completely made up. My hair is ironed sleek and straight, and my outfit is a simple, short black dress and strappy Manolo heels. I didn't bring any fancy outfits other than this one. Even without any options, I feel confident with my look.

At nine o'clock sharp, the bell to my room rings. I slowly open it, only to see Slade's mouth dropping as he takes me in from my heels to my eyes. He's wearing a black suit and white shirt, which is what I assume is his work uniform for events like these. Slade is typically so casual that seeing him all dressed like this turns my insides to fire. He stands there, still, without saying a word or taking his eyes off me.

Finally, he says, "Lauren." My name rolls off his breath. "You ready?"

I nod, clutching my black purse to my side.

"Do you have a shawl or jacket or something? Eve was complaining that it's chilly in the restaurant."

I turn back and take out a folded black pashmina scarf from one of the cabinet drawers. It's not what I would choose if I had my full wardrobe in front of me, but it'll do.

He takes my hand as we walk into the elevator. The ride downstairs is quiet and warm as his thumb rubs up and down over my knuckles.

"You look incredible. I had to physically restrain myself from stripping you in your room."

"Is that right?" Beneath my question is a dare and request. My insides clench.

"Yes. But I know all about you and your fancy dresses ..." His voice trails off as he checks me out.

I laugh because my wardrobe isn't the easiest to put on or take off, and no one knows it better than Slade.

"Well, for your information"—the elevator door opens, and we step out—"there are no buttons on this one, not even a zipper."

"Easy access, eh?"

"Maybe ... for the right man," I sass.

He laughs again. "Baby, I'm the only man."

I raise my eyebrows, but he ignores my attitude laced in question, holding my hand harder to his. We walk through the gorgeous, serene lobby to see a long red carpet outside of the entrance to the restaurant.

Slade clears his throat. "I'll be working at the party. But you'll enjoy yourself. Some big celebrities and fashion people are here."

His demeanor shifts as we get closer to the restaurant but not in a bad way. His chest inflates, and his stride quickens. This is Slade in his element, focused and razor sharp. He cracks his knuckles, and my insides clench. He's so hot; I can barely stand it.

He bends down to kiss my lips, and I lean up into him, wrapping my arms around his neck. His warm tongue is slow, deep, and delicious in my mouth, full of promise for more later. I should be afraid, but with the way he's treating me now with so much kindness and love, it isn't hard to tell myself that this morning wasn't as bad as I thought.

I'm glassy-eyed when he lets me go, moving his lips to my ear. "Only man," he says protectively.

Chills slide over my arms.

When he leaves, I'm breathless with need. But then, like an unannounced rainstorm, my internal alarm shrieks in warning. I have to figure out what's going on with him. It's as though all of the events of this morning have been erased from his memory and mine. It wasn't my imagination; what I saw was real. He's acting like all is well, and nothing is off. I know in my gut that this issue with him is only growing by the day.

No, I won't let myself freak out. I want to enjoy the evening. It's been ages since I actually had fun somewhere. I'll have a few cocktails with Eve and let loose. Tomorrow though, I'll deal with Slade.

I open my bag and check the time on my phone. I'll get a drink at the bar and hopefully bump into Eve, who should be inside. There's no way they're on the carpet, posing for any photos. As much as Vincent is famous in name, he's very careful to not show his face anywhere on the internet or on social media in particular. Eve mentioned how Vincent already paid off the photographers to exclude him in every single photo.

I enter without nerves, feeling back in my element. In LA, club and restaurant openings are part of my social calendar. After years of being in the scene, my friends and I know all of the big restaurateurs, who love to have hot, single women frequenting their parties. Even while engaged, Sanam still ditches Reza to be at the big parties.

"Once you leave the circuit, there might not be a spot for you again," she once cautioned.

Hook, the newest addition to the Milestone's restaurant list, is already full of people standing and mingling while waiters walk around with trays of delicious hors d'oeuvres. I'm offered a miniature lettuce wrap filled with vegetable squab, and I take it. It melts in my mouth, but I resist the temptation to call the waiter back for more. Other than that yoga class, I haven't been exercising at all. I'm sure I'll pay for these calories in pounds. Whatever. I'll just add it to my list of things I'm ignoring right now.

A line of chefs works behind a beautiful wooden sushi bar, slicing fish and putting together small plates. As the newest restaurant at the Mile, the entire event is full-on glamour. I recognize some famous faces, including the newest Victoria's Secret model. The crowd is New York and LA's finest, complete with A-list celebrities, just as Slade promised.

I order a dirty martini with Grey Goose vodka when Eve comes up next to me. We hug, and she looks absolutely gorgeous.

"Lauren," she starts, "Slade is seriously doing well for your complexion. I mean, you're glowing."

"He is amazing in bed. Like, off the charts," I brag, making the conscious choice to let tonight be about enjoyment and not hysteria.

Eve is so proud of her man. There is no way I'm taking any of that happiness away with my personal drama.

"Let's toast to that!"

She raises her flirty-looking pink martini, and I do the same. We clink our glasses and take our sips when I feel a body behind mine. Thinking it's Slade, I do an about-face with a huge smile. Who I see is super hot but not the man I was expecting.

Tall, dark, and sexy doesn't seem to mind my overly happy greeting. "Hey there, beautiful."

The way he's staring at me has my stomach fluttering.

I pause, mouth agape before I erupt in laughter. "Sorry for that wide-eyed hello. I thought you were someone else for a minute there."

He puts out his hand, brown eyes twinkling. "Alexander." His hand is soft, but his grip is warm.

"I'm Lauren."

"What brings you here to the opening?" He leans casually against the bar, raising a scruffy chin to the bartender before moving his gaze back to mine.

Dark, wavy hair, slightly too long, brushes against his forehead. I have the urge to put my fingers through the soft strands and push it back away from his face. He's handsome. More than that, he's a type I know well.

"I'm actually visiting a friend of mine who lives here." I turn to Eve and wink. "And you?"

"This is my restaurant." He turns to the eager bartender. "Macallan, rocks, please."

"Right away, sir."

Alexander looks back to me, and I can't stop the gush of, "Oh my God, really? It's beautiful! And the food is amazing." It seems that old habits die hard. "Have you been in this business a while?" My eyes widen, as they've done countless times before. A nagging voice tells me this is wrong, but I swat it away. My feelings for Slade are so strong, but Slade's not—

Eve whispers in my ear, "I'm going to check on Vincent. Have fun!" She gives me a dorky thumbs-up before stepping away.

I know how much she loves Slade, but we both know he's unavailable. Unfortunately, she has no idea just how unavailable he really is. My heart is at war.

Alexander continues, "This is actually the second Hook I've opened. First is in the Meatpacking District in New York City. But I'm planning on opening another in London within the next sixth months. Have you been to Lao?"

"Of course! I was just there last week in Vegas, and I love the one in LA."

"Those are mine, too." He gets slightly closer.

I can smell his expensive cologne, which is nothing like Slade, who's all tobacco and fresh laundry. Slade, who washes me and feeds me and—

"So, where do you live?" he asks, inching closer again.

"I'm in LA." I move an errant hair behind my ear, feeling almost nervous to have his attention. Even though I have nothing to feel bad about, in my gut, I know it's wrong.

Slade's words, "*Only man,*" echo around my mind.

"I'm from New York, but I spend lots of time out in California, too."

"Is that right?" My voice comes out shaky, the excited confidence from before dwindling.

He continues to talk, selling himself to me in all the ways he thinks will impress me. He mentions boating in the South of France this past summer, and I think about Slade shirtless on Lake Powell. He drops a line about visiting a new resort out in Cabo for Christmas and the New Year. My chest sinks. Where will I be during that time? Alone, back in LA. I suddenly feel sick. I want to leave.

But, of course, I do no such thing. I smile and nod, acting like I'm listening when, really, I'm waiting for an appropriate moment to excuse myself. And, with that thought, a chill roves up and down my arms; it feels as though I'm being watched. I turn left and right, but nothing seems out of the ordinary, and no one is looking at me. I wish I were wearing higher heels, so I could at least have a better view.

"You all right?" he asks, concerned, turning around for a moment as though to make sure nothing's wrong.

"If you don't mind, I'm going to use the ladies' room."

"Sure. Hopefully, I'll see you back here."

I strut off without a word, searching for the nearest restroom. The entire place feels too full. I can't be in a crowd like this. I've got to get out of here. Panic blooms in my stomach.

What starts out as a polite, "Excuse me," as I shuffle through the crowd becomes pushes. I can't stand here another second. The exit? It's no longer in my sight. I'm in the middle of champagne smiles and diamond stud earrings, and my eyes begin to water.

Someone takes my hand, but before I can see his face, he pivots and pulls me away. His grip isn't soft. It's rough and callous and heavy. I look up and see the back of a buzzed head. It's Slade. He briskly walks me straight through the employee exit until we're face-to-face in the dark night.

"Who the fuck was that guy back there?"

His interrogation has me shaking my head in confusion.

"Who?" I ask, breathless.

"That prissy fuck!" he yells.

"I walked away from him. And are you kidding me right now?" Anger takes the place of anxiety as I practically stand on my tiptoes to get closer to his face. "You have no right, Slade. I'm leaving in days. And you won't talk to me. You won't give me what I'm asking for."

"Oh, is that right?"

He lifts me up, pressing my back against the wall. It feels like concrete, scraping the back of my shoulder blades. I'm too riled up to tell him to put me down. To tell him that it hurts. I don't want to admit how soft I am or how fragile I feel.

"Last I checked, I've given you exactly what you asked for," he growls, putting his nose on my neck and breathing in, scenting me up and down my neck and down between my breasts, palming my ass and spreading me open.

Oh God. I can feel myself dripping. Angry, confused sex is a very bad idea. I'm mad but so turned on; my entire brain moves to static. I grip the back of his neck, shivering with want.

He takes one hand to unbutton his own pants before tearing the bottom of my dress.

"You're bare," he whispers, licking the tops of my breasts.

"Underwear lines."

Chuckling, he pulls down on my neckline, tonguing the lace over my nipples. Without any preamble, he slams into me. My mouth drops open in shock as he starts fucking me in earnest. I want it, but I'm also caught off guard. My back painfully rubs against the wall. I want to tell him to wait a second because all of this is happening almost too quickly, but my body has its own thought process. My insides are clenching with his rhythm, and I'm sure he can feel my body eagerly taking him in. My body betrays me because she loves it. His huge length hits every spot so deeply; it's only minutes before I'm shuddering with release.

He finishes right after me, zipping himself back up. My dress is tattered, and I already know, without looking, that my back is bloody. The burn makes itself known in every move I make. He didn't use a condom. Luckily, I'm on the pill.

I'm shaking when he says, "I'll take you back to my place."

I nod, unable to speak. I can't go back inside with a torn dress and bloody back, can I? I swallow down an awkward laugh. Of course not. The guests would likely call security, assuming I crashed the party. He takes my hand, and I wince with my first step.

He seems to notice my agony when he says, "Oh shit. Turn around."

Slade takes out his phone, flipping on the flashlight to check my back. He curses before calling someone. "I've got a personal thing. Can you cover me for an hour?" Pause. "Yeah." Pause. "Thanks."

Without words, he gently helps me into his truck. As he drives, our hands are threaded together. He lifts them up, kissing my knuckles and apologizing under his breath for hurting me. Mumbling, "I didn't mean it." And, "So fucking sorry."

Alicia's words bounce through my head. *"He wasn't always like this."*

I think back to the shooting in Vegas. He didn't have sex with me that night because he didn't want to hurt me or take advantage. It's my fault that I didn't speak up this time. I should have told him no and used my words. Instead, I just moaned. How can I blame him? *Excuses.*

I turn to my right, and I hiss from the stinging pain.

In his warm home, he brings me into his bathroom and wipes down my back with a washcloth dipped in hot water and soap before covering my abrasions with Neosporin. Gathering me into his chest, he brings me into his bed and tucks me into his sheets. I haven't said a word since we got here, but he doesn't seem to notice. When I'm set, he puts his shoes back on.

"I'll be back in a few hours. Do you need anything else?"

I shake my head. And then he leaves. I curl into the fetal position in his bed, smelling his sheets when I finally break down and cry.

18

Slade

I get back into the truck, cursing. I'm a total fuckup. Even when I'm straight, I continue to hurt her. I tore up her back, for Christ's sake! What's wrong with me? Speeding back to the Mile, I ask myself what it is I think I'm doing with a woman like her. My head pounds as my demons begin talking over one another. I need to go back home, have a few drinks, and take more pills if I'm going to survive another night. With a shaking hand, I flip open my glove compartment and take out three. I'm not sure which ones they are, but whatever. Just need something to numb my brain.

What are my options? I could tell her why I take them, so she can stay in safety. I can just be honest, tell her what's going on in my head, and stop the hiding and the lying. But do I trust her to keep my secret? If she tells Eve and Eve tells Vincent, my career is done. Vincent is my best friend, but after Eve, work will always come first. He's ruthless when it comes to cutting shit that's bad for business. Why would I be different? *No.* I slam the steering wheel. I'll keep popping the pills. They'll keep me afloat until this issue I've got disappears on its own. I have about a month's supply right now. That's enough. It's got to be.

I pull back into the restaurant, my eyes not far from this asshole Alexander. I know exactly who he is. Before Vincent gave him the lease to open Hook, I did a full background check. Vincent only wants the cleanest businessmen involved in the Mile.

In addition to Hook, he owns restaurants all over the United States and abroad. He's also in the club business. Never been married. Went to NYU. Began with small club promotions and slowly built up his own brand. The guy is completely kosher, and I want to wring his goddamn neck. He's exactly who Lauren should be with. Successful. Good-looking. And fucking sane.

I'm looking around the room, heart pumping wildly.

"You doing good?" Vincent asks, eyes lowered. He sees something's up with me.

"Yep. I'm going to watch the back entrance for a while." I move away, walking the perimeter of the restaurant until I find a nice dark corner to watch the crowd.

He follows at my heels.

"I didn't say I was finished talking to you." He turns me around. "Where the fuck is your head, Slade? You're falling, and don't think I don't see it."

"Falling?" I repeat, laughing. "I'm straighter than ever."

He crosses his arms in front of his chest. "Spoke to Rob, who told me he gave you some drugs to help you calm down and sleep. Have you tried to score more from anyone else? Harder shit?" His words are spoken dead seriously.

In another life, Vincent was the prince of the underground. He's fierce in his loyalty and friendship. But cross him or lie, and he'll cut you off at the knees.

Does he know about Lion and the MC? My fear becomes palpable. Without Vincent and the Milestone, I'll have nothing.

He swallows before a long, tense silence fills the space between us. I clench my fists.

"Your stone face doesn't fool me, Slade. I watched you on the boat.

See the changes in your demeanor; you've become erratic. It started slow, but I worry you'll become unreliable. You've got to get help ..." He pauses, the *or else* hanging in the air.

"No," I spit out.

"You know I love you like a brother. But I'm not asking you. I'm telling you. And if you refuse? We're done. I can't have my head of security be in denial about a drug problem. We have a huge project on our hands, bringing water onto the reservation. How can I do this with a man who lacks discipline and refuses to admit he has an addiction? You have to face this shit head-on. Getting help and facing reality makes you a man, not a pussy."

"I didn't see you opening your fucking heart after the shit you went through."

"That isn't true." He shakes his head. "First off, I had my woman by my side. We spoke to therapists separately and together."

My heart picks up. "That's fine. But it ain't me."

"Well, until you do, get the fuck out of here. I hate to show tough love, but having a dark undercurrent isn't healthy. We've got a billion-dollar operation here. A slipup won't be acceptable. And I'm not going to wait for it to happen. Get help or go home."

He stares, waiting for me to cave.

But I can't.

Instead, I turn away. It's time to go.

When I open my truck's door, Lauren's smell lingers. All I want to do is run back to my place and see her. My life continues to unravel, but at least I've got a few more days where she's near me. My heart beats straight through my chest. What did I take? I'm not even sure. I open the car window before pulling out a cigarette, smoking in a chain until I pull up to my driveway.

I quietly open and close my front door, not wanting to wake her. Pulling off my clothes, I watch her sleeping form in the dark. I enter my bathroom and turn on the sink. Cupping ice-cold water in my hands, I wash my face before scrubbing my hands with soap. Filling my cupped palms with water, I drink some.

My thoughts turn dark with how little control I have in my life. I wish I could go back in time and do things over, but I can't. I've lost my job, the one solid thing that's been giving my life meaning since leaving the SEAL Teams. What about the new construction project I've been helping with? Is that over now, too? Will Vincent no longer hire the veterans because of my fuckup?

I'm lucid enough to understand how desperate I feel. Getting help can't be the answer. It would only make shit worse. If I spoke about how I killed Rex ... if I spoke about my past and all the shit I'd done ... it would unleash the hardest memories, and that's something I can't do. I shiver, wishing I could add a padlock to my memories. I swipe across my eyes with my forearm, feeling the wetness coat my cheeks.

Initially, the move to Nevada was phenomenal. My memories of war were sealed in a large compartment in the back of my brain, buried securely between the fresh mountain air and heavy workload of starting a business. I was obsessed with working. I slept at night, only to be ready the next morning. I exercised and trained my body, so I could be efficient for the job.

I took a few days off to rest. My coffeemaker beeped, and an old memory sprang from some hidden compartment in my brain, pushing itself to the forefront. Since then, the random drip has turned into a flow. It's been an endless cycle of horrible nightmares, followed by restlessness as my memories continue to strike at random. I try to ignore them, but they're pecking on my subconscious and looming above me, just waiting for another moment to attack. I can't get relief, except with the drugs. Lauren helps, but I'm afraid for her safety when I'm not medicated.

I grip the sink, dropping my head low. *This isn't me, but it's me.*

God, I never should have brought Lauren into this. She senses everything and is trying to excuse my behavior.

The temptation to cry rises, but I splash water over my face, forcing my body to calm down. Men don't cry.

Climbing into the bed, I pull her soft body to mine, trying to enjoy this moment with my head lucid before the drugs go into effect. My hands glide into all that gorgeous, thick hair and soft, lush skin. It's overwhelming, how good she feels in my arms. I love this woman. I just want to close my eyes for a few minutes, and then I'll get up and take my pills. Just ... a few ... minutes ...

19

Lauren

I'm warm in bed, woken up from cursing. White puffs of smoke billow outside his bedroom window. He must be sitting on his small stoop outside, smoking. Climbing out of my warm, blanketed cocoon, I try not to shiver. The clock on the bedside table tells me it's 3:02 a.m.

I unlock the window before sliding it upward. "Come inside?" My voice cracks into the night. The cool air runs beneath his T-shirt I'm wearing and over my skin, prickling at the deep scratches on my back.

He turns his head and pulls out another. "I'll be in when I'm fuckin' ready, man." His voice is hard and brusque. A new cigarette enters his mouth. He lights up before wringing his hands, talking to someone I can't see.

My legs shake as I take a deep inhale of his exhales. It's leftover smoke mixed with his essence. I swallow it down.

In the middle of the night, without my strength of mind, my own subconscious slams straight into the forefront of my thoughts. How long have I been denying the fact that Slade has a bad case of PTSD?

Since the night of the shooting in Vegas. He turned into someone else in that club.

I shuffle to his nightstand and open the drawer, finding a clear Ziploc bag filled with what looks like an assortment of tablets in a variety of colors, all mixed together. I shake my head side to side, not wanting to believe what I'm seeing. *It can't be.* But it's here and ... undeniable.

Part of Slade is still in Afghanistan. The zoning out, followed by angry spells. It's all here, written in neon lights. I should have pried. Instead, I closed my eyes, pretending it was all fine. I didn't really want to know. Because the truth is, I only had two options: face the facts and turn away from him or ignore them and stay. I wanted him too badly, so I dug my head in the sand. But, now, I'm in love with him —and he's broken and wrecked.

When I move back to the window, his chiseled face is slightly lit by the red glow of his cigarette, sheared head dipped low. Mumbling to himself, he's speaking words I cannot hear. Suddenly, he stands. Like a criminal, I drop down to the floor, so he won't see me and think I was prying. What if he knows I opened his drawer? I move my gaze to the bedside table. Would he realize? Could he? I shiver.

Heavy steps come into the house, and the door creaks before shutting. I feel overwhelmed and insecure as kitchen drawers open and slam shut. Liquor cabinet maybe? Nothing I say will work. Is there a point to talk? Minutes later, another cabinet door opens and shuts. I'm not prepared for this! Quietly, I close the window and jump back into the bed, pretending I never left.

Closing my eyes, I feign sleep. He enters the bedroom. I open one eye. Slade can barely stand, smelling like warm smoke and bourbon.

"We'll be set to clear shortly," he shouts.

Is he on the phone? I squint both eyes. No. He's ... talking to the wall, to himself.

"Get some shut-eye, boys. Big day tomorrow." He starts laughing. "Shut up, Rex!" He smiles wide, jokingly.

Slade lays his large body on the bedroom floor and settles. Tears drip down my face in silence. Controlling a cry hurts like hell, my body coiling to stop from gasping. He's set in the fetal position, his spirit far from the safety of home.

I can't stay here on the bed while he's down on the cold wooden floor. Still, I wait five minutes to make sure he's truly sleeping. I watch the clock, keeping myself frozen until I'm sure the time has passed. Stepping off the bed, I pull the sheets and pillows with me and join him on the floor. I wonder if he skipped the drugs tonight. Maybe that's why he's vocal. Lifting his head, I place it on the pillow and cover us with the sheets. What I'm doing is so dangerous, but my heart won't let me do otherwise.

Sometime in the night, he moves above me. "Babe?"

I hum as he kisses the top of my head, my hair, and my shoulders. Warm lips press against my body as my shorts slide down. At last, my body awakens, not able to help itself against the massive man, his hardness pushing and wanting. I know who he is, and my body responds accordingly.

But does he know me?

"Slade," I whisper, "who am I?"

"You're mine, Lauren," he replies, pressing his forehead against mine. "Always mine."

His large body shudders as his thick fingers thread through my thin ones. Entering, he pushes within me as though he can't get close enough or deep enough. We slide against the floor from his movements until the wall stops us, my back burning. Slade clutches my body against his, like a line for his life. His desperation, like sweat, drips all over me.

I score his shoulders with my nails, replying with my body, *I'm here, and you're with me.*

My back burns, but I know he wouldn't hear me even if I spoke. He holds me tighter—so tight, too tight. I can't get out of his grip. Do I want to? It hurts to love him.

He needs me right now, and while my thinking is screwed up, I want to be the woman he possesses.

This entire night has been horrible, I think as he slams into me again and again.

"How much will I sacrifice?" I whisper blindly into the dark.

His hot, muscled body replies wordlessly as he continues to pound my body. Suddenly and without any warning, I splinter into a million pieces around him. My body has betrayed me.

"Mine," he shouts shortly after, exploding within me.

Heavy hands squeeze my torn back. He's pressing me so hard into his chest. My tears start to flow, salty and heavy.

He rolls over, and then, immediately, he falls asleep. I gingerly stand up, taking myself into the bathroom. I clean up before staring at my back in the mirror. Blood is everywhere.

20

Slade

The next morning, I wake up. Lauren's gone. She's not in the shower, and she's not in the kitchen. I pick up the phone, calling Vincent. My heart is in my fucking throat.

"Yo."

"Where's Lauren?" I ask without preamble, pacing back and forth across my bedroom floor.

"Hang on." The phone momentarily breaks before I hear, "Eve?"

"Yeah, babe?" I hear her soft voice in the background.

"Where's Lauren?"

A muffled response.

The phone crackles before Vincent's voice comes back on the line, clear as day. "You okay? Where are you right now, Slade?" There is an undercurrent of worry in Vincent's voice.

"Home," I grunt, my heart pounding.

"I'm stopping over."

"Like hell you are. Where. The fuck. Is Lauren?" I can feel my muscles vibrate.

"We don't know ... but you sound like shit. Let me just come over and—"

I hang up the phone and wash up in record time, riding my bike over to the Mile. Lauren cannot leave my home. No fucking way. She owes me more time. She swore she'd be here for two weeks, and she still has days left. I expect her to spend them in my bed with me. I'll convince her to come back. She has to.

I park right in front of the main entrance, not bothering to park in the lot. Sprinting through the white marble lobby, I jump in the elevator. Luckily, I go directly up to her floor. Strutting down the hall, I get to her room and knock.

The door swings open.

"Hey—" She pauses in shock.

Clearly, she didn't think I was the one knocking. I step inside.

"Where the hell did you go?" My voice comes out louder and angrier than I intended, but fuck that shit. I'm mad. How dare she just get up and run. We've got a few days left.

"You've got to calm down, Slade." Her voice quivers.

"Calm down? I'm not going to calm down when you ran out on me in the middle of the night after making me wild for you!" I yell, pivoting left and slamming my fist into the drywall.

She jumps, and I turn back toward her, taking a step closer. I can't control *this*. My feelings are bigger than I am. She looks so scared, like I'm a goddamn menace.

I swallow, shaking my head. She's misunderstanding. I need to get her to understand.

"Just wait. I'm not going to hurt you, Lauren—"

"Stay away from me," she pants, backing up.

Her fear riles me up. How dare she be afraid of me. I'd never hurt her!

She continues moving away.

"Just—fucking—stop running from me!"

Her head shakes side to side, and then she spins around, running into the bathroom and shutting the door with a slam.

I bang against the door, screaming, "Open up! Open the fucking door!"

"Get out, Slade! I'm leaving this place. I refuse to stay here near you," she yells.

I walk up and down the small hotel room, fury boiling in my veins. I just need some benzos. That'll calm me down. I feel in my pockets, but they're empty. In my anger, I left without them.

You're a junkie, my conscience chimes. *You're fucked up.*

I drop myself into the corner of her room and begin doing push-ups. *I need to calm down. I have to relax.* I repeat this to myself as I pump out fifty reps.

Finally, I settle some.

I walk back to the bathroom door, knocking. "I'm not going to hurt you, Lauren. I won't. Come out." I keep my voice steady, clenching and then unclenching my fists. My emotions are haywire.

"You're not stable," she answers through the door, her voice stronger and more confident than before. "When I'm with you, I don't know which version of you I'm going to get. Yes, I have feelings for you. I-I ..." Her voice trails off on a stammer.

I want to hear the words *I love you.* I realize it's too soon. People don't normally fall in love so fast. But we did, and I know it as the truth. I see it in her eyes. In the way she moves. Lauren loves me, and I love her. Still, I hold my breath, waiting for them. What if she needs more time for the truth to reach her? I know what I know. Can she see that I would do anything for her? She must know at least that.

"We're good together," she continues. "But you aren't dealing with your issues, and it's too much for me to handle. I'm getting scared." She gasps. "I see these women come in and out of the Center, and what's the difference between them and me? They date men who claim love, but they are abusive."

My eyes widen. Abuse? What the fuck is she talking about?

"I tried to ignore the parallels," she continues, "but they're there."

I hear her crying. I'm helpless. I need to comfort her, but she won't open the door.

Wait. What did she say?

"Abusive?" I huff out loud. "Parallels?"

It's as if she's speaking Chinese right now. I close my eyes and lean my head on the door. What she's saying is causing me physical pain. My chest feels splintered, cracked.

"Yes. You get up in my face if I cross an imaginary line. You're taking drugs, Slade. I-I know you are," she stutters.

Drugs? She ... knows. Shame and fury enter the spaces in my chest. I'm eroding.

"There's a crack in the rock. A heavy rain comes down and seeps into that crack along with sediment and natural debris, which then carve away at the inside edges." Eve's voice echoes.

She said this, right? Lake Powell? Yes. No. My mind can't be trusted.

I look down. I'm sweating. My T-shirt is soaked.

"I found a baggie of pills in your nightstand," Lauren says. "You drink constantly. Your smoking is nonstop. You wake up in the night, talking to yourself. You're sleeping on the floor, next to the bed. You need help, Slade. And last night ..." She pauses, and then the door swings open. Her face is soaked with tears.

I suck in a hard breath. My sweet girl is in pain.

"Last night was frightening. You hurt me against the wall in the alley."

She steps forward, smacking my chest. My mouth gapes open, but no air gets through.

"You woke up around three a.m., and you were outside and then on the ground. Then, we had sex. I've been ignoring all the signs, but they're there. And I'd be with you through it, but you won't talk to me. You know how I feel about you. But you won't tell me what's happening, and you're lying!" she screams loudly, punching me in the chest, hurt and angry and in fucking pain.

My temper flares up, giving me fuel to speak.

I step up to her terrified face, covering her mouth with my hand. "Enough!" I scream.

I can't hear this shit anymore. I'm frantic. I take her by the arms, shaking her. I need to keep her quiet. She's making it all sound worse than it is. I've got to make her understand!

"I'm fine. I'm going to be fine!"

What the fuck is happening here? To me? To us?

My shirt is heavy from sweat. Her face is completely terrified. I stop.

A flash in front of my eyes. Rex crumbling to the floor. He's on fire. I've got to get to him ...

Lauren screams. I blink. I'm hurting her.

Turning her body around, I hold her wrists tightly behind her back with one hand and lift her shirt with the other. I need to see it with my own eyes. Her back is ... it's ... raw. Sliced. Cut up and streaked. Blue bruises line her shoulder blades.

Is this me? Did I do this? *Who am I?*

"Let me go," she cries, begging. Her face is red and wet.

But I can't let go. I need to refocus my brain. My anger is opaque smoke, infiltrating every sinew within my body and impossible to see through. I need to take something. Without drugs, I'm insane.

I turn her back around, scanning her stomach, wondering what I've done. She has handprints on her hips.

From me? I can't remember. *We had sex last night. I was rough.*

I'm trembling as a fresh round of sweat breaks out on my forehead. I'm a lowlife. Damaged goods. I finally release her wrists.

"You were awake," she sobs. "Talking. I can't—" Her breaths are erratic.

Like a thump, my chest shuts. It's a horrible suction. A vacuum. The whole world zeroes in on me, like one of those TV shows where the lens focuses on one character, and everything else becomes a blurred static. Everything I've been hiding, maneuvering around, and controlling has been slammed back into my face. As though every private truth of mine has been scooped out from my lungs and then flung from Lauren's mouth for me to eat. Emotional force-feeding. I step backward. I made a mistake and should have listened to my gut. I don't deserve Lauren. I don't deserve anyone. I'm nothing but smashed glass.

She puts a hand to her mouth, as though realizing I'm falling to pieces. "Slade, I don't—just wait a second—we can—"

Lifting a hand in the air, I tell her, "Don't talk to me." I turn away, walking swiftly out of the room as she follows at my heels.

"Please—Slade—"

I ignore her. I can barely hear her actually. All I hear is a loud swooshing sound between my ears. Somehow, I find myself on my bike, turning on the engine. I see Lauren from my side-eye, her quickly moving mouth, but no words are coming out. I take off into the mountains, leaving her in the dust.

When I get to the base of the mountain, I pull out my gun from my saddlebag along with a flask full of liquor. Walking up the trail, I ask myself how I got here. My mind wanders to last year at Joe's gym. That's where it all began, I suppose. With Joe, the gym's owner, and James, another trainer, getting punched in the face.

"How many times do I have to tell ya? These men who come in here to train with us aren't actually trying to fight. Jesus Christ, Slade. For one seventy-five an hour, they just want to sweat a little bit and then go home to tell their friends they train at a boxing gym. They wanna tell people they box. They don't actually wanna box." His jaw twitches as he raises his hands in the air in an animated gesture. "All you need to do is make 'em sweat. Can you do that for me?"

"Yes, sir." I can feel my nostrils flare as I take a deep inhale and exhale through my nose, the black T-shirt I'm wearing stretching against my chest.

The last thing I would do is tell him that Leon, the asshole finance guy I'm paid to train, kept talking shit and asking me—no, begging me—to take a good swing at him. Idiot thought he could take it—from an ex-Navy SEAL, no less. These Wall Street types think they own the goddamn world. They want to prove their superiority every-fuckin'-where. I've got to keep this job. The money from the house sale has been floating me, but I need an income.

Joe is right. These guys are here for a good sweat. It's glorified cardio, so they can look chiseled at the beach in the Caribbean or wherever these rich guys vacation. They don't actually want to fight. God forbid they damage their pretty faces.

Regardless, I'm not a man who gives excuses. At the end of the day, I hit that asshole too hard in the face. Sure, he'd asked for it. But I did it, and now, my job is on the line.

"Can you?" he asks again angrily. "I gave you this job as a favor. I know leaving the service is hard. I remember it, son. But you cannot take out your aggression here. One more wrong move, and you're out." He points an old finger, crooked from probably multiple breaks, over his shoulder. "Don't make me regret taking you on."

I can see it in his eyes. He hopes it won't come to that. Still, Joe has a business to run, and he can't have a loose cannon on his staff.

We both turn to find James grumbling loudly as he leans against the window facing the street. He's holding an ice pack over his eye.

"What happened to you?" Joe asks, thick white brows furrowed together.

"Borignone," he spits out the last name like a curse. "I can't work with him anymore. He's too big. Too strong. Find someone else, Joe. Boy got out of prison, and I swear, he's twice the size as he was when he went in. He throws punches like his damn life is on the line, and I'm not down with that. Plus, Maria swore she'd divorce me if I came home with another bang to the head. What the fuck am I gonna tell her now?" The right side of his face pulses red, the bruise threatening to be nasty.

"Why'd he hit you? You don't spar."

Baring his teeth, he yells, "I couldn't hold up the damn pad!" His face flashes red, anger covering up embarrassment.

His eyes dare us to laugh. Joe chuckles despite the threat. I try not to, but my smile stretches wide. It's funny.

Like Joe, James's accent is thick New York. Growing up on a farm in Virginia, I never thought anyone actually spoke like these men in real life. Maybe just in the movies. But, as it turns out, the accent is real.

A fire engine goes off somewhere outside, and my heart skips. I'm still not used to the nonstop noise of Manhattan. Close to a year in this city, and sleep is still impossible. I need to leave, but the main question is, Where to?

Joe faces me, a smile moving from ear to ear. "Well, son, looks like today's your lucky day after all. Between the two o' you?" He points to Borignone, who's doing push-ups on a corner mat. "Not sure who's angrier."

I walk into the gym, toward the back. Here he is, the Mafia man. Ex-convict. Son of Antonio Borignone, boss of the largest Mafia on the East Coast. What if I piss him off and he decides to throw his goons on me? I shrug to myself. That would be an ironic way to die. Borignone thinks he's dangerous, but I've got nothing to lose other than my life. I win.

I push my emotions aside as I step over to the hulking lunatic. He hooks two sixteen kilogram kettlebells onto a weight belt around his waist. Pull-ups. I'm impressed, but my face shows nothing.

He completes his set and drops to the ground for push-ups. After that, he asks, "You the new guy? Hope you're ready to spar." His black eyes are hard, as though he's seen some serious damage. I know the look well because I wear it myself. He doesn't look over thirty, but it's obvious he's lived heavy. There's just something about him that's different. Commanding.

"Gotta get permission from Joe." My voice comes out strong and sure.

He laughs. The motherfucker actually cackles at me like I'm some brownnoser.

"Joe knows what I do. If he told you to work with me, it's because he knows you can take a punch." He looks me up and down as though he's estimating my weight.

"Two-oh-five." I crack my knuckles as he moves to tape his. "Don't." I gesture to the white roll in his hands. "It'll weaken your grip."

He looks up at me in silence before nodding. He places the tape by the grimy window and enters the ring. He's bouncing from foot to foot while I confirm with Joe, who shrugs and tells me it's my own life.

It's on.

I pull my shirt off, and he does the same. His shoulder is tatted up with the infamous Borignone insignia, surrounded by an intricate tribal design. We go at it, and I get some good punches in.

I fuckin' love this. Boy is a beast, but it's a damn good thing I am, too. I'm in my element, smiling as my body starts to pound from the grind, the motions natural.

Minutes later, and we're both soaked in sweat.

"Holy fuck, man." He drops his hands to his knees, panting. "You're good. Where'd you learn to fight?"

I throw him a towel. "Navy."

Moving to the water cooler, I pour myself a swallow. He follows behind me.

"Vincent."

He puts out his hand to shake, knuckles red and angry. I take it.

I WALK TO HIGHER GROUND, remembering how it only took a month for Vincent and me to become good friends. Vincent took a chance on me when I was lost, offering me a job any guy on the SEAL Teams would have killed for—head of security at the soon-to-be-famous Milestone. The opportunity spurred me into action, causing me to reconnect with Rob and Mike. The three of us started VST, the Vulcan Security Team. We have plans to expand our operations beyond the Milestone, but with my head all fucked up like this, that obviously can't happen anymore. This job grounded me for a while though. Kept me straight and focused.

Finding a tall and flat rock about a mile uphill, I sit. It's time to face the haunting truth. I'm here, but I'm also still *there*. Building my career at the Milestone kept me afloat, but that's done.

And then Lauren ... I thought maybe I could make it work. For just a little while at least, she'd be mine. When I was with her, my hurt was washed down and shrunken. Her beauty and intelligence. We had *something*. That's ruined now, too.

I'm taking drugs to stay buoyant, but what for? What's even left for me here?

I pull on the ends of my cropped hair before screaming out at the top of my lungs, my skin breaking out again in perspiration. What's the point in waiting? I'm exhausted and humiliated. Out of my mind. I've got ... no one left. I break down, crying and cursing the earth. Staring down at the gun in my palm, I know what I need to do.

21

Lauren

I immediately call Eve, and she curses when she hears my tears. I can barely get a word out, but she lets me know she's on her way to my room. Twenty minutes later, she shows up with a cold bottle of wine and a cozy sweat outfit.

"I've done something terrible," I stutter out as she sits next to me on the bed. "There's a side to Slade I haven't really discussed with you in detail, but when he came over, I sort of just opened my mouth and told him so many things at once and I think I—"

She places a warm hand on my shoulder. "Take a breath, and let's just start from the beginning." Her eyes are concerned.

I break down, giving her all the dirty and dark facts, even dropping the bomb about the drugs I found inside his bedside table. When I get to last night, during the opening of Hook, her mouth drops open.

"It's my fault. I shouldn't have let him fuck me against the wall like that."

"Let me see your back. Lift your shirt." Her voice is no nonsense. This is the lawyer born and raised in New York City.

I turn around and let her raise it herself.

"Oh. My. God. Lauren, he hurt you. He really hurt you!"

"He didn't mean it." I turn around in a rush. "He was upset because I was talking to this guy, and—"

"Do you hear yourself? Do you? You sound like one of the women at our Center, trying to make excuses."

"It's not like that ..."

I take in a hard breath as Alicia's face smashes through my mind's eye. The parallels between her and me aren't imaginary. They are real. I'm making excuses, just as she did. I'm allowing a man to hurt me, physically and verbally. I stood up for myself to Slade, but I'm still trying to protect him to the outside.

"You're allowed to be sexually wild with a man who respects you, but did he notice the pain in your face while you were having sex? There is no way you enjoyed that, Lauren. You must have been in agony." She sadly bites her lip, but her voice is outraged. "The pattern of instability ..." she continues. "I can't believe Vincent hasn't picked up on this. And where did that asshole go after you told him off?" She turns her head, looking at the door.

"I don't know. He ran as though I'd stabbed him. It's not his fault —what he does at night when he sleeps. He obviously has a severe case of PTSD. But the drugs I found, obviously illegal. The drinking ..." I think about all the words I said to Slade only moments ago and the words I didn't say.

"He needs help. That's for sure. But it's on Vincent and me, not you."

"Why not me?"

"Because you've got a life to set up. You've been through enough shit these last weeks. Go back to California and straighten yourself out. That's what you came here for. Look up degrees in social work. Think about your options. As I said before, there is always a place for you here, regardless of Slade. You should have a good life, Lauren. More than good."

"But he would give me a good life!" I exclaim. "He just needs a little time maybe. I know I have to leave here. But I don't want to give him up ..."

I clench my fists, knowing deep within me that I simply cannot turn a blind eye to the fact that Slade has major problems and that he's taken those issues out on me. If I don't leave, I'll end up as another Alicia. And that's not acceptable. I told him off. I can't follow up by running back to him, begging forgiveness for something I shouldn't be sorry for.

"Slade is an incredible man. But he's abusing drugs and getting up in your face and hurting you. You need to step away from him. He's got to work out his problems. Let this be a new start for you. A fresh start at life. You survived the shooting in Vegas and, now, all of this." She shakes her head, decision made. "You've got to move on and see if he'll get better. And then you'll see if the timing works. Right now, he doesn't deserve you."

I start to cry again. Is he all alone? A dark thought crosses my mind. "Vincent should find him."

"Don't worry. He's already on his way. Slade called us in a panic when he couldn't find you. Vincent got on his bike at the same time I came over."

"Can you text him? Vincent, I mean. I want to make sure Slade's okay." My eyes move above her shoulder, remembering his agony.

"Just relax. Vincent has it under control. And, anyway, I don't think you should hear about Slade. Your feelings are on high. I think, in a few weeks, when the dust has settled, you'll be able to come to terms with what went on this week. If Slade wants you, he has to get better for you. Otherwise? No dice."

I chuckle at her word choice, hiccuping from my cry. "No dice?"

She shrugs, a small smile on her lips. "Let him get better, okay? Then, you can try again."

Everything about this is so fucked up. "Maybe you're right. I'm not feeling so well."

My head swims as Eve makes her way to the minibar, pulling out the wine opener. She uncorks the bottle and pours two glasses.

I should tell her, I think.

"I might be falling in love with him." My body sways with the words said out loud. "There's more we need to learn about each other, but the base is there. We're just ... right for each other. No, it wasn't a lot of time. But I knew we'd get there. I think he feels the same."

Her eyes tear up. "I know, honey. But the reality still stands. You've got to let him get better. Otherwise, there's no chance for a healthy future. Think about your kids and family one day. Slade needs to get professional help if he's going to be that good man you know he can be."

I nod, sniffling. Rationally, I know she isn't wrong. This is the same advice I would give her if the tables were turned. But my heart has other ideas.

"I'm sure he'll call you. Just step back and trust me." She hands me a glass. "Let's get drunk. Do you want the jet to take you back tonight? I'm not so sure staying here is a good idea, considering."

"All right then."

I easily drink it down, as though it were water.

THREE DAYS HAVE GONE by since I came home. No one here knows I'm back, and I've taken full advantage of that fact. And by full advantage, I mean, not leaving my beautiful white four-poster bed unless it's to use the bathroom or open the door for the delivery guy, who has already come twice, bringing cartons of cookie dough ice cream. Binge-eating and watching a Netflix series, I alternate between missing Slade, wanting to punch Slade, and crying.

Eve has called a few times, but I haven't answered. I'm just not sure I'm ready to hear from her. Everything that happened between Slade and me is still so fresh. Painful memories mixed with the best days of my life. Nothing of what happened has been digested. Instead, it's all still sitting in my gut, weighing me down.

I open my phone, scrolling through my calendar when I groan. Sanam's wedding is this Saturday. I crawl to the edge of my bed to get a look inside my closet. My blush-toned gown hangs inside, pressed and ready. My shoes are still in the box and should add an extra five inches to my five-foot-three height. Sanam sent me photos of how she wants my hair and makeup to be done, and my appointments are all scheduled. Nothing to do now but let my life unfold. I look down at my stomach and know I've got to get my shit together if I'm going to fit into my dress.

I do the unthinkable and call Jonathan, letting him know I'm back early and ready to come in. He's ecstatic over the phone. Next, I let my parents know I'm back. They're amazingly supportive, glad to hear I decided to return early and asking me to come over for dinner tonight. I look and feel like shit, but it's time I get my ass into the shower and put some clothes on. Getting clean and dressed in something other than sweatpants will help.

My mind doesn't leave Slade, but I hold fast to Eve's earlier advice. He needs to find himself and get better before a woman can enter his life. I trust Vincent and Eve have his best interests at heart. Slade will be okay.

In the bathroom, I paint my face full of makeup. Drying tears with a small piece of toilet paper, I coat on each layer in the same way I've done for years. I don't know who I am, but this is how Lauren dresses. This is how Lauren makes herself up. The soft, natural face with minimal makeup and flat shoes of Nevada are officially behind me.

Dinner with my mom and dad goes well. They think my general malaise is from the shooting, and I don't correct them. If I tell them about Slade, they'll dig, and I'll have to tell them everything. If they knew the details, they'd be shocked and mortified, casting judgment. It would only make it harder for me to move forward from everything. We eat, and I smile.

SANAM'S WEDDING IS BEAUTIFUL. Perfect in all the ways that matter to her. I exit the ballroom, filled with champagne and steak, gowns and diamonds. The entire ceiling is coated with red roses, nothing of the original painted white showing. Even the arms of the crystal chandeliers are wrapped in thin green vines. It smells and looks like a dreamy rainforest.

Sanam just changed into her third gown for the evening, this one a short and heavily beaded dress. Her makeup continues to hold up despite the broken capillaries in her eyes from vomiting earlier tonight.

"STAYING at a size double zero takes work, Lauren." She wipes her mouth using the back of her arm, heaving.

I wasn't supposed to overhear her puking, but I did.

"I know," I reply soothingly. "Weddings are stressful. Soon, you'll be Mrs. Nader, and you'll be honeymooning on the Riviera. Your life will be amazing, and all of this will have been worth it."

My words aren't true but meant to pacify. She's about to walk down the aisle. Now isn't the time for her to hear an earful of reality.

She wraps me in her skinny arms. "So lucky to have you. I don't deserve you. We didn't even discuss what happened in Vegas ..."

"Don't think about that now." I swat my hand in front of my face, as though clearing the air. "It's your wedding!" I exclaim excitedly, plastering a large, fake grin on my face.

Three hours later and primped to the hilt, she is ready for showtime. Vera Wang satin gown, hair in an Audrey Hepburn–style bun, makeup cleanly airbrushed.

Her last words, "Soon for you," are said with genuine kindness as she squeezes my manicured hands in her own.

In her own way, she loves me.

Taking the elevator downstairs with her entourage of hairstylist, makeup artist, and mother, she's as happy tonight as she'll ever be.

WATCHING her dance with her husband, the truth comes. After years of friendship with Sanam, I want a divorce. What we have between us is no longer who I am or what I want to be associated with. Still, I'm not evil. I promised to be here for her tonight, and I'd never shirk my responsibilities as her maid of honor.

I find myself dancing with the bride in the center of the dance floor. A circle of guests surrounds us, clapping. Beneath candy-coated smiles are vultures, eager to check out every detail of the beautiful bride—diamond Harry Winston watch, four-carat diamond stud earrings from Tiffany, gigantic rock on her left hand flushed with a shimmering eternity band. As an afterthought, they gloss over her single friend—me. One of Sanam's cousins is pushed to where we are dancing, and I take it as my cue to leave. Thank God.

Finding the exit, I step out and deeply breathe the fresh air. I look down, seeing a man sitting on one of the steps off to the right, smoking. Leaning forward onto his elbows, he looks familiar with his broad shoulders and longish dark brown hair skimming his collar. He moves, and I can clearly see his profile.

"Alexander?"

He blows out a puff of smoke before turning. His eyebrows rise as he gives me a megawatt smile. "Hey there."

He quickly puts out his half-finished cigarette as though not to offend me, stepping on it with a shiny black shoe. I wish he hadn't. The smell reminds me of Slade.

I miss him so much. It's been a week. Seven painful days of burying myself in work and preparations for this wedding. Slade hasn't called, and I refuse to call Eve for information. I deserve an apology from him. I can't be that girl who calls her best friend for scraps of information on a man. I spent my twenties doing that, and those days are done. I'm looking for the man of my life, and I refuse to play games. Still, my heart feels on the verge of shattering.

"Do you have another?" I ask, gesturing to his pack of Marlboros.

He opens it in offering. I bend down to slide out a cigarette before he stands, lighting me up with his silver Zippo. He sits back on the step, and I unceremoniously plop myself next to him. My gown pools around me. If my dress gets dirty, I'll live.

"How did you get your start in the restaurant business?" I need him to change the subject going on repeat in my mind—Slade and the fact that he hasn't reached out.

Alexander, not shy in the least, starts talking. But, as opposed to the last time, it doesn't sound like he's boasting. I'm honestly impressed with his rags-to-riches story. He started out doing small-time club promotions at NYU. After befriending one of the club owners, they partnered up. Alexander would run the operation, and his friend would find the money. Over time, he made enough connections in the business to raise his own money for ventures. Seven restaurants and four nightclubs later, he's still going strong.

"And what about you?" He turns his dark gaze to mine.

I can feel his interest, but I ignore it. I don't want to give him any ideas, but I'm also not ready to return to the party.

"I'm actually considering getting a master's in social work. I've been working as a legal secretary for a while, but I'm not really liking it anymore, and I don't want to go to law school either."

"Good plan." He nods. "Every lawyer I know hates it."

"Don't I know it." I inhale the smoke into my lungs, and it turns me slightly light-headed. Perks of being a nonsmoker, I guess. Taking a moment to assess the man before me, I ask, "How old are you?"

"Just turned twenty-eight last week."

"Oh my God. You're a baby!" I exclaim.

"Hardly." He doesn't smile.

"You are to me." I shake my head, feeling miserable over my number.

"And how old are you?"

My inner voice screams, *Almost thirty-three.*

I could be his big sister! But there's no way in hell I'm telling him that. I'd just be opening myself up to scrutiny. By my reaction, I'm sure he's figured out I'm older than he is. Alexander doesn't need to know my concrete age. So, I do what any woman would do in my position. I shrug and smile seductively.

I look at my watch, realizing we've been outside together for too long. "I should go back inside and check on Sanam."

Our friendship might be over, but I would never disappear at her wedding.

"How do you know the bride?" he asks.

"We met in college. Our parents are Iranian, too, so that's something."

"Ah." He nods. "I get it. I'm here for Reza. I've opened up a restaurant in one of his buildings in downtown LA."

"Of course you have," I reply dryly.

"How about you give me your phone number? I'd love to take you out." His grin is breathtaking but still wrong.

"I don't think so. I've sort of been through a bunch of stuff, and I feel like, right now, I need to take it slow."

"This means, no dates?" He opens his hands to me, all charm.

"Nope."

"Well, give me your e-mail at least. I'll invite you to my next opening."

"Sure." I give it, and he nods. "Bye, Alexander," I say in a singsong voice.

"Bye, beautiful," he shouts to the back of my swaying blush-toned gown.

22

Lauren

Work today is insane. Jonathan has been driving me crazy all morning with bullshit tasks. Nothing is complicated, but it's all tedious.

On a good note, I've already begun studying for the GRE exam, so I can apply for a master's degree in social work. Those few days I worked with Eve were enough for me to realize that helping women and children is where I see myself growing professionally. The jury is still out as to whether or not I'll work with her out in Nevada, but regardless, I want to take this path. My parents are happy, too, that I've found something that fulfills me and finally made a move toward it.

My father insisted that it wasn't law he was hell-bent on, but he wanted me to "be settled in a career."

I apologized for always giving him the runaround in regard to law school, but he understood.

Once I stopped avoiding what had happened with Slade, Eve and I got back in touch. She was annoyed that I hadn't answered her previous calls, but thankfully, she understood why. Still, I asked her not to say a word about He Who Shall Not Be Named.

If he has anything to tell me, he'll have to do it himself. It's been eight weeks and nothing but radio silence from his end. It hurts and angers me. The dust has settled, and I see our situation for what it was. Slade treated me like shit, and I took it because my feelings for him were so strong. His good parts were extraordinary, but his bad ones brought me six feet under. I thought I was resilient and the kind of woman who'd never get caught up in an abusive relationship, but I ultimately caved to his will. I'm disgusted by myself, but most of all, I'm hurt.

My personal inbox pings, and I click on the tab.

Alexander Kasovitz <a.kasovitz@gmail.com>
To: Lauren Amini
Subject: Lounge Furniture

Question: lounge furniture in the bar area of a restaurant. White or black?

I SMILE. But, in my defense, I really try not to. Ever since the wedding, Alexander and I have been e-mailing about random things. Favorite movies—his: *Fight Club*, mine: *The Notebook*. Best vacation—his: Peru, after graduating from NYU with some of his buddies; mine: Paris with Sanam four years ago when we went with empty suitcases and returned with them full to the brim.

He's witty and funny, and he seems to always be doing something interesting. Me, on the other hand? Boring-ville. Not that I mind. I've had enough drama to last a lifetime, and this past month has been spent trying to find some sort of equilibrium. It's all about finding my career path and letting my heart settle. I don't get excited when I hear from Alexander. But, after what I went through with Slade, it does feel good to have some healthy attention even if it isn't going anywhere.

Looking down at my screen, I click REPLY.

Lauren Amini <Lauren.amini@gmail.com>
To: Alexander Kasovitz
Re: Lounge Furniture

I love white, but the lighting should be dim. Otherwise, it's tacky.

Alexander Kasovitz <a.kasovitz@gmail.com>
To: Lauren Amini
Re: Lounge Furniture

Why don't you come check it out? The space is almost complete. We've got white furniture coming in on Tuesday. I'd love your opinion.

Lauren Amini <Lauren.amini@gmail.com>
To: Alexander Kasovitz
Re: Lounge Furniture

Oh, puh-lease! You have so many restaurants. I'm sure you've got some fancy designer. What would you need me for?

Alexander Kasovitz <a.kasovitz@gmail.com>
To: Lauren Amini
Re: Lounge Furniture

You're honest. You're not trying to sell me something. And you've got great taste. Who else would I need?

I EXHALE, massaging my temples. Slade and I are over. He was horrible, and to add insult to injury, he still hasn't contacted me. I groan, hating the fact that his name is even on my mind. He doesn't deserve my time or attention.

Maybe I should force myself to just go out with Alexander, for the sake of staying busy. He has been trying to see me since the wedding, and I keep denying him. What harm could it do anyway? The wall around my heart is so high; Alexander couldn't make a dent. Maybe I'll have some fun though. I deserve it, right?

Lauren Amini <Lauren.amini@gmail.com>
To: Alexander Kasovitz
Re: Lounge Furniture

Let me know when.

I HIT SEND and immediately regret it. No! I won't allow myself to regret anything. It's just looking at furniture for his restaurant. That's all. I refuse to feel guilty for having a good time. Slade and I are completely over. He hurt me, and I hate him. The end.

Alexander Kasovitz <a.kasovitz@gmail.com>
To: Lauren Amini
Re: Lounge Furniture

Friday night. 7 p.m. I'll text you the address. Send me your number?

FRIDAY NIGHT COMES in a blink of an eye. I don't return home to doll myself up but instead go straight from work. This isn't a formal date, so I have no reason to drive myself crazy. Anyway, the days of taking hours to get dressed are behind me.

My white blouse is tucked into gray wide-leg pants, and my black heels are simple and sophisticated. With my makeup subdued and clean, there's nothing about me that screams sexy, and I prefer it that way. Sure, I added a little shimmery copper-toned eye shadow to my lids and texturizing dry spray to my roots—thankfully back to blonde —before stepping out of the office. But that's just because I want to look presentable.

The drive over is quick. I'm in awe as I walk into the space that's to be the newest and hottest restaurant in LA. It's stunning! There are already reservations booked up for a month out, and it hasn't even opened yet. The only reason I know this is because, before leaving work, I caved, Googling Alexander Kasovitz and this new restaurant. And then I called Eve to ask her opinion on me going out with Alexander, a younger guy.

"AGE DOESN'T MATTER. Do you like him? If you do, you should go. And, if you don't, you shouldn't. But, Lauren, there's something I think you should know about Sla—"

"No," I snap. "Please, just don't." I bite my cheek, trying to maintain calm. "The whole ordeal is just ... embarrassing. He treated me like shit the week I was there and hasn't contacted me since. Of course, I'm dying to know what you want to tell me. But I can't play that game."

"I know. But there are things you don't know. I think, if I told you about them, you'd feel better."

"Please don't make excuses. I don't need you being Slade's mouthpiece. If he can't tell me himself, then I'd rather just delete him from my thoughts. I'm not letting him off the hook by speaking through you. If he wants to talk, he can be a big boy and call me himself."

She blows out air, as though exasperated.

"*So, what did Vincent say about him?*"

"*Slade?*"

"*No. Alexander.*"

"*Oh. He told me, 'He's cool.'*"

"*Does that mean, like, he's a six out of ten?*" *I worriedly press my lips together. It's not a date, but I also have no patience to see a guy who's an asshole.*

"*It means that Vincent doesn't do business with shady guys. I'm sure Alexander runs a clean operation. Anything more than that, I don't know.*"

An uncomfortable silence moves between us.

I clear my throat. "*Okay. Well, I've got to get there. I'm just going to go and have fun. I don't need to marry the guy. Slade might have gone through some stuff, but he was on drugs, and he is a liar. I can't even believe you're trying to discuss him with me after you saw what he did. Do you know I have discoloration on my back?*" *I look around the office floor, relieved that no one seems to be listening to my conversation.*

"*Don't be mad at me for wanting to tell you,*" *she says in a rush.* "*You know I love you. I understand you're still angry, and you have every right to be. Slade is in a bad spot, but he's not a stranger. You guys had some amazing times. You know who he really is. I know you do.*"

"*I'm going out with Alexander, okay? Slade cannot be part of my thought process right now.*" *I grab my purse and strut out of the office.*

"*Just trust your heart. If you want a date with Alexander, go for it. I'm friends with Slade, but I'm friends with you, too. Best friends. I'm not the enemy.*"

I exhale through my nose. "*I'm sorry I got upset. I know you only want to help.*"

"*I get it. I really do. Go and enjoy your date. You deserve it.*"

MY HEELS CLICK against the dark wooden floor. There is a lounge in the front of the restaurant, complete with a bar and low white couches, and then a separate dining room in the back.

The shiny wooden tables in the main restaurant are already out, large to accommodate big groups and smaller ones around the perimeter. There is also a long, rectangular table in the center of the space, which I assume is for communal dining. Raising my head, I count seven huge chandeliers hanging from the massive ceiling. Well, I'm impressed.

Suddenly, the lights dim.

"Hey." I hear a masculine voice behind me, and I turn around, startled. "Sorry, I was playing with the lighting. Don't want you thinking it's tacky." He laughs. In a trim navy suit and white shirt, unbuttoned at the top, he looks like casual elegance personified.

"I realize what I'm about to say might be too much information way too soon, but I just want to get it off my chest." I bite my lip.

He nods, waiting for me to continue.

"There was someone else recently. And we didn't date long, but he did a serious number on me. I'm not in the state of mind to get into anything real with anyone. Whatever this is between us, it's capped at fun."

He raises his dark eyebrows. "Lauren, you don't even know me. Why not give us a chance? I'm not asking for love right now. Not yet. If fun is what you need, I can do that. For now."

He gives me a sexy grin, and I know Alexander's got the patience of a saint. He's already invested a month into coaxing me to go out with him, and he's accomplished it. My little speech didn't seem to bring him down at all. If anything, he looks like a man ready for a challenge.

"Just a little time, okay. But it will be temporary. I'm older than you, if you haven't noticed, and eventually, I want to find someone to settle down with. Once I'm back to myself, of course. So, right now, with us, it's just fun."

"Fun and temporary," he repeats in all seriousness. "I get it." There's a sheen in his eye like he doesn't actually believe what he's saying. "Let me show you around."

I nod.

We spend about thirty minutes walking through the restaurant.

My body tightens with nerves anytime his hand grazes my back, but I do my best to stay relaxed.

"Did you notice the second entrance outside? That'll be for the nightclub downstairs. But there's also access via the restaurant, if you want to have dinner here before heading down."

"Oh, I love that!" I exclaim, clapping my hands together. "Old ladies like me hate driving from spot to spot. I love the idea of one place for dinner, downstairs for dancing, and then back home."

He chuckles. "That's the plan." Not bothering to respond to my *old lady* comment, he guides me out of the restaurant. "Ready for dinner?"

I roll my eyes. How presumptuous of him. I check my phone, and there are no missed calls. I click on e-mails next. Nothing but clothing flash sales on my personal account and correspondence from the lawyers on my work e-mail. If I were in a movie, I would hear from Slade right now. I hate him for what he did to me, but I hate him more for not calling me to explain. I need to move on, but instead, I'm stuck in this painful in-between. I still love him, and I despise myself for it. How can I love a man who treated me the way he did? I'm no better than the women from the Center. I'm sure Eve could give me some sort of closure, but I refuse to take it from anyone other than the offender. He shouldn't have a *get out of jail* pass. If there's something he wants me to know, he's going to have to tell me himself.

"Sushi work for you? I know a place ..." He smiles.

Swallowing hard, I tell Alexander, "Okay."

Dinner is easy and fun. He makes me smile and laugh. He tells me about his crazy family in New York City and even mentions Mafia connections. It's all said in jest, but something tells me there's truth within his jokes. All in all, Alexander is the perfect gentleman. After we eat, he drives me back to my car.

"Next week?" he asks, holding my car door open for me.

I sit inside the leather driver's seat and twist my hands together. Could I? Should I?

He interrupts my thoughts and says, "Don't answer yet. I'll call you."

He is being patient, and it warms my heart.

Gratitude moves into my chest, but I simply nod. He shuts the car door, and I buckle up, turning on the ignition. Alexander is a great guy, and I'm doing nothing wrong. And yet, guilt sits heavily in my chest. Of course, it's Slade. I *miss* him. Yes, Alexander is wonderful. But, no, he doesn't give me that same excitement for life as Slade did. He doesn't *move* me.

I pull out of the parking lot and grip the steering wheel, frustrated at myself for comparing.

AFTER WASHING my face and slathering my skin with an anti-wrinkle serum, I put on a comfortable pair of plaid pajamas and turn on my laptop. Sitting upright on my bed, I skim through my e-mails. The name I see sitting in my inbox has my heart skidding to a stop. With a shaking hand, I click.

Slade McCormack <S.McCormack@TheMilestoneResort.com>
To: Lauren Amini
Subject: Hello

Lauren,

It's been eight weeks since we've seen each other or spoken. There are so many things I wanted to tell you but couldn't. The truth is, I shouldn't be contacting you. Not yet. Not while my life is still in shambles.

When you're done with this letter, you might think that I wrote it because I want your sympathy. It's not the case. I realize that, after what I've done, I don't deserve forgiveness or your friendship. I only want to share the truth because you ought to have it. We weren't together long, but I swear it when I say, you mean something to me.

More than anyone else ever has. I hurt you, physically and emotionally. And I am so sorry. Hopefully, after this letter, you will understand why I acted the way I did.

I left the SEAL Teams because I killed my best friend, Rex. It wasn't my bullet, but I didn't stop the one that shot him. My failure caused his death. After he died, I couldn't go on. I wasn't acting straight. Doing my job became impossible, and I retired before they could discharge me.

I came home to an empty house. Not only were my parents gone, but my brother had also recently died in combat in Iraq. After selling my family home, I got on the road. Stopping in New York City, I met Vincent at a boxing gym. We became friends, and he offered me the job at the Milestone to run security for him.

Things were decent for a while after that. Until they weren't. Flashbacks began to assault me for any reason or no reason at all. I brought a sweet girl to my place and had an incident in my sleep. She woke with my hand around her neck, choked out. She was physically fine afterward, but I wasn't.

Pills to help me relax was where it all began. And then pills to help bring me up. Pills to settle my nerves when things got overly stressful in my head. Mixing them with liquor when needed.

When we shared a room in Vegas, I didn't trust myself to be near you in the night. I slept on the floor after drinking a glass of vodka from the minibar and swallowing a few pills. I did the same when we shared a room near Lake Powell. I knew my nightmares could put you in danger, and instead of telling you or anyone else the truth, I self-medicated, taking medication I was never prescribed, all depending on my mood.

When my regular supplier no longer had what I needed, I went off to find harder stuff. I'm ashamed to admit it, but that night when I took you to the motorcycle club? I was scoring drugs from a guy named Lion. I know what you're thinking, and the answer is, yes, it's the same Lion. The president of the MC, ex-husband of Alicia who came into your Center. He hooked me up.

Memories from war were crippling me, and I felt that nothing but drugs could keep me afloat. I was already in too deep. If Vincent knew I had a problem, he'd fire me—which he did that night Hook opened. If you knew about my issue, I thought you'd run—which you did after I completely fucked up. I thought the drugs would balance me. But all they did was screw me up even worse. I deserved to lose you and my job.

After our huge fight in your hotel room, Vincent found me with a gun in my mouth. I was in the middle of the mountainside with nothing left to lose. He got me to a hospital, although I have to admit that I'm not sure how he got me there. I must have blocked it all out. *Rock bottom* is what they call it. But I call it *get help or die*.

After switching from psychiatrist to psychiatrist, I've finally found a doctor who seems to understand me.

Dr. Sullivan was a Marine, and that got my attention. Unlike these other doctors who were sitting in medical school, studying and living in freedom, while I was sacrificing my time and my life. Sully made the same sacrifices. He understands the world I lived in. The first time we met, it was like he knew exactly what I was going through. When he explained that, sometimes, there wasn't even a trigger but that my emotions would go haywire with random bursts of irritability and anger, I was shocked. Not because he was wrong, but because he was *right*. He told me to go get an MRI, and for once, I actually listened. I'm waiting now on the results.

I hope you're well. It's hard for me to sleep, knowing what I put you through. Memories of war are hell, but losing you has been its own form of torture. I'm so sorry for what I did.

Slade

I READ the e-mail over again. And then again. I've replayed our ending a thousand times in my head. This past month, I've fantasized about him returning to me. His huge, heavy body on top of mine in the night. Tracing the bone frog tattoo on his damp chest, sweaty from sex. His lips groaning against mine. Slade saving me and ... loving me. Sitting on the back of his bike when he takes me to the mountains. Cooking dinner. Laughing. I imagined all the things I wish we'd had time for, like watching a movie on his couch. More meals together.

Tears fill my eyes. Because I don't think any of that will ever happen. I was furious at his disappearance, but it wasn't his fault. He's ... sick.

Written in his own plain language is the truth. Slade is an addict who tried to kill himself. I'm in love with a man who's broken. Beyond repair maybe.

My heart feels like it's cracking in my chest, vibrating from the realization. I want to write back and tell him ... tell him how I feel, too. Tell him that I'll be there for him through it all. But I won't because I can't sacrifice myself for him. I've bled.

A healthy relationship can't grow from disability. We had a beautiful week, but there was pain, too. And I can't let us fall into the same pattern. Eve is right. Slade must get better on his own. I might lose him by not replying to this e-mail, but the alternative might be worse.

Shutting down my computer, I cuddle up under my soft covers and bring my legs to my chest in a fetal position. I won't reply. I can't. I want Slade but not at the expense of my life.

THREE DAYS LATER BEFORE BED, another e-mail shows up in my inbox.

Slade McCormack <S.McCormack@TheMilestoneResort.com>
To: Lauren Amini
Re: Hello

Hey Lauren,

I got the results of the MRI, and I wanted to share them with you. It turned out that, even while my brain is resting, I have spontaneous activity in my temporal lobes. This causes my temper to rage for no reason at all. My PTSD is severe, but Sully says it's manageable. I'm on a good path.

Vincent and I also worked some things out. I'm taking a leave of absence while I sort out my personal shit, but my job at the Mile will be waiting for me.

For all the times I flew off the handle and lost control, I'm sorry. For the time I hurt you up against the wall during the opening of Hook, I'm sorry. For that same night, when we had sex on the floor and I was completely out of my mind, I'm so sorry. For pulling the gun on you, I'm so sorry. For the lies. For the deceit. For taking advantage of your kind and open heart.

Lauren, you never deserved it. Even though my temper was out of my own control, I still withheld what I was going through, which is the same as a lie. The medications I took made things worse. It was illegal and dangerous and wrong. And, regardless of all the excuses on earth, I realize that I acted in ways that were completely unaccept-able. I'm a grown man who doesn't shirk away from responsibilities or problems. That's not who I am at my core. But it's what I did.

Using a combination of medication and psychotherapy, Dr. Sullivan has me in a twelve-week course of treatment where I talk about my trauma. He also has me write in detail about my time overseas. I started off pretty generally, just jotting down notes about how I got into the SEAL Teams in the first place. But, slowly, I've been getting into the gritty parts. Turns out, opening up doesn't make things worse, as I initially thought it would. It sets the pain free so that I don't have to wallow in it alone.

He's put me on some medication, but all of it is now under his control, not mine. I am putting my trust in him.

I hope you are well. You're on my mind every minute of every day.

Slade McCormack <S.McCormack@TheMilestoneResort.com>
To: Lauren Amini

Subject: How are you?

Lauren,

You're the most wonderful woman I've ever met. Have I ever told you that? Harming you was one of the worst things I've ever done. I know hearing from me might not be what you want, but I care about you too much to just walk away. I know you want a husband. You want a family. You want a life of your own filled with love. I want that for you, too. I don't know when or if I'll be better. Or if I'll ever be in a position to be good enough for you. Or even if I got my shit together, if you'd ever forgive me for the pain I caused. I wish I could swear that I'd be healed completely one day, but to say that would be a lie.

You don't reply to my e-mails. I know I don't deserve your time. I want to beg though. Beg that you'll give me a chance to get out of this. I've been through war. I've come home, only to realize that hell isn't always in a moment but can live in memories. But then I saw you at the hospital that night when Vincent was in a coma, and I was literally struck dumb by your beauty. It didn't take long for me to know your level of stunning is so much more than skin deep. Lauren, if you only knew how just your presence fills me up inside.

I'm missing you.

Slade McCormack <S.McCormack@TheMilestoneResort.com>
To: Lauren Amini
Subject: Hi there

Lauren,

How is everything going? Are you doing okay? Eve keeps me updated on you. She tells me you're going for the master's in social work. I'm so glad for you. You should never settle for anything less than you deserve. And you deserve to love your career.

Lauren, somehow, with you, I want to speak. With you, I want to open my guts and spill what's in my heart. This is not how I normally operate. I have always kept things inside. Maybe it's because you are so pure. There's a strength within you that calls to me. I've always been tough. Tough in the face of hardship. I think maybe my hardness was also related to fear when it came to you. I feared rejection. I didn't think you would ever love someone like me. Between my nightmares and drug abuse, I realized my worth was limited. I kept an iron curtain between my heart and yours. You should have a man without these hang-ups. You deserve more. Even if I learn to control these issues, Sully tells me they might never be gone completely. Still, I wish there was a way I could erase my problems. I want to be the type of man who deserves you. I'm going to try.

Slade McCormack <S.McCormack@TheMilestoneResort.com>
To: Lauren Amini
Subject: Hey there

Hi Lauren,

How are you? How is school? I'm getting a good handle on myself, and Sully is trying to get me to alter my thinking. Remember when we talked about mental strength and how important it is to keep your thoughts in line? I'm working on that. Lots of what happened is in the past, but I'm trying to change the way I see it in my rearview mirror. I still can't say it was an accident that Rex died because I should have seen the bullet coming. Protecting my brothers was my duty, and I failed. Sully wants to keep working on changing my mindset, but in this, I'm unchangeable. The best I can do is make peace with my errors. And that's why I went out to Texas—to visit his parents. Their home was a simple Tudor on a tree-lined block with an American flag on a tall pole in the front yard. Not exactly where I envisioned my pessimistic friend to live—he was always angry about something—but hey, beneath it all, Rex was completely dependable and the best type of man with honor and love in his heart. It makes sense that his upbringing was with warmth. Mine was, too. My parents loved me and Aaron, and they loved each other as well. I'm thankful for that.

Rex's mom and dad opened the door together, and his mom burst into tears. Is this how my mother would have greeted me had she been alive when I returned home?

We sat on a large, floral L-shaped couch in their living room, talking about what a brave son they had before they showed me photos of Rex as a baby and through school. Rex with his little league baseball trophy—he played first base. Rex's ninth birthday party at the ice-skating rink. The house was full of pride for their only son.

"Real hero he was," his mother exclaimed, tears filling her soft blue eyes, just like Rex's.

I choked up during my apology for not having saved him.

His father, flushed with emotion, embraced me. "It's not your fault. He died a true hero."

I finally broke down.

Leaving their home was bittersweet, but we promised to stay in touch. "You'll invite us to your wedding, right, Slade?"

The moment she said that, I thought of you on your wedding day and the lucky guy who would call himself your husband. Would you wear shoes like you wore to Vincent and Eve's wedding, all strappy and high? I still laugh about that.

When I was back in the car, "Black Hole Sun" came on the radio. I know you hate that song. I wanted to call you.

Eve and Vincent both think I should wait longer before I pick up the phone, at least until the twelve weeks are up, but it's taking all my self-control and then some. I miss you so badly. Do you miss me?

Lauren Amini <Lauren.amini@gmail.com>
To: Slade McCormack
Subject: Hello

Slade,

I've been getting your e-mails over the last month. Since I got the first,
I have written on and off again but wasn't able to press Send. To tell
you the truth, I just didn't know how to start.

You hurt me. You really did. I ignored my instincts because I was
enamored by you. Because you brought these feelings out of me that I
had never felt before. You're gorgeous and so intelligent. You're a hero.
In your eyes, I saw the best version of myself. With you, things
seemed to make sense. Like I could be the woman I always wanted to
be. Independent and strong and happy.

But then again, with you, I was yelled at. I was physically bruised and
emotionally beaten. I don't ever want to feel that way again. I won't.

I understand that you've been suffering from severe PTSD. I think I
realized it at the time but was steadfast in my denial. I know what you
went through overseas was horrifying. I read all of these Navy SEAL
books in an attempt to understand better, but I had to stop. All I
could see in them was you.

I'm also so sorry about what happened with Rex, but I'm glad to
hear you visited his family. I'm sure that was closure for you.
Maybe now, instead of feeling agony with the thought of him, you'll
be soothed by the fact that his family does not blame you. It
sounds like they really like you. I'm not surprised. You're a
great man.

I haven't been sleeping well, and so I saw a therapist. She tells me that
replying to you is not a good idea. She seems to think you're toxic and
dangerous. Don't worry; I haven't seen her since that session. You
aren't dangerous. You're going through a hard time, and I understand
that. I believe you'll get through it.

I'm not sure how I'll feel in a few months. Or next year. Or even
tomorrow. I'm trying to take my life day by day and concentrate on

work and bettering myself. What I went through with you was very painful, and I'm still having trouble with digesting it all.

Otherwise, things with me are good. As you know from Eve, I'm going for my master's. Online courses make things a lot easier. I work during the day at Crier and study at night. Almost no time for shopping. Surprised?

I know you want to hear more, but I'm not sure what else to say. I'm praying for you in your recovery.

Sincerely,
Lauren

Slade McCormack <S.McCormack@TheMilestoneResort.com>
To: Lauren Amini
Subject: Hi

Lauren,

Do me a favor and never see that therapist again. She's a moron. Yes, I fucked up. In some ways, I'm a wreck. I plan to rise above it. I'm going to show you, if you'll let me, that I'm not that horrible man you saw glimpses of.

What hurts me the most is the thought that I hardened you. You are so trusting and full of love. I ribbed you over your shopping habits, but I love it. I love the clothes you wear and how you've got so much style. I might not know about things like shoe types, but I do know that you always look gorgeous. Like, that bathing suit you wore on the lake. Or the strappy shoes at Vincent and Eve's wedding. The dress with a million buttons. Your blue cotton pajamas with lace on the edges. I notice everything about you, even when you think I don't. Please don't change. You are the most beautiful woman on earth, inside and out. I wish I'd told you this more when we were together. Vincent told me once that you weren't naive. He thought that maybe your kindness would be construed as that. I tried not to scoff. There is nothing naive about you, Lauren. You are good and kind and see the best in people. It's a part of you that I love. Don't lose faith just because of my fuckup.

Do you think I can call you? Maybe, if we spoke, I could explain everything more clearly.

Missing you.

23

Slade

It's been two weeks since my last e-mail, and she didn't respond. I drop my car off in the airport's parking lot and get on a flight to California. Maybe it's extreme, and I should take things more slowly. But fuck slow. I know who I want and what I want, and it's Lauren. E-mails aren't enough. The fact that there is another man trying to inch himself into her life doesn't make me want to slow down either. Did I do some digging on Alexander? Of course I did. Even though I recognize how badly I fucked up, I still know that she and I belong together. Alexander is nothing but filler.

THE LAW OFFICE where Lauren works is easy enough to find in the Financial District of Los Angeles. Stepping off the elevator and entering on the fifth floor, I tell the secretary who I'm looking for. On an annoying giggle, she points toward the Real Estate Transaction team where Lauren is the head legal secretary. I see her, focused in concentration as she stares at two monitors. Loads of files litter her desk. I stand there, waiting for her to lift her face. And then ... she does.

I swallow hard as her mouth parts in surprise. No words come out.

"Coffee?" I sound like myself, but my insides ache.

As I slide my hands to the back pockets of my jeans, nerves unseen tingle through my fingers. I want a cigarette, but I've cut back to only one in the morning and one at night.

My eyes scan her face and find emotion. Anger, hurt, and relief are all there for me to see.

She purposefully stands before stepping around her desk. I blink, and she's against my chest. I can't help but lift her into my arms, smelling the perfume inside her neck. It's flowery and soft and mixed with her own scent.

I love her.

I thought I was prepared to see her, but the feelings unleashed within me are larger than I thought. Wild almost. I want to mark her in the best of ways. Prove to her that I am who I am and that she has to give me another shot.

When I slowly put her down, she nods. "Yeah. Coffee. Okay."

Grabbing her purse from a desk drawer, she straightens out her black skirt that's slim against her hips, hitting right below the knee. A lacy-looking blouse is tucked inside the skirt. As always, she's so classy. I look down at my own clothes—a pair of worn jeans and a white henley shirt—and stand straighter. Maybe I should have dressed better.

Shit.

As she walks by my side to leave the office, I resist the urge to throw her onto the floor and kiss her until she melts.

She brings me to a small coffee shop around the corner, and I order a nonfat latte for her and a black cup of decaf for me. I get our drinks and bring them to where she sits.

"It's been a while," she starts.

"I had to get my shit together. I was spiraling within a bad place. My doctor thought it was best I complete twelve weeks with him before I came to see you. Vincent and Eve wanted me to wait even longer, but I didn't listen." I hoped for some small conversation first, but I guess I'm getting into it. "I know I'm a lot to handle. But I'm working on it all. I've gotten help, and it's going really well."

I want to take her hand in mine, but she's toying with the rim of her coffee cup, listening intently.

"That's great, Slade." She tries to smile, but it comes out sad.

"Can we try again?" I lean my elbows on the wooden table between us, wanting to get closer. "I know we had a shaky start. Actually, two shaky starts if you want to count the wedding. But I want you to know that I did plan on calling you back after that night. But, somehow, out of nowhere, my nightmares began pouring through my psyche. Things began to go from bad to worse, and I didn't think I was in the right mind to date you. And then we saw each other at the club, and ... I wanted it. Wanted you, so badly. And then the shooting in Vegas. Everything got worse after that. Still, I wanted you. From the moment I met you at the hospital, you were the one I couldn't stop thinking about. I wasn't good in the way you deserved. But I want you to give me another chance." I'm rambling, and I can't seem to stop it.

She sits back, as though unsure. I feel my pulse beating more quickly. The reality that she might say no is bigger than I thought.

"I know you don't trust me after everything, but—"

"Wait." She lifts a hand, stopping me. "I need you to understand that I won't ever tolerate lying. I will not allow someone to go behind my back. I spent the last few months thinking about what we had. And, truthfully, I'm angry with myself for letting it get that far. You can't take advantage of my feelings for you. You kept apologizing. Toying with me. You were on drugs ... lying to my face."

I grab her hand, in absolute awe of this strong, independent woman, and I resist the urge to vow everlasting love. I deserve her words and anger. But that doesn't mean I'm going to give up.

"I know. The medicine Dr. Sullivan put me on is working, and we don't plan on staying on them forever either. He thinks, over time, I'll be able to wean off. I betrayed your trust. And Vincent's and Eve's, too. But give me another chance to prove I'm better than the man you knew."

"But who are you?"

I sit back, feeling knifed. "I'm me." My voice lowers to a whisper. "You know who I am."

"Well, were you always on drugs when we were together?"

"No. Not always. It isn't like that. Look, let's just be friends. Start slower this time. Use the distance to our advantage."

"Slower?" She snorts in disbelief.

"That's right. We'll talk on the phone. I'll come visit on the weekends. Or every other. Whatever you want. We'll rebuild from a flat but stronger spot. You should meet Sully, too. He's heard all about you, and maybe he can help give you a better understanding about what I'm dealing with. But you and I have something special between us. And I don't want to let it go. I can't."

"Rebuild? I see you're still the same Boy Scout."

"You know it." I reach my hands to hers, threading our fingers together. "See?" I stare into her eyes, willing her to understand. "I'm me. You know me, Lauren."

"Well"—she pulls her hands away from me and pushes hair behind her ears—"you've said you don't want marriage or a family or anything long-term. I'm putting out my cards. I want love, Slade. I won't do a short-term thing. Not again. I hope to find love with someone, and I can't waste my time."

"No." I shake my head. "I want it, too. I swear, I do. Always have. Just got derailed for a while, but that's done now. Let's try. Start with friendship, so I can prove it to you. Can you give me that?"

Again, I slide my hands around hers. A light squeeze from hers tells me she's in. But then she opens and closes her mouth, like she wants to say something.

In a rush, she says, "I'm sort of dating someone."

My world slows down. "Huh?"

"Yeah. Nothing serious. Just a few dates here and there."

"End it."

"What?"

"You heard me. When I say friendship, I mean, we won't rush into getting physical again. There's only one man for you. And it's me. I fucked up, but it's time now to let me make it right. You and I belong together. And that's all there is. Tell him you won't be seeing him again."

Tears fill her eyes as she nods. "Yeah."

24

Lauren
Six Months Later

"I've removed all the boxes from your room. Your office is officially ready!" Eve's voice is so upbeat; it's almost laughable.

"Who are you, and what have you done with my serious friend?" I sit on top of a huge cardboard box, the words *Shoes* and *Bags* written in thick black Sharpie. I gave most of my accessories away to Goodwill, but when push came to shove, I had to keep some.

"What can I tell you? Being pregnant has turned me upside down." Eve's eyes sparkle with the words, and my heart fills with happiness for her, just as it always does when she mentions her pregnancy. "I'm just glad you'll be in full swing at the Center when he's born."

"And I'm just glad the world gets a miniature Vincent Borignone!" I fan myself, and she laughs.

"The universe had better get ready for this monster. I have a feeling he's got a big future." She rubs her round belly. "He's kicking like crazy. Big already, just like his dad."

"Oh, let me feel!" I rush over, pressing my hands to her stomach.

Tears fill my eyes as I feel the shift within her stomach. Fetal movement. "I'm so happy for you, Eve."

"How's school?" she asks, turning the conversation back to me as she drops herself on the beautiful L-shaped leather couch we bought for the living room.

"It's great. Almost there."

I have been working toward my social work degree online. The plan is that I'll pick up my pace at the Center during the day when Eve has her baby, but until then, I'm taking as many credits as I can handle. Luckily for us, the timing works perfectly.

Slade and Vincent walk into the new house, all big muscles and serious demeanors. With Slade's hair freshly buzzed and scruff lining his chin, he's the sexiest man I've ever seen.

"Slade, *hi*." My voice comes out all breathy.

Eve and I have been waiting for Slade and Vincent to help with the unpacking since we got here twenty minutes ago.

After giving up my place in California, Slade and I decided to live together out here in Nevada. Slade insisted that property values were just going up, particularly because the reservation was making big money off the casino at the Milestone, and it was attracting so much business to the area.

"The smart move would be for us to buy a bigger place. Trust me. A nice-sized house is a good investment," he said.

His dark and thoughtful eyes always seem to know things I don't.

So, I did what anyone in my position would do when her brilliant, gorgeous, ex-military boyfriend gives her real estate advice; I listened!

During one of my visits two months ago, Eve and I saw this house, a bungalow-style two bedroom, and I fell in love. While it needed work, the entire place just felt right.

"You could even fit a swing set in the back," she gushed.

Slade came right away with his perfect posture and muscled body and nodded. "This'll do. I'll put the time in."

He can be so *serious*, not that I'm complaining. When he gets all intense and introspective, I feel this surge of pride for him. It also turns me on like nothing else.

The kitchen is now painted pale blue and completely redone with a new refrigerator, freezer, dishwasher, and cabinetry. The living room and dining room are a gorgeous, warm cream color. The horrible carpet was lifted, and the floors are now thick wooden planks, freshly sanded in a neutral beige tone. Slade was against "good ole beige," but I insisted it would match whatever furniture we decided on. Luckily, he caved.

The best part was, Slade did all the work himself. I even got to watch when I was here. Slade, shirtless and sweating and doing physical labor? I'll take it any day of the week.

"How could I trust it was done right if I didn't do it myself?" he said.

I laughed and told him it was sweet. "My Boy Scout," I jokingly said before handing him a glass of cold water filled with ice. But, really, my heart was filled to the brim.

The bedroom though, I haven't seen since we bought the place.

"Just wait here," he told me.

My parents met Slade a few months ago. He brought a beautiful bouquet of white peonies, ate three plates of Persian food my mom had cooked, and even spoke some words in Farsi that I'd taught him. Luckily, he didn't show off the dirty words he knew. My mother was immediately smitten.

My dream wasn't for my parents to simply like Slade. I wanted them to love him and welcome him. Not that I'd stop seeing Slade on account of my parents. But still, it would be so great if they were happy with him. Life would be so much *better*.

After a cigar with my father on the deck, they came back inside, smiling, while my father tapped him on the back like a friend would. Slade's gaze devoured mine with that crazy sexy, quiet smirk, and I knew he was in the fold.

"DID you tell him about your bachelor's degree?" I whisper as my parents step into the kitchen, leaving us alone in the living room.

"I told him everything." He winks, lust in his eyes.

"What do you mean, everything?" I place a hand on my hip as my thoughts turn to what he did to me last night on my kitchen floor. I flush.

When he wags his brows at me, I smack him in the arm, eliciting a warm chuckle from him. He knows exactly what I'm thinking, and he's teasing me over it.

Moving an errant hair behind my ear, he tells me, "I told him all about the college program I'm doing online to get my degree, just like I promised my mother I'd do. Told him about bringing fresh water onto the reservation, so the tribal members no longer have to drive hours back and forth for clean water. He's a great guy, your dad. You didn't tell me how well we'd get along."

"I guess I wanted to surprise you."

"Lauren, no one is as funny as you are." He chuckles.

"I've got to keep you guessing, don't I?"

His eyes turn to flames. "Since you like surprises so much"—he pauses, and I try not to laugh because we both know me and surprises don't get along—"be ready for a surprise from me tonight."

"Oh, yeah? What kind of surprise?" I smile, draping my arms around his narrow waist and looking into his eyes. God, he's hot. "I can't wait."

His eyes drift to the kitchen and then come back down to me. "Don't want to ruin my good name by taking you right here on his living room couch. So, you'd better stop with those heated eyes."

"What heated eyes?" I lick my lips, gaze moving from his face down to the zipper in his navy slacks.

The fact that he got nicely dressed for my family makes me so crazy happy that I can barely contain it. I love him casual and gruff, but this clean-cut side is so sexy, too.

"Gotta learn a better game face, babe." He laughs playfully. "Maybe you should put on those huge, round bug-style glasses to hide it?"

My jaw drops and eyes widen before we break into laughter. "You'll never let me live that down, huh?"

"Don't think so."

"I'm enjoying tonight, but I can't wait to move out with you next month."

He growls low in his throat, "You've got no idea."

"Dessert?" My parents ask, entering the room

I see their faces, and I just know. Slade and I might be opposites, but somehow, we're just right in all the ways it counts.

"BABE, I want you to see our room." He moves a few boxes over, eyes twinkling.

Vincent and Eve smile, like they know something I don't.

"Finally!" I exclaim, clapping my hands together.

He's kept this bedroom from me since we bought the place. Something about dangerous fumes or toxic chemicals. Whatever it is, he scared me into staying out of it.

He pulls a silver key from his pocket and opens the lock. He takes my hand and leads me into the bedroom. My jaw drops. The walls are painted in a dusty gray. The bed is a beautiful white four-poster, complete with a fluffy white duvet cover and gray throw pillows.

"Did Eve help?" I ask.

Silver candles line the windowsills. The room is soft and Zen-like.

"Nope."

"Wait." I take in a breath before practically shrieking, eyes scanning the room. "*You* did this?" I wonder how he pulled this off.

"Boy Scouts can do all sorts of things. But first, closet."

He opens the door before flipping on a light, and I scream, jumping up and down in glee. It's a walk-in with racks for shoes, sections for bags, and rows of hanging space. It's ten times better than my closet in LA. And, to think, I gave away all those clothes and accessories. *Ugh!*

"And look. For your platforms and wedges." He winks, pointing to a shoe rack.

I laugh. "I've trained you well, huh?" I'm in awe. "Slade, where are you going to put your—" My gaze drops.

Slade isn't standing up. He's on ... one knee. My hands fly to cover my mouth. A small black box appears in his hands, tiny inside his large, callous palms.

"The first night I met your father, I spoke to him alone. We not only talked about the ways I was moving forward in my life, but I also told him how I was going through a hard time and dealing with issues post-war. He wasn't too keen about you being with a man who has PTSD, but once I let him know that I'd do anything to be the man you deserved and how hard I was working toward that goal, he came around.

"Lauren, I want to be the father of your children. I think, the night of Vincent and Eve's wedding, I knew you were the one. You know how badly I wanted you, but my demons were a wrench in my life. But your laughter, your smile, your depth, your soul? It all speaks to me. It saved me. I will always love you. Be my wife, Lauren."

He removes the ring and slides it onto my left hand. A simple round solitaire, surrounded with delicate red rubies. "The stone belonged to my mother, but I had it reset."

I drop to my knees, too, and he immediately wraps me up in his huge arms.

"Yes, Slade. Yes."

I burst into tears because we've come so far. The last six months, we've been traveling between Nevada and California. Long rides on his bike. Sunday night dinners with my family when he was in town. The never-ending phone calls. Conversations about life. His past. Mine. Helping to put together his broken pieces, displaced since war. I saw his doctor a few times, too. And counseling us together has worked wonders. I learned that I wouldn't be able to put him back exactly how he had been before war, but a new creation could be made. It would be different but amazing in its own way. Lucky for me, I love Slade as he is.

During his initial visits out to LA, we slept in separate beds. We both knew the situation wouldn't be forever, but it was the safest move, considering the fact that his nightmares were still being dealt with and Dr. Sullivan was still testing out doses of medications. It didn't take too long for us to feel that we could handle being side by side. And, when we did, it felt like returning home.

· · ·

"BABY?" *he whispers in the dark.*

"Yeah?"

"Will you stay here, next to me? Can we try to do a night together? If I move too much or seem to be getting restless in my sleep, just wake me. Want you in this bed by my side. I'm ready, if you are."

SOMEHOW, with distance, we grew immeasurably closer. I fell in love with his mind and his passion and dedication. He hired hundreds of US veterans to work on building water pipelines on the reservation, and I know it was incredible to him. Healing even.

"Come. I have another surprise set up for you."

Hand in hand, we enter our beautiful kitchen, tears streaming down my face. A large bottle of champagne on ice and a spread of cheese and vegetables and dips and Vincent and Eve and my parents, too! Were they hiding here all this time? My mom hugs me in her beautiful cream-colored pantsuit, and my father shakes Slade's hand. Vincent and Eve are all smiles with their new baby on the way, and I know that my life is just beginning. It might not always be easy, but there's nowhere else I'd rather be.

ALSO BY JESSICA RUBEN

Want to learn more about Vincent and Eve from **Warrior Undone**? Catch them in Jessica's Top 30 Amazon and International Bestselling series, Vincent and Eve: The Complete Series , available now and FREE with Kindle Unlimited!

You can find details on ALL of my books on my website, www.JessicaRubenAuthor.com

Vincent and Eve Series

Rising: Vincent and Eve, Book 1

Reckoning: Vincent and Eve, Book 2

Redemption: Vincent and Eve, Book 3

Vincent and Eve: The Complete Series (Box Set)

Mafia Kingdom Series

(All independent standalone books, to be read in any order!)

Light My Fire: A Dark Mafia Romance

Love Her Madly: A Dark Mafia Romance

Break On Through: An Arranged Marriage, Mafia Romance

Mafia Kingdom: The Complete Series (Box Set)

Holiday Springs Series, co-written with USA Today Bestselling Author MJ Fields

The Broody Brit: A Hot Single Father Second Chance Romance

The Irresistible Irishman: For St Patrick's Day

Continue reading for an excerpt from Light My Fire: A Dark Mafia Romance (Mafia Kingdom, Book 1)

light my FIRE

a MAFIA KINGDOM *novel*

BESTSELLING AUTHOR
JESSICA RUBEN

LIGHT MY FIRE EXCERPT

Kosovo, 1998

Jakup sits with his legs crossed, cigar smoke leaking from his pencil-thin lips as he howls, "We cannot fold! The KLA will win this war in the end. It has to." His voice reverberates through the home like thunder.

My hands clutch themselves together like magnets.

The top of my wooden staircase has a direct view of the living room. Hiding behind a large green plant mother recently brought inside, I watch the conversation unfold.

My father leans forward in his chair. "Serb police need to all be gunned down, once and for all. Over thirty of our children were killed this week. In the streets! They're animals, Jakup. We need independence. We need freedom. These atrocities cannot stand." Father's voice shakes with emotion. "But when will the US intervene? All they talk about is Monica Lewinsky, and meanwhile, the stakes here"—he points to the ground with a firm finger—"are rising."

I shift, the words *children ... gunned ... killed* bang against my head.

Father must hear my stressful thoughts because he calls up, "Elira, come down now."

Mother told me to stay upstairs today. "You're only ten," she said. "Your place is by my side."

But mother is not home; she's at the market, gathering food with my older brother, Agron. And as Father always says, I'm his right hand when mama isn't home.

Step by step, I move downstairs. Nerves envelop me, but thankfully, my legs do as they're told.

Over the last three months, men have been coming and going from our home, using our farm to train. We've been cooking the biggest meals.

"Like there's a party every day," mama said.

We're freedom fighters and members of the KLA, the Kosovo Liberation Army. My father along with Jakup are the two main party leaders. Albanians in Kosovo want to be free from Serbian rule. We want to govern ourselves. And my papa is going to bring us there.

"Jakup, this is my daughter, Elira."

I sit on the chair beside his, sitting tall and strong, just like he taught me.

Rubbing my back with his warm hand, his touch says, *Don't be nervous.*

I turn to him and nod. I'm not scared.

Jakup puts out a hand, and I do the same, hoping I look adult.

He laughs. "I can see it in your eyes; you're smart. You'll go places one day. And your father and I will clear the path for—"

The front door is kicked open. Gunfire. I turn my head to hide in my father's chest, but he throws me beneath the table. I curl up by a wooden leg, ducking my head low. Shots ring loud. Stomping and then yelling coming from the kitchen, too.

There's a war in the house! Can they see me? Will they get me? My entire body shakes. *Do I stay, or do I run?*

Suddenly, a hand grabs my leg like a vise, dragging me out from beneath my wooden cave. I want to scream and kick, but nothing comes from my mouth. My legs are lead. My voice is gone; it's vanished.

I'm forced to stand when a gun is brought to my temple. It's hard and cold. Wetness leaks beneath the pink flowery dress my mama sewed last week, dripping down my leg like a broken faucet. Suddenly, mama is before me. My father is lying on the floor, his head shattered. My brain turns to chaos and buzzes with light. Something within me floats from my chest.

Has God come to take my soul?

The gun is pressed harder against my head. He's screaming, "Where are the men hiding, Blerina?"

She doesn't reply, sweat soaking the front of her black hair.

He chuckles darkly. "Tell me, or I'll blow your daughter to bits."

Her mouth opens and shuts before her green eyes turn resolute. She stands taller, steadfast in her beliefs. My throat stings because my mind knows. The most important men in the resistance meet and train here. Their deaths could mean the end of our freedom, which everyone tells me is more important than the lives we've lost. She will never fold. My heart sinks, knowing my end is here and now.

Children in the streets ...

Children in the streets ...

My body will be among them.

BOOM!

My mother screams. I'm on the ground with a huge man on top of me. Blood and bone against my skin. From the corner of my eye, I see Nico, huge and looming, shooting his gun.

BOOM. BOOM. BOOM.

I don't take a breath as the chaos re-erupts around me.

Silence and stench. The room spins. I'm nailed onto the floor, something unmovable crushing me under.

Mama is down on her haunches, pushing the weight off my body and lifting me in her strong arms. She walks up the steps.

Am I a corpse, watching from above?

Her tears drip onto my face, telling me I'm alive.

Methodically, she turns on the bath before stripping me of my dress and underwear. I put my thumb in my mouth, a soothing habit I broke years ago. She places me in the bath and scrubs my skin until it's raw. I don't dare move.

The steam tells me the water is hot, but I can barely feel it. After a few minutes, she pulls me out, wrapping me in my towel, still damp from last night. Pink pajamas are slipped over my head. It's still morning, but we continue our nightly rituals until I'm tucked into bed.

"Now, don't move, Elira. Rest until I return."

"Don't leave me!" I finally cry as she reaches the door. My voice is loud, but it doesn't sound like mine. It's rough and too high-pitched.

Her eyes widen, like I just made a big mistake. I cover my lips with my hands.

Did the Serbs hear me? Are they back?

Before she can exit, my door swings open, and my mouth poises to scream. It's Nico, taking up my entire doorway.

"I'll stay with her, Blerina."

Mama trembles, folding herself into her own arms. He's eighteen but much bigger than she is. Nico is the biggest.

"Nabergjan is next on the Serb radar. This wasn't just a single hit but the start of terror in our village." He folds his heavy arms across his chest. A gun hangs around his waist, and I know there's a knife on him, too.

I hold my breath, listening.

"I will find arrangements for you to take Elira and Agron out as soon as possible. Your work is done." His voice is measured as he gives his decree.

"But—"

"Don't argue with me. It's for your safety." He cracks his knuckles. "Bring Elira tea. Now."

She nods in obedience. Father always said Nico is young but brighter and crueler than the rest. When Nico speaks, everyone listens and follows his orders. He fights for our freedom like the other men, but he is different, too. He's unlike the others in the way he carries himself—with so much strength and determination. Nothing can get in his way.

Mama's pale lips quiver, like she wants to say more. She leaves.

He comes next to me when I ask, "Why is she g-going down?" My voice is a whisper as I clutch on to him.

His white shirt is damp. Instinctively, I tuck my head into his chest. It's instant relief.

He pulls me closer, allowing me to take him in. "She's got to clean up the mess downstairs. You saw your father, didn't you? And Jakup?" His voice is firm and honest.

I look up into his deep, dark eyes. For me, Nico brings only truth. He holds my shoulder, like I'm a friend he's trying to comfort. From his touch, my heartbeat slows.

"They're dead now. But don't worry. I will find and kill the Serbs who got away. You have my word." He pauses, eyes narrowing into slits. "I'll never let them get away with this." His voice is harder than I've ever heard it.

A knock at the door. I freeze, but it's only my mother entering with a cup in her hands. Mint leaves float at the top, sugar already melted. She leaves it on my bedside table, and Nico gestures for her to leave. I should say I want my Mama, but I don't. He's all I need.

He stands, and I whisper-beg, "D-don't leave me."

The cup looks like a toy in his hands. "I will not leave your side. Not yet."

I sit up, my legs still beneath the covers. Gazing at him, not breathing, I watch as he gently blows the steam. He lifts the cup to my lips, and I slowly drink. It's hot and sweet. When it's finished, he leaves the bed to place it on the small table by my window.

How can the sun be shining when my father is dead?

I move inside my covers, feeling physically comatose from my internal pain. My feelings and thoughts are scattered like dead bodies in the streets. Life's leftovers for anyone to poach.

He sets himself next to me, the sheet a division between us. We're separate, but I can feel his body heat. He hugs me to his broad chest. I nestle my head beneath his chin as his hands move around my body like a vise. I like when he holds me like this. There's no way I can move, but why would I want to? He's hard, but nothing can hurt me when I'm in here. Slowly, I feel myself settling into safety. The warm tea has coated my stomach, softening the pain.

I try to calm my body, remembering yesterday. Nico chased me around the house and threw me over his shoulder and tickled me until tears dripped down my face. Before dinner, he told me about democracy. We reviewed my English words. *Bed. Chair. Pajamas. Slippers. Toothbrush.*

Nico is sort of like my father but not. He's kind of like a brother or a teacher but not that either. He's the man I love. Some girls know their favorite color. I know the man I will marry one day. Still, he's always out of reach. Too old. Too handsome. Too powerful. But one day, I won't be a child anymore. And I'll show him I'm worthy to be by his side, as his queen.

Mother tells me, when I was born, he came with his father to bring some fruit to celebrate my birth. I had been crying, seemingly inconsolable, and he asked to hold me. The moment I went into his arms, I calmed.

"She likes you," his father said.

After his family was killed by Serb forces, he came around to help my father with the KLA.

He whispers, "You were so brave, Elira."

He kisses the top of my hair, still damp. It reaches down my back in black waves. Sometimes, it gets knotted at the bottom, but I normally keep it in one long braid. Mother forgot to fix it after my bath. Anxiety returns to my chest. I lift my face, so I can see Nico's eyes. They're darker than night.

"My hair," I start. "It's always braided when I rest. Mama forgot!"

"Sit up. I used to do this for Elsa when she was small."

He separates my hair into three sections and begins to braid. When he's done, I lie back down, feeling better.

His skin is tanned from spending days in the hot sun. My white hands are pale compared to his. I trace the planes and angles of his face, memorizing his hard-looking, prominent cheekbones and straight black hair. I should feel shy to touch him in this way, but I don't. He never gave me permission to, but I have it. If I didn't, he would stop me. Nico isn't a man who ever lets things happen without his permission.

Just last week, Zamir didn't follow Nico's protocol when finding a Serb officer on the street. Nico had him beaten, threatening to never let him near the KLA again. Some people were scared, saying Nico shouldn't hurt one of our own. Others said Nico did right; he can't have a team who doesn't listen to their commander. Plus, Zamir's actions could have resulted in many people's deaths.

He shuts his eyes, a smirk filling his lips as I draw.

Women always giggle and smile around Nico, even when he doesn't try to make them laugh. Especially Bardha. Her huge breasts are always pulling against her shirt. And she tries to stay outside to get bronze on her face even though she should be helping in the kitchen. She talks about Nico. How "big" he is and how "good" he is in bed, but I don't see why that's special. Everyone can see how big he is. And, of course, he's good in bed. Aren't we all good when we sleep? So, why does she say it like it's a secret?

A few weeks ago, me and Bardha were rolling out dough for the lunch pies.

I asked her, "Why do you laugh when Nico is near? Why does your voice get squeaky like a mouse in the attic when he speaks with you?"

But she just rolled her eyes and told me I couldn't understand —yet.

"Nico is the kind of man who doesn't just talk about change. He makes change," she said. "Just last week, he organized ten of our men against fifty Serbian police, and Nico won! He leads like no one else. He's going to be the one to win our independence. I can feel it."

"Is he nice to you?" My hands balled into fists as I silently prayed the answer was no.

"No." She shook her head and smiled as though my question were silly. "Nico is a warrior. He fears no man on this earth. He is not the eldest, and yet he has earned the greatest respect because of the battles he's won on our streets. He has no great family lineage, but he has the confidence of a king. A man like Nico will never be nice. But that doesn't mean he isn't good ... in other ways." She winked.

Before I could respond that Nico was nice to *me*, she kissed my cheek and walked away. For days, I thought about what I could say to her. I still haven't had the chance. I'm not sure I ever will. Without Papa, nothing can be the same.

From my chest, the words, "I'm not safe here anymore," bubble out from my mouth.

His eyes flit open. "You will always be safe. I swear it. And my oath is my bond, Elira."

"What if those men come back for me?" The reality of this hits me, and panic begins to build.

"They can't. Those men are now in hell, where they belong. When you move into the afterlife, there is no return. And the ones who ran, I will find." A sneer mars his face.

Into his chest, I ask, "What if their children come for me?" My heart beats faster. Revenge is the natural order.

"I'll kill them, too." He shifts, so he can hold me closer. "Don't you know I will kill anyone who tries to hurt you?"

"Uh-huh." I nod quickly, eyes wide.

He's scary right now, eyes with such undisguised hatred and maliciousness that, for a moment, my voice fails me. This is the Nico men fear. I want to give myself up to crying convulsively, but Nico's strength holds my emotions up like a pillar. I won't cry. Not in front of him.

"Okay." I swallow hard, maintaining eye contact.

He holds the back of my head, as though to make sure I listen intently. "You are allowed to grieve for your father, and you should. You are allowed to be afraid, too. Giving yourself time to hurt will make you resilient. If you don't, the pain will eat at you and weaken you. When mourning is over, you must emerge to be the strong girl I know you to be."

"How do you know I'm strong?" I want reassurance. I want him to tell me who I am and what I'll be because his word is everything.

"What happened last week when you took the pie from the oven and burned yourself?"

"I rinsed my arm with cold water and put cream on."

"I watched how you dealt with the pain. Other girls or boys would scream or cry. Not you."

It was painful, but I didn't want to cause trouble or add to my mother's load. I burned my arm badly, but I know it will heal.

"And when you saw Alek's mother fallen, with a wound in the street, what did you do?"

"I-I got help."

"Right. You saw she needed aid, knew you couldn't bring her in yourself, and got someone strong to lift her. That's exactly right. Smart and intelligent people see a problem and do not cower. They find an answer. That's what you have always done. You are different from other girls, Elira. Better. I saw it from the moment you were born." He smiles, tapping my head. "But if you want to grow your strength, you'll make sure to deal with all problems as they come. Understand?"

I'm suddenly breathless. The loss of my papa, our home's protector, begins to leak into my consciousness. "I can't go downstairs. Papa is gone now. What will we do?"

The enormity of his death has only slightly touched the surface of my mind. It's too much for me to handle. I want to hide. Scream and cry. Instead, I sit frozen and still. His isn't the first death I've seen, but it's the first one that will permanently change my life.

He exhales, mood softening. "Your father is in heaven now, but you will continue with your mother and Agron. I see big things in your future." His voice is resolute.

"Big things?"

"Yes." He shifts his body, tucking an arm behind his head. "Remember what I told you about America?"

In the English he taught me, I tell him, "America is free and B-big Mac hamburg and gold in street."

He lets out a small laugh. "That's right. It's time to get you there.

Now that your father is no longer alive, I don't want you staying in Kosovo."

"But ... how? Isn't it hard to get into America?"

"Yes. But I know someone who will bring you there. I wanted you to leave sooner, but your mother wouldn't leave without your father."

"And what about you?" Worry fills my chest. I've heard of the country, but I can barely imagine the things I've heard.

"My place is here. I must finish this war."

My pillow turns damp with tears. *Am I crying?*

"Just sleep now. I will take care of everything."

"My feet are cold." I crouch my legs up.

Nico stands, taking another blanket from my closet. He covers me.

My voice shivers. "I'm scared, Nico." Heat seeps into my body quickly, but I still shiver like it's ten below.

He smooths the hair from my forehead. "A rose is afraid to open its petals until light coaxes it open."

"You're light," I whisper, my body growing heavier by the second. It's only moments more before I fall off to sleep.

* * *

The next three days, I refuse to leave my closet. I hide behind my hanging clothes with my back against the hard wall. Nico tells Mama it's okay, to let me sit until I'm ready to come out, but she is worried. *Doesn't she understand I cannot be seen?* Those men know where we live. They will come back. Each day, Nico swears I am safe but doesn't force me out. Instead, he tells me to sit and cry until I'm ready to emerge. He's giving me one week.

Nico knocks three times before entering the closet—our secret code. Sweat beads between his brows. I want to put my nose into his shirt and take in more of him. He's fresh dirt, grass, and soap. His scent makes me a good kind of dizzy.

"How are you, kid?" He squats low, bringing his large hands together.

"I'm hungry," I whisper, slightly embarrassed. Turns out, I'd rather be safe than full.

He grunts in annoyance. "Agron was supposed to come up an hour ago. Did he not?"

Not wanting to get my brother in trouble, I only shrug. "He must be busy."

He shuts his eyes in annoyance. "Your brother needs to learn to follow orders. He has many personalities, that Agron. You never know who you'll get."

Standing wordlessly, he leaves. I try not to cry at his hasty departure.

Nico returns, knocking again before opening the door. I'm sure it annoys him, but he does it anyway. My eyes widen in surprise as he steps in with a plate full of food.

"Fried potatoes and sour cream. Green tomatoes and fresh bread. Flija. Spinach pie." Piece by piece, like I am one of the baby lambs on our farm, he feeds me.

"How did you find this?" I chew.

He doesn't answer but lifts more for me to take.

"Is this yours?" I swallow, but the food sits like a lump in my throat.

Agron forgot to save me food, and Nico gave me his to eat.

My eyes fill with tears. "No. You need this. I don't."

"Shh. When you're full, I'm satisfied."

"Are you going to marry me when I'm older?" It's my secret wish —not so secret anymore.

He laughs and pats my head. "We'll see, kid. We have a long time before thoughts of that."

I flush, embarrassed. Nico carries me into the white bathroom and stands by the door, so I can wash up and use the toilet before placing me back inside my closet, nestled into fresh-smelling clothes.

That night, I sleep deeply.

"Elira, you cannot stay in here anymore." Mama is here, on her knees, trying to coax me out.

I tell her, "Only Nico."

"Nico is training the men, my sweet pea. Talk to me. Tell me. Open your heart."

"I miss Papa," I finally wail. The moment I say it, it's as though a dam is broken. I cry harder than I thought possible, shaking in her arms.

Clutching me against her chest, she says, "Yes, as do I. But this is the price we must pay. There are things in this world larger than we are. There will be time to mourn for him but not yet."

"I was going to die," I stutter out. "He was going to shoot me—"

"You were. God has other plans for you, it seems. Now, come out. Let me feed you at the kitchen table. The sunlight will be good."

Holding hands, we trek downstairs. The house is quiet and creaky. The sun is barely up, and the men haven't arrived to eat. I sit on the wooden chair with my feet curled into my chest. She gives me two boiled eggs. Fresh bread with butter. I eat hungrily.

Faster, faster—before they come.

Mama sits beside me. "Elira, I know how much you love Nico. But I worry for you. He is a man, and you're still a child."

"So?" My voice is loud and defensive. I can feel the heat crawling into my face.

"Don't speak. Just listen." Her words are firm. "When you were born, you wouldn't stop crying. Nico came over—"

"And he held me, and I stopped my tears. I know this story." I sulk.

"Nico has always had a soft spot for you. A place he has for no one else. But I do not want you to become attached to him. He is dangerous. He is always in the front line of all things. You must keep some distance between the two of you."

"Why?" I demand.

"Because you are a good girl. A smart girl. A man like Nico isn't for you. Not now and not later. You will grow up and find a man worthy. A doctor maybe. Not a man with violence in his veins. He's a man who likes power. He's grown accustomed to it, it seems." Her eyes cloud.

I shake my head, refusing to listen. "Nico isn't violent with me."

"Listen to me, Elira. The things he has done, I cannot repeat. I don't like him being near you, but what choice do I have? Now that Father and Jakup are gone, what he says goes. But if you create some space—"

"You can't make him stay away!" I yell, my voice shaking.

"No, I can't," she says admittedly. "But I want you to pull away. Don't look at him with adoration. Don't allow him in your room. It isn't appropriate anymore," she pleads. "You'll be eleven soon, too old to have a man who is not your brother or f-father alone with you." Tears fill her eyes at the mention of Papa. She opens and closes her mouth as though there is more to say, but nothing comes out. Her words are gone.

She lifts my plate in her hands and walks to the sink. Her back shakes as she turns on the water, head dropping low. Without another word, I run upstairs and into my closet. Shutting the door, I sit down in the corner. They can't find me here.

In the middle of the night, I'm awoken. It's Nico.

"Come on, kid. Time to go to America."

"Huh?" I'm confused, mouth dry.

"Yes. You will go with your mom and brother by horseback now to Montenegro. From there, someone will bring you to a place called Pennsylvania. You'll be safe there."

"I can't leave!" I scream, punching his hard, muscled chest as he drags me out.

He covers my mouth with his heavy hand. "You must. The arrangements came together very fast. I know it's short notice, but it's the safest way."

He lifts me over his massive shoulder and takes me downstairs. I want to yell, but fear has paralyzed my voice once again.

He whispers, "Don't be afraid. Soon, you will be free."

"When will I see you?" I plead.

Agron holds me tightly, keeping me away from Nico. *I want to stay!*

"One day, we will meet again. I swear it."

My brother clutches me atop his horse. And we're off.

* * *

WANT TO KEEP READING?

Click HERE: Light My Fire: A Dark Mafia Romance

Or, purchase the **Mafia Kingdom** box set and enjoy three deliciously dark romances: Mafia Kingdom: The Complete Series

Pssst: All books are FREE with Kindle Unlimited!

STAY IN TOUCH WITH JESSICA

Readers,

Please consider leaving a review on your purchase platform and Goodreads! It's an invaluable way to support an independent author, and would mean more to me than you can imagine.

Want to know about all the sales, updates, or news I have? Sign up for my newsletter:

http://jessicarubenauthor.com/newsletter/

Interested in hanging out with me and chatting all things bookish? Join my Facebook group, Jessica's Jet-Setters:

https://bit.ly/2lHuCaZ

I love to hear from readers! Please reach out to me via my website:

http://www.jessicarubenauthor.com

ACKNOWLEDGMENTS

The journey has been wild and there are people to thank!

Firstly, my husband. Every hero I write is born out of my love for you. My kids, without whom I could not function. You guys are truly the greatest blessings in my life.

Thank you, Autumn, at Wordsmith Publicity, for putting my books on the map. For supporting me through every step of the process and for being you. I don't just adore you. I freakin' love you!

To Sarah Hansen at Okay Creations, who created my gorgeous cover that truly embodies the words within.

Thank you to all of the incredible book bloggers! I never believed people would read my work, but then you all spread the word...got my books out...I'm in awe of what you all do. And to all the bookstagrammers! How you all manage to take such stunning book photos is astounding. Thank you!

Thank you to my best friends and beta readers who gave me the push and confidence I needed to publish my work. I love you guys so much. Caitlin, Alex, Jana, Keeana, Ronna, Jayme, Roxy, and Candice. Thank you to my Master Beta Reader, Leigh Ford. Without you...well, I won't say. Because I don't want to even think about a situation where you weren't in my life or involved in my character's lives.

To Jonathan, the man who inspired Slade. When I saw you and listened to your stories, I just felt it. Thank you for your service. Thank you for opening your heart to me. You're an incredible man and I am proud to know you.

To Jessica's Jet Setters!! You ladies rock. Your support and love keep me going.

To the readers. Thank you for making my dreams come true.